A C
Night with Consequences

SHARON KENDRICK

LYNNE GRAHAM

MELANIE MILBURNE

MILLS & BOON

First Published in Great Britain 2021
By Mills & Boon, an imprint of HarperCollins*Publishers* Ltd
1 London Bridge Street, London, SE1 9GF
www.harpercollins.co.uk

HarperCollins*Publishers*
1st Floor, Watermarque Building,
Ringsend Road, Dublin 4, Ireland

ISBN: 9780-263-30275-2

MIX
Paper from responsible sources
FSC™ C007454

This book is produced from independently certified FSC™ paper to ensure responsible forest management.

For more information visit: www.harpercollins.co.uk/green

Printed and bound in Spain
by CPI, Barcelona

THE ITALIAN'S CHRISTMAS SECRET

SHARON KENDRICK

For the vivacious and beautiful Amelia Tuttiett—
who is a great raconteur and always fun to be
with. She is also a brilliant ceramic artist.

Thanks for all the inspiration, Mimi!

CHAPTER ONE

'Mr Valenti?'

The woman's soft voice filtered into Matteo's thoughts and he made no effort to hide his exasperation as he leaned back against the leather seat of the luxury car. He'd been thinking about his father. Wondering if he intended carrying out the blustering threat he'd made just before Matteo had left Rome—and if so, whether or not he could prevent it. He gave a heavy sigh, forcing himself to accept that the ties of blood went deeper than any others. They must do. He certainly wouldn't have tolerated so much from one person if they hadn't been related. But family were difficult to walk away from. Difficult to leave. He felt his heart clench. Unless, of course, they left you.

'Mr Valenti?' the soft voice repeated.

Matteo gave a small click of irritation and not just because he loathed people talking to him when it was clear he didn't want to be disturbed. It was more to do with the fact that this damned trip hadn't gone according to plan, and not just because he hadn't seen a single hotel he'd wanted to buy. It was as much to do with the small-boned female behind the steering wheel who was irritating the hell out of him.

'Cos' hai detto?' he demanded until the ensuing silence reminded him that the woman didn't speak Italian, that he was a long way from home—in fact, he was in the middle of the infernal English countryside with a woman driver.

He frowned. Having a woman chauffeur was a first for him and when he'd first seen her slender build and startled blue eyes, Matteo had been tempted to demand a replacement of the more burly male variety. Until he reminded himself that the last thing he needed was to be accused of sexual prejudice. His aristocratic nostrils flared as he glanced into the driver's mirror and met her eyes. 'What did you say?' he amended, in English.

The woman cleared her throat, her slim shoulders shifting slightly—though the ridiculous peaked cap she insisted on wearing over her shorn hair stayed firmly in place. 'I said that the weather seems to have taken a turn for the worse.'

Matteo turned his head to glance out of the window where the deepening dusk was almost obscured by the violent swirl of snowflakes. He'd been so caught up in his thoughts that he'd paid scant attention to the passing countryside but now he could see that the landscape was nothing but a bleached blur. He scowled. 'But we'll be able to get through?'

'I certainly hope so.'

'You hope so?' he echoed, his voice growing harder. 'What kind of an answer is that? You do realise that I have a flight all geared up and ready to go?'

'Yes, Mr Valenti. But it's a private jet and it will wait for you.'

'I am perfectly aware that it's a *private jet* since I happen to own it,' he bit out impatiently. 'But I'm due at a party in Rome tonight, and I don't intend being late.'

With a monumental effort Keira stifled a sigh and kept her eyes fixed on the snowy road ahead. She needed to act calm and stay calm because Matteo Valenti was the most important customer she'd ever driven, a fact her boss had drummed into her over and over again. Whatever happened, she mustn't show the nerves she'd been experiencing for the past few days—because driving a client of this calibre was a whole new experience for her. Being the only woman and the more junior driver on the payroll, she usually got different sorts of jobs. She collected urgent packages and delivered them, or picked up spoilt children from their prep school and returned them to their nanny in one of the many exclusive mansions which were dotted around London. But even mega-rich London customers paled into insignificance when you compared them with the wealth of Matteo Valenti.

Her boss had emphasised the fact that this was the first time the Italian billionaire had ever used their company and it was her duty to make sure he gave them plenty of repeat business. She thought it was great that such an influential tycoon had decided to give Luxury Limos his business, but she wasn't stupid. It was obvious he was only using them because he'd decided on the trip at the last minute—just as it was obvious she'd only been given the job because none of the other drivers were available, this close to Christmas. According to her boss, he was an important hotelier looking to buy a development site in England, to expand his growing empire of hotels. So far they had visited Kent, Sussex and Dorset—though they'd left the most far-flung destination of Devon until last, which wouldn't have been how *she* would have arranged it, especially not with the pre-holiday traffic being what it was. Still, she wasn't being employed to sort out his schedule for him—she was here to get him safely from A to B.

She stared straight ahead at the wild flurry of snowflakes. It was strange. She worked *with* men and *for* men and knew most of their foibles. She'd learnt that in order to be accepted it was better to act like one of the boys and not stand out. It was the reason she wore her hair short—though not the reason she'd cut it in the first place. It was why she didn't usually bother with make-up, or wearing the kind of clothes which invited a second look. The tomboy look suited her just fine, because if a man forgot you were there, he tended to relax—though unfortunately the same rule didn't seem to apply to Matteo Valenti. She'd never met a less relaxed individual.

But that wasn't the whole story, was it? She clutched the steering wheel tightly, unwilling to admit the real reason why she felt so self-conscious in his company. Because wasn't the truth that he had blown her away the moment they'd met, with the most potent brand of charisma she'd ever encountered? It was disturbing and exciting and scary all at the same time and it had never happened to her before—that thing of looking into someone's eyes and hearing a million violins start playing inside your head. She'd gazed into the darkest eyes she'd ever seen and felt as if she could drown in them. She'd found herself studying his thick black hair and wondering how it would feel to run her fingers through it. Failing that, having a half-friendly working relationship would have satisfied her, but that was never going to happen. Not with a man who was so abrupt, narrow-minded and *judgmental*.

She'd seen his expression when she'd been assigned to him, his black gaze raking over her with a look of incredulity he hadn't bothered to disguise. He'd actually had the nerve to ask whether she felt *confident* behind the wheel of such a powerful car and she had been tempted to coolly inform him that yes, she was, thank you very much. Just as she was confident about getting underneath the bonnet and taking the engine to pieces, should the need arise. And now he was snapping at her and making no attempt to hide his irritation—as if she had some kind of magical power over the weather conditions which had suddenly hit them from out of the blue!

She shot a nervous glance towards the heavy sky and felt another tug of anxiety as she met his hooded dark eyes in the driver's mirror.

'Where are we?' he demanded.

Keira glanced at the sat-nav. 'I think we're on Dartmoor.'

'You think?' he said sarcastically.

Keira licked her lips, glad he was now preoccupied with staring out of the window instead of glaring so intently at her. Glad he was ignorant of the sudden panicked pounding of her heart. 'The sat-nav lost its signal a couple of times.'

'But you didn't think to tell me that?'

She bit back her instinctive response that he was unlikely to be an expert on the more rural parts of the south-west since he'd told her he hardly ever visited England. Unless, of course, he was implying that his oozing masculinity was enough to compensate for a total lack of knowledge of the area.

'You were busy with a phone call at the time and I didn't like to interrupt,' she said. 'And you said…'

'I said what?'

She gave a little shrug. 'You mentioned that you'd like to travel back by the scenic route.'

Matteo frowned. Had he said that? It was true he'd been distracted by working out how he was going to deal with his father, but he didn't remember agreeing to some guided tour of an area he'd already decided wasn't for him, or his hotels. Hadn't it simply been a case of agreeing to her hesitant suggestion of an alternative route, when she'd told him that the motorways were likely to be busy with everyone travelling home for the Christmas holiday? In which case, surely she should have had the sense and the knowledge to anticipate something like this might happen.

'And this snowstorm seems to have come from out of nowhere,' she said.

With an effort Matteo controlled his temper, telling himself nothing would be achieved by snapping at her. He knew how erratic and *emotional* women could be—both in and out of the workplace—and had always loathed overblown displays of emotion. She would probably burst into tears if he reprimanded her, followed by an undignified scene while she blubbed into some crumpled piece of tissue and then looked at him with tragic, red-rimmed eyes. And scenes were something he was at pains to avoid. He liked a life free of drama and trauma. A life lived on his terms.

Briefly, he thought about Donatella waiting for him at a party he wasn't going to be able to make. At the disappointment in her green eyes when she realised that several weeks of dating weren't going to end up in a swish Roman hotel bedroom, as they'd planned. His mouth hardened. He'd made her wait to have sex with him and he could tell it had frustrated the hell out of her. Well, she would just have to wait a little longer.

'Why don't you just get us there as safely as possible?' he suggested, zipping shut his briefcase. 'If I miss the party, it won't be the end of the world—just so long as I get home for Christmas in one piece. You can manage that, can't you?'

Keira nodded, but inside her heart was still racing faster than it should have been considering her sedentary position behind the wheel. Because she was rapidly realising that they were in trouble. Real trouble. Her windscreen wipers were going like crazy but no sooner had they removed a thick mass of white flakes, there were loads more their place. She'd never known such awful visibility and found herself wondering why she hadn't just risked the crowds and the traffic jams and gone by the most direct route. Because she hadn't wanted to risk a displeasure she suspected was never very far from the surface with her billionaire client. Matteo Valenti wasn't the kind of person you could imagine sitting bumper to bumper on a road of stationary traffic while children in Santa hats pulled faces through the back windows. To be honest, she was surprised he didn't travel round by helicopter until he'd informed her that you got to see a lot more of the natural lie of the land from a car.

He seemed to have informed her about quite a lot of things. How he didn't like coffee from service stations and would rather go without food than eat something 'substandard'. How he preferred silence to the endless stream of Christmas songs on the car radio, though he didn't object when once she changed the station to some classical music, which she found strangely unsettling—particularly when a glance in the mirror showed her that he had closed his eyes and briefly parted his lips. Her heartbeat had felt *very* erratic after that particular episode.

Keira slowed down as they drove past a small house on which an illuminated Santa Claus was driving his sleigh above a garish sign proclaiming *Best Bed & Breakfast on Dartmoor!* The trouble was that she wasn't used to men like Matteo Valenti—she didn't imagine a lot of people were. She'd watched people's reactions whenever he emerged from the limousine to cast his eye over yet another dingy hotel which was up for sale. She'd witnessed women's gazes being drawn instinctively to his powerful physique. She'd watched their eyes widen—as if finding it hard to believe that one man could present such a perfect package, with those aristocratic features, hard jaw and sensual lips. But Keira had been up close to him for several days and she realised that, although he looked pretty perfect on the surface, there was a brooding quality underneath the surface which hinted at danger. And weren't a lot of women turned on by danger? As she clamped her fingers around the steering wheel, she wondered if that was the secret of his undeniable charisma.

But now wasn't the time to get preoccupied about Matteo Valenti, or even to contemplate the holidays which were fast approaching and which she was dreading. It was time to acknowledge that the snowstorm was getting heavier by the second and she was losing control of the big car. She could feel the tyres pushing against the weight of the accumulating drifts as the road took on a slight incline. She could feel sweat suddenly beading her brow as the heavy vehicle began to lose power and she realised that if she wasn't careful…

The car slid to a halt and Keira's knuckles whitened as she suddenly realised there were no distant tail lights in front of them. Or lights behind them. She glanced in the mirror as she turned off the ignition and forced herself to meet the furious black stare which was being directed at her from the back seat.

'What's going on?' he questioned, his tone sending a shiver rippling down Keira's spine.

'We've stopped,' she said, turning the key again and praying for them to start moving but the car stayed exactly where it was.

'I can see that for myself,' he snapped. 'The question is, *why* have we stopped?'

Keira gulped. He must have realised why. Did he want her to spell it out for him so he could shovel yet more blame on her? 'It's a heavy car and the snow is much thicker than I thought. We're on a slight hill, and…'

'And?'

Face facts, she told herself fiercely. You know how to do that. It's a difficult situation, but it's not the end of the world. She flicked the ignition and tried moving forward again but despite her silent prayers, the car stubbornly refused to budge. Her hands sliding reluctantly from the wheel, she turned round. 'We're stuck,' she admitted.

Matteo nodded, biting back the angry exclamation which was on the tip of his tongue, because he prided himself on being good in an emergency. God knew, there had been enough of those over the years to make him an expert in crisis management. Now was not the time to wonder why he hadn't followed his instincts and demanded a male driver who would have known what he was doing, instead of some slip of a girl who didn't look strong enough to control a pushbike, let alone a car this size. Recriminations could come later, he thought grimly—and they would. First and foremost they needed to get out of here—and to do that, they needed to keep their wits about them.

'Where exactly are we?' he said, speaking slowly as if to a very small child.

She swivelled her head to look at the sat-nav for several silent seconds before turning to meet his gaze again.

'The signal has cut out again. We're on the edge of Dartmoor.'

'How close to civilisation?'

'That's the trouble. We're not. We're miles from anywhere.' He saw her teeth dig into her lower lip as if she were trying to draw blood from it. 'And there's no Wi-Fi connection,' she finished.

Matteo wanted to slam the flat of his hand against the snow-covered window but he sucked in an unsteady breath instead. He needed to take control.

'Move over,' he said roughly as he unclipped his seat belt.

She blinked those great big eyes at him. 'Move over where?'

'Onto the passenger seat,' he gritted out as he pushed open the car door to brace himself against a flurry of snowflakes. 'I'm taking over.'

He was pretty much covered in ice by the time he got into the car and slammed the door shut, and the bizarre thought which stuck in his mind was how deliciously warm the seat felt from where her bottom had been sitting.

Furious for allowing himself to be distracted by something so basic and inappropriate at a time like this, Matteo reached for the ignition key.

'You do know not to press down too hard on the accelerator, don't you?' she said nervously. 'Or you'll make the wheels spin.'

'I don't think I need any driving lessons from someone as incompetent as you,' he retorted. He started the engine and tried moving forward. Nothing. He tried until he was forced to surrender to the inevitable, which deep down he'd known all along. They were well and truly stuck and the car wasn't going anywhere. He turned to the woman sitting beside him who was staring at him nervously from beneath her peaked cap.

'So. Bravo,' he said, his words steeped in an anger he could no longer contain. 'You've managed to get us stranded in one of the most inhospitable parts of the country on one of the most inhospitable nights of the year—just before Christmas. That's some feat!'

'I'm so sorry.'

'Saying sorry isn't going to help.'

'I'll probably get the sack,' she whispered.

'You will if I have anything to do with it—that's if you don't freeze to death first!' he snapped. 'If it were down to me, I would never have employed you in the first place. But the consequences to your career are the last thing on my mind right now. We need to start working out what we're going to do next.'

She reached into the glove compartment for her mobile phone but he wasn't surprised to see her grimace as she glanced down at the small screen. 'No signal,' she said, looking up.

'You don't say?' he said sarcastically, peering out of the window where the howling flakes showed no signs of abating. 'I'm guessing there's no nearby village?'

She shook her head. 'No. Well, we did pass a little B&B just a while back. You know, one of those places which offer bed and breakfast for the night.'

'I'm in the hotel trade,' he said silkily. 'And I'm perfectly aware of what a B&B is. How far was it?'

She shrugged. 'Less than a mile, I'd guess—though it wouldn't be easy to reach in this kind of conditions.'

'No kidding?' Matteo eyed the virtual white-out which was taking place outside the window and his heart thundered as he acknowledged the real danger of their situation. Because suddenly this was about more than just missing his flight or disappointing a woman who had been eager to make him her lover; this was about survival. Venturing outside in this kind of conditions would be challenging—and dangerous—and the alternative was to hunker down in the car for the night and wait for help to arrive tomorrow. Presumably she would have blankets in the boot and they could continue to run the heater. His lips curved into a grim smile. And wasn't the traditional method of generating heat to huddle two bodies together? But he gave the idea no more than a few seconds' thought before dismissing it—and not just because she didn't look as if she had enough flesh on her bones to provide any degree of comfort. No. To take the risk of staying put while the snow came down this fast would be nothing short of madness, for there was no guarantee anyone would find them in the morning.

He ran his gaze over her uniform of navy blue trousers and the sturdy jacket which matched her cap. The material curved over the faint swell of her breasts and brushed against her thighs and was hardly what you would call *practical*—certainly not appropriate to face the elements at their worst. He sighed. Which meant he would have to give her his overcoat and freeze to death himself. 'I don't suppose you have any warmer clothes with you?'

For a few seconds, she seemed to brighten. 'I've got an anorak in the boot.'

'An anorak?'

'It's a waterproof jacket. With a hood.' She removed her peaked chauffeur's cap and raked her fingers through her short dark hair and Matteo felt inexplicably irritated by the brief smile which had lightened her pale face.

Was she expecting praise for having had the foresight to pack a coat? he wondered acidly.

'Just get it and put it on,' he bit out. 'And then let's get the hell out of here.'

CHAPTER TWO

KEIRA HAD TO work hard to keep up with Matteo as he battled his way through the deep snow because his powerful body moved much faster than hers, despite the fact that he'd insisted on bringing his suitcase with him. Thick, icy flakes were flying into her eyes and mouth and at times she wondered if she was imagining the small lighted building in the distance—like some bizarre, winter version of an oasis.

Despite putting on the big pair of leather gloves he'd insisted she borrow, her fingers felt like sticks of ice and she gave a little cry of relief when at last they reached the little house. Thank heavens she *hadn't* imagined it because she didn't like to think about Matteo Valenti's reaction if she'd brought him here on a wild goose chase. He might have insisted on her borrowing his gloves, but even that had been done with a terse impatience. She saw his unsmiling look as he kicked a pile of snow away from the wooden gate and pushed it open, and she stumbled after him up the path to stand beneath the flashing red and gold lights of the illuminated sign overhead. She was shivering with cold by the time he'd jammed his finger on the doorbell and they heard some tinkly little tune playing in the distance.

'Wh-what if…wh-what if nobody's in?' she questioned from between teeth which wouldn't seem to stop chattering.

'The light's on,' he said impatiently. 'Of course somebody's in.'

'They m-might have gone away for Christmas and left the lights on a timer to deter burglars.'

'You really think burglars are going to be enticed by a place like *this*?' he demanded.

But their bad-tempered interchange was brought to a swift halt by the sound of a lumbering movement from within the house and the door was pulled open by a plump, middle-aged woman wearing a flowery apron which was smeared with flour.

'Well, bless my soul!' she said, opening the door wider as she peered out into the gloom. 'You're not carol singers, are you?'

'We are not,' answered Matteo grimly. 'I'm afraid our car has got snowed in a little way down the road.'

'Oh, you poor things! What a night to be outside! Come in, come in!'

Keira felt like bursting into tears of gratitude as Matteo's palm positioned itself in the small of her back and propelled her inside the bright little hallway. During the seemingly endless journey here, she'd been convinced they weren't going to make it, and that their two frozen figures would be discovered the next day, or the day after that. And hadn't she been unable to stop herself from wondering whether anyone would have actually *cared* if she died?

But now they were standing dripping in a small hallway which had boughs of holly and strands of glittery tinsel draped absolutely everywhere. A green plastic tree was decked with flashing rainbow lights and from a central light hung a huge bunch of mistletoe. Keira's eyes were drawn in fascination to the row of small, fluffy snowmen waddling in a perfectly symmetrical line along a shelf—her attention only distracted by the realisation that puddles of water were growing on the stone tiles beneath their feet. Years of being told to respect property—especially when it *wasn't your own*—made Keira concentrate on the mess they were making, rather than the glaringly obvious fact that she and her bad-tempered Italian client were gate-crashing someone else's Christmas.

'Oh, my goodness—look at the floor!' she said, aware of the faint look of incredulity which Matteo Valenti was slanting in her direction. 'We're ruining your floor.'

'Don't you worry about that, my dear,' said the woman in her warm West Country accent. 'We get walkers coming in here all the time—that'll soon clean up.'

'We'd like to use your phone if that's okay,' said Matteo, and Keira watched as the woman looked at him, her mouth opening and closing comically as if she'd only just realised that she had six feet three inches of brooding masculine gorgeousness in her house, with melting snow sliding down over his black cashmere coat.

'And why would you want to do that, dear?' questioned the woman mildly.

Matteo did his best not to flinch at the overfamiliar response, even though he despised endearments from complete strangers. Actually, he despised endearments generally. Didn't they say that you always mistrusted what you weren't used to? Suppressing a frustrated flicker of anger at having found himself in this intolerable situation, he decided he needed to own it. Better to calmly spell out their needs, since his driver seemed incapable of doing anything with any degree of competence. 'Our car has become imbedded in the snow just down the road a little,' he said, directing an accusing glare at the woman who was currently pulling off her bulky waterproof jacket and shaking her short dark hair. 'We should never have taken this route, given the weather. However, what's done is done and we can't do anything about that now. We just need to get out of here, as quickly as possible, and I'd like to arrange that immediately.'

The woman nodded, her bright smile remaining unfaltering. 'I don't think that's going to be possible, dear. You won't get a rescue truck to dig you out—not tonight. Why, nothing's going to get through—not in these conditions!'

It was the confirmation of his worst fears and although Matteo was tempted to vent his rage, he was aware it would serve no useful purpose—as well as insulting the woman who'd been kind enough to open her house to them. And she was right. Who could possibly get to them tonight—in weather like this? He needed to face facts and accept that he was stuck here, in the middle of nowhere—with his incompetent driver in tow. A driver who was staring at him with eyes which suddenly looked very dark in her pale face. He frowned.

Of all the females in the world to be stranded with—it had to be someone like her! Once again his thoughts drifted to the luxurious party he would be missing, but he dismissed them as he drew in a deep breath and forced himself to say the unimaginable. 'Then it looks as if we're going to have to stay here. I assume you have rooms for hire?'

The woman's wide smile slipped. 'In December? Not likely! All my rooms are fully booked,' she added proudly. 'I get repeat trade all through the year, but especially at this time of year. People love a romantic Christmas on Dartmoor!'

'But we need somewhere to stay,' butted in Keira suddenly. 'Just until morning. Hopefully the snow will have stopped by then and we can get on our way in the morning.'

The woman nodded, her gaze running over Keira's pale cheeks as she took the anorak from her and hung it on a hook. 'Well, I'm hardly going to turn you out on a night like this, am I? Especially not at this time of the year—I'm sure we can find you room at the inn! I can put you in my daughter's old bedroom at the back of the house. That's the only space I have available. But the dining room is completely booked out and so I'm afraid I can't offer you dinner.'

'The meal doesn't matter,' put in Matteo quickly.

'Maybe if you could send something to the room when you have a moment?'

Keira felt numb as they were shown up some rickety stairs at the back of the house, and she remained numb as the landlady—who informed them that her name was Mary—opened the door with a flourish.

'You should be comfortable enough in here,' she said. 'The bathroom is just along the corridor though there's not much water left, and if you want a bath, you'll have to share. I'll just go downstairs and put the kettle on. Make yourselves at home.'

Mary shut the door behind her and Keira's heart started racing as she realised that she was alone in a claustrophobic space with Matteo Valenti. Make themselves at home? How on earth were they going to do that in a room this size with *only one bed*?

She shivered. 'Why didn't you tell her that we didn't want to share?'

He shot her an impatient look. 'We are two people and she has one room. You do the math. What alternative did I have?'

Keira could see his point. Mary couldn't magic up another bedroom from out of nowhere, could she? She looked around. It was one of those rooms which wasn't really big enough for the furniture it contained. It was too small for a double bed, but a double bed had been crammed into it nonetheless, and it dominated the room with its homemade patchwork quilt and faded pillow cases on which you could just about make out some Disney characters, one of which just happened to be Cinderella.

There were no signs of Christmas in here but on every available surface seemed to be a photo. Photos of someone who was recognisably Mary, looking much younger and holding a series of babies, then toddlers, right through gangly teenagers until the inevitable stiff wedding photos—and then yet more babies. Keira licked her lips. It was a life played out in stills. A simple life, probably—and a happy life, judging by the smile which was never far from Mary's face. Keira was used to cramped and cluttered spaces but she wasn't used to somewhere feeling homely—and she could do absolutely nothing about the fierce pang of something which felt like envy, which clutched at her heart like a vice.

She lifted her eyes to meet Matteo's flat gaze. 'I'm sorry,' she said.

'Spare me the platitudes,' he snapped, pulling out the mobile phone from the pocket of his trousers and staring at it with a barely concealed lack of hope. 'No signal. Of course there isn't. And no Wi-Fi either.'

'She said you could use the landline any time.'

'I know she did. I'll call my assistant once I've removed some of these wet clothes.' He loosened his tie before tugging it off and throwing it over the back of a nearby chair, where it dangled like some precious spiral of gunmetal. His mouth hardened with an expression of disbelief as he looked around. '*Per amor del cielo!* Who even uses places like this? We don't even have our own bathroom.'

'Mary told us we could use the one along the corridor.'

'She also told us that we'd need to share a bath because there wasn't enough hot water!' he flared. '*Sharing a bath? Not enough hot wate*r*?* Which century are we supposed to be living in?'

Keira shrugged her shoulders awkwardly, suspecting that Matteo Valenti wasn't used to the vagaries of small-town English landladies, or the kind of places where ordinary people stayed. Of course he wasn't. According to her boss, he owned luxury hotels all over his own country—he even had some scattered over America, as well as some in Barbados and Hawaii. What would he know about having to traipse along a chilly corridor to a bathroom which, like the rest of the house, obviously hadn't been modernised in decades?

'It's an English eccentricity. Part of the place's charm,' she added lamely.

'Charm I can do without,' he responded acidly. 'Good plumbing trumps charm every time.'

She wondered if he was deliberately ignoring something even more disturbing than the bathroom facilities...or maybe she was just being super-sensitive about it, given her uneasy history. Awkwardly she raked her fingers through her spiky hair, wondering what it was which marked her out from other women. Why was it that on the only two occasions she'd shared a bed with a man, one had been passed out drunk—while the other was looking at her with nothing but irritation in his hard black eyes?

He was nodding his head, as if she had spoken out loud. 'I know,' he said grimly. 'It's my idea of a nightmare, too. Sharing a too-small bed with an employee wasn't top of my Christmas wish list.'

Don't react, Keira told herself fiercely. And don't take it personally. Act with indifference and don't make out like it's a big deal.

'I expect we'll survive,' she said coolly, then began to rub at her arms through the thin jacket as she started to shiver.

He ran a speculative gaze over her and an unexpected note of consideration crept into his voice. 'You're cold,' he said, his eyes lingering on her thighs just a fraction too long. 'And your trousers are soaking.'

'You don't say?' she said, her voice rising a little defensively, because she'd never been very good at dealing with unsolicited kindness.

'Don't you have anything else you can wear?' he persisted.

Embarrassment made her even more defensive and Keira glared at him, aware of the heat now staining her cheeks. 'Yes, of course I do. I always make sure I carry an entire change of clothes with me whenever I embark on a drive from London to Devon,' she said. 'It's what every driver does.'

'Why don't you skip the sarcasm?' he suggested. 'And go and take a hot bath? You can borrow something of mine.'

Keira looked at him suspiciously, taken aback by the offer and not quite sure if he meant it. Without his cashmere coat he stood resplendent in a dark charcoal suit which, even to her untutored eye, she could tell was made-to-measure. It must have been—because surely your average suit didn't cater for men with shoulders as broad as his, or legs that long. What on earth could Matteo Valenti have in his suitcase which would fit *her*? 'You carry women's clothes around with you, do you?'

An unexpected smile lifted the corners of his mouth and the corresponding race of Keira's heart made her hope he wasn't going to do a lot of smiling.

'Funnily enough, no,' he said drily, unzipping the leather case. 'But I have a sweater you can use. And a soap bag. Here. Go on. Take it.'

He was removing the items from his case and handing them to her and Keira was overcome by a sudden gratitude. 'Th-thanks. You're very kind—'

'*Basta!* Spare me the stumbling appreciation. I'm not doing it out of any sense of *kindness*.' His mouth hardened. 'This day has already been a disaster—I don't want to add to the misery by having you catch pneumonia and finding myself with a wrongful death suit on my hands.'

'Well, I'll do my best not to get sick then,' she bit back. 'I'd hate to inconvenience you any more than I already have done!'

Her fingers digging into his sweater, Keira marched from the room to the bathroom along the corridor, trying to dampen down her rising feelings of anger. He really was the most hateful person she'd ever met and she was going to have to endure a whole night with him.

Hanging his sweater on the back of the door, she quickly assessed the facilities on offer and for the first time that day, she smiled. Good thing *she* was used to basics. To her the avocado-coloured sink and bath were nothing out of the ordinary, though she shuddered to think how Mr Cynical was going to cope. When she'd been growing up, she and her mother had lived in places with far worse plumbing than this. In fact, this rather tatty bathroom felt almost *nostalgic*. A throwback to tougher times, yes, but at least it had been one of those rare times when she'd known emotional security, before Mum had died.

Clambering into the tiny bath, she directed the leaking shower attachment over her head and sluiced herself with tepid water before lathering on some of Matteo's amazing soap. And then the strangest thing started happening. Beneath her massaging fingers she could feel her nipples begin to harden into tight little nubs and for a moment she closed her eyes as she imagined her powerful client touching her there, before pulling her hands away in horror. What on earth was *wrong* with her?

Leaving the plug in situ and climbing out of the tub, she furiously rubbed herself dry. Wasn't the situation bad enough without her fantasising about a man who was probably going to make sure she got fired as soon as they reached civilisation?

She put on her bra, turned her knickers inside out and slithered Matteo's grey sweater over her head. It was warm and very soft—it was just unfortunate that it only came to mid-thigh, no matter how hard she tugged at the hem. She stared into the mirror. And the problem with that was, what? Was she really naïve enough to think that the Italian tycoon would even *notice* what she was wearing? Why, judging from his attitude towards her up until now, she could probably waltz back in there completely naked and he wouldn't even bat those devastatingly dark eyelashes.

But about that Keira was wrong—just as she'd been wrong in making the detour via Dartmoor—because when she walked back into the bedroom Matteo Valenti turned around from where he had been standing gazing out of the window and, just like the weather outside, his face froze. It was extraordinary to witness, that unmistakable double take when he saw her, something which never normally happened when Keira walked into a room. His eyes narrowed and grew smoky and something in the atmosphere seemed to subtly shift, and change. She wasn't used to it, but she wasn't going to deny that it made her skin grow warm with pleasure. Unless, of course, she was totally misreading the situation. It wouldn't be the first time, would it?

'Is everything okay?' she asked uncertainly.

Matteo nodded in response, aware that a pulse had begun to hammer at his temple. He'd just finished a telephone conversation with his assistant and as a consequence he'd been miles away, staring out of the window at the desolate countryside and having the peculiar sensation of realising that nobody could get hold of him—a sensation which had brought with it a surprising wave of peace. He had watched his driver scuttle off towards the bathroom in her unflattering navy trouser suit, only now she had returned and…

He stared and swallowed down the sudden lump which had risen in his throat. It was inexplicable. What the hell had she done to herself?

Her short, dark hair was still drying and the heat

of the shower must have been responsible for the rosy flush of her cheeks, against which her sapphire eyes looked huge and glittery. But it was his sweater which was responsible for inflicting a sudden sexual awakening he would have preferred to avoid. A plain cashmere sweater which looked like a completely different garment when worn by her. She was so small and petite that it pretty much swamped her, but it hinted at the narrow-hipped body beneath and the most perfect pair of legs he had ever seen. She looked…

He shook his head slightly. She looked *sexy*, he thought resentfully as lust arrowed straight to his groin, where it hardened and stayed. She looked as if she wanted him to lay her down on the bed and start kissing her. As if she were tantalising him with the question of whether or not she was wearing any panties. He felt he was in a schoolboy's fantasy, tempted to ask her to bend down to pick up some imaginary object from the carpet so he could see for himself if her bottom was bare. And then he glared because the situation was bad enough without having to endure countless hours of frustration, daydreaming about a woman he couldn't have—even if he was the kind of man to indulge in a one-night stand, which he most emphatically wasn't.

'*Sì*, everything is wonderful. *Fantastico,*' he added sarcastically. 'I've just made a phone call to my assistant and asked her to make my apologies for tonight's party. She asked if I was doing something nice instead and I told her that no, I was not. In fact, I was stuck on a snowy moor in the middle of nowhere.'

'I've left you some hot water,' she said stiffly, deciding to ignore his rant.

'How will I be able to contain my excitement?' he returned as he picked up the clothes he had selected from his case and slammed his way out of the room.

But he'd calmed down a little by the time he returned, dressed down in jeans and a sweater, to find her stirring a pot of tea which jostled for space on a tray containing sandwiches and mince pies. She turned her face towards him with a questioning look.

'Are you hungry?' she said.

It was difficult to return her gaze when all he wanted to do was focus on her legs and that still tantalising question of what she was or wasn't wearing underneath his sweater. Matteo shrugged. 'I guess.'

'Would you like a sandwich?'

'How can I refuse?'

'It's very kind of Mary to have gone to the trouble of making us some, especially when she's trying to cook a big turkey dinner for eight people,' she admonished quietly. 'The least we can do is be grateful.'

'I suppose so.'

Keira tried to maintain her polite smile as she handed him a cup of tea and a cheese sandwich, telling herself that nothing would be gained by being rude herself. In fact, it would only make matters worse if they started sparring. She was the one in the wrong and the one whose job was on the line. If she kept answering him back, who was to say he wouldn't ring up her boss and subject him to a blistering tirade about her incompetence? If she kept him sweet, mightn't he be persuaded not to make a big deal out of the situation, maybe even to forget it had ever happened and put it down to experience? She needed this job because she loved it and things to love in Keira's life happened too rarely for her to want to give them up without a fight.

She noticed that he said nothing as he ate, his expression suggesting he was merely fuelling his impressive body rather than enjoying what was on offer—but Keira's hunger had completely deserted her and that was a first. She normally had a healthy appetite, which often surprised people who commented on her tiny frame. But not today. Today food was the last thing on her mind. She broke off the rim of one of the mince pies and forced herself to chew on it and the sugar gave her a sudden rush, but all she could think about was how on earth they were going to get through the hours ahead, when there wasn't even a radio in the room—let alone a TV. She watched the way the lamplight fell on her client's face—the hardness of his features contrasting with the sensual curve of his lips—and found herself wondering what it might be like to be kissed by a man like him.

Stop it, she urged herself furiously. Just *stop* it. You couldn't even maintain the interest of that trainee mechanic you dated in the workshop—do you really fancy your chances with the Italian billionaire?

A note of desperation tinged her voice as she struggled to think of something they could do which might distract her from all that brooding masculinity. 'Shall I go downstairs and see if Mary has any board games we could play?'

He put his empty cup down and his eyes narrowed. 'Excuse me?'

'You know.' She shrugged her shoulders helplessly. 'Cards, or Scrabble or Monopoly. Something,' she added. 'Because we can't just spend the whole evening staring at each other and dreading the night ahead, can we?'

He raised his dark eyebrows. 'You're dreading the night ahead, are you, Keira?'

A shimmer of amusement had deepened his voice and Keira realised that, not only was it the first time he'd actually used her name, but that he'd said it as no one had ever said it before. She could feel colour flushing over her cheekbones and knew she had to stop coming over as some kind of unworldly idiot. 'Well, aren't you?' she challenged. 'Don't tell me your heart didn't sink when you realised we'd have to spend the night here.'

Matteo considered her question. Up until a few moments ago he might have agreed with her, but there was something about the girl with the spiky black hair which was making him reconsider his original assessment. It was, he thought, a novel situation and he was a man whose appetites had been jaded enough over the years to be entertained by the novel. And Keira whatever-her-name-was certainly wasn't your average woman. She wasn't behaving as most women would have done in the circumstances. She had suggested playing a game as if she actually meant it, without any purring emphasis on the word *playing*, leaving him in no doubt how she intended the 'game' to progress—with him thrusting into her eager body. People called him arrogant, but he preferred to think of himself as a realist. He'd never been guilty of under-assessing his own attributes—and one of those was his ability to make the opposite sex melt, without even trying.

He focussed his gaze on her, mildly amused by the competitive look in her eyes which suggested that her question had been genuine. 'Sure,' he said. 'Let's play games.'

Picking up the tray, she went downstairs, reappearing after a little while with a stack of board games, along with a bottle of red wine and two glasses.

'There's no need to be snobby about the vintage,' she said, noticing his expression as he frowningly assessed the label on the bottle. 'It was very sweet of Mary to offer us a festive drink and I'm having a glass even if you aren't. I'm not driving anywhere tonight and I don't want to offend her, not when she's been so kind.'

Feeling surprisingly chastened, Matteo took the bottle and opened it, pouring them each a glass and forcing himself to drink most of his in a single draught as he lowered himself into the most uncomfortable chair he'd ever sat in.

'Ready?' she questioned as she sat cross-legged on the bed, with a blanket placed discreetly over her thighs as she faced him.

'I guess,' he growled.

They played Monopoly, which naturally he won—but then, he'd spent all his adult life trading property and had learnt early that there was no commodity more precious than land. But he was surprised when she suggested a quick game of poker and even more surprised by her skill with the cards.

Matteo wondered afterwards if he'd been distracted by knowing her legs were bare beneath the blanket. Or if he'd just spent too long gazing at her curling black lashes, which remarkably didn't carry a trace of mascara. Because wasn't the truth that he was finding his pocket-sized driver more fascinating with every moment which passed? She was certainly managing to keep her face poker-straight as she gazed at her cards and inexplicably he found himself longing to kiss those unsmiling lips.

He swallowed. Was she aware that her coolness towards him was fanning a sexual awareness which was growing fiercer by the second? He didn't know—all he *did* know was that by the time they'd drunk most of the bottle of wine, she had beaten him hands-down and it was an unfamiliar experience.

He narrowed his eyes. 'Who taught you to play like that?'

She shrugged. 'Before I became a driver, I worked as a car mechanic—mostly with men,' she added airily. 'And they liked to play cards when the workshop was quiet.'

'You worked as a *car mechanic*?'

'You sound surprised.'

'I am surprised. You don't look strong enough to take a car to pieces.'

'Appearances can be deceptive.'

'They certainly can.' He picked up the bottle and emptied out the last of the wine, noticing her fingers tremble as he handed her the glass. She must be feeling it too, he thought grimly—that almost tangible buzz of *electricity* when his hand brushed against hers. He crossed one leg over the other to hide the hard throb of his erection as he tried—and failed—to think of something which didn't involve his lips and her body.

'Mr Valenti,' she said suddenly.

'Matteo,' he instructed silkily. 'I thought we agreed we should be on first-name terms, given the somewhat *unusual* circumstances.'

'Yes, we did, but I...

Keira's words tailed away as he fixed her with a questioning look, not quite sure how to express her thoughts. The alcohol had made her feel more daring than usual—something which she'd fully exploited during that game of cards. She'd known it probably wasn't the most sensible thing to defeat Matteo Valenti and yet something had made her want to show him she wasn't as useless as he seemed to think she was. But she was now aware of her bravado slipping away. Just as she was aware of the tension which had been building in the cramped bedroom ever since she'd emerged from the bathroom.

Her breasts were aching and her inside-out panties were wet. Did he realise that? Perhaps he was used to women reacting that way around him but she wasn't one of those women. She'd been called frigid by men before, when really she'd been scared—scared of doing what her mother had always warned her against. But it had never been a problem before, because close contact with the opposite sex had always left her cold and the one time she'd ended up in bed with a man he had been snoring in a drunken stupor almost before his head had hit the pillow. So how was Matteo managing to make her feel like this—as if every pore were screaming for him to touch her?

She swallowed. 'We haven't discussed what we're going to do about sleeping arrangements.'

'What did you have in mind?'

'Well, it looks as if we've got to share a bed—so obviously we've got to come to some sort of compromise.' She drew a deep breath. 'And I was thinking we might sleep top and tail.'

'Top and tail?' he repeated.

'You know.'

'Obviously I don't,' he said impatiently. 'Or I wouldn't have asked.'

Awkwardly, she wriggled her shoulders. 'It's easy. I sleep with my head at one end of the bed and you sleep with yours at the other. We used to do it when I was in the Girl Guides. Sometimes people even put pillows between them, so they can keep to their side and there's no encroaching on the other person's space.' She forged on but it wasn't easy when he was staring at her with a growing look of incredulity. 'Unless you're prepared to spend the night in that armchair?'

Matteo became aware of the hardness of the overstuffed seat which made him feel as if he were sitting on spirals of iron. 'You honestly think I'm going to spend the night sitting in this damned chair?'

She looked at him uncertainly. 'You want *me* to take the chair?'

'And keep me awake all night while you shift around trying to get comfortable? No. I do not. I'll tell you exactly what's going to happen, *cara mia.* We're going to share that bed as the nice lady suggested. But don't worry, I will break the habit of a lifetime by not sleeping naked and you can keep the sweater on. *Capisci?* And you can rest assured that you'll be safe from my intentions because I don't find you in the least bit attractive.'

Which wasn't exactly true—but why make a grim situation even worse than it already was?

He stood up and as he began to undo the belt of his trousers, he saw her lips fall open. 'Better close those big blue eyes,' he suggested silkily, a flicker of amusement curving his lips as he watched all the colour drain from her cheeks. 'At least until I'm safely underneath the covers.'

CHAPTER THREE

KEIRA LAY IN the darkness nudging her tongue over lips which felt as dry as if she'd been running a marathon. She'd tried everything. Breathing deeply. Counting backwards from a thousand. Relaxing her muscles from the toes up. But up until now nothing had worked and all she could think about was the man in bed beside her. *Matteo Valenti. In bed beside her.* She had to keep silently repeating it to herself to remind herself of the sheer impossibility of the situation—as well as the undeniable temptation which was fizzing over her.

Sheer animal warmth radiated from his powerful frame, making her want to squirm with an odd kind of frustration. She kept wanting to fidget but she forced herself to lie as still as possible, terrified of waking him up. She kept telling herself that she'd been up since six that morning and should be exhausted, but the more she reached out for sleep, the more it eluded her.

Was it because that unwilling glimpse of his body as he was about to climb into bed had reinforced all the fantasies she'd been trying not to have? And yes, he'd covered up with a T-shirt and a pair of silky boxers—

but they did nothing to detract from his hard-packed abdomen and hair-roughened legs. Each time she closed her eyes she could picture all that hard, honed muscle and a wave of hunger shivered over her body, leaving her almost breathless with desire.

The sounds coming from downstairs didn't help. The dinner which Mary had mentioned was in full flow and bothering her in ways she'd prefer not to think about. She could hear squeals of excitement above the chatter and, later, the heartbreaking strains of children's voices as they started singing carols. She could picture them all by a roaring log fire with red candles burning on the mantle above, just like on the front of a Christmas card, and Keira felt a wave of wistfulness overwhelm her because she'd never had that.

'Can't sleep?' The Italian's silky voice penetrated her spinning thoughts and she could tell from the shifting weight on the mattress that Matteo Valenti had turned his head to talk to her.

Keira swallowed. Should she pretend to be asleep? But what would be the point of that? She suspected he would see through her ruse immediately—and wasn't it a bit of a relief not to have to keep still any more? 'No,' she admitted. 'Can't you?'

He gave a short laugh. 'I wasn't expecting to.'

'Why not?'

His voice dipped. 'I suspect you know exactly why not. It's a somewhat *unusual* situation to be sharing a bed with an attractive woman and having to behave in such a chaste manner.'

Keira was glad of the darkness which hid her sudden

flush of pleasure. Had the gorgeous and arrogant Matteo Valenti actually called her *attractive*? And was he really implying that he was having difficulty keeping his hands off her? Of course, he might only be saying it to be polite—but he hadn't exactly been the model of politeness up until now, had he?

'I thought you said you didn't find me attractive.'

'That's what I was trying to convince myself.'

In the darkness, she gave a smile of pleasure. 'I could go downstairs and see if I could get us some more tea.'

'Please.' He groaned. 'No more tea.'

'Then I guess we'll have to resign ourselves to a sleepless night.' She plumped up her pillow and sighed as she collapsed back against it. 'Unless you've got a better suggestion?'

Matteo gave a frustrated smile because her question sounded genuine. She wasn't asking it in such a way which demanded he lean over and give her the answer with his lips. Just as she wasn't accidentally brushing one of those pretty little legs against his and tantalising him with her touch. He swallowed. Not that her virtuous attitude made any difference because he'd been hard from the moment he'd first slipped beneath the covers, and he was rock-hard now. Hard for a woman with terrible hair whose incompetence was responsible for him being marooned in this hellhole in the first place! A different kind of frustration washed over him as the lumpy mattress dug into his back until he reminded himself that apportioning blame would serve little purpose.

'I guess we could talk,' he said.

'What about?'

'What do women like best to talk about?' he questioned sardonically. 'You could tell me something about yourself.'

'And what good will that do?'

'Probably send me off to sleep,' he admitted.

He could hear her give a little snort of laughter. 'You do say some outrageous things, Mr Valenti.'

'Guilty. And I thought we agreed on Matteo—at least while we're in bed together.' He smiled as he heard her muffled gasp of outrage. 'Tell me how you plan to spend Christmas—isn't that what everyone asks at this time of year?'

Beneath the duvet, Keira flexed and unflexed her fingers, thinking that of all the questions he *could* have asked, that was the one she least felt like answering. Why hadn't he asked her about cars so she could have dazzled him with her mechanical knowledge? Or told him about her pipedream of one day being able to restore beautiful vintage cars, even though realistically that was never going to happen. 'With my aunt and my cousin, Shelley,' she said grudgingly.

'But you're not looking forward to it?'

'Is it that obvious?'

'I'm afraid it is. Your voice lacked a certain...enthusiasm.'

She thought that was a very diplomatic way of putting it. 'No, I'm not.'

'So why not spend Christmas somewhere else?'

Keira sighed. In the darkness it was all too easy to forget the veneer of nonchalance she always adopted when people asked questions about her personal life.

She kept facts to a minimum because it was easier that way. If you made it clear you didn't want to talk about something, then eventually people stopped asking.

But Matteo was different. She wasn't ever going to see him again after tomorrow. And wasn't it good to be able to say what she felt for once, instead of what she knew people expected to hear? She knew she was lucky her aunt had taken her in when that drunken joy-rider had mown down her mother on her way home from work, carrying the toy dog she'd bought for her daughter's birthday. Lucky she hadn't had to go into a foster home or some scary institution. But knowing something didn't always change the way you felt inside. And it didn't change the reality of being made to feel like an imposition. Of constantly having to be grateful for having been given a home, when it was clear you weren't really wanted. Trying to ignore all the snide little barbs because Keira had been better looking than her cousin Shelley. It had been the reason she'd cut off all her hair one day and kept it short. Anything for a quiet life. 'Because Christmas is a time for families and they're the only one I have,' she said.

'You don't have parents?'

'No.' And then, because he seemed to have left a gap for her to fill, she found herself doing exactly that. 'I didn't know my father and my aunt brought me up after my mother died, so I owe her a lot.'

'But you don't like her?'

'I didn't say that.'

'You didn't have to. It isn't a crime to admit it. You

don't have to like someone, just because they were kind to you, Keira, even if they're a relative.'

'She did her best and it can't have been easy. There wasn't a lot of money sloshing around,' she said. 'And now my uncle has died, there's only the two of them and I think she's lonely, in a funny kind of way. So I shall be sitting round a table with her and my cousin, pulling Christmas crackers and pretending to enjoy dry turkey. Just like most people, I guess.'

There was a pause so long that for a moment Keira wondered if he *had* fallen asleep, so that when he spoke again it startled her.

'So what *would* you do over Christmas?' he questioned softly. 'If money were no object and you didn't have to spend time with your aunt?'

Keira pulled the duvet up to her chin. 'How much money are we talking about? Enough to charter a private jet and fly to the Caribbean?'

'If that's what turns you on.'

'Not particularly.' Keira looked at the faint gleam of a photo frame glowing in the darkness on the other side of the room. It was a long time since she'd played make-believe. A long time since she'd dared. 'I'd book myself into the most luxurious hotel I could find,' she said slowly, 'and I'd watch TV. You know, one of those TVs which are big enough to fill a wall—big as a cinema screen. I've never had a TV in the bedroom before and it would be showing every cheesy Christmas film ever made. So I'd lie there and order up ice cream and popcorn and eat myself stupid and try not to blub too much.'

Beneath the thin duvet, Matteo's body tensed and not just because of the wistfulness in her voice. It had been a long time since he'd received such an uncomplicated answer from anyone. And wasn't her simple candour refreshing? As refreshing as her lean young body and eyes which were *profundo blu* if you looked at them closely—the colour of the deep, dark sea. The beat of his heart had accelerated and he felt the renewed throb of an erection, heavy against his belly. And suddenly the darkness represented danger because it was cloaking him with anonymity. Making him forget who he was and who she was. Tempting him with things he shouldn't even be thinking about. Because without light they were simply two bodies lying side by side, at the mercy of their senses—and right then his senses were going into overdrive.

Reaching out his arm, he snapped on the light, so that the small bedroom was flooded with a soft glow, and Keira lay there with the duvet right up to her chin, blinking her eyes at him.

'What did you do that for?'

'Because I'm finding the darkness…distracting.'

'I don't understand.'

He raised his eyebrows. 'Don't you?'

There was a pause. Matteo could see wariness in her eyes as she shook her head, but he could see the flicker of something else, something which made his heart pound even harder. Fraternising with the workforce was a bad idea—everyone knew that. But knowing something didn't always change the way you felt. It didn't stop your body from becoming so tight with lust that it felt like a taut bow, just before the arrow was fired.

No,' she said at last. 'I don't.'

'I think I'd better go and sleep in that damned armchair after all,' he said. 'Because if I stay here any longer I'm going to start kissing you.'

Keira met his mocking black gaze in astonishment. Had Matteo Valenti just said he wanted to *kiss* her? For a moment she just lay there, revelling in the sensation of being the object of attraction to such a gorgeous man, while common sense pitched a fierce battle with her senses.

She realised that despite talking about the armchair he hadn't moved and that an unspoken question seemed to be hovering in the air. Somewhere in a distant part of the house she heard a clock chiming and, though it wasn't midnight, it felt like the witching hour. As if magic could happen if she only let it. If she listened to what she wanted rather than the voice of caution which had been a constant presence in her life ever since she could remember. She'd learnt the hard way what happened to women who fell for the wrong kind of man—and Matteo Valenti had *wrong* written on every pore of his body. He was dangerous and sexy and he was a billionaire who was way out of her league. Shouldn't she be turning away from him and telling him yes, to please take the armchair?

Yet she wasn't doing any of those things. Instead of her eyes closing, the tip of her tongue was sliding over her bottom lip and she was finding it impossible to drag her gaze away from him. She could feel a molten heat low in her belly, which was making her ache in a way which was shockingly exciting. She thought about the holidays ahead. The stilted Christmas lunch with her aunt beaming at Shelley and talking proudly of her daughter's job as a beautician, while wondering how her only niece had ended up as a car mechanic.

Briefly Keira closed her eyes. She'd spent her whole life trying to be good and where had it got her? You didn't get medals for being good. She'd made the best of her dyslexia and capitalised on the fact that she was talented with her hands and could take engines apart, then put them back together. She'd found a job in a man's world which was just about making ends meet, but she'd never had a long-term relationship. She'd never even had sex—and if she wasn't careful she might end up old and wistful, remembering a snowy night on Dartmoor when Matteo Valenti had wanted to kiss her.

She stared at him. 'Go on, then,' she whispered. 'Kiss me.'

If she thought he might hesitate, she was wrong. There was no follow-up question about whether she was sure. He framed her face in his hands and the moment he lowered his lips to hers, that was it. The deal was done and there was no going back. He kissed her until she was dizzy with pleasure and molten with need. Until she began to move in his arms—restlessly seeking the next stage, terrified that any second now he would guess how laughingly inexperienced she was and push her away. She heard him laugh softly as he slid his fingers beneath the sweater to encounter the bra which curved over her breasts.

'Too much clothing,' he murmured, slipping his hand round her back to snap open the offending article and shake it free.

She remembered thinking he must have done this lots of times before and maybe she should confess how innocent she was. But by then he'd started circling her nipples with the light caress of his thumb and the moment passed. Desire pooled like honey in her groin and Keira gave a little cry as sensation threatened to overwhelm her.

'Sta' zitto,' he urged softly as he pulled the sweater over her head and tossed it aside, the movement quickly followed by the efficient disposal of his own T-shirt and boxers. 'Stay quiet. We don't want to disturb the rest of the house, do we?'

Keira shook her head, unable to answer because now he was sliding her panties down and a wild flame of hunger was spreading through her body. 'Matteo,' she gasped as his fingers moved down over her belly and began to explore her molten flesh. He stoked her with a delicacy which was tantalising—each intimate caress making her slide deeper into a brand-new world of intimacy. Yet strangely, it felt familiar. As if she knew exactly what to do, despite being such a novice. Did he tell her to part her legs or were they opening of their own accord? She didn't know. All she knew was that once he started stroking his fingertip against those hot, wet folds, she thought she might pass out with pleasure. 'Oh,' she whispered, on a note of wonder.

'Oh, what?' he murmured.

'It's...incredible.'

'I know it is. Now, touch me,' he urged against her mouth.

Keira swallowed. Did she dare? He was so big and proud and she didn't really know what to do. Swallowing down her nerves, she took him between her thumb and forefinger and began to stroke him up and down with a featherlight motion which nearly made him shoot off the bed.

'*Madonna mia!* Where did you learn to do *that*?' he gasped.

She guessed it might destroy the mood if she explained that car mechanics were often blessed with a naturally sensitive touch. Instead, she enquired in a husky voice which didn't really sound like her voice at all, 'Do you like it?'

'Do I like it?' He swallowed. 'Are you crazy? I love it.'

So why was he halting her progress with the firm clamp of his hand around her wrist, if he loved it so much? Why was he was blindly reaching for the wallet which he'd placed on the nightstand? He was pulling out a small foil packet and Keira shivered as she realised what he was about to do. This might be the craziest and most impulsive thing which had ever happened to her—but at least she would be protected.

He slid on the condom and she was surprised by her lack of fear as she wound her arms eagerly around his neck. Because it felt right. Not because he was rich and powerful, or even because he was insanely good-looking and sexy, but because something about him had touched her heart. Maybe it was the way his voice had softened when he'd asked her those questions about Christmas. Almost as if he *cared*—and it had been a long time since anybody had cared. Was she such a sucker for a few crumbs of affection that she would give herself completely to a man she didn't really know? She wasn't sure. All she knew was that she wanted him more than she'd ever wanted anything.

'Matteo,' she said as he pulled her into his body.

His eyes gleamed as he looked down at her. 'You want to change your mind?'

His consideration only made her want him more. 'No,' she whispered, her fingertips whispering over his neck. 'No way.'

He kissed her again—until she'd reached that same delicious melting point as before and then he moved to straddle her. His face was shadowed as he positioned himself and she tensed as he made that first thrust and began to move, but although the pain was sharp it was thankfully brief. She saw his brow darken and felt him grow very still before he changed his rhythm. His movements slowed as he bent her legs and wrapped them tightly around his waist so that with each long thrust he seemed to fill her completely.

As her body relaxed to accommodate his thickness, Keira felt the excitement build. Inch by glorious inch he entered her, before pulling back to repeat the same sweet stroke, over and over again. She could feel her skin growing heated as all her nerve-endings bunched in exquisitely tight anticipation. She could feel the inexorable build-up of excitement to such a pitch that she honestly didn't think she could take it any more. And then it happened. Like a swollen dam bursting open, waves of intense pleasure began to take her under. She felt herself shatter, as if he needed to break her apart before she could become whole again, and she pressed her mouth against his sweat-sheened shoulder. Dimly, she became aware of his own bucked release as he shuddered above her and was surprised by the unexpected prick of tears to her eyes.

He pulled out of her and rolled back against the pillows to suck in a ragged breath. With a sudden shyness, Keira glanced across at him but his eyes were closed and his olive features shuttered, so that suddenly she felt excluded from the private world in which he seemed to be lost. The room was quiet and she didn't dare speak—wondering what women usually said at moments like this.

Eventually he turned to her, his eyebrows raised in question and an expression on his face she couldn't quite work out.

'So?'

She wanted to hang on to the pleasure for as long as possible—she didn't want it all to evaporate beneath the harsh spotlight of explanation—but he seemed to be waiting for one all the same.

She peered up at him. 'You're angry?'

He shrugged. 'Why should I be angry?'

'Because I didn't tell you.'

'That you were a virgin?' He gave an odd kind of laugh. 'I'm glad you didn't. It might have shattered the mood.'

She tucked a strand of hair behind her ear. 'Aren't you going to ask me why?'

'You chose me to be your first?' His smile now held a faint trace of arrogance. 'I could commend you for your excellent judgment in selecting someone like me to be your first lover, but it's not really any of my business, is it, Keira?'

For some reason, that hurt, though she wasn't going to show it. Had she been naïve enough to suppose he might exhibit a chest-thumping pride that she had chosen him, rather than anyone else? 'I suppose not,' she said, her toes moving beneath the rumpled bedclothes in a desperate attempt to locate her only pair of panties.

'I just hope you weren't disappointed.'

'You must know I wasn't,' she said, in a small voice.

He seemed to soften a little at that, and brushed back a few little tufts of hair which had fallen untidily over her forehead. '*Sì*, I know. And for what it's worth, it was pretty damned amazing for me, too. I've never had sex with a virgin before but I understand it's uncommon for it to be as good as that the first time. So you should feel very pleased with yourself.' He began to stroke her hair. 'And you're tired.'

'No.'

'Yes,' he said firmly. 'And you need to sleep. So why don't you do that? Lie back and let yourself drift off.'

His words were soothing but Keira didn't want to sleep, she wanted to talk. She wanted to ask him about himself and his life. She wanted to know what would happen now—but there was something in his voice which indicated he didn't feel the same. And mightn't stilted conversation destroy some of this delicious afterglow which felt so impossibly fragile—like a bubble which could be popped at any moment? So she nodded obediently and shut her eyes and within seconds she could feel herself drifting off into the most dreamy sleep she'd ever known.

Matteo watched as her eyelashes fluttered down and waited until her breathing was steady before removing his arm from where it had been resting around her shoulders, but, although she stirred a little, she didn't waken. And that was when the reality of what he'd done hit him.

He'd just seduced a member of staff. More than that, he'd taken her innocence.

Silently, he cursed. He'd broken two fundamental rules in the most spectacular way. His chest was tight as he switched off the lamp and his mind buzzed as he attempted to ignore the naked woman who lay sleeping beside him. Yet that was easier said than done. He wanted nothing more than to push his growing erection inside her tight body again, but he needed to work out the most effective form of damage limitation. For both of them.

He stared up at the shadowy ceiling and sighed. He didn't want to hurt her and he could so easily hurt her. Hurting was something he seemed to do to women without even trying, mainly because he couldn't do love and he couldn't do emotion—at least that was what he'd been accused of, time after time. And Keira didn't deserve that. She'd given herself to him with an openness which had left him breathless and afterwards there had been no demands.

But none of that detracted from the reality of their situation. They came from worlds which were poles apart, which had collided in this small bedroom on the snowy outreaches of Devon. For a brief time they had come together in mindless pleasure but in truth they were nothing more than mismatched strangers driven by the stir of lust. Back in Italy he had been given an ultimatum which needed addressing and he needed to consider the truth behind his father's words.

'Give me an heir, Matteo,' he had breathed. *'Continue the Valenti name and I will give you your heart's desire. Refuse and I will sign the estate over to your stepbrother and his child.'*

Matteo's heart kicked with pain. He had to decide how much he was willing to sacrifice to maintain his links to the past. He needed to return to his world. And Keira to hers.

His jaw tightened. Would he have stopped if he'd known he was her first? He might have *wanted* to stop but something told him he would have been powerless to pull back from the indescribable lure of her petite body. His throat dried as he remembered that first sweet thrust. She had seemed much too small to accommodate him, but she had taken him inside her as if he had been intended to fit into her and only her. He remembered the way she'd touched him with that tentative yet sure touch. She'd made him want to explode. Had the newness of it been responsible for her joyful response—and for the tears which had trickled against his shoulder afterwards, but which she'd hastily blotted away?

Suddenly he could understand the potent power wielded by virgins but he could also recognise that they were a responsibility. They still had dreams—because experience hadn't yet destroyed them. Would she be expecting him to take her number? For him to fly her out to Rome for a weekend of sex and then see what happened? Hand in hand for a sunset stroll along Trastevere, Rome's supposedly most romantic neighbourhood? Because that was never going to happen. His jaw tightened. It would only raise up her hopes before smashing them.

He heard her murmur something in her sleep and felt the heavy weight of his conscience as he batted possibilities back and forth. What would be the best thing he could do for Keira—this sexy little driver with the softest lips he'd ever known? Glancing at his watch, he saw from the luminous dial that it was just before midnight and the rest of the house had grown silent. Could he risk using the landline downstairs without waking everyone? Of course he could. Slipping from the sex-scented bed, he threw on some clothes and made his way downstairs.

He placed the call without any trouble, but his mood was strangely low after he'd terminated his whispered conversation and made his way back to the bedroom. With the light from the corridor flooding in, he stared at Keira's face, which was pillowed on a bent elbow. Her lips were curved in a soft smile and he wanted to kiss them. To take her in his arms and run his hands over her and do it all over again. But he couldn't. Or rather, he shouldn't.

He was careful not to touch her as he climbed into bed, but the thought of her out-of-bounds nakedness meant that he lay there sleeplessly for a long, long time.

CHAPTER FOUR

A PALE LIGHT woke her and for a moment Keira lay completely still, her head resting against a lumpy pillow as her eyes flickered open and she tried to work out exactly where she was. And then she remembered. She was in a strange bedroom on the edge of a snowy Dartmoor—and she'd just lost her virginity to the powerful billionaire she'd been driving around the country!

She registered the sweet aching between her legs and the delicious sting of her nipples as slowly she turned her head to see that the other half of the bed was empty. Her pulse speeded up. He must be in the bathroom. Quickly, she sat up, raking her fingers through her mussed hair and giving herself a chance to compose herself before Matteo returned.

The blindingly pale crack of light shining through the gap in the curtains showed that the snow was still very much in evidence and a smile of anticipation curved her lips. Maybe they'd be stuck here today too—and they could have sex all over again. She certainly hoped so. Crossing her arms over her naked breasts, she hugged herself tightly as endorphins flooded through her warm body. Obviously, she'd need to reassure him that although she was relatively inexperienced, she certainly wasn't naïve. She knew the score—she'd heard the men in the workshop talking about women often enough to know what they did and didn't like. She would be very grown up about what had happened. She'd make it clear that she wasn't coming at this with any *expectations*—although, of course, if he wanted to see her again when the snow had been cleared she would be more than happy with that.

And that was when she noticed the nightstand—or rather, what was lying on top of it. Keira blinked her eyes in disbelief but as her vision cleared she realised this was no illusion as she stared in growing horror at the enormous wad of banknotes. She felt as if she were taking part in some secretly filmed reality show. As if the money might suddenly disintegrate if she touched it, or as if Matteo would suddenly appear from out of hiding. She looked around, realising there *was* nowhere to hide in this tiny room.

'Matteo?' she questioned uncertainly.

Nobody came. Of course they didn't. She stared at the money and then noticed the piece of paper which was lying underneath it. It took several seconds before she could bring herself to pick it up and as she began to read it she was scarcely able to believe what she was seeing.

Keira, he had written—and in the absence of any affectation like *Dear* or *Darling*, she supposed she ought to be grateful that he'd got her name right, because Irish names were notoriously difficult to spell.

I just wanted to tell you how much I enjoyed last night and I hope you did, too. You looked so peaceful sleeping this morning that I didn't want to wake you—but I need to be back in Italy as soon as possible.

You told me your dream was to spend Christmas in a luxury hotel and I'd like to make this possible, which is why I hope you'll accept this small gift in the spirit with which it was intended.

And if we'd been playing poker for money, you would certainly have walked away with a lot more than this!

I wish you every good thing for your future.

Buon Natale.

Matteo.

Keira's fingers closed tightly around the note and her feeling of confusion intensified as she stared at the money—more money than she'd ever seen. She allowed herself a moment of fury before getting up out of bed, acutely aware that for once she wasn't wearing her usual nightshirt, and the sight of her naked body in the small mirror taunted her with memories of just what she and the Italian had done last night. And once the fury had passed she was left with hurt, and disappointment. Had she really been lying there, naïvely thinking that Matteo was going to emerge from the bathroom and take her in his arms when the reality was that he couldn't even bear to face her? What a stupid fool she'd been.

She washed and dressed and went downstairs, politely refusing breakfast but accepting a mug of strong tea from Mary, who seemed delighted to relay everything which had been happening while Keira had been asleep.

'First thing I know, there's a knock on the door and it's a man in one of those big four-wheel drives,' she announced.

'Which managed to get through the snow?' questioned Keira automatically.

'Oh, yes. Because Mr Valenti ordered a car with a snow plough. Apparently he got on the phone late last night while everyone was asleep and organised it. Must have been very quiet because nobody heard him.'

Very quiet, thought Keira grimly. He must have been terrified that she would wake up and demand he take her with him.

'And he's ordered some men to dig your car out of the snow. Said there was no way you must be stranded here,' said Mary, with a dreamy look on her careworn face. 'They arrived about an hour ago—they should be finished soon.'

Keira nodded. 'Can I pay you?'

Mary beamed. 'No need. Your Mr Valenti was more than generous.'

Keira's heart pounded; she wanted to scream that he wasn't 'her' anything. So the cash wasn't there to pay for the B& B or help her make her own journey home, because he'd already sorted all that out. Which left only one reason for leaving it. Of course. How could she have been so dense when the bland words of the accompanying letter had made it perfectly clear? The comment about the poker and the disingenuous suggestion she take herself off to a luxury hotel were just a polite way of disguising the very obvious. A wave of sickness washed over her.

Matteo Valenti had *paid her for sex.*

Operating on a dazed kind of autopilot, Keira made her way back to her newly liberated car, from where she slowly drove back to London. After dropping the car off at Luxury Limos, she made her way to Brixton, acutely aware of the huge wad of cash she was carrying. She'd thought of leaving it behind at Mary's, but wouldn't the kindly landlady have tried to return it and just made matters a whole lot worse? And how on earth would she have managed to explain what it was doing there? Yet it felt as if it were burning a massive hole in her pocket—haunting her with the bitter reminder of just what the Italian really thought of her.

The area of Brixton where she rented a tiny apartment had once been considered unfashionable but now, like much of London, the place was on the up. Two days before Christmas and the streets had a festive air which was bordering on the hysterical, despite the fact that the heavy snows hadn't reached the capital. Bright lights glittered and she could see Christmas trees and scarlet-suited Santas everywhere she looked. On the corner, a Salvation Army band was playing 'Silent Night' and the poignancy of the familiar tune made her heart want to break. And stupidly, she found herself missing her mother like never before as she thought about all the Christmases they'd never got to share. Tears pricked at the backs of her eyes as she hugged her anorak around her shivering body, and never had she felt so completely alone.

But self-pity would get her nowhere. She was a survivor, wasn't she? She would get through this as she had got through so much else. Dodging the crowds, she started to walk home, her journey taking her past one of the area's many charity shops and as an idea came to her she impulsively pushed open the door of one. Inside, the place was full of people trying on clothes for Christmas parties and New Year—raiding feather boas and old-fashioned shimmery dresses from the crowded rails. The atmosphere was chaotic and happy but Keira was grim-faced as she made her way to the cash desk. Fumbling around in her pocket, she withdrew the wad of cash and slapped it down on the counter in front of the startled cashier.

'Take this,' Keira croaked. 'And Happy Christmas.'

The woman held up a hand. 'Whoa! Wait a minute! Where did you—?'

But Keira was already pushing her way out of the shop, the cold air hitting the tears which had begun streaming down her cheeks. Her vision blurred and she stumbled a little and might have fallen if a steady arm hadn't caught her elbow.

'Are you okay?' a female voice was saying.

Was she okay? No, she most definitely was not. Keira nodded, looking up at a woman with platinum hair who was wearing a leopard-skin-print coat. 'I'm fine. I just need to get home,' she husked.

'Not like that, you're not. You're not fit to go anywhere,' said the woman firmly. 'Let me buy you a drink. You look like you could use one.'

Still shaken, Keira allowed herself to be led into the bright interior of the Dog and Duck where music was playing and the smell of mulled wine filled her nostrils. The woman went up to the bar and returned minutes later with a glass of a brown mixture resembling medicine, which was pushed across the scratched surface of the table towards her.

'What's this?' Keira mumbled, lifting the glass and recoiling from the fumes.

'Brandy.'

'I don't like brandy.'

'Drink it. You look like you're in shock.'

That much was true. Keira took a large and fiery swallow and the weird thing was that she *did* feel better afterwards. Disorientated, yes—but better.

'So where did you get the money from?' the blonde was asking. 'Did you rob a bank or something? I was in the charity shop when you came in and handed it over. Pretty dramatic gesture, but a lovely thing to do, I must say—especially at this time of the year.'

Afterwards Keira thought that if she hadn't had the brandy then she might not have told the sympathetic blonde the whole story, but the words just started tumbling out of her mouth and they wouldn't seem to stop. Just like the tears which had preceded them. It was only when the woman's eyes widened when she came out with the punchline about how Matteo had left her a stack of money and done a runner that she became aware that something in the atmosphere had changed.

'So he just disappeared? Without a word?'

'Well, he left a note.'

'May I see it?'

Keira put the brandy glass down with a thud. 'No.'

There was a pause. 'He must be very rich,' observed the blonde. 'To be able to be carrying around that kind of money.'

Keira shrugged. 'Very.'

'And good-looking, I suppose?'

Keira swallowed. 'What does that have to do with anything?'

The blonde's heavily made-up eyes narrowed. 'Hunky Italian billionaires don't usually have to pay women for sex.'

It was hearing someone else say it out loud which made it feel a million times worse—something Keira hadn't actually thought possible. She rose unsteadily to her feet, terrified she was going to start gagging. 'I… I'm going home now,' she whispered. 'Please forget I said anything. And…thanks for the drink.'

Somehow she managed to get home unscathed, where her cold, bare bedsit showed no signs of the impending holiday. She'd been so busy that she hadn't even bought herself a little tree, but that now seemed like the least of her worries. She realised she hadn't checked her phone messages since she'd got back and found a terse communication from her aunt, asking her what time she was planning on turning up on Christmas Day and hoping she hadn't forgotten to buy the pudding.

The pudding! Now she would have to brave the wretched shops again. Keira closed her eyes as she pictured the grim holiday which lay ahead of her. How was she going to get through a whole Christmas, nursing the shameful secret of what she'd done?

Her phone began to ring, the small screen flashing an unknown number; in an effort to distract herself with the inevitable sales call, Keira accepted the call with a tentative hello. There was an infinitesimal pause before a male voice spoke.

'Keira?'

It was a voice she hadn't known until very recently but she thought that rich, Italian accent would be branded on her memory until the end of time. Dark and velvety, it whispered over her skin just as his fingers had done. Matteo! And despite everything—the wad of money and the blandly worded note and the fact that he'd left without even saying goodbye—wasn't there a great lurch of hope inside her foolish heart? She pictured his ruffled hair and the dark eyes which had gleamed with passion when they'd looked at her. The way he'd crushed his lips hungrily down on hers, and that helpless moment of bliss when he'd first entered her.

'Matteo?'

Another pause—and if a silence could ever be considered ominous, this one was. 'So how much did she pay you?' he questioned.

'Pay me?' Keira blinked in confusion, thinking that bringing up money wasn't the best way to start a conversation, especially in view of what had happened. 'What are you talking about?'

'I've just had a phone call from a...a *journalist*.'

He spat out the word as if it were poison. 'Asking me whether I make a habit of paying women for sex.'

Keira's feeling of confusion intensified. 'I don't…' And then she realised and hot colour flooded into her cheeks. 'Was her name Hester?'

'So you *did* speak to her?' He sucked in an unsteady breath. 'What was it, Keira—a quickly arranged interview to see what else you could squeeze out of me?'

'I didn't plan on talking to her—it just happened.'

'Oh, really?'

'Yes, really. I was angry about the money you left me!' she retorted.

'Why? Didn't you think it was enough?' he shot back. 'Did you imagine you might be able to get even more?'

Keira sank onto the nearest chair, terrified that her wobbly legs were going to give way beneath her. 'You bastard,' she whispered.

'Your anger means nothing to me,' he said coldly. 'For *you* are nothing to me. I wasn't thinking straight. I couldn't have been thinking straight. I should never have had sex with you because I don't make a habit of having one-night stands with strangers. But what's done can't be undone and I have only myself to blame.'

There was a pause before he resumed and now his voice had taken on a flat and implacable note, which somehow managed to sound even more ominous than his anger.

'I've told your journalist friend that if she prints one word about me, I'll go after her and bring her damned publication down,' he continued. 'Because I'm not someone you can blackmail—I'm just a man who allowed himself to be swayed by lust and it's taught me a lesson I'm never going to forget.' He gave a bitter laugh. 'So, goodbye, Keira. Have a good life.'

CHAPTER FIVE

Ten months later

'I HOPE THAT baby isn't going to cry all the way through lunch, Keira. It would be nice if we were able to eat a meal in peace for once.'

Tucking little Santino into the crook of her arm, Keira nodded as she met her aunt's accusing stare. She would have taken the baby out for a walk if the late October day hadn't been so foul and blustery. Or she might have treated him to a long bus ride to lull him to sleep if he hadn't been so tiny. As it was, she was stuck in the house with a woman who seemed determined to find fault in everything she did, and she was tired. So tired. With the kind of tiredness which seemed to have seeped deep into her bones and taken up residence there. 'I'll try to put him down for his nap before we sit down to eat,' she said hopefully.

Aunt Ida's mouth turned down at the corners, emphasising the deep grooves of discontentment which hardened her thin face. 'That'll be a first. Poor Shelley says she hasn't had an unbroken night since you moved in. He's obviously an unsettled baby if he cries so much. Maybe it's time you came to your senses and thought about adoption.'

Keira's teeth dug into her bottom lip as the word lodged like a barb in her skin.

Adoption.

A wave of nausea engulfed her but she tried very hard not to react as she stared down into the face of her sleeping son. Holding onto Santino even tighter, she felt her heart give a savage lurch of love as she told herself to ignore the snide comments and concentrate on what was important. Because only one thing mattered and that was her baby son.

Everything you do is for him, she reminded herself fiercely. *Everything.* No point in wishing she hadn't given away Matteo's money, or tormenting herself by thinking how useful it might have been. She hadn't known at the time that she was pregnant—how could she have done? She'd handed over that thick wad of banknotes as if there were loads more coming her way—and now she just had to deal with the situation as it was and not what it could have been. She had to accept that she'd lost her job and her home in quick succession and had been forced to take the charity of a woman who had always disapproved of her. Because how else would she and Santino have managed to cope in an uncaring and hostile world?

You know exactly how, prompted the ever-present voice of her conscience but Keira pushed it from her mind. She could *not* have asked Matteo for help, not when he had treated her like some kind of *whore.* Who had made it clear he never wanted to see her again.

'Have you registered the child's birth yet?' Aunt Ida was asking.

'Not yet, no,' said Keira. 'I have to do it within the first six weeks.'

'Better get a move on, then.'

Keira waited, knowing that there was more.

Her aunt smiled slyly. 'Only I was wondering whether you were going to put the mystery father's name on the birth certificate—or whether you were like your poor dear mother and didn't actually know who he was?'

Keira's determination not to react drained away. Terrified of saying something she might later regret, she turned and walked out of the sitting room without another word, glad she was holding Santino because that stopped her from picking up one of her aunt's horrible china ornaments and hurling it against the wall. Criticism directed against her she could just about tolerate—but she wouldn't stand to hear her mother's name maligned like that.

Her anger had evaporated by the time she reached the box-room she shared with Santino, and Keira placed the baby carefully in his crib, tucking the edges of the blanket around his tiny frame and staring at him. His lashes looked very long and dark against his olive skin but for once she found herself unable to take pleasure in his innocent face. Because suddenly, the fear and the guilt which had been nagging away inside her now erupted into one fierce and painful certainty.

She couldn't go on like this. Santino deserved more than a mother who was permanently exhausted, having to tiptoe around a too-small house with people who didn't really like her. She closed her eyes, knowing there was somebody else who didn't like her—but someone she suspected wouldn't display a tight-lipped intolerance whenever the baby started to cry. Because it was *his* baby, too. And didn't all parents love their children, no matter what?

A powerful image swam into her mind of a man whose face she could picture without too much trying. She knew what she had to do. Something she'd thought about doing every day since Santino's birth, and in the nine months preceding it, until she'd forced herself to remember how unequivocally he'd told her he never wanted to see her again. Well, maybe he was going to have to.

Her fingers were shaking as she scrolled down her phone's contact list and retrieved the number she had saved, even though the caller had hung up on her the last time she'd spoken to him.

With a thundering heart, she punched out the number. And waited.

Rain lashed against the car windscreen and flurries of falling leaves swirled like the thoughts in Matteo's mind as his chauffeur-driven limousine drove down the narrow suburban road. As they passed houses which all looked exactly the same, he tried to get his head round what he'd learned during a phone call from a woman he'd never thought he'd see again.

He was a father.

He had a child.

A son. His heart pumped. In a single stroke he had been given exactly what he needed—though not necessarily what he wanted—and could now produce the grandson his father yearned for.

Matteo ordered the driver to stop, trying to dampen down the unfamiliar emotions which were sweeping through his body. And trying to curb his rising temper about the way Keira had kept this news secret. How *dared* she keep his baby hidden and play God with his future? Grim-faced, he stepped out onto the rain-soaked pavement and a wave of determination washed over him as he slammed the car door shut. He was here now and he would fix this—to his advantage. Whatever it took, he would get what he wanted—and he wanted his son.

He hadn't told Keira he was coming. He hadn't wanted to give her the opportunity to elude him. He wanted to surprise her—as she had surprised him. To allow her no time to mount any defences. If she was unprepared and vulnerable then surely that would aid him in his determination to get his rightful heir. Moving stealthily up the narrow path, he rapped a small bronze knocker fashioned in the shape of a lion's head and moments later the door was opened by a woman with tight, curly hair and a hard, lined face.

'Yes?' she said sharply. 'We don't buy from the doorstep.'

'Good afternoon,' he said. Forcing the pleasantry to his unwilling lips, he accompanied it with a polite smile. 'I'm not selling anything. I'd like to see Keira.'

'And you are?'

'My name is Matteo Valenti,' he said evenly. 'And I am her baby's father.'

The woman gasped, her eyes scanning him from head to toe, as if registering his cashmere coat and handmade shoes. Her eyes skated over his shoulder and she must have observed the shiny black car parked so incongruously among all the sedate family saloons. Was he imagining the look of calculation which had hardened her gimlet eyes? Probably not, he thought grimly.

'You?' she demanded.

'That's right,' he agreed, still in that same even voice which betrayed nothing of his growing irritation.

'I had no idea that...' She swallowed. 'I'll have to check if she'll see you.'

'No,' Matteo interrupted her, only just resisting the desire to step forward and jam his foot in the door, like a bailiff. 'I *will* see Keira—and my baby—and it's probably best if we do it with the minimum of fuss.' He glanced behind him where he could see the twitching of net curtains on the opposite side of the road and when he returned his gaze to the woman, his smile was bland. 'Don't you agree? For everyone's sake?'

The woman hesitated before nodding, as if she too had no desire for a scene on the doorstep. 'Very well. You'd better come in.' She cleared her throat. 'I'll let Keira know you're here.'

He was shown into a small room crammed with porcelain figurines but Matteo barely paid any attention to his surroundings. His eyes were trained on the door as it clicked open and he held his breath in anticipation—

expelling it in a long sigh of disbelief and frustration when Keira finally walked in. Frustration because she was alone. And disbelief because he scarcely recognised her as the same woman whose bed he had shared almost a year ago—though that lack of recognition certainly didn't seem to be affecting the powerful jerk of his groin.

Gone was the short, spiky hair and in its place was a dark curtain of silk which hung glossily down to her shoulders. And her body. He swallowed. What the hell had happened to *that*? All the angular leanness of before had gone. Suddenly she had hips—as well as the hint of a belly and breasts. It made her look softer, he thought, until he reminded himself that a woman with any degree of softness wouldn't have done what she had done.

'Matteo,' she said, her voice sounding strained—and it was then he noticed the pallor and the faint circles which darkened the skin beneath her eyes. In those fathomless pools of deepest blue he could read the vulnerability he had wanted to see, yet he felt a sudden twist of something like compassion, until he remembered what she had done.

'The very same,' he agreed grimly. 'Pleased to see me?'

'I wasn't—' She was trying to smile but failing spectacularly. 'I wasn't expecting you. I mean, not like this. Not without any warning.'

'Really? What did you imagine was going to happen, Keira? That I would just accept the news you finally saw fit to tell me and wait for your next instruction?' He walked across the room to stare out of the window and saw that a group of small boys had gathered around his limousine. He turned around and met her eyes. 'Perhaps you were hoping you wouldn't have to see me at all. Were you hoping I would remain a shadowy figure in the background and become your convenient benefactor?'

'Of course I wasn't!'

'No?' He flared his nostrils. 'Then why *bother* telling me about my son? Why now after all these months of secrecy?'

Keira tried not to flinch beneath the accusing gaze which washed over her like a harsh ebony spotlight. It was difficult enough seeing him again and registering the infuriating fact that her body had automatically started to melt, without having to face his undiluted fury.

Remember the things he said to you, she reminded herself. But the memory of his wounding words seemed to have faded and all she could think was the fact that here stood Santino's father and that, oh, the apple didn't fall far from the tree.

For here was the adult version of the little baby she'd just rocked off to sleep before the doorbell had rung. Santino was the image of his father, with his golden olive skin and dark hair, and hadn't the midwife already commented on the fact that her son was going to grow up to be a heartbreaker? Keira swallowed. Just like Matteo.

She felt an uncomfortable rush of awareness because it wasn't easy to acknowledge the stir of her body, or the fact that her senses suddenly felt as if they'd been kicked into life. Matteo's hair and his eyes seemed even blacker than she remembered and never had his sensual lips appeared more kissable. Yet surely that was the last thing she should be thinking of right now. Her mind-set should be fixed on practicalities, not foolish yearnings. She felt disappointed in herself and wondered if nature was clever enough to make a woman desire the father of her child, no matter how contemptuously he was looking at her.

She found herself wishing he'd given her some kind of warning so she could at least have washed her hair and made a bit of effort with her appearance. Since having a baby she'd developed curves and she was shamefully aware that her pre-pregnancy jeans were straining at the hips and her baggy top was deeply unflattering. But the way she looked had been the last thing on her mind. She knew she needed new clothes but she'd been forced to wait, and not just because of a chronic shortage of funds.

Because how could she possibly go shopping for clothes with a tiny infant in tow? Asking her aunt to babysit hadn't been an option—not when she was constantly made aware of their generosity in providing a home for her and her illegitimate child, and how that same child had disrupted all their lives. The truth was she hadn't wanted to spend her precious pennies on new clothes when she could be buying stuff for Santino. Which was why she was wearing an unflattering outfit, which was probably making Matteo Valenti wonder what he'd ever seen in her. Measured against his made-to-measure sophistication, Keira felt like a scruffy wrongdoer who had just been dragged before an elegant high court judge.

She forced a polite smile to her lips. 'Would you like to sit down?'

'No, I don't want to *sit down*. I want an answer to my question. Why did you contact me to tell me that I was a father? Why now?'

She flushed right up to the roots of her hair. 'Because by law I have to register his birth and that brought everything to a head. I've realised I can't go on living like this. I thought I could but I was wrong. I'm very…grateful to my aunt for taking me in but it's too cramped. They don't really want me here and I can kind of see their point.' She met his eyes. 'And I don't want Santino growing up in this kind of atmosphere.'

Santino.

As she said the child's name Matteo felt a whisper of something he didn't recognise. Something completely outside his experience. He could feel it in the icing of his skin and sudden clench of his heart. 'Santino?' he repeated, wondering if he'd misheard her. He stared at her, his brow creased in a frown. 'You gave him an Italian name?'

'Yes.'

'Why?'

'Because when I looked at him—' her voice faltered as she scraped her fingers back through her hair and turned those big sapphire eyes on him '—I knew I could call him nothing else but an Italian name.'

'Even though you sought to deny him his heritage and kept his birth hidden from me?'

She swallowed. 'You made it very clear that you never wanted to see me again, Matteo.'

'I didn't know you were pregnant at the time,' he bit out.

'And neither did I!' she shot back.

'But you knew afterwards.'

'Yes.' How could she explain the sense of alienation she'd felt—not just from him, but from everyone? When everything had seemed so *unreal* and the world had suddenly looked like a very different place. The head of Luxury Limos had said he didn't think it was a good idea if she carried on driving—not when she looked as if she was about to throw up whenever the car went over a bump. And even though she hadn't been sick—not once—and even though Keira knew that by law she could demand to stay where she was, she didn't have the energy or the funds to investigate further. What was she going to do—take him to an industrial tribunal?

She'd been terrified her boss would find out who the father of her unborn child was—because having sex with your most prestigious client was definitely a sacking offence. He'd offered her a job back in the workshop, but she had no desire to slide underneath a car and get oil all over her hands, not when such a precious bundle was growing inside her. Eventually she'd accepted a mind-numbingly dull job behind the reception desk, becoming increasingly aware that on the kind of wages she was being paid, she'd never be able to afford childcare after the birth. She'd saved every penny she could and been as frugal as she knew how, but gradually all her funds were running out and now she was in real trouble.

'Yes, I knew,' she said slowly. 'Just like I knew I ought to tell you that you were going to be a father. But every time I picked up the phone to call you, something held me back. Can't you understand?'

'Frankly, no. I can't.'

She looked him straight in the eye. 'You think those cruel words you said to me last time we spoke wouldn't matter? That you could say what you liked and it wouldn't hurt, or have consequences?'

His voice grew hard. 'I haven't come here to argue the rights and wrongs of your secrecy. I've come to see my son.'

'He's sleeping.'

'I won't wake him.' His voice grew harsh. 'You've denied me all this time and you will deny me no longer. I want to see my son, Keira, and if I have to search every room in the house to find him, then that's exactly what I'm going to do.'

It was a demand Keira couldn't ignore and not just because she didn't doubt his threat to search the small house from top to bottom. She'd seen the brief tightening of his face when she'd mentioned his child and another wave of guilt had washed over her. Because she of all people knew what it was like to grow up without a father. She knew about the gaping hole it left—a hole which could never be filled. And yet she had sought to subject her own child to that.

'Come with me,' she said huskily.

He followed her up the narrow staircase and Keira

was acutely aware of his presence behind her. You couldn't ignore him, even when you couldn't see him, she thought despairingly. She could detect the heat from his body and the subtle sandalwood which was all his and, stupidly, she remembered the way that scent had clung to her skin the morning after he'd made love to her. Her heart was thundering by the time they reached the box-room she shared with Santino and she held her breath as Matteo stood frozen for a moment before moving soundlessly towards the crib. His shoulders were stiff with tension as he reached it and he was silent for so long that she started to get nervous.

'Matteo?' she said.

Matteo didn't answer. Not then. He wasn't sure he trusted himself to speak because his thoughts were in such disarray. He looked down at the baby expecting to feel the instant bolt of love people talked about when they first set eyes on their own flesh and blood, but there was nothing. He stared down at the dark fringe of eyelashes which curved on the infant's olive-hued cheeks and the shock of black hair. Tiny hands were curled into two tiny fists and he found himself leaning forward to count all the fingers, nodding his head with satisfaction as he registered each one. He felt as if he were observing himself and his reaction from a distance and realised it was possession he felt, not love. The sense that this was someone who belonged to him in a way that nobody ever had before.

His son.

He swallowed.

His *son*.

He waited for a moment before turning to Keira and he saw her dark blue eyes widen, as if she'd read something in his face she would prefer not to have seen.

'So you played God with all our futures,' he observed softly. 'By keeping him from me.'

Her gaze became laced with defiance.

'You paid me for sex.'

'I did not *pay you for sex*,' he gritted out. 'I explained my motivation in my note. You spoke of a luxury you weren't used to and I thought I would make it possible. Was that so very wrong?'

'You know very well it was!' she burst out. 'Because offering me cash was insulting. Any man would know that.'

'Was that why you tried to sell your story to the journalist, because you felt "insulted"?'

'I did not *sell my story* to anyone,' she shot back. 'Can't you imagine what it was like? I'd had sex for the first time and woke to find you gone, leaving that wretched pile of money. I walked into a charity shop to get rid of it because it felt...well, it felt tainted, if you must know.'

He grew very still. 'You gave it away?'

'Yes, I gave it away. To a worthy cause—to children living in care. Not realising I was pregnant at the time and could have used the money myself. The journalist just happened to be in the shop and overheard—and naturally she was interested. She bought me a drink and I hadn't eaten anything all day and...' She shrugged. 'I guess I told her more than I meant to.'

Matteo's eyes narrowed. If her story was true it

meant she hadn't tried to grab some seedy publicity from their brief liaison. *If it was true.* Yet even if it was—did it really change anything? He was here only because her back was up against the wall and she had nowhere else to turn. His gaze swept over the too-tight jeans and baggy jumper. And this was the mother of his child, he thought, his lips curving with distaste.

He opened his mouth to speak but Santino chose that moment to start to whimper and Keira bent over the crib to scoop him up, whispering her lips against his hair and rocking him in her arms until he had grown quiet again. She looked over his head, straight into Matteo's eyes. 'Would you…would you like to hold him?'

Matteo went very still. He knew he *should* want that, but although he thought it, he still couldn't *feel* it. There was nothing but an icy lump where his heart should have been and as he looked at his son he couldn't shift that strange air of detachment.

His lack of emotional empathy had never mattered to him before—only his frustrated lovers had complained about it and that had never been reason enough to change, or even *want* to change. But now he felt like someone on a beach who had inadvertently stepped onto quicksand. As if matters were spinning beyond his control.

And he needed to assert control, just as he always did.

Of course he would hold his son when he'd got his head round the fact that he actually *had* a son. But it would be in conditions favourable to them both—not in some tiny bedroom of a strange house while Keira stood studying him with those big blue eyes.

'Not now,' he said abruptly. 'There isn't time. You need to pack your things while I call ahead and prepare for your arrival in Italy.'

'What?'

'You heard me. He isn't staying here. And since a child needs a mother, then I guess you will have to come, too.'

'What are you talking about?' She rocked the child against her breast. 'I know it's not perfect here but I can't just walk out without making any plans. We can't just go to *Italy*.'

'You can't put out a call for help and then ignore help when it comes. You telephoned me and now you must accept the consequences,' he added grimly. 'You've already implied that the atmosphere here is intolerable so I'm offering you an alternative. The only sensible alternative.' He pulled a mobile phone from the pocket of his cashmere overcoat and began to scroll down the numbers. 'For a start, you need a nursery nurse to help you.'

'I don't *need* a nurse,' she contradicted fiercely. 'Women like me don't have nurses. They look after their babies themselves.'

'Have you looked in the mirror recently?'

It was an underhand blow to someone who was already feeling acutely sensitive and once again Keira flushed. 'I'm sorry I didn't have a chance to slap on a whole load of make-up and put on a party dress!'

He shook his head. 'That wasn't what I meant. You look as if you haven't had a decent night's sleep in weeks and I'm giving you the chance to get some rest.' He forced himself to be gentle with her, even though his instinct was always to push for exactly what he wanted. And yet strangely, he felt another wave of compassion as he looked into her pale face. 'Now, we can do this one of two ways. You can fight me or you can make the best of the situation and come willingly.' His mouth flattened. 'But if you choose the former, it will be fruitless because I want this, Keira. I want it very badly. And when I want something, I usually get it. Do you believe me?'

The mulish look which entered her eyes was there for only a second before she gave a reluctant nod. 'Yes,' she said grudgingly. 'I believe you.'

'Then pack what you need and I'll wait downstairs.' He turned away but was halted by the sound of her voice.

'And when we get there, what happens then, Matteo?' she whispered. 'To Santino?' There was a pause. 'To us?'

He didn't turn back. He didn't want to look at her right then, or tell her he didn't think there was an 'us'. 'I have no crystal ball,' he ground out. 'We'll just have to make it up as we go along. Now pack your things.'

He went downstairs, and, despite telling himself that this was nothing more than a problem which needed solving, he could do nothing about the sudden and inexplicable wrench of pain in his heart. But years of practice meant he had composed himself long before he reached the tiny hallway and his face was as hard as granite as he let himself out into the rainy English day.

CHAPTER SIX

GOLDEN SUNLIGHT DANCED on her closed eyelids and warmed her skin as Keira nestled back into the comfortable lounger. The only sounds she could hear were birdsong and the buzz of bees and, in the far distance, the crowing of a cock—even though it was the middle of the day. Hard to believe she'd left behind a rain-washed English autumn to arrive in a country where it was still warm enough to sit outside in October. And even harder to believe that she was at Matteo Valenti's Umbrian estate, with its acres of olive groves, award-winning vineyards and breathtaking views over mountains and lake. In his private jet, he'd announced he was bringing her here, to his holiday home, to 'acclimatise' herself before he introduced her to his real life in Rome. She hadn't been sure what he meant by that but she'd been too exhausted to raise any objections. She'd been here a week and much of that time had been spent asleep, or making sure that Santino was content. It felt like being transplanted to a luxury spa cleverly hidden within a rustic setting—with countless people working quietly in the background to maintain the estate's smooth running.

At first she'd been too preoccupied with the practical elements of settling in with her baby to worry about the emotional repercussions of being there. She'd worried about the little things, like how Matteo would react when he discovered she wasn't feeding Santino herself. Whether he would judge her negatively, as the whole world seemed to do if a woman couldn't manage to breastfeed. Was that why, in a rare moment of candour, she'd found herself explaining how ill she'd been after the birth—which meant breastfeeding hadn't been possible? She thought she'd glimpsed a brief softening of the granite-like features before his rugged features resumed their usual implacable mask.

'It will be easier that way,' he'd said, with a shrug. 'Easier for the nursery nurse.'

How *cold* he could be, she thought. Even if he was right. Because despite her earlier resistance, she was now hugely appreciative of the nursery nurse they'd employed. The very day after they'd arrived, he had produced three candidates for her to interview—top-notch women who had graduated from Italy's finest training establishment and who all spoke fluent English. After asking them about a million questions—but more importantly watching to see how well they interacted with her baby—Keira had chosen Claudia, a serene woman in her mid-thirties whom she instinctively trusted. It meant Keira got all the best bits of being a mother—cuddling and bathing her adorable son and making goo-goo noises at him as she walked him around the huge estate—while Claudia took over the dreaded three o'clock morning feed.

Which meant she could catch up with the sleep she so badly needed. She'd felt like a complete zombie when she arrived—a fact not helped by the disorientating experience of being flown to Italy on Matteo's luxury jet then being picked up by the kind of limousine which only a year ago she would have been chauffeuring. The drive to his Umbrian property had passed in a blur and Keira remembered thinking that the only time emotion had entered Matteo's voice was when they drove through the ancient gates and he began to point out centuries-old landmarks, with an unmistakable sense of pride and affection.

She almost wished Santino had been a little older so he could have appreciated the silvery ripple of olive trees, heavy with fruit and ready for harvest, and the golden pomegranates which hung from the branches like Christmas baubles. She remembered being greeted by a homely housekeeper named Paola and the delicious hot bath she took once the baby had been settled. There had been the blissful sensation of sliding between crisp, clean sheets and laying her head on a pillow of goosedown, followed by her first full night's sleep since before the birth. And that was pretty much how she'd spent the last seven days, feeling her vitality and strength returning with each hour that passed.

'You're smiling,' came a richly accented voice from above her as a shadow suddenly blotted out the sun.

Shielding her eyes with the edge of her hand, Keira peered up to see Matteo towering over her and her smile instantly felt as if it had become frozen. She could feel her heart picking up speed and the tug of silken hunger in the base of her belly and silently she cursed the instinctive reaction of her body. Because as her strength had returned, so too had her desire for Matteo—a man who she couldn't quite decide was her jailer or her saviour. Or both.

Their paths hadn't crossed much because he'd spent much of the time working in a distant part of the enormous farmhouse. It was as if he'd unconsciously marked out different territories for them, with clear demarcation lines which couldn't be crossed. But what she'd noted above all else was the fact that he'd kept away from the nursery, using the *excuse* that his son needed to settle in before getting used to too many new people. Because that was what it had sounded like. An excuse. A reason not to touch the son he had insisted should come here.

She'd seen him, of course. Glimpses in passing, which had unsettled her. Matteo looking brooding and muscular in faded denims and a shirt as he strode about the enormous estate, conversing in rapid Italian with his workers—or wearing a knockout charcoal suit just before driving to Rome for the day and returning long after she'd gone to bed.

Another image was burnt vividly into her mind, too. She'd overslept one morning and gone straight to the nursery to find Claudia cradling Santino by the window and telling him to watch 'Papa' going down the drive. *Papa*. It was a significant word. It emphasised Matteo's importance in their lives yet brought home how little she really knew about the cold-hearted billionaire. Yet that hadn't stopped her heart from missing a beat as he'd speeded out of the estate in his gleaming scarlet sports car, had it?

'It makes me realise how rarely I see you smile,' observed Matteo, still looking down at her as he stood silhouetted by the rich October sun.

'Maybe that's because we've hardly seen one another,' said Keira, flipping on the sunglasses which had been perched on top of her head, grateful for the way they kept her expression hidden. Not for the first time, she found it almost impossible to look at the man in front of her with any degree of impartiality, but she disguised it with a cool look. 'And you're a fine one to talk about smiling. You don't exactly go around the place grinning from ear to ear, do you?'

'Perhaps our forthcoming trip to Rome might bring a smile to both our faces,' he suggested silkily.

Ah yes, the trip to Rome. Keira felt the anxious slam of her heart. She licked her lips. 'I've been meaning to talk to you about that. Do we really have to go?'

In a movement which distractingly emphasised the jut of his narrow hips, he leaned against the sun-baked wall of the farmhouse. 'We've agreed to this, Keira. You need to see the other side of my life, not just this rural idyll. And I'm mainly based in Rome.'

'And the difference is what?'

'It's a high-octane city and nothing like as relaxed as here. When I'm there I go to restaurants and theatres. I have friends there and get invited to parties—and as the mother of my baby, I will be taking you with me.'

She sat up on the lounger, anxiety making her heart thud even harder against her ribcage. 'Why bother?

Why not just leave me somewhere in the background and concentrate on forming a relationship with your son?'

'I think we have to examine all the possibilities,' he said carefully. 'And number one on that list is to work out whether we could have some kind of life together.' He lifted his brows. 'It would certainly make things a whole lot easier.'

'And you're saying I'll let you down in my current state, is that it?'

He shrugged his broad shoulders with a carelessness which wasn't very convincing. 'I think we're both aware that you don't have a suitable wardrobe for that kind of lifestyle. You can't wear jeans all the time and Paola mentioned that you only seem to have one pair of boots.'

'So Paola's been spying on me, has she?' Keira questioned, her voice dipping with disappointment that the genial housekeeper seemed to have been taking her inventory.

'Don't be absurd. She was going to clean them for you and couldn't find any others you could wear in the meantime.'

Keira scrambled up off the lounger and stared into his hard and beautiful features. He really came from a totally different planet, didn't he? One which was doubtless inhabited by women who had boots in every colour of the rainbow and not just a rather scuffed brown pair she'd bought in the sales. 'So don't take me with you,' she said flippantly. 'Leave me behind while you go out to all your fancy places and I can stay home and look after Santino, wearing my solitary pair of boots.'

A flicker of a smile touched the corners of his lips, but just as quickly it was gone. 'That isn't an option, I'm afraid,' he said smoothly. 'You're going to have to meet people. Not just my friends and the people who work for me, but my father and stepmother at some point. And my stepbrother,' he finished, his mouth twisting before his gaze fixed her with its ebony blaze. 'The way you look at the moment means you won't fit in. Not anywhere,' he continued brutally. 'And there's the chance that people will talk about you if you behave like some kind of hermit, which won't make things easy for you. Apart from anything else, we need to learn more about each other.' He hesitated. 'We are parents, with a child and a future to consider. We need to discuss the options open to us and that won't be possible if we continue to be strangers to one another.'

'You haven't bothered coming near me since we got here,' she said quietly. 'You've been keeping your distance, haven't you?'

'Can you blame me? You were almost on your knees with exhaustion when you arrived.' He paused as his eyes swept over her again. 'But you look like a different person now.'

Keira was taken aback by the way her body responded to that slow scrutiny, wondering how he could make her feel so many different things, simply by looking at her. And if that was the case, shouldn't she be protecting herself from his persuasive power over her, instead of going on a falsely intimate trip to Rome?

'I told you. I don't want to leave the baby,' she said stubbornly.

'Is that what's known as playing your trump card?' he questioned softly. 'Making me out to be some cruel tyrant who's dragging you away from your child?'

'He's only little! Not that you'd know, of course.' She paused and lifted her chin. 'You've hardly gone near him.'

Matteo acknowledged the unmistakable challenge in her voice and he felt a sudden chill ice his skin, despite the warmth of the October day. How audacious of her to interrogate him about his behaviour when her own had hardly been exemplary. By her keeping Santino's existence secret he had been presented with a baby, instead of having time to get used to the idea that he was to become a father.

Yet her pointed remark about his lack of interaction struck home, because what she said was true. He *had* kept his distance from Santino, telling himself that these things could not be rushed and needed time. And she had no right to demand anything of him, he thought bitterly. He would do things according to *his* agenda, not hers.

'Rome isn't far,' he said coolly. 'It is exactly two hundred kilometres. And I have a car constantly on standby.'

'Funnily enough that's something I *do* remember—being at your beck and call!'

'Then you will know there's no problem,' he said drily. 'Particularly as my driver is solid and reliable and not given to taking off to remote areas of the countryside in adverse weather conditions.'

'Very funny,' she said.

'We can be back here in an hour and a half should the need arise. We'll leave here at ten tomorrow morning—and be back early the next day. Less than twenty-four hours in the eternal city.' He gave a faintly cynical laugh. 'Don't women usually go weak at the knees at the prospect of an unlimited budget to spend on clothes?'

'Some women, maybe,' she said. 'Not me.'

But Keira's stubbornness was more than her determination not to become a rich man's doll. She didn't *know* about fashion—and the thought of what she might be expected to wear scared her. Perhaps if she'd been less of a tomboy, she might have flicked through glossy magazines like other women her age. She might have had some idea of what did and didn't suit her and would now be feeling a degree of excitement instead of dread. Fear suddenly became defiance and she glared at him.

'You are the bossiest man I've ever met!' she declared, pushing a handful of hair over her shoulder.

'And you are the most difficult woman I've ever encountered,' he countered. 'A little *gratitude* might go down well now and again.'

What, gratitude for his high-handedness and for making her feel stuff she'd rather not feel? Keira shook her head in frustration as she tugged her T-shirt down over her straining jeans.

'I'll be ready at ten,' she said, and went off to find Santino.

She put the baby in his smart new buggy to take him for a walk around the estate, slowly becoming aware that the weather had changed. The air had grown heavy and sultry and heavy clouds were beginning to accumulate on the horizon, like gathering troops. When eventually they returned to the farmhouse, Santino took longer than usual to settle for his sleep and Keira was feeling out of sorts when Paola came to ask whether she would be joining Signor Valenti for dinner that evening.

It was the first time she'd received such an invitation and Keira hesitated for a moment before declining. Up until now, she'd eaten her supper alone or with Claudia and she saw no reason to change that routine. She was going to be stuck with Matteo in Rome when clearly they were going to have to address some of the issues confronting them. Why waste conversation during a stilted dinner she had no desire to eat, especially when the atmosphere felt so close and heavy?

Fanning her face with her hand, she showered before bed but her skin still felt clammy, even after she'd towelled herself dry. Peering up into the sky, she thought she saw a distant flash of lightning through the thick curtain of clouds. She closed the shutters and brushed her hair before climbing into bed, but sleep stubbornly eluded her. She wished the occasional growl of thunder would produce the threatened rain and break some of the tension in the atmosphere and was just drifting off into an uneasy sleep when her wish came true. A loud clap of thunder echoed through the room and made her sit bolt upright in bed. There was a loud whoosh and heavy rain began to hurl down outside her window and quickly she got up and crept into Santino's room but, to her surprise, the baby was sound asleep.

How did he manage to do that? she thought enviously—feeling even more wide awake than before. She sighed as she went back to bed and the minutes ticked by, and all she could think about was how grim she was going to look, with dark shadowed eyes and a pasty face. Another clap of thunder made her decide that a warm drink might help relax her. And wasn't there a whole stack of herb teas in the kitchen?

To the loud tattoo of drumming rain, she crept downstairs to the kitchen with its big, old-fashioned range and lines of shiny copper pots hanging in a row. She switched on some low lighting and not for the first time found herself wistfully thinking how *homely* it looked—and how it was unlike any place she had imagined the urbane Matteo Valenti would own.

She had just made herself a cup of camomile tea when she heard a sound behind her and she jumped, her heart hammering as loudly as the rain as she turned to see Matteo standing framed in the doorway. He was wearing nothing but a pair of faded denims, which were clinging almost indecently to his long and muscular thighs. His mouth was unsmiling but there was a gleam in his coal-dark eyes, which made awareness drift uncomfortably over her skin and suddenly Keira began to shiver uncontrollably, her nipples tightening beneath her nightshirt.

CHAPTER SEVEN

THE WALLS SEEMED to close in on her and Keira was suddenly achingly conscious of being alone in the kitchen with a half-naked Matteo, while outside she could hear the rain howl down against the shuttered windows.

With a shaking hand she put her mug down, her eyes still irresistibly drawn to the faded jeans which hugged his long and muscular thighs. He must have pulled them on in a hurry because the top button was undone, displaying a line of dark hair which arrowed tantalisingly downwards. Soft light bathed his bare and gleaming torso, emphasising washboard abs and broad shoulders.

She realised with a start that she'd never seen his naked torso before—or at least hadn't really noticed it. She'd been so blown away when they'd been having sex that her eyes hadn't seemed able to focus on anything at all. But now she could see him in all his beauty—a dark and forbidding beauty, but beauty all the same. And despite all the *stuff* between them, despite the fact that they'd been snapping at each other like crocodiles this afternoon, she could feel herself responding to him, and there didn't seem to be a thing she could do about it.

Beneath her nightshirt her nipples were growing even tighter and her breasts were heavy. She could feel a warm melting tug at her groin and the sensation was so intense that she found herself shifting her weight uncomfortably from one bare foot to the other. She opened her mouth to say something, but no words came.

He stared at her, a strange and mocking half-smile at his lips, as if he knew exactly what was happening to her. 'What's the matter, Keira?' he queried silkily. 'Can't sleep?'

She struggled to find the correct response. To behave as anyone else would in the circumstances.

Like a woman drinking herb tea and not wishing that he would put his hand between her legs to stop this terrible aching.

'No. I can't. This wretched storm is keeping me awake.' She forced a smile. 'And neither could you, obviously.'

'I heard someone moving around in the kitchen, so I came to investigate.' He stared down at her empty cup. 'Is the tea working?'

She thought about pretending but what was the point? 'Not really,' she admitted as another crash of thunder echoed through the room. 'I'm still wide awake and I'm probably going to stay that way until the storm dies down.'

There was a pause while Matteo's gaze drifted over her and he thought how pale she looked standing there with her nightshirt brushing against her bare thighs and hair spilling like dark silk over her shoulders. Barefooted, she looked *tiny*—a tantalising mixture of vulnerability and promise—and it felt more potent than anything he'd ever experienced. She was trying to resist him, he knew that, yet the look in her eyes told him that inside she was aching as much as he was. He knew what he was going to do because he couldn't put it off any longer, and although the voice of his conscience was sounding loud in his ears, he took no notice of it. She needed to relax a little—for all their sakes.

'Maybe you should try a little distraction technique,' he said.

Her eyes narrowed. 'Doing what?'

'Come and look at the view from my study,' he suggested evenly. 'It's spectacular at the best of times, but during a storm it's unbelievable.'

Keira hesitated because it felt as if he were inviting her into the lion's lair, but surely anything would be better than standing there feeling totally out of her depth. What else was she going to do—go back to bed and lie there feeling sorry for herself? And they were leaving for Rome tomorrow. Perhaps she should drop her guard a little. Perhaps they should start trying to be friends.

'Sure,' she said, with a shrug. 'Why not?'

His study was in a different wing of the house, which hadn't featured in the guided tour he'd given her at the beginning of the week—an upstairs room sited at the far end of a vast, beamed sitting room. She followed him into the book-lined room, her introspection vanishing the instant she saw the light show taking place outside the window. Her lips fell open as she stood watching the sky blindingly illuminated by sheet lightning, which lit up the dark outlines of the surrounding mountains. Each bright flash was reflected in the surface of the distant lake, so that the dramatic effect of what she was seeing was doubled. 'It's…amazing,' she breathed.

'Isn't it?'

He had come to stand beside her—so close that he was almost touching and Keira held her breath, wanting him to touch her, *praying* for him to touch her. Did he guess that? Was that why he slid his arm around her shoulders, his fingers beginning to massage the tense and knotted muscles?

She looked up into the hard gleam of his eyes, startled by the dark look of hunger on his face.

'Shall we put a stop to all this right now, Keira?' he murmured. 'Because we both know that the damned storm has nothing to do with our inability to sleep. It's desire, isn't it? Two people lying in their lonely beds, just longing to reach out to one another.'

His hands had slipped to her upper arms, and as his hard-boned face swam in and out of focus Keira told herself to break away and escape to the sanctuary of her room. Yet her body was stubbornly refusing to obey. All she could seem to focus on were his lips and how good it felt to have him touching her like this. She'd never stood in a storm-lit room with a half-dressed man, completely naked beneath her frumpy nightshirt, and yet she knew exactly what was going to happen next. She could feel it. Smell it. She swayed. Could almost *taste* the desire which was bombarding her senses and making her pounding heart the only thing she could hear above the loud hammer of the rain.

'Isn't that so?' he continued, brushing hair away from

her face as the pad of his thumb stroked its way over her trembling lips. 'You want me to kiss you, don't you, Keira? You want it really quite badly.'

Keira resented the arrogance of that swaggering statement—but not enough to make her deny the truth behind it. 'Yes,' she said. 'Yes, I do.'

Matteo tensed, her whispered assent sharpening his already keen hunger, and he pulled her against his body and crushed his mouth over hers. And, oh, she tasted good. Better than good. Better than he remembered—but maybe that was because her kiss had lingered in his memory far longer than it should have done. He tried to go slowly but his usual patience fled as his hands began to rediscover her small and compact body. Before she had been incredibly lean—he remembered narrow hips and the bony ladder of her ribcage. But now those bones had disappeared beneath a layer of new flesh, which was soft and tempting and just ripe for licking.

Her head tipped back as he rucked up her nightshirt, his hand burrowing beneath the bunched cotton until he had bared her breast. He bent his head to take one taut rosebud in between his lips and felt her fingers digging into his bare shoulders as he grazed the sensitive areola between his teeth. Already he felt as if he wanted to explode—as if he would die if he'd didn't quickly impale her. Was the fact that she'd borne his child the reason why he was feeling a desire which felt almost *primitive* in its intensity? Was that why his hands were trembling like this?

'Do you know how long I've been wanting to do this?' he husked, his fingers sliding down between her breasts and caressing their silken weight. 'Every second of every day.'

Her reply was a muffled gasp against his mouth. 'Is that why you've stayed away from me?'

'That's exactly why.' He let his fingertips trickle down over her belly and heard her catch her breath as they travelled further downwards. 'You needed to rest and I was trying to be a...*gentleman*,' he growled.

'And how does this qualify as being...*oh*!' Her words faded away as he slid his hand between her legs, brushing over the soft fuzz of hair to find the molten heat beneath.

'You were saying?' he breathed as he dampened his finger in the soft, wet folds before starting to stroke the little bud which was already so tight.

He heard her give a shaky swallow. 'Matteo, this is...is...'

He knew exactly what it was. It was arousing her to a state where she was going to come any second, and while it was turning him on to discover how close to the edge she was—it was also making his own frustration threaten to implode. With a necessary care which defied his hungry impatience, he eased the zip of his jeans down over his straining hardness—breathing a sigh of relief as his massive erection sprang free. The denim concertinaed around his ankles but he didn't care. He knew propriety dictated he should take them off, but he couldn't. He couldn't wait, not a second longer.

Impatiently he pushed her back against his desk, shoving aside his computer and paperwork with uncharacteristic haste. And the moment the moist tip of his penis touched her, she seemed to go wild, clawing eagerly at his back—and it took more concentration than he'd ever needed to force himself to pull back. Through the distracting fog of desire, he recalled the condom concealed in a drawer of his desk and by the time it was in place he felt as excited as a teenage boy as his hungry gaze skated over her.

Like a sacrifice she lay on the desk, her arms stretched indolently above her head as he leaned over to make that first thrust deep inside her. And this time there was no pain or hesitation. This time there was nothing but a gasped cry of pleasure as he filled her. Greedily, he sank even deeper and then he rode her—and even the crash of something falling from the desk wasn't enough to put him off his stroke. Or maybe it was just another crash of thunder from the storm outside. Who cared? He rode her until she came, her frantic convulsions starting only fractionally before his own, so that they moved in perfect time before his ragged groan heralded the end and he slumped on top of her, her hands clasped around the sweat-sheened skin of his back.

He didn't say anything at first, unwilling to shatter the unfamiliar peace he felt as he listened to the quietening of his heart. He felt spent. As if she had milked him dry. As if he could have fallen asleep right there, despite the hardness of the wooden surface. He forced himself to open his eyes and to take stock of their surroundings. Imagine if they were discovered here in the morning by one of the cleaners, or by Paola—already surprised that, not only had he brought a woman here, but he had a baby son.

A son he had barely seen.

Guilt formed itself into an icy-cold knot deep in his chest and was enough to dissolve his lethargy. Untwining himself from Keira's arms, he moved away from the desk, bending to pull up his jeans and zip them. Only then did he stare down at her, where she lay with her eyes closed amid the debris of his wrecked desk. Her cotton nightshirt was rucked right up to expose her beautiful breasts and her legs were bent with careless abandon. The enticing gleam between her open thighs was making him grow hard again but he fought the feeling—telling himself he needed to start taking control. He would learn about his son in time—he *would*—but for now his primary purpose was to ensure that Santino remained a part of his life, and for that to happen he needed Keira onside.

So couldn't their powerful sexual chemistry work in his favour—as effective a bargaining tool as his vast wealth? Couldn't he tantalise her with a taste of what could be hers, if only she was prepared to be reasonable? Because Keira Ryan was unpredictable. She was proud and stubborn, despite the fact that she'd been depending on other people's charity for most of her life, and he was by no means certain that she would accede to his wishes. So maybe it was time to remind her just who was calling the shots. He bent and lifted her into his arms, cradling her against his chest as her eyelashes fluttered open.

'What are you doing?' she questioned drowsily.

'Taking you back to bed.'

She yawned. 'Can't we just stay here?'

He gave an emphatic shake of his head. 'No.'

Keira closed her eyes again, wanting to capture this feeling for ever—a feeling which went much deeper than sexual satisfaction, incredible though that side of it had been. She had felt so close to Matteo when he'd been deep inside her. *Scarily* close—almost as if they were two parts of the same person. Had he felt that, too? Her heart gave a little leap of hope. Couldn't they somehow make this work despite everything which had happened? Couldn't they?

Resting her head against his warm chest, she let him carry her through the house to her own room, not pausing until he had pulled back the duvet and deposited her in the centre of the soft bed. Only then did her eyelids flutter open, her heart missing a beat as she took in his gleaming torso and powerful thighs. She stared up at him hopefully. Was he going to lose the jeans and climb in beside her, so she could snuggle up against him as she so desperately wanted to do and stroke her fingers through the ruffled beauty of his black hair?

She watched as his gaze swept over her, the hectic glitter of hunger in their ebony depths unmistakable. And she waited, because surely it should be *him* asking her permission to stay? She didn't know very much about bedroom etiquette, but instinct told her that. She recognised that she'd been a bit of a pushover back there, and it was time to show the Italian tycoon that he might need to work a little harder this time.

'So?' She looked at him with what she hoped was a welcoming smile.

'That's better. You don't smile nearly enough.' His finger traced the edges of her lips as he leaned over her. 'All the bad temper of this afternoon banished in the most pleasurable way possible.' He stroked an exploratory finger over the tightening nipple beneath her nightshirt. 'Was that what you needed all along, Keira?'

It took a few moments for his meaning to sink in and when it did, Keira could hardly believe her ears. A powerful wave of hurt crashed over her. Was that all it had been? Had he made love to her as a way of soothing her ruffled emotions and making her more *amenable*? As if he were some kind of *human sedative*? She wanted to bite down hard on her clenched fist. To demand how someone so cold-blooded could possibly live with himself. But she forced herself to remain silent because only that way could she cling onto what was left of her battered pride. Why give him the satisfaction of knowing he'd hurt her? If he was going to act so carelessly, then so would she. And why be so surprised by his callous behaviour when he hadn't shown one fraction of concern for his baby son. Matteo Valenti was nothing but a manipulative and cold-blooded *bastard*, she reminded herself.

Hauling the duvet up to her chin, she closed her eyes. 'I'm tired, Matteo,' she said. 'Would you mind turning off the light as you go?'

And then, deliberately manufacturing a loud yawn, she turned her back on him.

CHAPTER EIGHT

KEIRA DIDN'T SAY a word to Matteo next morning, not until they were halfway to Rome and his powerful car had covered many miles. The fierce storm had cleared the air and the day had dawned with a sky of clear, bright blue—but the atmosphere inside the car was heavy and fraught with tension. She was still feeling the painful tug of saying goodbye to Santino, though he'd been happily cradled in Claudia's arms when the dreaded moment had arrived. But as well as the prospect of missing her baby, Keira was still smarting from what had happened the night before.

She'd woken up with a start soon after dawn, wondering why her body felt so…

Slowly she had registered her lazy lethargy and the sweet aching between her legs.

So…*used.*

Yes, used, that was it. *Used.* Vivid images had flashed through her mind as she remembered what had happened while the storm raged outside. Matteo unzipping his jeans and pushing her onto his desk. Matteo rucking up her nightdress before thrusting into her and making her cry out with pleasure. It had hardly been the stuff of fairy tales, had it? So why not concentrate on the reality, rather than the dumb romantic version she'd talked herself into when she was lying quivering beneath his sweat-sheened body?

He had cold-bloodedly seduced her after days of acting as if she didn't exist. He had invited her to witness the storm from the best vantage point in the house and, although it had been the corniest request in the world, she had agreed. Trotting behind him like some kind of puppy dog, she'd had sex with him. Again. Keira closed her eyes in horror as she remembered the way she'd clawed at his bare back like some kind of wildcat. Did her inexperience explain the fierce hunger which had consumed her and made her unable to resist his advances? Or was it just that Matteo Valenti only had to touch her for her to come apart in his arms?

And now the trip to Rome, which she'd already been dreading, was going to be a whole lot worse. Bad enough being in the kind of car she'd lusted after during her days as a mechanic—and having it driven by *someone else*—without the knowledge of how smug Matteo must be feeling. Why, he hadn't even wanted to spend the night with her! He'd just deposited her in her bed like some unwanted package and behaved as if what had happened had been purely functional. Like somebody scratching an itch. Was that how it had been for him, she wondered bitterly? Had he seen her as a body rather than a person?

'So, are you going to spend the next twenty-four hours ignoring me?' Matteo's voice broke into her rebellious thoughts as they passed a signpost to a pretty-looking place called Civita Castellana.

Keira wanted to pretend she hadn't heard him but that was hardly the way forward, was it? She mightn't be happy with the current state of affairs, but that didn't mean she had to lie down and passively accept it. Unless she was planning on behaving like some sort of victim—allowing the powerful tycoon to pick her up and move her around at will, without her having any say in the matter. It was time she started asserting herself and stopped beating herself up. They'd had sex together as two consenting adults and surely that put them on some kind of equal footing.

So *ask* him.

Take some of the control back.

She turned her head to look at his profile, trying not to feel affected by that proud Roman nose and the strong curve of his shadowed jaw. His silk shirt was unbuttoned at the neck, offering a tantalising glimpse of olive skin, and he exuded a vitality which made him seem to glow with life. She could feel a trickle of awareness whispering over her body and it made her want to fidget on the plush leather car seat.

She wanted him to touch her all over again. And when he touched her she went to pieces.

Firmly pushing all erotic possibilities from her mind, she cleared her throat. 'So why this trip, Matteo?'

There was a pause. 'You know why. We've discussed this. We're going to buy you some pretty clothes to wear.'

His words were deeply patronising and she wondered

if that had been his intention—reminding her that she fell way short of his ideal of what a woman should be. 'I'm not talking about your determination to change my appearance,' she said. 'I mean, why bring me to Italy in the first place? That's something we haven't even discussed. What's going to happen once you've waved your magic wand and turned me into someone different? Are you planning to return me to England in your fancy plane and make like this was all some kind of dream?'

His mouth hardened into a flat and implacable line. 'That isn't an option.'

'Then what *are* the options?' she questioned quietly.

Matteo put his foot down on the accelerator and felt the powerful engine respond. It was a reasonable question, though not one he particularly wanted to answer. But he couldn't keep on putting off a conversation they needed to have because he was wary of all the stuff it might throw up. 'We need to see whether we can make it work as a couple.'

'A *couple*?'

He saw her slap her palms down on her denim-covered thighs in a gesture of frustration.

'You mean, living in separate parts of the same house? How is that in any way what a *couple* would do?' She sucked in a breath. 'Why, we've barely *seen* one another—and when we have, it isn't as if we've done much talking!'

'That can be worked on,' he said carefully.

'Then let's start working on it right now. Couples aren't complete strangers to one another and we are. Or at least, you are. I told you a lot about my circumstances on the night we…' Her voice wavered as she corrected herself before growing quieter. 'On that night we spent together in Devon. But I don't know you, Matteo. I still don't really know anything about you.'

Matteo stared at the road ahead. Women always asked these kinds of questions and usually he cut them short. With a deceptively airy sense of finality, he'd make it clear that he wouldn't tolerate any further interrogation because he didn't want anyone trying to 'understand' him. But he recognised that Keira was different and their situation was different. She was the mother of his child and she'd given birth to his heir—not some socially ambitious woman itching to get his ring on her finger. He owed her this.

'What do you want to know?' he questioned.

She shrugged. 'All the usual stuff. About your parents. Whether or not you have any brothers or sisters. That kind of thing.'

'I have a father and a stepmother. No siblings,' he said, his voice growing automatically harsher and there wasn't a damned thing he could do to stop it. 'But I have a stepbrother who's married, with a small child.'

He could feel her eyes on him. 'So your parents are divorced?'

'No. My mother is dead.'

'Like mine,' she said thoughtfully.

He nodded but didn't say anything, his attention fixed on the road ahead, trying to concentrate on the traffic and not on the bleak landscape of loss.

'Tell me about your father,' she said. 'Do you get on well with him?'

Some of the tension left his body as he overtook a truck and he waited until he had finished the manoeuvre before answering. He wondered if he should give her the official version of his life, thus maintaining the myth that all was well. But if she stayed then she would soon discover the undercurrents which surged beneath the surface of the powerful Valenti clan.

'We aren't close, no. We see each other from time to time, more out of duty than anything else.'

'But you mentioned a stepmother?'

'You mean the latest stepmother?' he questioned cynically. 'Number four in a long line of women who were brought in to try to replace the wife he lost.'

'But…' She hesitated. 'None of them were able to do that?'

'That depends on your definition. I'm sure each of them provided him with the creature comforts most men need, though each marriage ended acrimoniously and at great financial cost to him. That's the way it goes, I guess.' His hands tightened around the steering wheel. 'But my mother would have been a hard act for any woman to follow—at least according to the people who knew her.'

'What was she like?' she prompted, and her voice was as gentle as he'd ever imagined a voice could be.

Matteo didn't answer for a long time because this was something nobody ever really asked. A dead mother was just that. History. He couldn't remember anyone else who'd ever shown any interest in her short life.

He could feel the tight squeeze of his heart. 'She was beautiful,' he said eventually. 'Both inside and out. She was training to be a doctor when she met my father—an only child from a very traditional Umbrian family who owned a great estate in the region.'

'The farmhouse where we've been staying?' she questioned slowly. 'Is that…?'

He nodded. 'Was where she grew up, *sì*.'

Keira nodded as slowly she began to understand. She gazed out of the window at the blue bowl of the sky. Did that explain his obvious love for the estate? she wondered. The last earthly link to his mum?

'Does your father know?' she questioned suddenly. 'About Santino?'

'Nobody knows,' he said harshly. 'And I won't let it be known until we've come to some kind of united decision about the future.'

'But a baby isn't really the kind of thing you can keep secret. Won't someone from the farm have told him? One of the staff?'

He shook his head. 'Discretion is an essential quality for all the people who work for me and their first loyalty is to me. Anyway, my father isn't interested in the estate, only as…'

'Only as what?' she prompted, her curiosity sharpened by the harsh note which had suddenly entered his voice.

'Nothing. It doesn't matter. And I think we've had enough questions for today, don't you?' he drawled. He lifted one hand from the steering wheel to point straight ahead. 'We're skirting Rome now and if you look over there you'll soon be able to see Lake Nemi.'

Her gaze followed the direction of his finger as she tried to concentrate. 'And that's where you live?'

'That's where I live,' he agreed.

They didn't say much for the rest of the journey, but at least Keira felt she knew a little more about him. And yet it was only a little. He had the air of the enigma about him. Something at the very core of him which was dark and unknowable and which seemed to keep her at arm's length. Behind that formidable and sexy exterior lay a damaged man, she realised—and something about his inner darkness made her heart go out to him. *Could* they make it as a couple? she wondered as they drove through a beautiful sheltered valley and she saw the silver gleam of the lake. Would she be a fool to want that?

But the stupid thing was that, yes, she did want that, because if Santino was to have any kind of security—the kind she'd always longed for—then it would work best if they *were* a couple. Her living with Matteo Valenti as his lover and mother to his son…would that be such a bad thing?

Her daydreaming was cut short by her first sight of Matteo's villa and she began to wonder if she was crazy to ever imagine she would fit in here. Overlooking Lake Nemi, the apricot-coloured house was three storeys high, with high curved windows overlooking acres of beautifully tended gardens. And she soon discovered that inside were countless rooms, including a marble-floored dining room and a ballroom complete with a lavish hand-painted ceiling. It felt more like being shown round a museum than a house. Never had her coat felt more threadbare or the cuffs more frayed as it was plucked from her nerveless fingers by a stern-faced butler named Roberto, who seemed to regard her with complete indifference. Was he wondering why his powerful employer had brought such a scruffy woman to this palace of a place? Keira swallowed. Wasn't she wondering the same thing herself?

After ringing the farmhouse and being told by Paola that Santino was lying contentedly in his pram in the garden, Keira accepted the tiny cup of espresso offered by a maid in full uniform and sat down on a stiff and elegant chair to drink it. Trying to ignore the watchful darkness of Matteo's eyes, she found herself thinking about the relaxed comfort of the farmhouse and felt a pang as she thought about her son, wondering if he would be missing his mama. As she drank her coffee she found herself glancing around at the beautiful but cavernous room and suppressed a shiver, wondering how much it must cost to heat a place this size.

'Why do you live here?' she questioned suddenly, lifting her gaze to the dark figure of the man who stood beside the vast fireplace.

He narrowed his eyes. 'Why wouldn't I? It has a fresher climate than the city, particularly in the summer months when it can get very hot. And it's a valuable piece of real estate.'

'I don't doubt it.' She licked her lips. 'But it's *enormous* for just one person! Don't you rattle around in it?'

'I'm not a total hermit, Keira,' he said drily. 'Sometimes I work from here—and, of course, I entertain.'

The question sprang from her lips before she could stop it. 'And bring back loads of women, I expect?'

The look he shot her was mocking. 'Do you want me to create the illusion that I've been living a celibate life all these years?' he asked softly. 'If sexual jealousy was the reason behind your question?'

'It wasn't!' she denied, furious with herself for having asked it. Of *course* Matteo would have had hundreds of women streaming through these doors—and it wasn't as if he were her *boyfriend*, was it? Her cheeks grew red. He never had been. He was just a man who could make her melt with a single look, no matter how much she fought against it. A man who had impregnated her without meaning to. And now he was observing her with that sexy smile, as if he knew exactly what she was thinking. As if he was perfectly aware that beneath her drab, chain-store sweater her breasts were hungering to feel his mouth on them again. She could feel her cheeks growing warm as she watched him answer his mobile phone to speak in rapid Italian and when he'd terminated the call he turned to look at her, his hard black eyes scanning over her.

'The car is outside waiting to take you into the city centre,' he said. 'And the stylist will meet you there.'

'A stylist?' she echoed, her gaze flickering uncertainly to her scuffed brown boots.

'A very famous stylist who's going to take you shopping.' He shrugged. 'I thought you might need a little guidance.'

His condescension only intensified Keira's growing feelings of inadequacy and she glared at him. 'What, in case I opt for something which is deeply unsuitable?'

His voice was smooth. 'There is a different way of looking at it, Keira. I don't expect you've been given unlimited use of a credit card before, have you?'

Something in the way he said it was making Keira's blood boil. 'Funnily enough, no!'

'So what's the problem?'

'The problem is *you*! I bet you're just loving this,' she accused. 'Does flashing your wealth give you a feeling of power, Matteo?'

He raised his eyebrows. 'Actually, I was hoping it might give you a modicum of pleasure. So why don't you go upstairs and freshen up before the car takes you into the city?'

Keira put her empty cup down on a spindly gold-edged table and rose to her feet. 'Very well,' she said, forcing her stiff shoulders into a shrug.

'By the way,' he said as he gestured for her to precede him, 'I notice you didn't make any comment about my driving on the way here.'

'I thought it might be wise, in the circumstances.'

'But as a professional, you judged me favourably, I hope?'

She pursed her lips together. 'You were okay. A little heavy on the clutch, perhaps—but it's a great car.'

She took a stupid and disproportionate pleasure from the answering humour which gleamed from his eyes before following him up a sweeping staircase into a sumptuous suite furnished in rich brocades and velvets, where he left her. Alone in the ballroom-sized bathroom, where water gushed from golden taps, Keira dragged the hairbrush through her hair, wondering what on earth the stylist was going to think about being presented with such unpromising raw material.

But the stylist was upbeat and friendly—even if the store on the Via dei Condotti was slightly terrifying. Keira had never been inside such an expensive shop before—although in her chauffeuring days she'd sat outside places like it often enough, waiting for her clients. A slim-hipped woman named Leola came forward to greet her, dressed in an immaculate cream dress accessorised with gleaming golden jewellery and high-heeled patent shoes. Although she looked as if she'd stepped straight off the catwalk, to her credit, she didn't seem at all fazed by Keira's appearance, as she led her around the shop and swished her fingertips over rail after rail of clothes.

In the chandelier-lit changing room, she whipped a tape measure around Keira's newly abundant curves. 'You have a fantastic figure,' she purred. 'Let's show it off a little more, shall we?'

'I'd rather not, if you don't mind,' said Keira quickly. 'I don't like to be stared at.'

Leola raised perfectly plucked black eyebrows by a centimetre. 'You are dating one of the city's most eligible bachelors,' she observed quietly. 'And Matteo will expect people to stare at you.'

Keira felt a shimmer of anxiety as she tugged a blue cashmere dress over her head and pulled on some navy-blue suede boots. What possible response could she make to that? What would the stunning Leola say if she explained that she and Matteo weren't 'dating', but simply parents to a darling little boy? And even that wasn't really accurate, was it? You couldn't really describe a man as a parent when he regarded his newborn infant with the caution which an army expert might display towards an unexploded bomb.

Just go with the flow, she told herself. Be amenable and do what's suggested—and after you've been dressed up like a Christmas turkey, you can sit down with the Italian tycoon and talk seriously about the future.

She tried on hip-hugging skirts with filmy blouses, flirty little day dresses and sinuous evening gowns, and Keira was reeling by the time Leola had finished with her. She wanted to protest that there was no way she would wear most of these—that she and Matteo hadn't even discussed how long she would be staying—but Leola seemed to be acting on someone else's orders and it wasn't difficult to work out whose orders they might be.

'I will have new lingerie and more shoes sent by courier to arrive later,' the stylist explained, 'since I understand you're returning to Umbria tomorrow. But you certainly have enough to be going on with. Might I suggest you wear the red dress this evening? Matteo was very specific about how good he thought you would look in vibrant colours. Oh, and a make-up artist will be visiting the house later this afternoon. She will also be able to fix your hair.'

Keira stared at the slippery gown of silk-satin which was being dangled from Leola's finger and shook her head. 'I can do my own hair,' she said defensively, wondering if dressing up in all this finery was what Matteo usually expected for dinner at home on a weekday evening. 'And I can't possibly wear that—it's much too revealing.'

'Yes, you can—and you must—because you look amazing in it,' said Leola firmly, before her voice softened a little. 'Matteo must care for you a great deal to go to so much trouble. And surely it would be unwise to displease him when he's gone to so much trouble.'

It was a candid remark which contained in it a trace of warning. It was one woman saying to another—don't look a gift horse in the mouth. But all it did was to increase Keira's sensation of someone playing dress-up. Of being moulded for a role in the billionaire's life which she wasn't sure she was capable of filling. Her heart was pounding nervously as she shook the stylist's hand and went outside to the waiting car.

And didn't she feel slightly ashamed at the ease with which she allowed the chauffeur to open the door for her as she slid onto the squishy comfort of the back seat? As if already she was turning into someone she didn't recognise.

CHAPTER NINE

THE CLOCK WAS striking seven and Matteo gave a click of impatience as he paced the drawing room, where an enormous fire crackled and burned. Where the hell *was* she? He didn't like to be kept waiting—not by anyone, and especially not by a woman who ought to have been bang on time and full of gratitude for his generosity towards her. He wondered how long it would have taken Keira to discover how much she liked trying on lavish clothes. Or how quickly she'd decided it was a turn-on when a man was prepared to buy you an entire new wardrobe, with no expense spared. He was just about to send Roberto upstairs to remind her of the time, when the door opened and there she stood, pale-faced and slightly uncertain.

Matteo's heart pounded hard in his chest because she looked… He shook his head slightly as if to clear his vision, but the image didn't alter. She looked *unrecognisable*. Light curls of glossy black tumbled over her narrow shoulders and, with mascara and eyeliner, her sapphire eyes looked enormous. Her lips were as red as her dress and he found himself wanting to kiss away her unfamiliar lipstick. But it was her body which commanded the most attention. *Santo cielo!* What a body! Scarlet silk clung to the creamy curve of her breasts, the material gliding in over the indentation of her waist, then flaring gently over her hips. Sheer stockings encased her legs and skyscraper heels meant she looked much taller than usual.

He swallowed because the transformation was exactly what he'd wanted—a woman on his arm who would turn heads for all the *right* reasons—and yet now he was left with intense frustration pulsing through his veins. He wanted to call their host and cancel and to take her straight to bed instead, but he was aware that such a move would be unwise. He had less than twenty-four hours to get Keira Ryan to agree to his plan—and that would not be achieved by putting lust before logic.

'You look...beautiful,' he said unsteadily, noticing how pink her cheeks had grown in response to his compliment, and he was reminded once again of her innocence and inexperience.

She tugged at the skirt of the dress as if trying to lengthen it. 'I feel a bit underdressed, to be honest.'

He shook his head. 'If that were the case then I certainly wouldn't let you leave the house.'

She raised her eyebrows. 'What, you mean you'd keep me here by force? Prisoner of the Italian tycoon?'

He smiled. 'I've always found persuasion to be far more effective than force. I assume Leola organised a suitable coat for you to wear?'

'A coat?' She stared at him blankly.

'It's November, Keira, and we're going to a party in

the city. It might be warmer than back in England, but you'll still need to wrap up.'

Keira's stomach did a flip. 'You didn't mention a party.'

'Didn't I? Well, I'm mentioning it now.'

She gave the dress another tug. 'Whose party is it?'

'An old friend of mine. Salvatore di Luca. It's his birthday—and it will be the perfect opportunity for you to meet people. It would be a pity for you not to have an audience when you look so very dazzling.' His gaze travelled over her and his voice thickened. 'So why not go and get your coat? The car's waiting.'

Keira felt nerves wash over her. She was tempted to tell him she'd rather stay home and eat a *panino* in front of the fire, instead of having to face a roomful of strangers—but she was afraid of coming over as some kind of social misfit. Was this some strange kind of interview to assess whether or not she would be up to the task of being Matteo's partner? To see if she was capable of making conversation with his wealthy friends, of getting through a whole evening without dropping a canapé down the front of her dress?

Her black velvet swing coat was lined with softest cashmere and Keira hugged it around herself as the driver opened the door of the waiting limousine, her heart missing a beat as Matteo slid onto the seat beside her. His potent masculinity was almost as distracting as the dark suit which fitted his muscular body to perfection and made him look like some kind of movie star on his way to an awards ceremony. 'You aren't driving, then?' she observed.

'Not tonight. I have a few calls I need to make.' His black eyes gleamed. 'After that I'm exclusively yours.'

The way he said it sent ripples of excitement whispering over her skin and she wondered if that had been deliberate. But there was apprehension too because Keira wasn't sure she would be able to cope with the full blaze of his undivided attention. Not when he was being so… *nice* to her.

She suspected he was on his best behaviour because he wanted her to agree to his masterplan—whenever he got around to unveiling it. And although he hadn't shown any desire to parent their son, something told her that he saw Santino as his possession, even if so far he had exhibited no signs of love. Because of that, she suspected he wouldn't let her go easily and the stupid part was that she didn't want him to. She was beginning to recognise that she was out of her depth—and not just because he was a billionaire hotelier and she a one-time car mechanic. She didn't have any experience of relationships and she didn't have a clue how to react to him. Part of her wished she were still in the driver's seat, negotiating the roads with a slick professionalism she'd been proud of until she'd ruined her career in the arms of the man who sat beside her, his long legs stretched indolently in front of him.

She forced herself to drag her eyes away from the taut tension of his thighs—and at least there was plenty to distract her as she gazed out of the window at the lights of the city and the stunning Roman architecture, which made her feel as if she'd fallen straight into the pages of a guide book.

Salvatore de Luca's apartment was in the centre of it all—a penthouse situated close to the Via del Corso and offering commanding views of the city centre. Keira was dimly aware of a maid taking her coat and a cocktail being pressed into her hand and lots of people milling around. To her horror she could see that every other woman was wearing elegant black and her own expensive scarlet dress made her feel like something which had fallen off the Christmas tree. And it wasn't just the colour. She wasn't used to displaying a hint of cleavage, or wearing a dress which came this high above the knee. She felt like an imposter—someone who'd been more at home with her hair hidden beneath that peaked hat, instead of cascading over her shoulders like this.

She saw a couple of the men give her glances which lingered more than they should have done—or was that just something Italian men did automatically? Certainly, Matteo seemed to be watching her closely as he introduced her to a dizzying array of friends and she couldn't deny the thrill it gave her to feel those dark eyes following her every move.

Keira did her best to chat animatedly, hugely grateful that nearly everybody spoke perfect English, but conversation wasn't easy. She was glaringly aware of not mentioning the one subject which was embedded deeply in her heart and that was Santino. She wondered when Matteo was planning to announce that he was a father and what would happen when he did. Did any of his friends have children? she wondered. This apartment certainly didn't look child-friendly and she couldn't imagine a toddler crawling around on these priceless rugs, with sticky fingers.

Escaping from the growing pitch of noise to the washroom, Keira took advantage of the relative calm and began to peep into some of the rooms on her way back to the party. Entering only those with open doors, she discovered a bewildering number of hand-painted salons which reminded her of Matteo's villa. His home wasn't exactly child-friendly either, was it?

The room she liked best was small and book-lined—not because she was the world's greatest reader but because it opened out onto a lovely balcony with tall green plants in pots and fabulous views over the glittering city. She stood there for a moment with her arms resting on the balustrade when she heard the clip-clop of heels enter the room behind her and she turned to see a tall redhead who she hadn't noticed before. Maybe she was a late arrival, because she certainly wasn't the kind of woman you would forget in a hurry. Her green gaze was searching rather than friendly and Keira had to concentrate very hard not to be fixated on the row of emeralds which gleamed at her slender throat and matched her eyes perfectly.

'So *you're* the woman who's been keeping Matteo off the scene,' the woman said, her soft Italian accent making her sound like someone who could have a very lucrative career in radio voice-overs.

Keira left the chilly balcony and stepped into the room. 'Hello, I'm Keira.' She smiled. 'And you are?'

'Donatella.' Her green eyes narrowed, as if she was

surprised that Keira didn't already know this. 'Your dress is very beautiful.'

'Thank you.'

There was a pause as Donatella's gaze flickered over her. 'Everyone is curious to know how you've managed to snare Italy's most elusive bachelor.'

'He's not a rabbit!' joked Keira.

Either Donatella didn't get the joke or she'd decided it wasn't funny because she didn't smile. 'So when did you two first meet?'

Aware of the sudden race of her heart, Keira suddenly felt *intimidated*. As if she was being backed into a corner, only she didn't know why. 'Just under a year ago.'

'When, exactly?' probed the redhead.

Keira wasn't the most experienced person when it came to social etiquette, but even she could work out when somebody was crossing the line. 'Does it really matter?'

'I'm curious, that's all. It wouldn't happen to have been two nights before Christmas, would it?'

The date was burned so vividly on Keira's memory that the affirmation burst from her lips without her even thinking about it. 'Yes, it was,' she said. 'How on earth did you know that?'

'Because he was supposed to be meeting me that night,' said Donatella, with a wry smile. 'And then I got a call from his assistant to say his plane couldn't take off because of the snow.'

'That's true. The weather was terrible,' said Keira.

'And then, when he got back—nothing. Complete

radio silence—even though the word was out that there was nobody else on the scene.' Donatella's green eyes narrowed thoughtfully. 'Interesting. You're not what I expected.'

Even though she hadn't eaten any of the canapés which had been doing the rounds, Keira suddenly felt sick. All she could think about was the fact that another woman had been waiting for Matteo while he'd been in bed with *her*. He must have had his assistant call Donatella while she'd been in the bath and then preceded to seduce *her*. Had it been a case of *any* woman would do as a recipient of all that hard hunger? A man who'd been intent on sex and was determined not to have his wishes thwarted? What if all that stuff about not finding her attractive had simply been the seasoned technique of an expert who'd recognised that he needed to get her to relax before leaping on her. She swallowed. Had he been imagining it was Donatella beneath him instead of her?

'Well, you know what they say…there's no accounting for taste.' From somewhere Keira dredged up a smile. 'Great meeting you, Donatella.'

But she was trembling by the time she located Matteo, surrounded by a group of men and women who were hanging onto his every word, and maybe he read something in her face because he instantly disengaged himself and came over to her side.

'Everything okay?' he questioned.

'Absolutely lovely,' she said brightly, for the benefit of the onlookers. 'But I'd like to go now, if you wouldn't mind. I'm awfully tired.'

His dark brows lifted. '*Certamente.* Come, let us slip away, *cara*.'

The practised ease with which the meaningless endearment fell from his lips made Donatella's words seem even more potent and in the car Keira sat as far away from him as possible, placing her finger on her lips and shaking her head when he tried to talk to her. She felt stupidly emotional and close to tears but there was no way she was going to break down in front of his driver. She knew better than most how domestic upsets could liven up a sometimes predictable job and that a chauffeur had a front-row seat to these kinds of drama. It wasn't until they were back in the villa, where a fire in the drawing room had obviously been kept banked for their return, that she turned to Matteo at last, trying to keep the edge of hysteria from her voice.

'I met Donatella,' she said.

'I wondered if you would. She arrived late.'

'I don't give a damn when she arrived!' She flung her sparkly scarlet clutch bag down onto a brocade sofa where it bounced against a tasselled cushion. 'She told me you were supposed to be meeting her the night we got stuck in the snow!'

'That much is true.'

She was so horrified by his easy agreement that Keira could barely choke out her next words. 'So you were in a sexual relationship with another woman when you seduced me?'

He shook his head. 'No, I was not. I'd been dating her for a few weeks, but it had never progressed beyond dinner and the occasional trip to the opera.'

'And you expect me to believe that?'

'Why wouldn't you believe it, Keira?'

'Because…' She sucked in a deep breath. 'Because you didn't strike me as the kind of man who would chastely court a woman like that.'

'Strangely enough, that's how I like to operate.'

'But not with me,' she said bitterly. 'Or maybe you just didn't think I was worth buying dinner for.'

Matteo tensed as he read the hurt and shame which clouded her sapphire eyes and was surprised how bad it made him feel. He knew he owed her an explanation but he sensed that this went deeper than anything he'd had to talk his way out of in the past, and part of him rebelled at having to lay his thoughts open. But he sensed there was no alternative. That despite the ease with which she had fallen into his arms, Keira Ryan was no pushover.

'Oh, you were worth it, all right,' he said softly. 'Just because we didn't do the conventional thing of having dinner doesn't change the fact that it was the most unforgettable night of my life.'

'Don't tell me lies!'

'It isn't a lie, Keira,' he said simply. 'It was amazing. We both know that.'

He saw her face working, as if she was struggling to contain her emotions.

'And then,' she said, on a gulp, 'when you got back—she says you didn't see her again.'

'Again, true.'

'Why not?' she demanded. 'There was nothing stopping you. Especially after you'd given me the heave-ho.'

If he was surprised by her persistence he didn't show it and Matteo felt conflicted about how far to go with his answer. Mightn't it be brutal to explain that he'd been so appalled at his recklessness that night that he'd decided he needed a break from women? If he told her that he'd never had a one-night stand before, because it went against everything he believed in, mightn't it hurt her more than was necessary? He didn't believe in love—not for him—but he believed in passion and, in his experience, it was always worth the wait. Deferred gratification increased the appetite and made seduction sweeter. And delaying his own pleasure reinforced his certainty that he was always in control.

Yet his usual fastidiousness had deserted him that snowy night when he'd found himself in bed with his petite driver, and it had affected him long after he'd returned to Italy. It wasn't an admission he particularly wanted to make but something told him it would work well in his favour if he did. What was it the Americans said? Ah, *sì*. It would buy him brownie points. 'I haven't had sex with anyone since the night I spent with you. Well, until last night,' he said.

Her eyes widened and the silence of the room was broken only by the loud ticking of the clock before she blurted out a single word.

'Why?' she breathed.

He bent to throw an unnecessary log onto the already blazing fire before straightening up to face the dazed disbelief which had darkened her eyes. He had tried convincing himself it had been self-disgust which had made him retreat into his shell when he'd returned to Rome, but deep down he'd known that wasn't the whole story.

'Because, annoyingly, I couldn't seem to shift you from my mind,' he drawled. 'And before you start shaking your head like that and telling me I don't mean it, let me assure you I do.'

'But why?' she questioned. 'I mean, why me?'

He paused long enough to let her know that he'd asked himself the same question. 'Who knows the subtle alchemy behind these things?' He shrugged, his gaze roving over her as he drank in the creamy curves of her flesh. 'Maybe because you were different. Because you spoke to me in a way that people usually don't. Or maybe because you were a virgin and on some subliminal level I understood that and it appealed to me. Why are you looking at me that way, Keira? You think that kind of thing doesn't matter? That a man doesn't feel an incomparable thrill of pleasure to discover that he is the first and the only one? Then you are very wrong.'

Keira felt faint and sank down onto the brocade sofa, next to her discarded clutch bag. His words were shockingly old-fashioned but that didn't lessen their impact on her, did it? It didn't stop her from feeling incredibly *desired* as his black gaze skated over her body and hinted at the things he might like to do to her.

Did her lips open of their own accord or did he somehow orchestrate her reaction from his position by the fireplace—like some puppet master twitching invisible strings? Was that why a hard gleam suddenly entered his eyes as he walked towards her and pulled her to her feet.

'I think we're done with talking, don't you?' he questioned unsteadily. 'Haven't I answered all your questions and told you everything you need to know?'

'Matteo, I—'

'I'm going to make love to you again,' he said, cutting right through her protest. 'Only this time it's going to be in a bed and it's going to be all night long. And please don't pretend you're outraged by the idea, when the look on your face says otherwise.'

'Or maybe you're just going to do it to pacify me?' she challenged. 'Like you did last night.'

'Last night we were in the middle of a howling storm and I wasn't really thinking straight, but today I am.'

And with that he lifted her up into his arms and swept her from the room and it occurred to Keira that no way would she have objected to such masterful treatment, even if he *had* given her the option. Because wasn't he making her feel like a woman who was completely desired—a woman for whom nothing but pleasure beckoned? Up the curving marble staircase he carried her, her ear pressed closely to his chest so she could hear the thundering of his heart. It felt like something from a film as he kicked the bedroom door shut behind them. Unreal. Just as the excitement coursing through her body felt unreal. Was it wrong to feel this rush of hungry pleasure as Matteo unzipped the scarlet dress and let it fall carelessly onto the silken rug? Or for her to gasp out words of encouragement from lips soon swollen by the pressure of his kiss?

Her bra swiftly followed and she gave a squeal of protesting pleasure as he hooked his fingers into the edges of her panties and ripped them apart and didn't that thrill her, too? Showing similar disregard for his own clothes, he tore them from his body like a man with the hounds of hell snapping at his ankles. But once they were both naked on the bed, he slowed things right down.

'These curves,' he said unevenly as his fingertips trickled over her breasts and hips.

'You don't like them?' she questioned breathlessly.

'Whatever gave you that idea? I seem to like you lean and I seem to like you rounded. Any way at all is okay with me, Keira.'

Slowly, he ran his fingertip from neck to belly before sliding it down between her thighs, nudging it lightly against her wet heat in a lazy and rhythmical movement. She shivered and had to stifle a frustrated moan as he moved his hand away. But then his mouth began to follow the same path as his fingers and Keira held her breath as she felt his lips acquainting themselves with the soft tangle of hair at her groin before he burrowed his head deep between her legs and made that first unbelievable flick of his tongue against her slick and heated flesh.

'Matteo!' she gasped, almost shooting off the bed with pleasure. 'What…what are you doing?'

He lifted his head and she saw pure devilry in his black eyes. 'I'm going to eat you, *cara mia*,' he purred, before bending his head to resume his task.

Keira let her head fall helplessly back against the pillow as he worked sweet magic with his tongue, loving the way he imprisoned her wriggling hips with the firm clamp of his hands. She came so quickly that it took her by surprise—as did the sudden way he moved over her to thrust deep inside her, while her body was still racked with those delicious spasms. She clung to his shoulders as he started a sweet, sure rhythm which set senses singing.

But suddenly his face hardened as he grew still inside her. 'How long do you think I can stop myself from coming?' he husked.

'Do you…?' She could barely get the words out when he was filling her like this. 'Do you *have* to stop yourself?'

'That depends. I do if you're going to have a second orgasm, which is my intention,' he murmured. 'In fact, I'm planning to make you come so often that you'll have lost count by the morning.'

'Oh, Matteo.' She closed her eyes as he levered himself to his knees and went even deeper.

She moaned as the finger moved between their joined bodies to alight on the tight nub between her legs and began to rub against her while he was deep inside her. The pleasure it gave her was almost too much to bear and it felt as if she were going to come apart at the seams. She gasped as pleasure and pressure combined in an unstoppable force. Until everything splintered around her. She heard him groan as his own body starting to convulse before eventually collapsing on top of her, his head resting on her shoulder and his shuddered breath hot and rapid against her neck.

His arms tightened around her waist and for countless seconds Keira felt as if she were floating on a cloud.

Had he really told her he hadn't slept with anyone else because he hadn't been able to get her out of his mind? Yes, he had. With a sigh of satisfaction, she rested her cheek against his shoulder and he murmured something soft in Italian in response.

She lay there for a long time after he'd fallen asleep, thinking that sex could blind you to the truth. Or maybe lull you into such a stupefied state that you stopped seeking the truth. He'd commented on her curves and admired them with his hands, but he'd made no mention of *why* her body had undergone such a dramatic transformation. She bit her lip. Because she'd carried his son and given birth to him—a fact he seemed to find all too easy to forget.

And she thought how—despite the heart-stopping intimacy of what had just taken place—she still didn't know Matteo at all.

CHAPTER TEN

SHE HAD TO say something. She *had* to. She couldn't keep pretending nothing was wrong or that there weren't still a million questions buzzing around in her head which needed answering.

Keira turned her head to look at the face of the man who lay sleeping beside her. It was a very big bed, which was probably a good thing since Matteo Valenti's naked body was taking up most of it. Morning light flooded in from the two windows they hadn't bothered closing the shutters on before they'd tumbled into bed the night before. From here she could see the green of the landscape which spread far into the distance and, above it, the endless blue of the cloudless sky. It was the most perfect of mornings, following the most perfect of nights.

She hugged her arms around herself and gave a wriggle of satisfaction. She'd never thought she could feel the way Matteo had made her feel. But the clock was ticking away and she needed to face reality. She couldn't keep pretending everything was wonderful just because they'd spent an amazing night together. He'd said he wanted to explore the possibility of them becoming a couple but there was more to being a couple than amazing sex. How could they keep ignoring the gaping hole at the centre of their relationship which neither of them had addressed? He for reasons unknown and she…

She turned her attention from the distraction of the view to the dark head which lay sleeping beside her. Was she too scared to ask him, was that it?

Because the most important thing was all out of kilter and the longer it went on, the worse it seemed. Matteo acted as if Santino didn't exist. *As if he didn't have a son.* To her certain knowledge, he'd never even cuddled him—why, he'd barely even asked after him.

It didn't matter how many boxes the Italian ticked—she could never subject Santino to a life in which he was overlooked. And trying to compensate for his father's lack of regard with her own fierce love wouldn't work. She'd grown up in a house where she had been regarded as an imposition and no way was she going to impose that on her darling son.

Which left her with two choices. She could carry on being an ostrich and ignore what was happening—or rather, what wasn't happening. Or she could address the subject when Matteo woke and make him talk about it. She wouldn't accuse him or judge him. Whatever he told her, she would try to understand—because something told her that was very important.

Quietly, she slipped from the bed and went to the bathroom and when she returned with brushed teeth and hair, Matteo was awake—his black gaze following her as she walked back towards the bed.

'Morning,' she said shyly.

'Is this the point where I ask whether you slept well and you lower your eyelids and say, *not really*?' he murmured.

Blushing like a schoolgirl, Keira slipped rapidly beneath the covers so that her naked body was no longer in the spotlight of that disturbingly erotic stare. It was all very well being uninhibited when the room was in darkness but the bright morning light was making her feel awfully vulnerable. Especially as she sensed that Matteo wasn't going to like what she had to say, no matter how carefully she asked the question. He drew her into his arms but she gave him only the briefest of kisses before pulling her lips away. Because he needed to hear this, and the sooner, the better.

'Matteo,' she said, rubbing the tip of her finger over the shadowed angle of his jaw.

His brows knitted together. 'Why does my heart sink when you say my name that way?' he questioned softly.

She swallowed. 'You know we have to go back to Umbria soon.'

'You think I'd forgotten? Which is why I suggest we don't waste any of the time we have left.'

He had begun to stroke a light thumb over one of her nipples and although it puckered obediently beneath his touch, Keira pushed his hand away. 'And we need to talk,' she said firmly.

'And that was why my heart sank,' he drawled, shifting his body to lie against the bank of pillows and fixing her with a hooded look. 'Why do women always want to talk instead of making love?'

'Usually because something needs to be said.' She

pulled in a breath. 'I want to tell you about when I was growing up.'

The look on his face said it all. Wrong place; wrong time. 'I met your aunt,' he said impatiently. 'Over-strict guardian, small house, jealous cousin. I get it. You didn't have such a great time.'

Keira shook her head as uncomfortable thoughts flooded into her mind. She needed to be completely honest, else how could she expect complete honesty in return? Yet what she was about to tell him wasn't easy. She'd never told anyone the full story. Even her aunt. Especially her aunt. 'I told you my mother wasn't married and that I didn't know my father. What I didn't tell you was that she didn't know him either.'

His gaze was watchful now. 'What are you talking about?'

Keira flushed to the roots of her hair because she could remember her mother's shame when she'd finally blurted out the story, no longer able to evade the curious questions of her young daughter. Would her mother be appalled if she knew that Keira was now repeating the sorry tale, to a man with a trace of steel running through his veins?

'My mother was a student nurse,' she said slowly, 'who came to London and found it was nothing like the rural farm she'd grown up on in Ireland. She was quite shy and very naïve but she had those Irish looks. You know, black hair and blue eyes—'

'Like yours?' he interrupted softly.

She shook her head. 'Oh, no. She was much prettier than me. Men were always asking her out but usually she preferred to stay in the nurses' home and watch something on TV, until one night she gave in and went to a party with a group of the other nurses. It was a pretty wild party and not her kind of thing at all. People were getting wasted and Mum decided she didn't want to stay.' She swallowed. 'But by then it was too late because someone had...had...'

'Someone had what, Keira?' he questioned as her words became strangled and his voice was suddenly so gentle that it made her want to cry.

'Somebody spiked her drink,' she breathed, the words catching like sand in her throat because even now, they still had the power to repulse her. 'She...she woke up alone in a strange bed with a pain between her legs, and soon after that she discovered she was pregnant with me.'

He gave a terse exclamation and she thought he was going to turn away in disgust but to her surprise he reached out to push away the lock of hair which had fallen over her flushed cheeks, before slipping his hand round her shoulder and pulling her against the warmth of his chest. *'Bastardo,'* he swore softly and then repeated it, for added emphasis.

She shook her head and could feel the taste of tears nudging at the back of her throat and at last she gave into them, in a way she'd never done before. 'She didn't know how many men had been near her,' she sobbed. 'She had to go to the clinic to check she hadn't been given some sort of disease and of course they offered her...' She swallowed away the tears because she saw from the tightening of his jaw that she didn't actually need to spell it out for him. 'But she didn't want that. She wanted me,' she said simply. 'There wasn't a moment of doubt about that.'

He waited until she had composed herself before he spoke again, until she had brushed the remaining tears away with the tips of her fingers.

'Why are you telling me all this, Keira?' he questioned softly. 'And why now?'

'Because I grew up without a father and for me there was no other option—but I don't want the same for my baby. For… Santino.' Her voice wavered as she looked into the hardness of his eyes and forced herself to continue, even though the look on his face would have intimidated stronger people than her. 'Matteo, you don't… you don't seem to feel anything for your son.' She sucked in a deep breath. 'Why, you've barely *touched* him. It's as if you can't bear to go near him and I want to try to understand why.'

Matteo released his hold on her and his body tensed because she had no right to interrogate him, and he didn't *have* to answer her intrusive question. He could tell her to mind her own damned business and that he would interact with his son when he was good and ready and not according to *her* timetable. Just because she wanted to spill out stuff about her own past, didn't mean he had to do the same, did it? But in the depths of her eyes he could read a deep compassion and something in him told him there could be no going forward unless she understood what had made him the man he was.

He could feel a bitter taste coating his throat. Maybe everyone kept stuff hidden away inside them—the stuff which was truly painful. Perhaps it was nature's way of trying to protect you from revisiting places which were too dark to contemplate. 'My mother died in childbirth,' he said suddenly.

There was a disbelieving pause as the words sank in and when they did, her eyes widened. 'Oh, Matteo. That's terrible,' she whispered.

Matteo instantly produced the self-protective clause which enabled him to bat off unwanted sympathy if people *did* find out. 'What is it they say?' He shrugged. 'That you can't miss what you've never had. And I've had thirty-four years to get used to it.'

Her muffled 'But…' suggested she was about to disagree with him, but then she seemed to change her mind and said nothing. Leaving him free to utter the next words from his set-piece statement. 'Maternal death is thankfully rare,' he bit out. 'My mother was just one of the unlucky ones.'

'I'm so sorry.'

'Yes,' he said. 'I think we've established that.' He chose his words carefully. 'I've never come into contact with babies before. To be honest, I've never even held one, but you're right—it isn't just inexperience which makes me wary.' His jaw tightened. 'It's guilt.'

'Guilt?' she echoed, in surprise.

He swallowed and the words took a long time in coming. 'People say they feel instant love for their own child but that didn't happen to me when I looked at Santino for the first time. Oh, I checked his fingers and his toes and was relieved that he was healthy, but I didn't *feel* anything.' He punched his fist against his heart and the words fell from his lips, heavy as stones. 'And I don't know if I ever can.'

Keira nodded as she tried to evaluate what he'd told her. It all made sense now. It explained why he'd thrown a complete wobbly when she'd kept her pregnancy quiet. What if history had grimly repeated itself and she'd died in childbirth as his mother had done? Nobody had known who the father of her baby was because she'd kept it secret. Wasn't it possible that Santino could have been adopted by her aunt and her cousin and grown up without knowing anything of his roots?

She felt another wrench as she met the pain in his eyes. What must it have been like for him—this powerful man who had missed out on so much? He had never experienced a mother's love. Never even felt her arms hugging him in those vital hours of bonding which followed birth. Who had cradled the tiny Matteo as the cold corpse of his mother was prepared for her silent journey to the grave, instead of a joyous homecoming with her newborn baby? No wonder he'd been so reluctant to get close to his little boy—he didn't know *how.*

'Didn't your father make up for the fact that you didn't have a mother?'

His mouth twisted and he gave a hollow laugh. 'People cope in their own way—or they don't. He left my care to a series of young nannies, most of whom he apparently slept with—so then they'd leave—or the new stepmother would fire them. But it didn't seem to matter how much sex he had or how many women he married, he never really got over my mother's death. It left a hole in his life which nothing could ever fill.'

Keira couldn't take her eyes away from his ravaged face. Had his father unconsciously blamed his infant son for the tragic demise of his beloved wife—would that explain why they weren't close? And had Matteo been angry with his father for trying to replace her? She wondered if those different stepmothers had blamed the boy for being an ever-present reminder of a woman they could never compete with.

And blame was the last thing Matteo needed, Keira realised. Not then and certainly not now. He needed understanding—and love—though she wasn't sure he wanted either. Reaching out, she laid her hand on his bunched and tensed biceps but the muscle remained hard and stone-like beneath her fingers. Undeterred, she began to massage her fingertips against the unyielding flesh.

'So what do we do next, now we've brought all our ghosts into the daylight?' she questioned slowly. 'Where do we go from here, Matteo?'

His gaze was steady as he rolled away from her touch, as if reminding her that this was a decision which needed to be made without the distraction of the senses. 'That depends. Where do you want to go from here?'

She recognised he was being open to negotiation and on some deeper level she suspected that this wasn't usual for him in relationships. Because this *was* a relationship, she realised. Somehow it had grown despite their wariness and private pain and the unpromising beginning. It had the potential to grow even more—but only if she had the courage to give him the affection he needed, without making any demands of her own in return. She couldn't *demand* that he learn to love his son, she could only pray that he would. Just as she couldn't demand that he learn to love *her*. 'I'll go anywhere,' she whispered. 'As long as it's with Santino. And you.'

She leaned forward to kiss him and Matteo could never remember being kissed like that before. A kiss not fuelled by sexual hunger but filled with the promise of something he didn't recognise, something which started his senses humming. He murmured something in objection when she pulled back a little, her eyes of *profondo blu* looking dark and serious, but at least when she wasn't kissing him he was able to think straight. He didn't understand the way she made him feel, but maybe that didn't matter. Because weren't the successes of life—and business—based on gut feeling as much as understanding? Hadn't he sometimes bought a hotel site even though others in the business had told him he was crazy—and turned it into a glittering success because deep down he'd known he was onto a winner? And wasn't it a bit like that now?

'I will learn to interact with my son,' he said.

'That's a start,' she said hesitantly.

The look on her face suggested that his answer had fallen short of the ideal—but he was damned if he was going to promise to love his son. Because what if he failed to deliver? What if the ice around his heart was so deep and so frozen that nothing could ever penetrate it? 'And I want to marry you,' he said suddenly.

Now the look on her face had changed. He saw surprise there and perhaps the faint glimmer of delight, which was quickly replaced by one of suspicion, as if perhaps she had misheard him.

'Marry me?' she echoed softly.

He nodded. 'So that Santino will have the security you never had, even if our relationship doesn't last,' he said, his voice cool but certain. 'And so that he will be protected by my fortune, which one day he will inherit. Doesn't that make perfect sense to you?'

He could see her blinking furiously, as if she was trying very hard to hold back the glitter of disappointed tears, but then she seemed to pull it all together and nodded.

'Yes, I think marriage is probably the most sensible option in the circumstances,' she said.

'So you will be my wife?'

'Yes, I'll be your wife. But I'm only doing this for Santino. To give him the legitimacy I never had. You do understand that, don't you, Matteo?'

She fixed him with a defiant look, as if she didn't really care—and for a split second it occurred to him that neither of them were being completely honest. 'Of course I understand, *cara mia*,' he said softly.

CHAPTER ELEVEN

KEIRA HEARD FOOTSTEPS behind her and turned from the mirror to see Claudia in a pretty flowery dress, instead of the soft blue uniform she usually wore when she was working.

'Is everything okay with Santino?' Keira asked the nursery nurse immediately, more out of habit than fear because she'd been cradling him not an hour earlier as she had dressed her baby son in preparation for his parents' forthcoming marriage.

Claudia smiled. 'He is well, *signorina.* His father is playing with him now. He says he is teaching him simple words of Italian, which he is certain he will remember when eventually he starts to speak.'

Keira smiled, turning back to her reflection and forcing herself to make a final adjustment to her hair, even though she kept telling herself that her bridal outfit was pretty irrelevant on what was going to be a purely functional wedding day. But Matteo's father and stepmother were going to be attending the brief ceremony, so she felt she had to make *some* sort of effort. And surely if she did her best it might lessen their inevitable disbelief that he was going to marry someone like her.

'What kind of wedding would you like?' Matteo had asked during that drive back from Rome after she'd agreed to be his wife.

Keira remembered hedging her bets. 'You first.'

She remembered his cynical laugh, too.

'Something small. Unfussy. I'm not a big fan of weddings.'

So of course Keira had agreed that small and unfussy would be perfect, though deep down that hadn't been what she'd wanted at all. Maybe there was a part of every woman which wanted the whole works—the fuss and flowers and clouds of confetti. Or maybe that was just her—because marriage had always been held up as the perfect ideal when she'd been growing up. There had been that photo adorning her aunt's sideboard—the bouquet-clutching image which had stared out at her over the years. She recalled visiting for Sunday tea when her mother was still alive, when attention would be drawn to Aunt Ida's white dress and stiff veil. 'Wouldn't you have loved a white wedding, Bridie?' Ida used to sigh, and Keira's mother would say she didn't care for pomp and ceremony.

And Keira had thought she was the same—until she'd agreed to marry Matteo and been surprised by the stupid ache in her heart as she realised she must play down a wedding which wasn't really a wedding. It was a legal contract for the benefit of their son—not something inspired by love or devotion or a burning desire to want to spend the rest of your life with just one person, so it didn't really count. At least, not on Matteo's part.

And hers?

She smoothed down her jacket and sighed. Because even more disturbing than her sudden yearning to wear a long white dress and carry a fragrant bouquet was the realisation that her feelings for Matteo had started to change. Was that because she understood him a little better now? Because he'd given her a glimpse of the vulnerability and loss which lay beneath the steely exterior he presented to the world? Maybe. She told herself not to have unrealistic expectations. Not to wish for things which were never going to happen, but concentrate on being a good partner. To give Matteo affection in quiet and unobtrusive ways, so that maybe the hard ice around his heart might melt a little and let her in.

He was doing his best to change, she knew that. In the busy days which followed their return from his Roman villa, he had meticulously paid his son all the attention which had been lacking before. Sometimes he would go to Santino if he woke in the night—silencing Keira's sleepy protests with a kiss. Occasionally, he gave the baby a bottle and, once, had even changed his nappy, even though he'd protested that this was one task surely better undertaken by women.

But as Keira had watched him perform these fatherly duties she had been unable to blind herself to the truth. That it *was* simply a performance and Matteo was just going through the motions. He was being a good father, just as he was a good lover—because he was a man who excelled in whatever he did. But it was duty which motivated him. His heart wasn't in it, that much was obvious. And as long as she accepted that, then she'd be fine.

She turned away from the mirror, wondering if there was anything she'd forgotten to do. Matteo's father, Massimo, and his wife, Luciana, had arrived only a short while ago because the traffic from Rome had been bad. Since they were due at the town hall at noon, there had been little opportunity for Keira to exchange more than a few words of greeting and introduce them to their new grandson. She'd been nervous—of course she had—she suspected it was always nerve-racking meeting prospective in-laws, and most people didn't have to do it on the morning of the wedding itself.

Massimo was a bear of a man, his build bulkier than Matteo's, though Keira could see a likeness around the jet-dark eyes. Her prospective stepmother-in-law, Luciana, was an elegant woman in her fifties, who had clearly embraced everything facial surgery had to offer, which had resulted in a disturbingly youthful appearance.

Keira picked up her clutch bag and went downstairs, her heart pounding with an anxiety which seemed to be increasing by the second. Was that because she'd seen Luciana's unmistakable look of disbelief when they'd been introduced? Was she wondering how this little Englishwoman from nowhere had wrested a proposal of marriage from the Italian tycoon?

But the expression on Matteo's face made Keira's stomach melt as she walked into the hallway, where everyone was waiting. She saw his eyes darken and the edges of his lips curve into an unmistakable smile of appreciation as he took her cold hand in his and kissed it.

'Sei bella, mia cara,' he had murmured softly. *'Molta bella.'*

Keira told herself he was only saying it because such praise was expected of the prospective groom, but she couldn't deny the feeling of satisfaction which rippled down her spine in response. Because she *wanted* him to look at her and find her beautiful, of course she did. She wasn't stupid and knew she couldn't take his desire for granted. Someone like her was always going to have to work to maintain it. Leola the stylist had been dispatched from Rome with a selection of wedding outfits and Keira had chosen the one she felt was the most flattering but also the most *appropriate.* Steadfastly pushing away the more floaty white concoctions, she had opted for functional rather than fairy tale. The silvery-grey material of the dress and jacket reminded her of a frosty winter morning but there was no doubt that it suited her dark hair and colouring. Only the turquoise shoes and matching clutch bag provided a splash of colour—because she had refused all Leola's inducements to carry flowers.

At least Massimo Valenti seemed enchanted by his grandson. Keira travelled in one of the cars with him to the nearly town and watched as he spent the entire journey cooing at the baby in delight. It made her wonder why he hadn't been close to his own son—but there was no time for questions because they were drawing up outside the town hall where Matteo was waiting to introduce her to the interpreter, which Italian law demanded.

Twenty minutes later she emerged from the building as a married woman and Matteo was pulling her into his arms, his hands resting on either side of her waist—but even that light touch was enough to make her want to dissolve with lust and longing.

'So. How does it feel to be Signora Valenti?' he questioned silkily.

Her heart was pounding as she stared up into the molten darkness of his eyes. 'Ask me again next week,' she said breathlessly. 'It feels a little unreal right now.'

'Maybe this will help you accept the reality,' he said, *'mia sposa.'*

And there, beneath the fluttering Italian flag of the town hall, his lips came down to claim hers with a kiss which left her in no doubt that he would rather they were somewhere private, preferably naked and horizontal. It set off an answering hunger and reminded Keira of the slightly incredible fact that he couldn't seem to get enough of her. Didn't he demonstrate that every night when he covered her trembling body with his own? And wasn't that *enough*? she wondered as they drove back to the farmhouse together, her golden ring glinting as she fussed around with Santino's delicate shawl. Was it just her inherently cautious nature which made her wonder if her relationship with Matteo was as superficial as the icing sugar sprinkled over the top of the chocolate wedding cake which Paola had baked?

Yet when he carried her over the threshold, it felt real. And when she returned from putting Santino down for a nap, having removed the silvery-grey jacket to reveal the filmy chiffon dress beneath, Matteo had been waiting in the shadowed hallway for her.

Pulling her into a quiet alcove, he placed his palm over her hammering heart and she licked her lips as her nipple automatically hardened beneath his touch.

'Ever wish you could just wave a magic wand and make everyone disappear?' he drawled.

She shivered as the light stroking of her nipple increased. 'Isn't that a little…anti-social?'

'I'm feeling anti-social,' he grumbled, his lips brushing over the curve of her jaw before moving upwards to tease her now trembling lips. 'I want to be alone with my new wife.'

Keira kissed him back as his words set off another whisper of hope inside her and she wondered if it was wrong to allow herself to hope, on this, her wedding day.

'You were the man who once told me about the benefits of waiting,' she teased him. 'Won't this allow you to test out your theory?'

Matteo laughed as she pulled away from him, the prim twitch of her lips contradicting the hunger in her eyes, and he shook his head slightly, wondering what kind of spell she had cast over him. He was used to the wiles of women yet Keira used none of them. She wasn't deliberately provocative around him and didn't possess that air of vanity of someone who revelled in her sexual power over a man. On the contrary, in public she was almost demure—while in private she was red-hot. And that pleased him, too. She pleased him and unsettled him in equal measure. She left him wanting more—but more of *what*, he didn't know. She was like a drink you took when your throat was dry yet when you'd finished it, you found that your thirst was just as intense.

He stroked his fingers down over her belly, his gaze steady as they stood hidden by the shadows of the staircase. Hard to believe that a child had grown beneath its almost-flat curve. 'I want you to know you are an amazing mother,' he said suddenly. 'And that Santino is blessed indeed.'

He saw the surprise behind the sudden brightness in her eyes, her mouth working as she struggled to contain herself.

'Don't make me get all emotional, Matteo,' she whispered. 'I've got to go in there and make conversation with your father and stepmother and I'm not going to make a very good impression if I've been blubbing.'

But he disregarded her soft plea, knowing he needed to express something which had slowly become a certainty. He owed her that, at least. 'I shouldn't have taken you to Rome when I did and made you leave the baby behind,' he admitted slowly. 'No matter how good the childcare we had in place. I can see now that it was a big ask for a relatively new mother in a strange country.'

He saw her teeth working into her bottom lip and he thought she might be about to cry, when suddenly she smiled and it was like the bright summer sun blazing all over him with warmth and light, even though outside it was cold and wintry.

'Thank you,' she said, a little shakily. 'I love you for saying that.'

He stilled. 'Really?'

A look of horror crossed her face as she realised what she'd said. 'I didn't mean—'

'Didn't you?' he murmured. 'How very disappointing.'

Keira told herself he was only teasing as he led her into the salon, but she felt as if she were floating on air as she took a grizzling Santino from Massimo's bear-like arms and rocked him dreamily against her chest. Had Matteo really just admitted he'd been in the wrong by taking her to Rome and told her she was a good mother? It wasn't so much the admission itself, more the fact he was beginning to accept that each and every one of them got it wrong sometimes—and that felt like a major breakthrough.

And had she really just let her guard down enough to tell him she loved him? It hadn't been in a dramatic way or because she'd expected an instant reciprocal response. She'd said it affectionately and Matteo needed that, she reckoned. How many times had he been told he'd been loved when he was growing up? Too few, she suspected.

Still high from the impact of their conversation, Keira refused the glass of vintage champagne which was offered and accepted a glass of some bittersweet orange drink instead.

But unusually, Santino grizzled in her arms and she wondered if it was the excitement of the day which was making him so fractious. Discreetly, she slipped away to the nursery to feed and change him before rocking him until he was sound asleep and carefully putting him in his crib.

She picked up the empty bottle and was just on her way out when she was startled by the sight of Luciana, who suddenly appeared at the nursery door in a waft of expensive scent. Keira wondered if she'd wandered into the wrong room or if she'd been hoping for a cuddle with Santino. But there was an odd smile on her new stepmother's face and, for some reason, whispers of trepidation began to slide over Keira's spine.

'Is everything okay, Luciana?' she questioned, hoping she sounded suitably deferential towards the older woman.

Luciana shrugged. 'That depends what you mean by *okay*. I was a little disappointed that my son and his family were not invited to the ceremony today.'

'Oh, well—you can see how it is.' Keira gave a nervous smile, because Matteo had hinted that there was no love lost between him and his stepbrother, Emilio. 'We just wanted a very small wedding.'

'Sì.' Luciana picked up a silver-framed photo of Santino and began to study it. 'And naturally, it would have been very *difficult* for Emilio.'

'Difficult?'

Luciana put the photograph down. 'In the circumstances.'

Keira blinked. 'What circumstances?'

Elegantly plucked eyebrows were raised. 'Because of the clause in my husband's will, of course.'

Keira's heart began to pound as some nameless dread crept over her. 'What clause?'

'Surely Matteo has told you?' Luciana looked surprised. 'Though perhaps not. He has always been a man who gives very little away.' Her expression became sly. 'You are aware that this house belonged to Massimo's first wife?'

'To Matteo's mother?' questioned Keira stiffly. 'Yes, I knew that. It's where she was born and where she grew up. It's one of the reasons he loves it so much.'

Luciana shrugged. 'Ever since Matteo reached the age of eighteen, Massimo has generously allowed his son to use the estate as his own. To all intents and purposes, this *was* Matteo's home.' She paused. 'But a strange thing happens to men as they grow older. They want to leave something of themselves behind.' Her surgically enhanced eyes gleamed. 'I'm talking, of course, about continuing the Valenti name. I am already a grandmother. I understand these desires.'

Keira's head was spinning. 'I honestly don't understand what you're getting at, Luciana.'

'Ah, I can see you know nothing of this.' Luciana gave a hard smile. 'It's very simple. He loves this house for obvious reasons, but he does not *own* it. And Massimo told him he intended bequeathing the entire estate to his stepson, unless Matteo produced an heir of his own with the Valenti name.' She shrugged her bony shoulders. 'I wondered if he would be prepared to sacrifice his freedom for an heir, not least because he has always shown a certain…*disdain* for women. And yet here you are—a pretty little English girl who arrived with a baby in her arms and got a wedding ring for her troubles. The perfect solution to all Matteo's problems!'

'You're saying that…that Matteo would have lost this house unless he produced an heir?'

'That's exactly what I'm saying. His gain, my son's loss.' Luciana shrugged. *'C'est la vie.'*

Keira felt so shocked that for a moment her limbs felt as if they were completely weightless. With a shaking hand, she put the empty bottle down on a shelf and swallowed, trying to compose herself—and knowing that she had to get away from Luciana's toxic company before she did or said something she regretted. 'Please excuse me,' she said. 'But I must get back to the wedding party.'

Did she imagine the look of disappointment which flickered across Luciana's face, or did she just imagine it? It didn't matter. She was going to get through this day with her dignity intact. Matteo had married her to get his hands on this property, so let him enjoy his brief victory. What good would come of making a scene on her wedding day?

Somehow she got through the rest of the afternoon, meeting Matteo's questioning stare with a brittle smile across the dining table, while everyone except her tucked into the lavish wedding breakfast. Did he sense that all was not well, and was that the reason why his black gaze seemed fixed on her face?

She was relieved when finally Massimo and Luciana left—though her father-in-law gave her the most enormous hug, which brought an unexpected lump to her throat. Leaving Matteo to dismiss Paola and the rest of the staff, Keira hurried to tend to Santino, spending far longer than necessary as she settled her baby son for the night.

At last she left the nursery and went into the bedroom but her hands were clammy as she pulled off her wedding outfit and flung it over a chair. Spurred on by Leola, she had been planning on surprising Matteo with the shortest dress she'd ever worn. A bottom-skimming dress for his eyes and no one else's. She'd wanted to wear it in anticipation of the appreciative look on his face when he saw it and to hint at a final farewell to her residual tomboy. But now she tugged on a functional pair of jeans and a sweater because she couldn't bear the thought of dressing up—not when Matteo's motives for marrying her were making her feel so *ugly* inside.

Although she would have liked nothing better than to creep into bed on her own and pull the duvet over her head to blot out the world, she knew that wasn't an option. There was only one acceptable course of action which lay open to her, but she couldn't deny her feeling of dread as she walked into the room which overlooked the garden at the back of the house, where Matteo stood beside the fire, looking impossibly handsome in his charcoal wedding suit. Don't touch me, she prayed silently, even though her body desperately wanted him to do just that—and maybe something had alerted him to her conflicted mood because his eyes narrowed and he made no attempt to approach her.

His face was sombre as he regarded her. 'Something is wrong.'

It was a statement, not a question, but Keira didn't answer straight away. She allowed herself a few more seconds before everything changed for ever. A final few seconds where she could pretend they were newlyweds about to embark on a shared life together. 'You could say that. I had a very interesting conversation with Luciana earlier.' She inhaled deeply and then suddenly the words came spilling out, like corrosive acid leaking from a car battery. 'Why didn't you tell me you were only marrying me to get your hands on an inheritance?' she demanded. 'And that this house would only become yours if you produced a legitimate child? I would have understood, if only you'd had the guts to tell me.'

He didn't flinch. His gaze was hard and steady. 'Because the inheritance became irrelevant. I married you because I care for you and my son and because I want us to make a future together.'

Keira wanted to believe him. The child-woman who had yearned for a long white dress and big bouquet of flowers longed for it to be the truth. But she couldn't believe him—it was a stretch too far. Once she'd thought he sounded like someone reading from a script when he'd been addressing a subject which would make most people emotional—and he was doing it again now.

I care for you and my son.

He sounded like a robot intoning the correct response, not someone speaking from the heart. And his lack of emotion wasn't the point, was it? She'd known about that from the start. She'd known the reason he was made that way and, filled with hope and with trust, had been prepared to make allowances for it. She bit her lip. When all the time he'd been plotting away and using her as a pawn in his desire to get his hands on this estate.

'I understand that you're known as an elusive man who doesn't give anything away,' she accused shakily. 'But how many more people are going to come out of the woodwork and tell me things about you that I didn't know? Can you imagine how it made me feel to hear that from Luciana, Matteo? To know you'd been buttering me up to get me to marry you? I thought… I thought you were doing it for your son's future, when all the time it was because you didn't want to lose a piece of land you thought of as rightfully yours! You don't want a family—not really—you've just used me as some kind of incubator!'

'But there's a fundamental flaw in your argument,' he grated. 'If inheriting the estate meant so much to me, then why hadn't I fathered a child with someone else long before I met you?'

'Because I don't think you really like women,' she said slowly. 'Or maybe you just don't understand them. You never knew your mother and she died so tragically that it's inevitable you idealised her. She would have had flaws, just like we all do—only you never got to see them. No woman could ever have lived up to her and maybe that's one of the reasons why you never settled down.' She sucked in a deep breath. 'And then I came along and took the decision away from you. A stolen night, which was never meant to be any more, suddenly produced an heir. You didn't have to go through the whole tedious ritual of courting a woman you didn't care for in order to get yourself a child. Fate played right into your hands, didn't it, Matteo? Suddenly you had everything you needed, without any real effort on your part.'

His face blanched. 'You think I am so utterly ruthless?'

She shrugged. 'I don't know,' she said, and there was

a crack in her voice. 'Maybe you do care—a little. Or as much as you ever can. But you're missing the point. I thought growing up without a father was difficult, but at least I knew where I stood. It may have been grim at times but it was honest and you haven't been honest with me.' She swallowed. 'It feels like I'm in the shadows of your life—like someone in the wings watching the action on stage. I see the way you are with the baby—and with me—and it comes over as a performance, not real. How could it be, when Santino and I were only ever a means to an end?'

Matteo flinched as he met the accusation in her eyes, because nobody had ever spoken quite so candidly to him. 'For someone so tiny, you certainly don't pull any punches, do you, Keira?'

'What's the point in pulling punches? All we have left is the truth,' she said wearily. 'You've got what you wanted, Matteo. We're married now and your son has been legitimised. You have continued the Valenti name and will therefore inherit the estate. You don't need me any more.'

Matteo felt his chest tighten and his instinct was to tell her that she was right—and that he *didn't* need anyone. He'd spent his whole life not needing anyone because there had been nobody there to lean on, nobody to get close to—why change that pattern now? But some unknown emotion was nudging at his conscience as something deep inside him told him this was different.

'And what if I say I do need you?' he said hoarsely as he attempted to articulate the confusion of thoughts which were spinning around inside his head.

Her eyes widened, but he could see a wariness in their depths of *profondo blu*. 'You do?' she queried uncertainly.

The moment it took for her to ask the question was all Matteo needed to shift things into perspective, because he knew he mustn't offer her false promises or false hope. She deserved more than that. So stick to the facts, he urged himself grimly. You're good with facts. Allow her to consider all the advantages of remaining here, as his wife.

'Of course,' he said. 'And logistically it makes perfect sense.'

'Logistically?' she echoed, her voice a little faint.

'Sure.' He shrugged. 'If we're all living together under one roof as a family, it will be much better for Santino. Better than having a father who just jets in and sees him on high days and holidays.'

'There is that, of course,' she said woodenly.

'And I've married you now, Keira,' he said softly. 'I have given you the security of bearing my name and wearing my ring. Your future is assured. You don't need to worry about money ever again.'

'You think that's what it's all about?' she questioned, her voice trembling. 'Money?'

'Not all of it, no—but a big part of it. And we have plenty of other reasons to keep our marriage going.' He curved her a slow smile. 'What about the sexual chemistry which exists between us? That fact that you are the hottest woman I've ever had in my bed?'

She gasped as if she had been winded before staring at him—as if she were looking at someone she'd never seen before. 'You just don't get it, do you, Matteo? You list all the reasons I should stay with you and yet you haven't mentioned anything which really *matters*!'

He flinched with pain as he met the undiluted anger in her gaze, but at the same time a strange sense of relief washed over him as he realised that he no longer had to try. She was going and taking their child with him and he would just have to learn how to deal with that. And anyway, he thought grimly—why would he want to prolong a relationship when it could hurt like this? Hadn't he vowed never to let anyone hurt him, ever again?

'Okay, I get it. What do you want?'

With an effort he held up the palms of his hands, in silent submission, and the sudden wobble of her lips made him think she might be about to backtrack—maybe to soften the blows which she'd just rained on him, but all she said was, 'I'd like us to separate.'

He told himself it was better this way. Better to go back to the life he was used to and be the person he knew how to be, rather than chase after the glimmer of gold which Keira Ryan had brought shimmering into his life.

'Tell me what you want, in practical terms,' he said flatly.

He could see her throat constricting as she nodded.

'I'd like to return to London as soon as possible and to rent somewhere before I decide to buy,' she said, before sucking in a deep breath. 'But I want you to know that I'll take only what is necessary for our needs and you're not to worry. I don't intend to make a great hole in your wealth, Matteo.'

And even that got to him, because he couldn't even level the charge of greed against her. She wasn't interested in his money, he realised, and she never had been. She'd taken the cash he'd thoughtlessly left beside the bed and had given it away to charity. She'd fought like mad against him buying her a fancy wardrobe. She was a jewel of a woman, he realised—a bright and shining jewel. But it was too late for them. The cold, pinched look on her beautiful face told him that. So let her go, he told himself. Set her free. At least you can give her that.

'That can all be arranged,' he said. 'But in turn, I need your reassurance that I can continue to see my son.'

There was surprise on her face now and he wondered if secretly she had expected him to cut all ties with his own flesh and blood.

'Of course. You can see as much of Santino as you wish,' she said quietly. 'I will never deny you your son, Matteo, and I hope you will see him very often, because he...he needs you. You're his daddy.'

A lump rose in his throat as he moved away from the blaze of the fire.

'I'd like to say goodnight to him now,' he said and she nodded and made as if to follow him.

'Alone,' he gritted out.

But Matteo's heart was heavy as he walked towards the nursery—as if a dark stone had lodged itself deep inside his chest. The night light made the room appear soft and rosy and Matteo stared down at the sleeping child. He remembered the first time he had seen him. When he had counted his fingers and toes like someone learning basic mathematics, and had felt nothing.

But not this time.

This time he could barely make out any detail of his sleeping son, his vision was so blurred. Too late, his heart had cracked open and left room for emotion to come flooding in, powerfully and painfully. And Santino stirred as Matteo's tears fell like rain onto the delicate white shawl.

CHAPTER TWELVE

It was raining by the time Keira got back from her walk and she had just let Charlie off his lead when she noticed the letter lying in the centre of the hall table, where Claudia must have left it. She pulled a face. Another one.

The envelope carried an Italian stamp and the airmail sticker seemed to wink at her. Quickly, she slid it into a drawer to lie on top of all the others, because she couldn't quite bring herself to throw them away. Her reluctance to dispose of the growing pile of correspondence was just about equal to her reluctance to read them, because they were from Matteo—she recognised his handwriting. And why would she wish to read them and risk making the hole in her heart even bigger? Why was he even *writing* to her when she'd told him it was better if all correspondence took place between their respective solicitors? Why had he arrogantly elected to take no notice?

Because she was fighting like crazy not to go under. Not to give into the tears which pricked at her eyes at night when she lay in bed missing the warm embrace of her estranged husband. She was determined to pour all her energies into being there for Santino—into being the best mother she possibly could—and she couldn't manage that if her heart stayed raw and aching from thinking about Matteo all the time.

She'd wondered whether his determination to keep in close contact with his son would have faded once she and Santino had left Umbria but to her surprise, it hadn't. He'd already paid two visits and they'd only been back in England a little over a fortnight. On both those occasions she had absented herself from the house, leaving Claudia in charge of the baby—Claudia who had been happy to accompany her from Umbria when Keira had made the emotional return to her homeland.

She supposed people might think it a form of cowardice that she couldn't bear the thought of confronting the man with whom she hadn't even shared a wedding night. But that was too bad. It didn't matter what anyone else thought, only what was right for her and her son. Sooner or later she hoped she'd be able to greet him with a genuine air of indifference but for now she didn't trust herself not to burst into noisy howls of sorrow and to tell him how much she was missing him.

With the money he'd settled on her, she was renting a house. A house with a garden and a front door which wasn't shared—the kind of house in Notting Hill where she used to drop off her prep-school charges when she was working at Luxury Limos. And she'd bought a dog, too. A scruffy little thing with a lop-sided ear and the saddest eyes she'd ever seen. The staff at the rescue centre had told her he'd been badly beaten and was fearful and shy, but he had taken one look at Keira and hurled himself at her with a series of plaintive yelps. Charlie was the best thing to have happened to them since they'd returned to England and had reinforced her intention to give Santino a proper childhood. The kind she'd never had—with a dog and a mother who was always waiting for him when he got home from school.

Pulling off her rain-soaked coat, she went upstairs to the nursery where Claudia was just putting Santino down to sleep. The nursery nurse straightened up as Keira entered the room and she found herself wondering why Claudia's cheeks were so pink. Walking over to the crib, Keira stared down into the sleepy eyes of her son, her heart turning over with love.

'He looks happy,' she murmured as she leaned over to plant a soft kiss on his silken cheek.

'He should be!' said Claudia. 'After you took him out for such a long walk this morning.'

'Good thing I did. At least we missed the rain,' said Keira, with an idle glance out of the window as she drew the curtains.

There was a pause. 'Would you mind if I went out earlier than planned?' asked Claudia.

'Of course I don't mind.' Keira smiled because she knew that Claudia had struck up a close friendship with a man she'd met at the Italian Embassy. 'Hot date?'

Claudia smiled as she put her forefinger over her lips and Keira was so preoccupied with tidying up the nursery that she barely registered the nursery nurse leaving the room, though she did hear the distant bang of the front door. She turned the light out and was just about to make her way downstairs when her mobile phone began to ring and she pulled it from the pocket of her jeans, frowning when she saw Matteo's name flashing up on the screen.

Fury began to bubble up inside her. She'd asked him not to write and he had ignored that. She'd asked him not to call her and he was ignoring that too! So why now, coming straight after yet another unwanted letter from him? She clicked the connection.

'This had better be urgent,' she said.

'It is.'

She frowned as she registered a curious echo-like quality to his voice. 'And?'

'I need to see you.'

She needed to see him too, but no good would come of it. Wouldn't it make her hunger for what she could never have and certainly didn't need—a man who had lured a woman into marriage just because he wanted to inherit a house? 'I thought we'd decided that wasn't a good idea.'

'No, Keira…*you* decided.'

Still that curious echo. Keira frowned. Shouldn't she just agree to see him once and get it over with? Steel her heart against her own foolish desires and listen to what he had to say? 'Very well,' she said. 'We'll put an appointment in the diary.'

'Now,' he bit out.

'What do you mean…*now*?'

'I want to see you now,' he growled.

'Matteo, you're in Italy and I'm in England and unless you've discovered the secret of teleportation, that's not going to happen.'

'I'm downstairs.'

She froze. '*What* did you say?'

'I'm downstairs.' The echo began to get louder. 'Coming up.'

Her heart slamming against her ribcage, Keira rushed from the nursery to see Matteo with his mobile phone held against his ear, making his way up the stairs towards her. His face was more serious than she'd ever seen it as he cut the connection and slid the phone into the pocket of his jeans.

'Hi,' he said, the casual greeting failing to hide the tension and the pain which were written across his ravaged features.

She wanted to do several things all at once. To drum her fists against his powerful chest, over and over again. And she wanted to pull his darkly handsome face to hers and kiss him until there was no breath left in her body.

'What are you doing here?' she demanded.

'I need to speak to you.'

'Did you have to go about it so dramatically? You scared me half to death!' She looked at him suspiciously. 'You don't have a key, do you?'

'I don't,' he agreed.

'So how did you get in?'

'Claudia let me in before she left.'

'Claudia let you in?' she repeated furiously. 'Why would she do something like that?'

'Because I asked her to.'

'And what you say goes, I suppose, because you're the one with the money,' she said contemptuously.

'No.' He sucked in a ragged breath. 'I'm the one with the broken heart.'

It was such an unbelievable thing for him to say that Keira assumed she'd misheard him, and she was too busy deciding that they needed to move out of Santino's earshot in case they woke him to pay very much attention to her husband's words. 'You'd better come with me,' she said.

Matteo followed the denim-covered sway of her bottom as they went downstairs, watching her long black ponytail swinging against her back with every determined stride she took. Her body language wasn't looking promising and neither was her attitude. But what had he expected—that she would squeal with delight when she saw him again? Welcome him into the embrace he had so missed—as if that whole great betrayal had never happened? His throat thickened. He had tried playing it slow and playing by her rules but he'd realised she would be prepared to push him away for ever if he let her.

And he couldn't afford to let her.

They reached a beautiful, high-ceilinged sitting room dominated by a tall Christmas tree, which glittered in front of one of the tall windows. Fragrant and green, it was covered with lights and tiny stars and on the top stood an angel with gossamer-fine wings. A heap of presents with ribbons and bows stood at the base of the giant conifer and Matteo thought it looked so homely. And yet he wasn't connected to any of it, was he? He was still the outsider. The motherless boy who had never really felt part of Christmas.

So what are you going to do about it, Valenti? he asked himself as she turned to face him and they stood looking at one another like two combatants.

'You wanted to talk,' she said, without preamble. 'So talk. Why did you sneak into my house like this?'

'You've been ignoring my letters.'

She nodded and the glossy black ponytail danced around her shoulders. 'I told you I wanted to keep all written communication between our respective solicitors.'

'You really think that my lawyer wants to hear that I love you?' he demanded, his breath a low hiss.

Her lips opened and he thought she might be about to gasp, before she closed them again firmly, like an oyster shell clamping tightly shut.

'And that I miss you more than I ever thought possible?' he continued heatedly. 'Or that my life feels empty without you?'

'Don't waste my time with your lies, Matteo.'

'They aren't lies,' he said unevenly. 'They're the truth.'

'I don't believe you.'

'I didn't think you would.' He sucked in a deep breath. 'Which is why I wrote you the letters.'

'The letters,' she repeated blankly.

'I know you got them, because I asked Claudia. What did you do with them, Keira—did you throw them away? Set light to them and watch them go up in flames?'

She shook her head. 'No. I didn't do that. I have them all.'

'Then, I wonder, could you possibly fetch them?'

Was it the word 'fetch' which brought Charlie bounding into the room, his tail wagging furiously and his once sad eyes bright and curious as he looked up at the strange man? Keira glared as she saw Matteo crouch down and offer his hand to the little dog, furious yet somehow unsurprised when the terrier edged cautiously towards him. The shock of seeing Matteo again had shaken her and weakened her defences, making her realise that she was still fundamentally shaky around him—and so she nodded her agreement to his bizarre request. At least leaving the room and his disturbing presence would give her the chance to compose herself and to quieten the fierce hammering of her heart.

Slowly she walked into the hallway to retrieve the pile of envelopes from the drawer and went back into the sitting room, holding them gingerly between her fingers, like an unexploded bomb. By now Charlie's tail was thrashing wildly, and as Matteo straightened up from stroking him the puppy gave a little whine of protest and she wondered how he had so quickly managed to charm the shy little dog. But the terrier had been discovered wriggling in a sack by the side of the road, she remembered, the only survivor among all his dead brothers and sisters. Charlie had also grown up without a mother, she thought—and a lump lodged in her throat.

'Here,' she croaked, holding the letters towards him.

'Don't you want to open them?' he said.

She shook her head. 'Not really.'

'Then maybe I'd better tell you what's in them,' he said, his eyes not leaving her face as he took them from her. 'They are all love letters. With the exception of one.'

He saw her eyes widen before dark lashes came shuttering down to cloak their sapphire hue with suspicion.

'What's that? A hate letter?' she quipped.

'I'm serious, Keira.'

'And so am I. Anyone can write down words on a piece of paper and not mean them.'

'Then how about I summarise them for you out loud?'

'No.'

But that one word was so whispered that he barely heard it and Matteo had no intention of heeding it anyway. 'Four words, actually,' he husked. 'I love you, Keira. So how about I say it again, just so there can be no misunderstanding? I love you, Keira, and I've been a fool. *Uno scemo!* I should have been honest with you from the start, but…' He inhaled deeply through his nostrils and then expelled the air on a shuddered breath. 'Keeping things locked away inside was the way I operated. The only way I knew. But believe me when I tell you that by the time I asked you to marry me, I wasn't thinking about the house any more. My mind was full of you. It still is. I can't stop thinking about you and I don't want to. So I'm asking you to give me another chance, Keira. To give *us* another chance. You, me and Santino. That's all.'

She didn't say anything for a moment and when she spoke she started shaking her head, as if what he was demanding of her was impossible.

'That's *all*?' she breathed. 'After everything that's happened? You don't know what you're asking, Matteo.'

'Oh, but I do,' he demurred. 'I'm asking you to be my wife for real. With nothing but total honesty between us from now on, because I want that. I want that more than anything.' His voice lowered. 'But I realise it can only work if you love me too. Once, in a shadowed hallway after we had taken our wedding vows, you whispered to me that you did, but you may not have meant it.'

Keira clamped her lips together to try to contain the stupid tremble of emotion. Of course she had meant it. Every single word. The question was whether he did, too. Was it possible that he really loved her, or was this simply a means to an end—the manipulative declaration of a man determined to get his rightful heir back into his life? Or maybe just pride refusing to let a woman walk away from him.

Yet something was stubbornly refusing to allow her to accept the bleaker version of his reasons for coming here today. Was it the anguish she could see in his black eyes—so profound that even she, in her insecurity, didn't believe she was imagining it? She flicked the tip of her tongue over her mouth, wondering if it was too late for them, until she realised what the reality of that would mean. Matteo gone from her life and free to make another with someone else, while she would never be able to forget him.

And she wasn't going to allow that to happen. Because how could she ignore the burning inside her heart and the bright spark of hope which was beginning to flood through her veins?

'I've tried not to love you,' she admitted slowly. 'But it doesn't work. I think about you nearly all the time and I miss you. I love you, Matteo, and I will be your wife, but on one condition.'

His body grew very still. 'Anything,' he said. 'Name it.'

She had been about to ask him never knowingly to hurt her, but she realised that was all part of the package. That hurt and pain were the price you paid for love and you just had to pray they didn't rear their bitter heads too often in a lifetime. She knew also that if they wanted to go forward, then they had to leave the bitterness of the past behind. So instead of demanding the impossible, she touched her fingertips to his face, tracing them slowly down over his cheek until they came to rest on his beautiful lips.

'That you make love to me,' she said, her voice softened by tears of joy. 'And convince me this really is happening.'

His voice was unsteady. 'You mean, right now?'

She swallowed and nodded, rapidly wiping underneath her eyes with a bent finger. 'This very second,' she gulped.

Framing her face within the palms of his hands, he looked at her for one long moment before he spoke. 'To the woman who has given me everything, because without you I am nothing. *Ti amo, mia sposa.* My beautiful, beautiful wife,' he husked, and crushed his lips down hard on hers.

EPILOGUE

OUTSIDE THE WINDOW big white flakes floated down from the sky, adding to the dazzling carpet which had already covered the vast sweep of lawn. Keira gazed at it and gave a dreamy sigh. It was unusual for snow to settle in this part of Umbria and she thought she'd never seen anything quite so magical, or so beautiful. She smiled. Well, except maybe one other time…

Looking up from where she was crouched beside the Christmas tree where she'd just placed a couple of presents, she saw Matteo walk into the room—with snowflakes melting against his dark hair. He'd been outside, putting the finishing touches to a snowman, which would be the first thing Santino saw when he looked out of his window tomorrow morning. Their son's first real Christmas, Keira thought, because last year he'd been too young to realise what was going on and she…

Well, if she was being honest, she could hardly remember last Christmas herself. She and Matteo had been busy discovering each other all over again—and finding out that things were different from how they'd been before. They couldn't have been anything *but* different once the constraints of the past were lifted and they'd given themselves the freedom to say exactly what was on their minds. Or in their hearts.

Matteo had given her the option of living in London, Rome or Umbria—and she'd opted for the sprawling Umbrian estate which had once belonged to his mother's family. She figured it was healthier for Santino to grow up in the glorious Italian countryside, especially now that they had acquired a beautiful black cat named Luca who, against all odds, had become a devoted companion to Charlie the terrier.

But it was more than that. This estate was Matteo's link with his roots. It represented continuity and stability—something which had been lacking in both their lives until now. One day Santino might listen to the call of his forebears and decide he didn't want to be a businessman, like his daddy. He might want to grow up and farm the fertile acres of this beautiful place. A place which might so nearly have disappeared from the family.

Because Keira had discovered that the very first letter Matteo had sent during their separation contained estate agent details marketing the property. He'd put it up for sale to demonstrate that the house meant nothing, if he didn't have her. They had quickly aborted the prospective sale, despite the frantic bidding war which had been taking place at the time. And had decided to make the estate their permanent home.

'What are you smiling at?' questioned Matteo softly as he walked over to the Christmas tree and pulled her to her feet.

Her contented expression didn't change. 'Do I need a reason?' She sighed. 'I'm just so happy, Matteo. Happier than I ever thought possible.'

'Well, isn't that a coincidence? Because I feel exactly the same way,' he said, his fingers beginning to massage her shoulders, their practised caress never failing to arouse her. 'Have I told you lately that I love you, Mrs Valenti?'

She pretended to frown. 'I think you might have mentioned it before you went out to build Santino's snowman. And just for the record, I love you, too. So very much.'

He bent his head and kissed her, deeply and passionately and it was some time before she broke off to graze her lips against the dark stubble of his angled jaw.

'Did you speak to your father?' she said.

'I did. And he's looking forward to Christmas lunch tomorrow. He says he'll be here soon after eleven and is bringing his new girlfriend.' His eyes gleamed down at her. 'And that we should prepare ourselves for what he calls a *significant* age gap.'

Keira giggled as she rested her head on Matteo's shoulder. Massimo had divorced Luciana in the spring and although Keira had tried to feel sad about it, she just couldn't. Not only had the older woman been a troublemaker—it transpired that she'd been unfaithful to her husband as well. And one night, soon after the decree nisi had come through and Matteo had been away on business, Keira and her father-in-law had dined together in Rome. He'd told her it wasn't a desire to manipulate which had made him threaten to disinherit Matteo if he didn't produce an heir—but concern that his son was becoming emotionally remote and would end up a rich and lonely old man.

'And then you stepped in and saved him and made him happy. Truly happy—and I cannot thank you enough for that, Keira,' he had whispered, his voice cracking a little. 'I know I wasn't a good father when he was growing up.' He had fallen silent for a moment and his eyes had grown reflective. 'I missed his mother so much and he…well, he looked so much like her, that sometimes it was painful to be around him.'

'Have you told him that, Massimo?' she had said quietly, pressing her hand over his across the table. 'Because I think you should.'

And he had. Keira closed her eyes, remembering the long overdue heart-to-heart between father and son, and the growing closeness of their relationship which had resulted.

Her mind flicked back to the present as Matteo began to caress her bottom, murmuring his appreciation that these days she almost always wore a dress. She liked wearing dresses, although she could still resurrect her inner tomboy when needed—and she suspected she was going to need to do that a lot if Santino played as much football as Matteo intended he should. 'Would you like part of your Christmas present tonight?' she whispered, snuggling up to him.

He pulled away to look at her and raised his eyebrows. 'Is that an offer I shouldn't refuse?'

'Put it this way—I'm wearing it underneath this dress and I need you to unwrap it for me. Matteo!' She giggled as he began to lead her towards the bedroom. 'I didn't mean *now*—I meant later.'

'Too bad,' he murmured, not lessening his pace by a fraction. 'Because I have something for you which can't wait.'

Actually, that wasn't quite true—he had two things for her. The first was sitting in the garage wrapped in a giant red bow ready to be untied on Christmas morning. A neglected Ferrari 1948 Spider sports car which he'd tracked down with great difficulty and at considerable expense, because she'd once told him it was her dream to restore beautiful vintage cars—and Matteo was rather partial to making his wife's dreams come true.

The second gift was rather different and he didn't give it to her until after he'd dealt with her outrageous panty thong with its matching boned bodice, which he damaged beyond repair in his eagerness to unhook it. And once he had her naked, he was distracted for quite some time…

His throat thickened with unexpected emotion as he pulled the small box from his discarded trousers and flipped open the lid to reveal a flawless white solitaire which sparkled like a giant star against dark velvet.

'What's this?' she questioned breathlessly, from among the sheets which were rumpled around her.

He lifted her left hand and slid the solitaire in place above her wedding band. 'I never gave you an engagement ring, did I? And I didn't give you a dream wedding either. A civil ceremony in a town hall was never something we were going to enjoy telling our grandchildren about.' He lifted her hand to his lips and kissed her fingertips. 'So I wondered if you'd like to renew our vows in my favourite church in Rome. You could wear a big white dress and do it properly this time, and we could throw a party afterwards. Or not—whichever you prefer. What I'm asking is, would you like to marry me again, Keira Valenti?'

Keira opened her mouth to say that she didn't care about pomp or ceremony, but that wasn't quite true. And weren't she and Matteo all about the truth, these days? She thought about something else, too, something which had been niggling away at her for a while now. Because weddings could bring people together and heal old wounds, couldn't they? Motherhood had changed her. Softened her. She realised now that her aunt might have been strict when she was growing up, but she'd given an orphaned little girl the home she'd badly needed and had stopped her from being taken into care. And didn't she owe her aunt Ida a great deal for that? Wasn't it time to invite her and Shelley to Italy, to share in her good fortune and happiness and to introduce Santino to some of *her* roots?

She wound her arms around Matteo's neck and looked into his beautiful black eyes, her heart turning over with emotion. 'Yes, Matteo,' she said breathlessly. 'I'll be proud to marry you. To stand before our family and friends and say the thing I'll never tire of saying, which is that I love you—and I'll love you for the rest of my life.'

* * * * *

THE ITALIAN'S CHRISTMAS CHILD

LYNNE GRAHAM

Christmas is one of my favourite times of year.

It's about family and friends, so this is dedicated to you.

CHAPTER ONE

THE MOORLAND LANDSCAPE on Dartmoor was cold and crisp with ice. As the four-wheel drive turned off the road onto a rough lane, Vito saw the picturesque cottage sheltering behind winter-bare trees with graceful frosted branches. His lean, strong face grim with exhaustion, he got out of the car ahead of his driver, only tensing as he heard the sound of yet another text hitting his phone. Ignoring it, he walked into the property while the driver emptied the car.

Instant warmth greeted him and he raked a weary hand through the dense blue-black hair that the breeze had whipped across his brow. There was a welcome blaze in the brick inglenook fireplace and he fought the sense of relief threatening to engulf him. He was not a coward. He had not run away as his ex-fiancée had accused him of doing. He would have stood his ground and stayed in Florence had he not finally appreciated that the pursuit of the paparazzi and outrageous headlines were only being fuelled by his continuing presence.

He had grudgingly followed his best friend Apollo's advice and had removed himself from the scene, recognising that his mother had quite enough to deal with when her husband was in hospital following a serious heart attack without also having to suffer the embarrassment of her son's newly acquired notoriety. Undeniably, his friend had much more experience than Vito had of handling scandals and bad publicity. The Greek playboy had led a far less restricted life than Vito, who had known from an early age that he would become the next CEO of the Zaffari Bank. His grandfather had steeped him in the history and traditions of a family that could trace its beginnings back to the Middle Ages when the Zaffari name had stood shoulder to shoulder with words like *honour* and *principle*. No more, Vito reflected wryly. Now he would be famous for ever as the banker who had indulged in drugs and strippers.

Not his style, not his style at all, Vito ruminated ruefully, breaking free of his thoughts to lavishly tip his driver and thank him. When it came to the drug allegations, he could only suppress a groan. One of his closest friends at school had taken something that had killed him at a party and Vito had never been tempted by illegal substances. And the whores? In truth Vito could barely remember when he had last had sex. Although he had been engaged until a week earlier, Marzia had always been cool in that department.

'She's a lady to her backbone.' His grandfather had sighed approvingly, shortly before his passing. 'A Ravello with the right background and breeding. She will make a superb hostess and future mother for your children.'

Not now, though, Vito thought, glancing at his phone to discover that his ex had sent him yet another text. *Dio mio*, what did she want from him now? He had perfectly understood her decision to break off their engagement and he had wasted no time in putting the house she had been furnishing for their future occupation back on the market. That, however, had proved to be a move that had evidently rankled, even though he had assured Marzia that she was welcome to keep every stick of furniture in the place.

What about the Abriano painting? she'd texted.

He pointed out that his grandfather's engagement gift would have to be returned. It was worth millions—how much more compensation was he to pay in terms of damages? He had offered her the house but she had refused it.

But in spite of his generosity, he still felt guilty. He had messed up Marzia's life and embarrassed her. For probably the first time in his life he had wronged someone. On the spur of the moment he had made a decision that had hit Marzia very hard and even the sincerest apology could not lessen the impact of it. But he could not have told his former fiancée the truth because he could not have trusted her to keep it secret. And if the truth came out, his sacrifice would be pointless and it would plunge the only woman he had ever loved into gross humiliation and heartbreak. Vito had made a very tough choice and he was fully prepared to take the heat for it.

That, indeed, was why vanishing off-grid for a couple of weeks over Christmas *still* felt disturbingly gutless to Vito, whose natural instincts were pre-emptive and forceful.

'Ritchie's a lying, cheating scumbag!' Holly's flatmate and best friend, Pixie, ranted furiously down the phone.

Holly grimaced and pushed her hand through her

heavy mane of black curling hair, her big blue eyes red-rimmed and sad as she checked her watch to see that she was still safely within her lunch hour. 'You're not going to get any argument from me on that score,' she said ruefully.

'He's as bad as that last guy who borrowed all the money from you,' Pixie reminded her with a typical lack of tact. 'And the one before that who wanted to marry you so that you could act as a carer for his invalid mother!'

Wincing at her disheartening past history with men, Holly reflected that she could not have done worse in the dating stakes had she drawn up a specific list of selfish, dishonest losers. 'Let's not look back,' she urged, keen to move on to more positive subjects.

Pixie refused to cooperate, saying, 'So, what on earth are you planning to do now for your festive break with me, stuck in London and Ritchie out of the picture?'

A sudden grin lit Holly's oval face with surprising enthusiasm. 'I'm going to make Christmas for Sylvia instead!'

'But she's staying with her daughter in Yorkshire over the holiday...*isn't she*?'

'No, Alice had to cancel Sylvia at the last minute. Her house has been flooded by a burst pipe. Sylvia was horribly disappointed when she found out and then when I walked in on Ritchie with his floozy today, I realised that I could take two pieces of bad luck and make something good out of them...'

'I really hate it when you pick yourself up off the floor and come over all optimistic again.' Pixie sighed dramatically. 'Please tell me you at least *thumped* Ritchie...'

'I told him what I thought of him…briefly,' Holly qualified with her innate honesty, for really she had been too squeamish to linger in the presence of her half-naked boyfriend and the woman he had chosen to cheat on her with. 'So, is it all right for me to borrow your car to go to Sylvia's?'

'Of course it is. How else would you get there? But watch out: there's snow forecast—'

'They always like to talk about snow this close to Christmas,' Holly demurred, unimpressed by the threat. 'By the way, I'm taking our Christmas tree and ornaments with me and I'd already bought and made all the trimmings for a festive lunch. I'm going to put on that Santa outfit you wore for the Christmas party at the salon last year. Sylvia loves a laugh. She'll appreciate it.'

'Sylvia will be over the moon when she finds you on the doorstep,' her friend predicted warmly. 'Between losing her husband and having to move because she couldn't manage the farmhouse alone any more, she's had a horrible year.'

Holly held firmly on to the inspiring prospect of her foster mother's happiness at her arrival while she finished her afternoon shift at the busy café where she worked. It was Christmas Eve and she adored the festive season, possibly because she had grown up mainly in foster care and had always been painfully conscious that she did not have a real family to share the experience with. In an effort to comfort her, Pixie had assured her that family Christmases could be a nightmare and that she was in love with an ideal of Christmas rather than the reality. But some day, somehow, Holly was determined to turn fantasy into reality with a husband and children of her own. That was her dream and in spite of recent setbacks she understood that it was hanging on to her dream that essentially kept her going through more challenging times.

Both she and Pixie had been fostered by Sylvia Ware from the age of twelve and the older woman's warm acceptance and understanding had been far superior to the uncaring and occasionally neglectful homes Holly and Pixie had endured as younger children caught up in the care system. Holly had long regretted not paying more heed to Sylvia's lectures about studying harder at school. Over the years Holly had attended so many different schools and made so many moves that she had simply drifted through her education, accepting that she would always be behind in certain subjects. Now at almost twenty-four, Holly had redressed that adolescent mistake by attending night classes to achieve basic qualifications but the road ahead to further education seemed so long and complex that it daunted her and she had instead chosen to study for a qualification in interior design online.

'And what use is that to you?' Pixie, who was a hairdresser, had asked baldly.

'I'm really interested in it. I love looking at a room and thinking about how I can improve it.'

'But people from our sort of background don't get hired as interior designers,' Pixie had pointed out. 'I mean, we're just ordinary workers trying to pay our bills, not people with fancy careers.'

And Holly had to acknowledge as she donned her friend's Santa outfit that there *was* nothing fancy or impressive about her likely to combat that discouraging assurance. Fortunately the short dress had been far too generously sized on her infinitely more slender friend.

Pixie might envy Holly's curves but Pixie could eat whatever she liked and never put on a pound while Holly was engaged in a constant struggle to prevent her curves from taking over. Her golden skin tone hailed from an unknown father. He might or might not have been someone her erratic mother had met abroad. On the other hand he might simply have been a man who lived in the same street. Her only parent had told her so many lies that Holly had long accepted that the truth of her fatherhood would never be known.

At four feet ten inches tall, Holly, like her mother, lacked height. She pulled on warm black winter tights under the bright red satin and corseted dress. Thrusting her feet into cowboy boots rather than the heels Pixie had sported for her party a year earlier, Holly scowled at her gaudy, busty reflection in the mirror and jammed on the Santa hat in a defiant move. OK, she looked comical, she acknowledged, but her appearance would make Sylvia laugh and overlook the disappointment of not having her own daughters around her to celebrate Christmas Day with, and that was what was truly important.

Planning to spend the night on the sofa in Sylvia's tiny living area, she packed her rucksack and carefully placed what remained of the decorations and the food into a box heavy enough to make her stagger on her final trip to the car. *At least the food wouldn't be going to waste*, she thought with determined positivity, until a flashback of the ugly scene she had interrupted with Ritchie and the receptionist at his insurance office cut through her rebellious brain.

Her tummy rolled with nausea and her battered heart clenched. *In the middle of the day as well*, she thought with a shudder. She couldn't imagine even having sex, never mind going at it on a desk in broad daylight. Possibly she wasn't a very adventurous person. In fact both she and Pixie were probably pretty strait-laced. At twelve years old they had shuddered over the ugly chaos of broken relationships in their mothers' lives and had solemnly decided to swear off men altogether. Of course once puberty had kicked in, with all its attendant confusing hormones, that rule had failed. At fourteen they had ditched their embargo on men while deciding that sex was the real danger and best avoided outside a serious relationship. *A serious committed relationship.* Holly's eyes rolled at the memory of their mutual innocence. And so far neither she nor her friend had managed to have a serious committed relationship with a man.

All that considered thought about steering clear of sexual relationships hadn't done her many favours either, Holly reflected with helpless insecurity. There had been men she really liked who ran a mile from what they saw as her outdated expectations and then there had been the others who stayed around for a few weeks or months, eager to be the first into her bed. Had she only ever been a sexual challenge to Ritchie? How long, for instance, had he been messing around with other women?

'Did you expect me to wait for you for ever?' Ritchie had shouted back at her, blaming her for his betrayal because she had held back on having sex with him. 'What's so special about you?'

Holly flinched at that ugly recollection because she had always known that there was nothing particularly special about her.

It was snowing as she drove off in the battered little hatchback that Pixie had christened Clementine, and she groaned. She loved the look of snow but she didn't like to drive in it and she hated being cold. Thank goodness for the car, she acknowledged, as she rattled out of the small Devon town where she lived and worked.

Snow was falling fast by the time she reached Sylvia's home, which was dismayingly dark. Perhaps the older woman was out at a church service or visiting a neighbour. Jamming down her hat over the mass of hair fighting to escape its confines, Holly rapped on the door and waited, stamping her feet to keep warm. After a couple of minutes she knocked again and then she followed the communal path to the little house next door, which was brightly lit, and knocked there instead.

'I'm sorry to bother you but I wondered if you knew where Mrs Ware has gone and if she'll be home soon,' Holly asked with a friendly smile.

'Sylvia left this afternoon. I helped her pack—she was in such a tizzy because she wasn't expecting anyone,' the elderly little woman at the door told her.

Holly frowned, her heart sinking. 'So, she went to her daughter's after all, then?'

'Oh, no, it wasn't the daughter who came, it was her son. Big tall chap in a suit. He's taking her back to Bruges or Belgium or some place,' the neighbour told her less certainly.

'Brussels. That's where Stephen lives. Do you know how long she'll be away?'

'A couple of weeks at least, she seemed to think...'

As deflated as a pricked balloon, Holly walked back to her car.

'You watch yourself driving home,' the old lady called after her. 'There's to be heavy snow tonight.'

'Thanks, I will,' Holly promised, forcing a smile. 'Merry Christmas!'

And a very merry Christmas it was going to be on her own, she thought unhappily, annoyed to find that her eyes were prickling with tears. After all, Sylvia was going to have the best possible Christmas with her son and the grandchildren she rarely saw. Holly was really, really pleased that Stephen had swooped in from abroad to save the day. He and his wife were rare visitors but he had at least made the effort and now his mother wouldn't have to spend her first Christmas as a widow alone. Holly sniffed and blinked back the tears, scolding herself for being so selfish. She was young and healthy and employed. She had nothing to complain about, nothing at all.

Maybe she was simply missing Pixie, she reasoned, as she drove with care on the steep, icy road that climbed up over the moors. Pixie's kid brother was in some sort of trouble and Pixie had taken time off to go and stay with him and sort it out. It was probably financial trouble but Holly wouldn't ask any awkward questions or offer unwelcome advice because she didn't want to hurt her friend, who was deeply attached to her horribly self-centred sibling. Everyone had problems, she reminded herself doggedly, tensing as she felt the tyres of the car shift into a near skid on the slippery surface and slowing her speed even more. She had far fewer problems than most people and had no excuse whatsoever for feeling sorry for herself.

Ritchie? Well, that wasn't an excuse. So, she had got hurt but then Pixie would point out that she was too soft in that line, too prone to thinking well of people and being knocked back hard when they let her down. Pixie was more of a cynic, strong on distrust as a means of self-defence, except when it came to her own brother.

Holly peered out of the windscreen because visibility was fading fast with the wipers unable to keep up with the heavy snow. She wasn't the dramatic type, she assured herself, as the car coasted down a hill that seemed steeper than it had seemed when she drove over it earlier that evening, but the weather was foul and the light snowfall she had dimly expected now bore a closer resemblance to a blizzard.

And then without the smallest warning, and to the accompaniment of her strangled scream, the car glided in the most terrifying slow motion off the road into a ditch where it tilted over and wedged fast with a loud, nerve-racking crunch of metal. After switching off the engine, Holly breathed in slow and deep to calm herself. She was alive, no other car was involved and nobody was hurt. There was much to be thankful for, she told herself bracingly.

Sadly that was a conviction that took a beating once she climbed out with some difficulty, owing to the angle the car had crashed at, to inspect the damage. The side wing of Pixie's elderly vehicle was crushed up against a large rock, which had presumably been placed to mark the entrance to the lane. *My goodness, how much will the repairs cost?* was her first fearful thought. It was *her* responsibility, not Pixie's.

A spark of fear assailed her only after she had examined her surroundings. The road was deserted and lay under a covering of unbroken snow. It was a bad night and it was Christmas Eve and she didn't think there would be much passing traffic, if any. As she stood there nursing her mobile phone and wondering what she was going to do, Holly had never felt more lonely. She had no close friend she could ring and drag out in such dreadful weather on such a special night. No, she was on her own, sink or swim. Consternation gripped her when she couldn't get a signal on her phone to use it. Only then did she turn round to look again at the lane she stood beside and there, like a faint beacon in the darkness, she saw the lights of what could only be a house and relief filled her to overflowing. Hopefully it was occupied and the occupant had a landline she could use to call for a breakdown truck.

Vito was savouring a glass of award-winning wine and wondering what to do with the evening when the knocker on the door sounded. Taken aback, he frowned because he hadn't heard a car and there were no lights outside. Did the local caretaker live within walking distance? He peered out through the spyhole and saw a red-and-white Santa hat. Someone was definitely at the wrong house because Vito hated Christmas. He yanked open the door and enormous blue eyes like velvet pansies looked up at him. At first he thought his visitor was a child and then his eyes dropped and took in the swell of breasts visible between the parted edges of her coat and he registered that, although she might be very small, she was all woman.

Holly stared up in wonderment at the male who appeared in the doorway. He looked like every fantasy male she had ever dreamt about meeting all rolled into one spectacular package. In fact he was so gorgeous with his black hair, designer stubble and dark, deep-set, mysterious eyes that he made her teeth clench in dismay because he didn't look approachable or helpful or anything that might have encouraged her. That he wore a very formal dark business suit with a white shirt and natty gold tie didn't help to relax her either.

'If you're looking for a party, you're at the wrong house,' Vito told her loftily, recalling his friend's warnings about how sneaky the paparazzi could be. If he'd thought about that risk, he wouldn't have answered the door at all.

'I'm looking for a phone. Mine has no reception here and my car went off the road at the foot of your lane,' Holly explained in a rush. 'Do you have a landline?'

Exasperation flashed through Vito, who had far too much sensitive information on his cell phone to consider loaning it to anyone. 'This isn't my house. I'll look and see,' he fielded drily.

As he turned on his heel without inviting her in out of the heavily falling snow, Holly grimaced and shivered because she wasn't dressed for bad weather, having only thrown on a raincoat to cover her outfit because she had known she would be warm inside the car. *Not Mr Nice Guy, anyway*, she thought ruefully. She had recognised the impatience in those electrifyingly dark magnetic eyes, watched the flare of his nostrils and the tightening of his wide, sculpted mouth as he'd bit back a withering comment. She was good at reading faces, even gorgeous ones, she conceded, as she shifted her feet in a vain effort to heat the blood freezing in her veins. She didn't think she had ever seen a more handsome man, no, not even on a movie screen, but personality-wise she reckoned that there was a good chance that he was chillier than an icicle.

'There is a phone… You may step inside to use it,' he invited grudgingly, his foreign accent edging every syllable in a very attractive way.

Holly reddened with discomfiture, already well aware that she was not a welcome visitor. She dug out her phone to scroll through numbers for Pixie's car mechanic, Bill, who ran a breakdown service. As she did so, she missed seeing the step in front of her and tripped over it, falling forward with a force that would have knocked the breath from her body had not strong arms snapped out to catch her before she fell.

'Watch out…' Taken aback by a level of clumsiness utterly unknown to a male as surefooted as a cat, Vito virtually lifted her into the porch. As her hair briefly brushed his face he was engulfed by the scent of oranges, sweet and sun-warmed. But it was only by touching her and seeing her face below the lights that he registered that she was almost blue with cold. '*Maledizione*, you're freezing! Why didn't you tell me that?'

'It's enough of an imposition coming to the door—'

'Yes, I would surely have been happier to trip over your frozen corpse on my doorstep in the morning!' Vito fielded scathingly. 'You should've told me—'

'You've got eyes of your own and an off-putting manner. I don't like bothering people,' Holly said truthfully while she frantically rubbed her hands over her raincoat in an effort to get some feeling back into her fingers before she tried to work her phone again.

Vito gazed down at her from his height of six foot one. He was bemused by her criticism when he was trying to be pleasant and when he could not recall when a woman had last offered him a word of criticism. Even in the act of breaking their engagement, Marzia had contrived not to speak a word of condemnation. Either a woman of saintly tolerance or one who didn't give a damn who he might have slept with behind her back? It was a sobering thought.

An off-putting manner? Could that be true about him? His grandfather had taught him to maintain distance between himself and others and he had often thought that a useful gift when it came to commanding a large staff, none of whom dared to take liberties with their authoritarian CEO.

Thoroughly irritated by the thoughts awakened by his visitor and that unfamiliar self-questioning mode, he swiped the phone from between her shaking fingers and said firmly, 'Go and warm up first by the fire and then make the call.'

'Are you sure you don't mind?'

'I will contrive to bear it.'

Halfway towards the wonderful blaze of the log fire illuminating the dim interior, Holly spun round with a merriment in her eyes that lit up her whole face and she laughed. 'You're a sarky one, aren't you?'

In the firelight her eyes were bright as sapphires and that illuminating smile made the breath catch in his throat because it lent her incredible appeal. And Vito was not the sort of male who noticed women very often and when he did he usually swiftly stifled the impulse. But for a split second that playful tone and that radiant smile knocked him sideways and he found himself staring. He scanned the glorious dark hair that fell free of the Santa hat as she whipped it off, before lowering his appreciative gaze to the wonderfully generous thrust of her breasts above a neat little waist, right down to the hem of the shimmering dress that revealed slim knees and shapely calves incongruously encased in cowboy boots. He threw his shoulders back, bracing as the pulse at his groin beat out a different kind of tension.

Holly connected momentarily with eyes of gold semi-veiled by the lush black sweep of his lashes and something visceral tightened low in her pelvis as she let her attention linger on his lean, hard bone structure, which was stunningly hard and male from his level dark brows to his arrogant classic nose and his strong, sculpted jawline. Just looking at him sent the oddest flash of excitement through her and she reddened uneasily, and deliberately spun back to the fire to hold her hands out to the heat. So, he was very good-looking. That didn't mean she had to gape like an awestruck fan at a rock star, did it? She was only inside his house to use the phone, she reminded herself in embarrassment.

She flexed her fingers. 'Where did you put my phone?'

As she half turned it was settled neatly into her hand and she opened it and scrolled through the numbers. He handed her the handset of the house phone and she pressed out Bill's number, lifting it to her ear while carefully not glancing again in her host's direction.

Vito was engaged in subduing his sexual arousal and reeling in shock from the need to do so. What was he? A teenager again? She wasn't his type…if he had a type. The women in his life had invariably been tall, elegant blondes and she was very small, very curvy and very, *very* sexy, he conceded involuntarily as she moved about the room while she talked, her luxuriant hair rippling across her shoulders, her rounded hips swaying. She was apologising for disturbing someone on Christmas Eve and she apologised at great length instead of getting straight to the point of her problem with her car.

What were the chances that she was a particularly clever member of the paparazzi brigade? Vito had flown into the UK on a private plane to a private airfield and travelled to the cottage in a private car. Only Apollo and his mother, Concetta, knew where he was. But Apollo had warned him that the paps went to extraordinary lengths to steal photos and find stories they could sell. His perfect white teeth gritted. At the very least, he needed to check that there was a broken-down car at the foot of the lane.

'Boxing Day?' Holly was practically whispering in horror.

'And possibly only if the snowplough has been through ahead of me,' Bill told her apologetically. 'I'm working flat out tonight as it is. Where exactly is the car?'

The older man was local and, knowing the road well, was able to establish where she was. 'Aye, I know the house down there—foreign-owned holiday home as far as I know. And you're able to stay there?'

'Yes,' Holly said in as reassuring a tone as she could contrive while wondering if she was going to have to bed down in Pixie's car. 'Do you know anyone else I could ring?'

She tried the second number but there was no response at all. Swallowing hard, she set the digital phone down. 'I'll go back to the car now,' she told Vito squarely.

'I'll walk down with you… See if there's anything I can do—'

'Unless you have a tractor to haul it out of the ditch I shouldn't think so.' Holly buttoned her coat, tied the belt and braced herself to face the great outdoors again.

As she straightened her shoulders she looked round the room with belated admiration, suddenly noticing that the opulent décor was an amazing and highly effective marriage of traditional and contemporary styles. In spite of the ancient brick inglenook fireplace, the staircase had a glass surround and concealed lights. But she also noticed that there was one glaring omission: there were no festive decorations of any kind.

Vito yanked on his cashmere coat and scarf over the suit he still wore.

'If you don't have boots, I can't let you go down there with me… You'll get your shoes soaked,' Holly told him ruefully, glancing at the polished, city-type footwear he sported with his incredibly stylish suit, which moulded to his well-built, long-legged frame as though specifically tailored to do so.

Vito walked into the porch, which boasted a rack of boots, and, picking out a pair, donned them. Her pragmatism had secretly impressed him. Vito was extremely clever but, like many very clever people, he was not particularly practical and the challenges of rural living in bad weather lay far outside his comfort zone.

'My name is Holly,' she announced brightly on the porch.

'Vito…er… Vito Sorrentino,' Vito lied, employing his father's original surname.

His mother had been an only child, a daughter when his grandfather had longed for a son. At his grandfather's request, Vito's father had changed his name to Zaffari when he married Vito's mother to ensure that the family name would not die out. Ciccio Sorrentino had been content to surrender his name in return for the privilege of marrying a fabulously wealthy banking heiress. There was no good reason for Vito to take the risk of identifying himself to a stranger. Right now the name Zaffari was cannon fodder for the tabloids across Europe and the news of his disappearance and current location would be worth a great deal of money to a profiteer. And if there was one gift Vito had in spades it was the gilded art of making a profit and ensuring that nobody got to do it at his expense.

His grandfather would have turned in his grave at the mere threat of his grandson plunging the family name and the family bank into such a sleazy scandal. Vito, however, was rather less naive. Having attended a board meeting before his departure, Vito was aware that he could virtually do no wrong. All the Zaffari directors cared about was that their CEO continued to ensure that the Zaffari bank carried on being the most successful financial institution in Europe.

CHAPTER TWO

'YOU SAID THIS wasn't your house,' Holly reminded him through chattering teeth as they walked out into the teeth of a gale laced with snow.

'A friend loaned it to me for a break.'

'And you're staying here alone?'

'*Sì*...yes.'

'By choice...*alone*...at Christmas?' Holly framed incredulously.

'Why not?' Vito loathed Christmas but that was none of her business and he saw no need to reveal anything of a personal nature. His memories of Christmas were toxic. His parents, who rarely spent time together, had squabbled almost continuously through the festive break. His mother had made a real effort to hide that reality and make the season enjoyable, but Vito had always been far too intelligent even as a child not to understand what was happening around him. He had seen that his mother loved his father but that her love was not returned. He had watched her humiliate herself in an effort to smooth over Ciccio's bad moods and even worse temper. He had listened to her beg for five minutes of her husband's attention. He had eventually grasped that the ideal goal composed of marriage, family and respectability could be a very expensive shrine to worship at. Had he not been made aware that it was his inherent duty to carry on the family line, nothing would have persuaded Vito into matrimony.

He studied the old car in the ditch with an amount of satisfaction that bemused him. It was a shabby ancient wreck of a vehicle. It had to mean that Holly was not a plant, not a spy or a member of the paparazzi, but a genuine traveller in trouble. Not that that reality softened his irritation over the fact that he was now stuck with her for at least one night. He had listened to the phone call she had made. Short of it being a matter of life or death, nobody was willing to come out on such a night. Of course he could have thrown his wealth at the problem to take care of it but nothing would more surely advertise his presence than the hiring of a helicopter to remove his unwanted guest, and he was doubtful that even a helicopter could fly in such poor conditions.

'As you see…it's stuck,' Holly pointed out unnecessarily while patting the bonnet of the car as if it were a live entity in need of comfort. 'It's my friend's car and she's going to be really upset about this.'

'Accidents happen…particularly if you choose to drive without taking precautions on a road like this in this kind of weather.'

In disbelief, Holly rounded on him, twin spots of high colour sparking over her cheekbones. 'It wasn't snowing this bad when I left home! There were no precautions!'

'Let's get your stuff and head back to the house.'

Suppressing the anger his tactless comment had roused with some difficulty, Holly studied him in astonishment. 'You're inviting me back to the house? You don't need to. I can—'

'I'm a notoriously unsympathetic man but even I could not leave you to sleep in a car in a snowstorm on Christmas Eve!' Vito framed impatiently. 'Now, may we cut the conversation and head back to the heat? Or do you want to pat the car again?'

Face red now with mortification, Holly opened the boot and dug out her rucksack to swing it up onto her back.

The rucksack was almost as big as she was, Vito saw in disbelief. 'Let me take that.'

'No…I was hoping you'd take the box because it's heavier.'

Stubborn mouth flattening, Vito reached in with reluctance for the sizeable box and hefted it up with a curled lip. 'Do you really need the box as well?'

'Yes, it's got all my stuff in it…*please*,' Holly urged. Her amazingly blue eyes looked up at him and he felt strangely disorientated. Her eyes were as translucent a blue as the Delft masterpieces his mother had conserved from his grandfather's world-famous collection. They trudged back up the lane with Vito maintaining a disgruntled silence as he carried the bulky carton.

'*Porca miseria!* What's in the box?'

'My Christmas decorations and some food.'

'Why are you driving round with Christmas decorations and food? Of course, you were heading to a party,' he reasoned for himself, thinking of what she wore.

'No, I wasn't. I intended to spend the night with my foster mother because I thought she was going to be on her own for Christmas. *But*…turns out her son came and collected her and she didn't know I was planning to surprise her, so when I went off the road I was driving home again.'

'Where's home?'

She named a town Vito had never heard of.

'Where are you from?'

'Florence…in Italy,' he explained succinctly.

'I do know where Florence is…it *is* famous,' Holly countered, glancing up at him while the snow drifted down steadily, quietly, cocooning them in the small space lit by his torch. 'So, you're Italian.'

'You do like to state the obvious, don't you?' Vito derided, stomping into the porch one step behind her.

'I hate that sarcasm of yours!' Holly fired back at him angrily, taking herself almost as much by surprise as she took him because she usually went out of her way to avoid conflict.

An elegant black brow raised, Vito removed the boots, hung his coat and scarf and then lifted the rucksack from her bent shoulders. 'What have you got in here? Rocks?'

'Food.'

'The kitchen here is packed with food.'

'Do you always know better than everyone else about everything?' Holly, whose besetting fault was untidiness, carefully hung her wet coat beside his to be polite.

'I very often *do* know better,' Vito answered without hesitation.

Holly spread a shaken glance over his lean, darkly handsome and wholly serious features and groaned out loud. 'No sense of humour either.'

'Knowing one's own strengths is not a flaw,' Vito informed her gently.

'But it is if you don't consider your faults—'

'And what are *your* faults?' Vito enquired saccharine smooth, as she headed for the fire like a homing pigeon and held her hands out to the heat.

Holly wrinkled her snub nose and thought hard. 'I'm untidy. An incurable optimist. Too much of a people-pleaser… That comes of all those years in foster care and trying to fit in to different families and different schools.' She angled her head to one side, brown hair lying in a silken mass against one creamy cheek as she pondered. In the red Santa get-up, she reminded him of a cheerful little robin he had once seen pacing on a fence. 'I'm too forgiving sometimes because I always want to think the best of people or give them a second chance. I get really cross if I run out of coffee but I don't like conflict and avoid it. I like to do things quickly but sometimes that means I don't do them well. I fuss about my weight but I *still* don't exercise…'

As Vito listened to that very frank résumé he almost laughed. There was something intensely sweet about that forthright honesty. 'Strengths?' he prompted, unable to resist the temptation.

'I'm honest, loyal, hardworking, punctual…I like to make the people I care about happy,' she confided. 'That's what put me on that road tonight.'

'Would you like a drink?' Vito enquired.

'Red wine, if you have it…' Moving away from the fire, Holly approached her rucksack. 'Is it all right if I put the food in the kitchen?'

She walked through the door he indicated and her eyebrows soared along with the ceiling. Beyond that door the cottage changed again. A big extension housed an ultra-modern kitchen diner with pale sparkling granite work surfaces and a fridge large enough to answer the storage needs of a restaurant. She opened it up. It was already generously packed with goodies, mainly of the luxury version of ready meals. She arranged her offerings on an empty shelf and then walked back into the main room to open the box and extract the food that remained.

Obviously, she was stuck here in a strange house with a strange man for one night at the very least, Holly reflected anxiously. A slight frisson of unease trickled down her spine. Vito hadn't done or said anything threatening, though, she reminded herself. Like her, he recognised practicalities. He was stuck with her because she had nowhere else to go and clearly he wasn't overjoyed by the situation. Neither one of them had a choice but to make the best of it.

'You brought a lot of food with you,' Vito remarked from behind her.

Holly flinched because she hadn't heard him approach and she whipped her head around. 'I assumed I would be providing a Christmas lunch for two people.'

Walking back out of the kitchen when she had finished, she found him frowning down at the tree ornaments visible in the box.

'What is all this stuff?' he asked incredulously.

Holly explained. 'Would it be all right if I put up my tree here? I mean, it is Christmas Eve and I won't get another opportunity for a year,' she pointed out. 'Christmas is special to me.'

Vito was still frowning. 'Not to me,' he admitted flatly, for he had only bad memories of the many disappointing Christmases he had endured as a child.

Flushing, Holly closed the box and pushed it over to the wall out of the way. 'That's not a problem. You're doing enough letting me stay here.'

Dio mio, he was relieved that she was only a passing stranger because her fondness for the sentimental trappings of the season set his teeth on edge. Of course she wanted to put up her Christmas tree! Anyone who travelled around wearing a Santa hat was likely to want a tree on display as well! He handed her a glass of wine, trying not to feel responsible for having doused her chirpy flow of chatter.

'I'm heading upstairs for a shower,' Vito told her, because even though he had worn the boots, his suit trousers were damp. 'Will you be all right down here on your own?'

'Of course… This is much better than sitting in a crashed car,' Holly assured him before adding more awkwardly, 'Do you have a sweater or anything I could borrow? I only have pyjamas and a dress with me. My foster mum's house is very warm so I didn't pack anything woolly.'

Vito had not a clue what was in his luggage because he hadn't packed his own case since he was a teenager at boarding school. 'I'll see what I've got.'

Through the glass barrier of the stairs, Holly watched his long, powerful legs disappear from view and a curious little frisson rippled through her tense body. She heaved a sigh. So, no Christmas tree. What possible objection could anyone have to a Christmas tree? Did Vito share Ebenezer Scrooge's loathing for the festive season? Reminding herself that she was *very* lucky not to be shivering in Pixie's car by the side of the road, she settled down on the shaggy rug by the hearth and simply luxuriated in the warmth emanating from the logs glowing in the fire.

Vito thought about Holly while he took a shower. It

was a major mistake. Within seconds of picturing her sexy little body he went hard as a rock, his body reacting with a randy enthusiasm that astonished him. For months, of course, his libido had very much taken a back seat to the eighteen-hour days he was working. This year the bank's revenues would, he reminded himself with pride, smash all previous records. He was doing what he had been raised to do and he was doing it extremely well, so why did he feel so empty, so joyless? Vito asked himself in exasperation.

Intellectually he understood that there was more to life than the pursuit of profit but realistically he was and always had been a workaholic. An image of Holly chattering by the fire assailed him. Holly with her wonderful curves and her weird tree in a box. She was unusual, not remotely like the sort of women Vito usually met, and her originality was a huge draw. He had no idea what she was likely to say next. She wasn't wearing make-up. She didn't fuss with her appearance. She said exactly what she thought and felt—she had no filter. Towelling off, he tried to stop thinking about Holly. Obviously she turned him on. Equally obviously he wasn't going to do anything about it.

Why the hell not? The words sounded in the back of his brain. That battered old car, everything about her spelled out the message that she came from a different world. Making any kind of a move would be taking advantage, he told himself grimly. Yet the instant he had seen Holly he had wanted her, *wanted* her with an intensity he hadn't felt around a woman since he was a careless teenager. It was the situation. He could relax with a woman who had neither a clue who he was nor any idea of the sleazy scandal currently clinging to his name. And why wouldn't he want her? After all, he was very probably sex-starved, he told himself impatiently as he tossed out the contents of one of his suitcases and then opened a second before finding a sweater he deemed suitable.

Holly watched Vito walk down the stairs with the fluid, silent grace of a panther. He had looked amazing in his elegant business suit, but in black designer jeans and a long-sleeved red cotton tee he was drop-dead gorgeous and, with those high cheekbones and that full masculine mouth, very much in the male-model category. She blinked and stared, feeling the colour rise in her cheeks, her self-consciousness taking over, for she had literally never ever been in the radius of such a very handsome male and it was just a little like bumping into a movie star without warning.

'Here… You can roll up the sleeves.' Vito tossed the sweater into her lap. 'If you want to freshen up, there's a shower room just before you enter the kitchen.'

Holly scrambled upright and grabbed her rucksack to take his advice. A little alone time to get her giddy head in order struck her as a very good idea. When she saw herself in the mirror in the shower room she was affronted by the wind-tousled explosion of her hair and the amount of cleavage she was showing in the Santa outfit. Stripping off, she went for a shower, exulting in the hot water and the famous-name shower gel on offer. Whoever owned the cottage had to be pretty comfortably off, she decided with a grimace, which probably meant that Vito was as well. He wore a very sleek gold-coloured watch and the fit of his suit had been perfection. But then what did she know about such trappings or the likely cost of them? Pixie would laugh to hear such musings when the closest Holly had ever got to even dating an office worker was Ritchie, the cheating insurance salesman.

She pulled on the blue sweater, which plunged low enough at the neck to reveal her bra. She yanked it at the back to raise it to a decent level at the front and knew she would have to remember to keep her shoulders back. She rolled up the sleeves and, since the sweater covered her to her knees, left off her tights. Her hair she rescued with a little diligent primping until it fell in loose waves round her shoulders. Frowning at her bunny slippers, she crammed them back in her rucksack, deciding that bare feet were preferable. Cosmetics-wise she was pretty much stuck with the minimal make-up she had packed for Sylvia's. Sighing, she used tinted moisturiser, subtle eyeliner and glossed her lips. Well, at short notice that was the best she could do. In any case it was only her pride that was prompting her to make the effort. After all, a male as sophisticated as Vito Sorrentino wouldn't look at her anyway, she thought with a squirming pang of guilty disappointment. Why on earth was she thinking about him that way?

And thinking about Vito that way put her back in mind of Ritchie, which was unfortunate. But it also reminded her that she hadn't taken her pill yet and she dug into her bag to remedy that, only to discover that she had left them at home. As to why a virgin was taking contraceptive precautions, she and Pixie both did on a 'better safe than sorry' basis. Both of their mothers had messed up their lives with early unplanned pregnancies and neither Holly nor Pixie wanted to run the same risk.

Of course a couple of years back Holly had had different and more romantic expectations. She had fondly imagined that she would eventually meet a man who would sweep her away on a tide of passion and she had believed that she had to protect herself in the face of such temptation. Sadly, nothing any boyfriend had yet made her feel could have fallen into a category that qualified as being *swept away*. Since then Holly had wondered if there was a distinct possibility that she herself simply wasn't a very passionate woman. Still, Holly reasoned wryly, there was nothing wrong with living in hope, was there?

Somehow Vito had been fully expecting Holly to reappear with a full face of make-up. Instead she appeared with her face rosy and apparently untouched, his sweater drooping round her in shapeless, bulky folds, her tiny feet bare. And Vito almost laughed out loud in appreciation and relief. What remained of his innate wariness was evaporating fast because no woman he had ever yet met could possibly have put less effort into trying to attract him than Holly. Before his engagement and even since it he had been targeted so often by predatory women that he had learned to be guarded in his behaviour around females, both inside and outside working hours. His rare smile flashed across his lean, strong face.

Holly collided involuntarily with molten gold eyes enhanced by thick black lashes and then that truly heart-stopping smile that illuminated his darkly handsome features, and her heart not only bounced in her chest but also skipped an entire beat in reaction. She came to an abrupt halt, her fingers dropping from her rucksack. 'Do you want me to make something to eat?' she offered shakily, struggling to catch her breath.

'No, thanks. I ate before you arrived,' Vito drawled

lazily, watching her shrug back the sweater so that it didn't slip too low at the front. No, she really *wasn't* trying to pull him and he was captivated as he so rarely was by a woman.

'Then you won't mind if *I* eat? I brought supper with me,' she explained, moving past him towards the kitchen.

She's not even going to try to entertain me, Vito reflected, positively rapt in admiration in receipt of that clear demonstration of indifference.

When had he become so arrogant that he expected every young woman he came into contact with to make a fuss of him and a play for him?

It wasn't arrogance, he reasoned squarely. He was as rich as Midas and well aware that that was the main reason for his universal appeal. He poured Holly a fresh glass of wine and carried it into the kitchen for her. She closed the oven, wool stretching to softly define her heart-shaped derrière.

'Do you have a boyfriend?' he heard himself enquire, seemingly before his brain had formed the question, while his attention was still lodged on the sweater that both concealed and revealed her lush curves.

'No. As of today I have an ex,' Holly told him. 'You?'

'I'm single.' Vito lounged back against the kitchen island, the fine fabric of his pants pulling taut to define long, muscular thighs *and*...the noticeable masculine bulge at his crotch. Heat surging into her cheeks, Holly dragged her straying attention off him and stared down at her wine. Since when had she looked at a man *there*? Her breath was snarled up in her throat and her entire body felt super sensitive.

'What happened today?' Vito probed.

'I caught Ritchie having sex with his receptionist on his lunch break,' Holly told him in a rush before she could think better of that humiliating admission. Unfortunately looking at Vito had wrecked her composure to such an extent that she barely knew what she was saying any more.

CHAPTER THREE

IN RECEIPT OF that startling confession, Vito had the most atrocious desire to laugh, but he didn't want to hurt Holly's feelings. Her cheeks had gone all pink again and her eyes were evasive as if that confession had simply slipped accidentally from her lips. He breathed in deep. 'Tough. What did you do?'

'Told him what I thought of him in one sentence, walked out again.' Holly tilted her chin, anger darkening her blue eyes as she remembered the scene she had interrupted. 'I hate liars and cheats.'

'I'm shockingly well behaved in that line. Too busy working,' Vito countered, relieved that she had not a clue about the scandal that had persuaded him to leave Florence and even less idea of who he was. In recent days he had been forced to spend way too much time in the company of people too polite to say what they thought but not too polite to stare at him and whisper. Anonymity suddenly had huge appeal. He finally felt that he could relax.

'So, why are you staying here all alone?' Holly asked, sipping her wine, grateful he had glossed over her gaffe about Ritchie without further comment.

'Burnout. I needed a break from work.' Vito gave

her the explanation he had already decided on in the shower. 'Obviously I wasn't expecting weather like this.'

He was unusually abstracted, however, ensnared by the manner in which the blue of his sweater lit up her luminous eyes. He was also wondering how she could possibly look almost irresistibly cute in an article of his clothing when the thick wool draped her tiny body like a blanket and only occasionally hinted at the treasures that lay beneath. What was the real secret of her appeal? he was asking himself in bewilderment, even though the secret was right in front of him. She had a wonderfully feminine shape, amazing eyes and a torrent of dark hair that tumbled round her shoulders in luxuriant loose curls. But what was most different about Holly was that she was genuine as so few people dared to be. She put on no show and said nothing for effect; indeed she followed a brand of candour that was blunt to the point of embarrassing.

'Why are you staring at me?' Holly asked baldly, straightening her spine and squaring her little shoulders for all the world as though she was bracing herself for him to say something critical.

'Am I?' Vito fielded, riveting dark eyes brimming with amusement as he straightened to leave the kitchen. 'Sorry… I didn't mean to make you uncomfortable.'

He was setting up a games console when Holly joined him with her plate of savoury snacks. 'I thought I'd have a game,' he told her, 'but perhaps you would rather watch TV—'

'No, what game is it?'

It was a war game Holly knew well. 'I'll play you,' she told him.

Vito shot her a startled glance. 'You play?'

'Of course I do. Every foster family had a console and you learned to play with the other kids to fit in,' she pointed out wryly.

'*Dio mio*...how many different families did you live with?'

'I never counted but there were a lot of them. I'd get settled somewhere and then someone somewhere would decide I should have another go at bonding with my mother, and I'd be shot back to her again for a few months.'

Vito was frowning as he set up the game. 'Your mother was still alive?'

'Just not a good parent. It never worked out with her,' Holly completed wryly, keen to gloss over the facts with as little detail as possible while she watched Vito, lean hips flexing down into powerful thighs as he bent down.

From her position kneeling on the floor, she could admire the fluidity of his long-fingered brown hands as he leant over the console. His every movement was incredibly graceful, she acknowledged. And when she glanced up at him she noticed the black density of his eyelashes and the definition that dark luxuriance lent to his already stunning dark eyes. Her nipples were tight little buds inside her bra and she felt hot.

'Your father?' Vito queried.

'I had no idea who my father was so he didn't come into the picture. But my mother still being around was the reason why I moved around so much, because she refused to allow me to be put up for adoption. Every time I went back to my mother and then had to leave her again to go back into care, I ended up with a new foster family.' Holly grimaced and shrugged. 'It was a messy way to grow up.'

Vito had always thought he had it rough with a tyrannical grandfather, warring parents and being an only child on whom huge expectations rested. But his glimpse at what lay on Holly's side of the fence sobered him and gave him an unsettling new perspective. He had always had security and he had always known he was loved. And although Holly had enjoyed neither advantage, she wasn't moaning about it, he thought with grudging appreciation.

As Vito lounged back on the sofa his six-pack abs rippled below the soft cotton stretched over his broad chest and Holly's mouth ran dry. He was amazingly beautifully built and the acknowledgement sent colour surging into her cheeks because she had never looked at a man's body and thought that before. But she couldn't take her eyes off him and it mortified her. It was as if she had been locked back into a teenager's body again because there was nothing sensible or controlled about what she was experiencing.

'We'll set the timer for a ten-minute challenge,' Vito told her lightly, doubting that she would last the game that long.

Fortunately, Holly didn't even have to think while she played him. In dark times the engrossing, mindless games had been her escape from the reality of a life that hurt too much. With the weapon she had picked she made kill after kill on screen and then the challenge was over and she had won.

'You're very fast,' Vito conceded with a slashing grin of appreciation, because once again he could not think of a single woman who, having chosen to play him, would not have then allowed him to win even though she was a better player. Of course that was a debatable point when he didn't actually know any other woman who could play.

'Lots of practice over the years,' Holly conceded, still recovering from the raw charisma of that wolfish grin that cracked right through his essential reserve. Gaming had relaxed him, warmed him up, melted that cool façade he wore to show the real man underneath. And now he didn't just strike her as heartbreakingly handsome, he was downright irresistible. She shifted uneasily in her seat, her body tense and so weirdly super sensitive that even her clothes seemed to chafe her tender skin.

'And the prize is…' Vito's attention locked like a missile to the soft pink fullness of her mouth and her nipples pinched into tight little points. 'You get to put your Christmas tree up.'

Holly sprang off the seat. 'Seriously?' she exclaimed in surprise.

'Seriously.' Vito focused on that sparkling smile and gritted his teeth in a conscious attempt to cool off and quell his hard-on. He didn't know what it was about her but one look from those melting blue eyes and he was hotter than hell. 'Go ahead…' He pinched one of the snacks on her plate by his feet. 'Any more of these?'

Holly laughed. 'I'll put more on before I get the tree sorted.'

Vito watched her rush about full of energy, and suppressed a rueful sigh. It didn't take a lot to make her happy. 'Why does Christmas mean so much to you?'

'I didn't have it when I was very small,' she admitted.

'How can you *not* have Christmas?'

'Mum didn't celebrate it. Well, not in the family sense. There was no tree, no present, nothing. She went out partying but I didn't know what the day was supposed to be until I went into care for the first time.'

Vito frowned. 'And how did that happen?'

Holly hesitated, eyes troubled as her oval face stiffened. 'You know, this is all very personal…'

'I'm curious…I've never met anyone who grew up in care before,' Vito told her truthfully, revelling in every fleeting expression that crossed her expressive little face. She was full to the brim with emotional responses. She was his exact opposite because she felt so much and showed even more. It shook him that he could find that ingenuousness so very appealing in a woman that he was challenged to look away from her.

Holly compressed her lips, those full pink lips with that dainty little cupid's bow that called to him on a far more primitive level. 'When I was six years old, Mum left me alone for three days over Christmas. I went to a neighbour because I was hungry and she called the police.'

Taken aback by that admission, Vito sat up very straight, dark-as-night eyes locked to her as she finished that little speech in an emotive surge. 'Your mother abandoned you?'

'Yes, but eventually she probably would have come back, as she'd done it before. I was put into a short-term foster home and the family gave me Christmas even though it was already over,' Holly told him with a fond smile of remembrance.

'And you've been making up for that loss ever since,' Vito said drily, shrugging off the pangs of sympathy assailing him, taking refuge in edgy cynicism instead. He didn't do emotion, avoiding such displays and feelings whenever he could because the memories of his mother's raw pain in the face of his father's rejections still disturbed him. As far as he was concerned, if you put your feelings out on display you were asking to be kicked in the teeth and it was not a risk he was prepared to take for anyone. Yet just looking at Holly he could tell that she had taken that same risk time and time again.

'Probably. As obsessions go, Christmas is a fairly harmless one,' Holly fielded before she got up to hurry into the kitchen and retrieve the snacks from the oven. After handing him the plate, she returned to winding the fairy lights round the small tree.

He watched the firelight flicker over her, illuminating a rounded cheekbone, a tempting stretch of gleaming thigh as she bent down, and the provocative rise of her curvy behind. 'How old are you, Holly?'

Holly attached an ornament to a branch and glanced over her shoulder at him. As soon as she collided with his spellbinding dark golden eyes, her heart raced, her mouth ran dry and her mind went blank. 'I'm twenty-four…tomorrow.'

Vito's gaze glittered in the firelight. 'It's both Christmas *and* your birthday.'

'Now it's your turn. Tell me about you,' Holly urged with unconcealed eagerness because everything about Vito Sorrentino made her insanely curious.

It should not have been an unexpected question but it hit Vito like a brick and he froze on the reality that having questioned her so thoroughly he could hardly refuse to respond in kind. He breathed in deep, squaring his broad shoulders, fighting his tension. 'I'm the only child of ill-matched parents. Holiday periods when my father was expected to play his part as a family man were always very stressful because he hated being forced to spend time with us. Christmas fell into that category.'

'Why haven't they separated?' He was so on edge talking about his family situation that it touched her heart. Such a beautiful man, so sophisticated and cool in comparison to her, so seemingly together and yet he too bore the damage of a wounding childhood. Holly was fascinated.

'My mother was raised to believe that divorce is wrong…and she loves my father. She's incredibly loyal to the people she loves.' Vito spoke very stiffly because he had never in his life before shared that much about his family dynamics. He had been taught to live by the same code of secretive silence and polite denial that his mother had always observed. Even if the roof was falling in, appearances still had to be conserved. Breaking that code of silence with an outsider filled him with discomfiture.

'That must've put a lot of pressure on you,' Holly remarked, soulful big blue eyes pinned to him with an amount of sympathy far beyond what he considered necessary.

And yet inexplicably there was something in Vito that was warmed by that show of support. He came up off the sofa as though she had yanked a chain attached to his body, and pulled her up into his arms, and in neither of those moves did he recognise conscious thought or decision. It was instinct, pure instinct to reach for Holly.

He tugged her close, long brown fingers flying up to tilt her chin, and gazed down into those inviting clear eyes of hers. A split second later, he kissed her.

In shock, Holly simply stood there, conflicting feelings pulling her in opposing directions. *Push him away, back off* now, one voice urged. *He finds me attractive, find out what it's like*, the other voice pleaded while she brimmed with secret pride. He touched her mouth slow and soft, nipping her lips lightly and teasingly, and she could hardly breathe. Her heart was thumping like a jackhammer inside her ribcage. His tongue eased apart the seam of her lips and flickered and a spasm of raw excitement thrilled down into her pelvis. With a hungry groan he tightened his arms round her.

Nothing had ever tasted as good as Vito's mouth on hers and she trembled in reaction, her whole body awakening. Her hands linked round his neck as the hard, demanding pressure of his mouth sent a delicious heat spiralling down through her. She felt wonderfully warm and safe for the first time ever. In that moment of security she rejoiced in the glorious feel of his mouth and the taste of the wine on his tongue. His fingers splayed to mould to her hips and trailed down the backs of her thighs. Tiny little shivers of response tugged at her as she felt a tightening sensation at her core and her breasts felt achingly full.

Vito lifted his dark head. Dark golden eyes sought hers. 'I want you,' he husked.

'I want you,' Holly framed shakily and it was the very first time she understood the need to say that to someone.

In all the years she had thought about having sex it had always been because sex was expected of her in a relationship, never because she herself was tempted. In the face of those expectations, her body had begun to seem like something to cede, and not fully her own. And that had been wrong, *so* wrong, she finally saw. It should be her choice and her choice alone. But she was learning that only now in Vito's arms and recognising the difference because she was finally experiencing a genuine desire for something more. And it was a heady feeling that left her bemused and giddy.

Staring up into Vito's dark, dangerous eyes, she stretched up on tiptoe to reach him, simply desperate to feel his beautiful mouth on hers again. And the sheer strength of that physical connection, the locking in of every simultaneous sensation that assailed her, only emphasised how right it felt to be with him that way.

This was what all the fuss was about, she thought joyously, the thrumming pulse of need that drove her, the tiny little tremors of desire making her tremble, the overwhelming yearning for the hard, muscular feel of his body against hers. And as one kiss led into another he drew her down onto the rug again and the heat of the fire on her skin burned no more fiercely than the raw hunger raging through her with spellbinding force.

With her willing collusion he extracted her from the sweater and released the catch on her bra. He studied the full globes he had bared with unhidden hunger. 'You have a totally amazing body, *gioia mia*.'

A deep flush lit Holly's cheeks and the colour spread because she was not relaxed about nudity. Yet there in the firelight with Vito looking at her as though he were unveiling a work of art, she was horribly self-conscious but she felt no shame or sense of inadequacy. Indeed, the more Vito looked, the more the pulse of heat humming between her thighs picked up tempo. Long fingers shaping the plump curves of her breasts, Vito flicked a tongue over a straining pink nipple and a hungry groan of appreciation was wrenched from him as he dallied there, toying with her sensitive flesh in a caress that made her hips squirm while a new sense of urgency gripped her.

'Kiss me,' she urged breathlessly as he tugged at the tender buds of her breasts and an arrow of burning heat pierced her feminine core, only increasing her agitation.

He crushed her ripe mouth beneath his again, his tongue plunging deep, and for a split second it satisfied the craving pulling at her, and then somehow even that wasn't enough any more. She shifted position restively, her legs sliding apart to let his hips slide between as she silently, instinctively sought more. Her hips rocked. She wanted and she *wanted*…

And then at last, as if he knew exactly what she needed, he smoothed his passage up a silken inner thigh and tugged off her panties. He stroked her, found the most needy place of all, and a current of almost unbearable excitement shot through Holly's veins. Suddenly in the hold of her own explosive response she was all heat and light and sensation. A long finger tested her slick, damp core and she whimpered, her teeth clenching, the ferocious need clawing cruelly at her as her spine arched, her body all too ready to take charge.

There was no room for thought in the passion that had swept her away in the way she had always dreamed. But it wasn't the same as her dream because what she was feeling was much more basic, much more wild and out of control than she had ever allowed herself to be. He moved to one side, yanking off his top, revealing an abdomen grooved with lean, hard muscle, and her hand slid greedily up over his chest, rejoicing in his sleek bronzed skin and the manner in which every muscle jerked taut the instant she touched him.

'I have no condoms,' Vito bit out in sudden frustration. 'But I had a health check a few weeks ago and I'm clean.'

'I'm on the pill,' Holly framed shakily, belatedly jolted into rational thought by the acknowledgement that she wasn't about to call a halt to their activities. And why was that? She had never wanted anything or anyone the way she wanted him and surely that was the way it was supposed to be? It felt right. *He* felt right.

Vito hauled in a shuddering breath of relief and came back down to her again, tasting her reddened mouth again with devouring appetite. Her hands smoothed over him, caressing every part of him she could reach from his wide brown shoulders to the satin-smooth expanse of his back. Desire drove her like an addictive drug. Beneath his touch she writhed, her reactions pitching her desire higher and higher until the mushroom of liquid-honey heat inside her flared up in ecstasy before spreading to every part of her. She gasped, shaken by an almost out-of-body feeling, her entire being singing with the potent rush of pleasure.

And then she felt him pushing at the heart of her, tilting her back for his entrance and she was wildly impatient, needing more, ready to try anything that he could give her. He filled her completely, thrusting deep with a slick, sure forcefulness that took her by surprise. The bite of pain was an equal surprise and she blinked back tears and sank her teeth into her lower lip, grateful that her face was against his shoulder where he couldn't see her reaction.

'You're incredibly wet and tight,' Vito growled in a roughened undertone. 'It's a hell of a turn-on, *gioia mia*.'

The pinch of discomfort evaporated as he moved

and she arched up to receive him. He vented a groan of all-male satisfaction as she joined in, no longer separate in thought and behaviour. That overpowering hunger kicked back in as his fluid, insistent thrusts filled her with renewed enthusiasm. In fact the wild, sweet rhythm of his sensual possession fired a blinding, pulsing excitement inside her. Locked with his, her body was snatched up into a passionate climax that flooded her with exquisite sensation.

Coiling back from her, Vito saw the blood on her thighs. '*Maledizione*…you're bleeding? Did I hurt you? Why didn't you stop me?'

Brutally summoned back to reality without warning, Holly snaked back from him and hugged her knees in sudden mortification. 'It's all right—'

'No, you being hurt is *not* all right in any way,' Vito shot back at her grimly.

Holly could feel a beetroot-red flush start at her toes and slowly burn up over her whole body. Lifting her head, she clashed reluctantly with glittering dark eyes of angry concern. 'I wasn't hurt…at least not the way you mean,' she explained grudgingly. 'I was a virgin… and obviously there was some physical evidence of it… which I wasn't expecting…'

'A virgin?' Vito exclaimed in raw disbelief. 'You were a *virgin*?'

Snatching up the sweater he had taken off her, Holly pulled it over her again, struggling to slide her arms back into the sleeves. 'Don't make such a big deal of it,' she urged while she was still safely submerged in the wool.

'It *is* a big deal!' Vito grated, springing upright to zip his trousers again and reach for his shirt.

Flushed and uncomfortable, Holly glanced at him

unwillingly. 'Maybe to me but I don't see why it should bother you!'

'Don't you indeed?' Vito riposted.

'No, I don't,' Holly countered on a rising note of anger because his reaction was the very last thing she had expected from him and the topic mortified her.

Dark eyes flashing gold, Vito studied her. 'You should've warned me. Why didn't you?'

Holly stood her ground, her vexation stifling her embarrassment. 'Because it was a private matter and none of your business.'

'Nothing of that nature stays private when you're having sex with someone!'

In discomfited retreat, Holly headed towards the shower room she had used earlier. 'Well, I'll take your word for that since it was my first experience.'

Vito was inflamed by her refusal to understand and chose to be blunt. 'I feel like I took advantage of you!' he admitted harshly.

Holly whirled back at the door. 'That's nonsense. I'm not a kid. My body, my choice.'

Vito snatched in a ragged breath, still reeling from the shock of her innocence. He hadn't told her who he was or indeed anything important about himself. She didn't, *couldn't* understand that in his position he was innately suspicious of anything as unexpected as their encounter and on top of it the very tardy revelation that she was a virgin. With his experience, that revelation had smacked of a possible sting of some kind and he had immediately wondered if she had some kind of hidden agenda. Now gazing into her troubled face, belatedly recognising the hurt and sadness there, he wanted to kick himself for treating her like some sort of scam artist.

'I'm sorry…' Vito breathed abruptly. 'I let my surprise push me into an overreaction, Holly. Of course, it's your choice…'

Some of her tension evaporated but her eyes remained guarded. 'I didn't even think of warning you. And if I *had* thought of it, I probably would've been too embarrassed to mention it.'

'I wrecked the moment,' Vito groaned in acknowledgement. He moved forward to close his arms round her and somehow, even after that uneasy exchange, it felt like the best thing in the world to Holly. Her stiffness slowly ebbing, she rested against him, drinking in the heat and the comfortingly hard, masculine contours of his lean, muscular body against hers. 'I also neglected to tell you that what we shared…it was amazing.'

'You're just saying that,' she mumbled.

'No. It *was* amazing, *cara mia*. Now let's go upstairs and shower,' Vito urged, easing her in a different direction, inexplicably keen to keep her close even though something in his brain was urging him to step back.

Amazing? Was that a polite lie? Just something a man said for the sake of it? He had flipped the situation on its head again and she didn't know how he had achieved that. She blinked in surprise as the lights illuminated a much bigger bedroom than she had expected, airily furnished in stylish tones of grey.

Vito pushed open the door of a very spacious en-suite. 'You first…unless you'd like company in the shower?'

Holly gave him a startled look. 'I don't think I'm ready for that yet.'

Vito laughed in appreciation and bent down to claim her swollen pink mouth with his own in a searing kiss that made every skin cell in her body sit up and take notice. 'I'll ask you again in the morning,' he warned her.

Holly's attention skated to the giant bed. 'We're going to share the bed?'

'There is only one bedroom here. I was planning to take the sofa.'

'No, I won't banish you to the sofa,' Holly breathed with a sudden grin as she slid past him into the en-suite while barely recognising her own thoughts or feelings. She only knew she didn't want him to sleep downstairs on the sofa and away from her. That felt wrong.

She stood in the shower feeling astonishingly light-hearted for a woman who had strayed from values that were as ingrained in her as her usual honesty. But making love with Vito had felt right and it was hard to credit that anything that had felt so natural and right could possibly be wrong. After all, they were both single and nobody was being hurt by their being together. What harm could it possibly do for her to go with the flow for a change in a relationship instead of trying to plan everything or wait for some extraordinary special sign? And why on earth was she feeling guilty about Ritchie when *he* had cheated on *her*?

It wasn't as though she had ever imagined that she was in love with Ritchie. She had only been seeing him for a few weeks and, even though he had been full of himself, he had been good company. Was what she felt with Vito a rebound attraction?

But how could it be? Ritchie couldn't be compared to Vito on any level. Vito utterly overshadowed his predecessor in every way. And just like her secret fantasy,

Vito had swept Holly away in the tide of passion she had always dreamt of experiencing. Of course, it wasn't going anywhere, she reminded herself staunchly, suppressing a pang of sorrow at that acknowledgement. There would be no ongoing relationship with Vito. She didn't need Vito to spell that out. What they had now was time out of time, separate from their normal lives and associations. Attraction had sparked purely because they were stuck together in a snowbound cottage, and she wasn't foolish enough to try and make more of it, was she?

She wrapped a towel round herself rather than put on his sweater again and crept out of the bathroom. Clad only in his jeans, which were unbuttoned at the waistband, Vito was towelling his hair dry. He tossed aside the towel, finger-combing his black hair carelessly off his brow. 'I used the shower downstairs.'

Holly hovered, suddenly awkward. 'I could have done that. This is your room, after all.'

Vito saw the wary uncertainty in her blue eyes and knew he had put it there. Holly was nothing at all like the women he was accustomed to meeting. Nevertheless he had initially judged her by the cynical standards formed by years of experience with such women. Yet he sensed that she would have been very shocked by the scandal that he had been forced to leave behind him. He had wounded her by questioning her innocence yet that same innocence of hers ironically drew him like a beacon. He crossed the room and closed both arms round her, responding to the inbuilt drive to bridge the gap between them. 'Tonight it's *our* room. Let's go to bed…' he urged.

And Holly thought about saying no and heading

down to the sofa. After all, she had broken her own rules and just because she had done that once didn't mean she had an automatic excuse to keep on doing it. Indeed, if having sex with Vito had been a mistake, she was honour-bound to choose the sofa over him.

But sleeping alone wasn't what she wanted and needed right then. She wanted to be with Vito. She wanted to make the most of the time they had together. She was even feeling sensible enough to know that it was fortunate that she wouldn't be with Vito for much longer, for she reckoned that given the opportunity she would fall for him like a ton of bricks. That, of course, would be totally, unforgivably stupid. And she might be a little sentimental, but stupid she was not.

She looked at Vito, even though she knew she really shouldn't, but there he was, etched in her head in an image that would burn for all time, she thought dizzily. He was beautiful, drop-dead beautiful and tonight…tonight he was all *hers…*

CHAPTER FOUR

At dawn, Holly sneaked out of bed and crept into the bathroom to freshen up. She grimaced at her reflection. Her hair was a mess. Her face reddened in places by Vito's stubble. Her mouth was very swollen and pink. And when she stepped into the shower she swallowed a groan because every muscle she possessed complained as if she had overdone it in a workout.

But no workout, she thought dizzily, could possibly have been more demanding than the stamina required for a night in bed with Vito Sorrentino. He was insatiable and he had made her the same way, she conceded in stupefaction. She felt as though she had changed dramatically in less than twelve hours. She had learned so much about herself and even more about sex. Her body ached in intimate places and a bemused smile tilted her lips as she emerged from the en-suite again.

Vito was sprawled across the bed, a glorious display of bronzed perfection. Luxuriant black lashes flickered as he focused on her. 'I wondered where you were,' he muttered.

'Bathroom,' she whispered, barely breathing as she slid back under the duvet.

Vito reached for her with a sleepy hand and pulled

her back against him. She shivered in contact with the raw heat and scent of him. 'Go back to sleep,' he told her thickly.

He wanted her again. What the hell was wrong with him? How could he want her again when he had already had her so many times? She had to be sore too, he reminded himself in exasperation. He was being a selfish bastard. As soon as he heard the deep, even tenor of her breathing sink into sleep, he eased out of the bed, went for a cold shower and got dressed.

Nothing in Vito's mental rule book covered what had happened the night before. He hadn't had a one-night stand in many years and none had been extraordinary on any level. Sex was sex, a temporary release and pleasure. He was practical about sex, cool about sex. His desire had never controlled him and he would never let it do so. But then he had never ever been intimate with a woman he wanted over and over again, and his voracious hunger for Holly even after having her downright unnerved him. What was wrong with him? Was he in some weird frame of mind after the trying ordeal of the publicity fallout he had endured over the past week? In his opinion it certainly wasn't normal to want a woman *that* much. It smacked of unbalance, of unhealthy obsession. It was fortunate that their time together had a built-in closing date, he told himself grimly.

Even so, it was Christmas Day as well as being Holly's birthday and it bothered him that he had nothing to give her. Vito was so accustomed to gift-giving and other people's high expectations of his gifts that he felt very uncomfortable in that situation. In an effort to make the day special for Holly he decided to make her breakfast in bed. He couldn't cook but how difficult could it be to make breakfast? He could manage orange juice and toast, couldn't he?

Holly was stunned when she blinked into drowsy wakefulness because Vito was sliding a tray of food on to her lap. She stared down in wonderment at the charred toast. 'You made me breakfast?'

'It's your birthday. It's not much but it's the best I can do.'

Holly tried not to look at him as though he were the eighth wonder of the world but that was certainly how he struck her at that moment because nobody had ever given Holly breakfast in bed before, no, not even when she was ill. It was a luxury she could barely even imagine and that Vito should have gone to that much effort to spoil her thrilled her. So, she didn't make a sound when her first sip of tea gave her a mouthful of the teabag that had not been removed and she munched through the charred toast without complaint. It was the thought that counted, after all, and that Vito *had* thought touched her heart. In addition, the effect of having Vito carelessly sprawled at the foot of the same bed sent her pulse rate rocketing. She remembered all the things they had done and tried desperately to feel guilty about them. But it didn't work. One look into those inky-black-lashed dark golden eyes of his and she was shot off to another planet.

'Thanks,' she said even though it took great effort to locate her voice.

'I'm not great in the kitchen. If it had only been for me I would have cooked one of the ready meals,' he admitted.

'It was very thoughtful of you.' Holly was registering how very lucky she was not to be facing roast meat for breakfast and she gratefully drank her orange juice, which was so cold it froze her teeth. As she drained the glass she pushed the tray away and he swept it up and put it on the floor.

He came back to the bed and moved towards her with the sinuous grace of a stalking cat and her mouth ran dry, her heartbeat racing. 'I was going to get up, organise lunch,' she framed shakily.

'Way too early for that, *bellezza mia*,' Vito husked, up close, his breath fanning her cheek and his luxuriant black hair brushing her chin as he bent his head to press his mouth to the pulse point below her ear.

And her whole body went into free fall as though he had hit a button. Breath fled her parted lips as she sank back into the pillows and gazed up at him with luminous blue eyes. 'Vito—'

He closed her mouth with the onslaught of his own. 'No, we don't talk,' he told her after kissing her breathless. 'We already know all we need to know about each other.'

'I don't even know what you do,' she began.

'I'm in business…and you?'

'Waitress…well, waitress with aspirations,' she adjusted jerkily when he tensed against her. 'I want to be an interior designer but it's more a dream than reality.'

'It takes work to turn dreams into reality.'

Holly smiled up at him. 'Vito… I've had to work hard for everything in life but sometimes getting a break relates more to resources and luck than slaving away.'

'This is getting way too serious,' Vito objected when he found himself on the brink of offering her advice.

Holly let her fingers drift up to brush his black hair off his brow, her attention locked to his lean, darkly handsome features even as her heart had sunk because she was scarily well attuned to his body language. 'Agreed. Let's stay away from the real world.'

His long, lean body relaxed against hers again and tears stung her eyes as she blinked against his shoulder. The news that she was a waitress had been too sharp a stab of reality for Vito, highlighting as it did the difference in their statuses. His clothing, even the variety and expense of the food in the refrigerator, not to mention the stylish opulence of her surroundings all told Holly that Vito inhabited a rather more privileged place in society than she did. And while here at the cottage without other people around, that difference didn't really matter. She knew it would matter very much outside these walls.

'I still want you,' Vito confided thickly, running the tip of his tongue along her collarbone.

Her tummy flipped, her feminine core clenched and she stiffened. Reality was intruding whether she wanted it to or not because she was too tender to engage again in the kind of intimacy he was probably envisaging. 'I can't,' she whispered tightly, a small hand smoothing down a denim-clad thigh, feeling the ripple of his muscles tightening in response.

'Maybe later,' Vito murmured sibilantly, fingers spearing into her hair to lift her mouth to his. 'But in the short term there are other things we can do, *gioia mia*.'

Holly laughed and buried her face in his shoulder. 'You're so shameless.'

'Why wouldn't I be? You've been brilliant. I can't understand why you were still untouched.'

'It was a promise I made to myself when I was very young…to wait. It just seemed sensible to wait until I was an adult and then…' Holly sighed. 'Somewhere along the line it became a burden, a tripwire in relationships that held me back from who I could be.'

Vito gazed down at her with a frown of incomprehension. 'But why me? Why did you choose me?'

'Maybe it was because you let me put my Christmas tree up,' she teased, because there were all too many reasons why she had chosen him and very few she was prepared to share. There was no safe way to tell a man that he had been her fantasy without him getting the wrong idea and assuming that she was feeling more than she was supposed to feel in terms of attachment.

Her fingers slid up caressingly to the firm bulge at his crotch and exerted gentle pressure and he groaned, dark head falling back, wide sensual mouth tightening, his broad chest vibrating against her. Holly leant over him, staring down into lustrous eyes that glittered like precious gold. 'Maybe it's because you act as though I'm the most ravishing female you've ever met, even though I'm perfectly ordinary. But perhaps that's your true talent. Maybe you treat all women the same way.'

'No. I've never been with any woman the way I've been with you…' Vito surveyed her with frowning force, probing that statement, worrying about it because it was true. He had never felt so comfortable with a woman or so relaxed. He hadn't once thought about work or about the shocking scandal he had left behind him in Italy. Furthermore Holly was completely unique on his terms because for the first time ever he was with a woman who didn't know who he was, cherished no financial expectations and in truth attached no undue importance to him. He was Mr Anonymous with Holly and he liked the freedom of that one hell of a lot.

Holly unzipped his jeans with a sense of adventure.

Her most driving need was to give him pleasure and she didn't understand it. Shouldn't she be more selfish? The catch in his breathing was followed by a long, unrestrained sound of rising hunger. She had distracted him with sex, she thought guiltily. She didn't want to talk about being a waitress, about any of the things that separated them as people in the outside world, and his unashamed sexual response to her gave her a shocking sense of power.

Heaven for Vito was the gentle friction of her mouth and the teasing, erotic stroke of her tiny fingers. His hand knotted in her hair and he trembled on the edge of release, gruffly warning her, but she didn't pull away. Then the sheer liberating wash of pleasure engulfed him and wiped him out.

Holly watched Vito sleep with a rueful grin. She went for another shower, donned the dress she had packed and dried her hair. Downstairs, she switched on the television and tuned it to a channel playing Christmas carols before going into the kitchen and beginning to organise the lunch she had prepared with such care. It shook her to acknowledge that she hadn't even known Vito Sorrentino existed the day before.

The shame and embarrassment she had fought off at dawn began to creep up again through the cracks in her composure. She had broken all her rules and for what? A one-night stand with a male she would probably never hear from or see again? How could she be proud of that? But would it have been any better to lose her virginity with a sleazy, cheating liar like Ritchie, who had pretended that she meant much more to him than she did?

She thought not. Anyway, it was too late for regrets, she reminded herself unhappily. What was done was done and it made more sense to move on from that point than to torture herself over what could not be changed. How much, though, had all the wine she had imbibed contributed to her recklessness? Her loss of inhibition? *Stop it, stop it*, she urged herself fiercely, *stop dwelling on it.*

Vito came down the stairs when she was setting the table. 'You should have wakened me.'

'You were up much earlier than I was,' she pointed out as she retrieved the starters from the kitchen. 'Hungry?'

Vito reached for her instead of a chair. 'Only for you.'

Her bright blue eyes danced with merriment. 'Now, where did you get that old chestnut from?'

In answer Vito bent his tousled dark head and kissed her and it was like an arrow of fire shooting through her body to the heart of her. She quivered, taken aback all over again by the explosive effect he had on her. His sensual mouth played with hers and tiny ripples of arousal coursed through her. Her breasts swelled, their buds tightening while heat and dampness gathered between her legs. It took enormous willpower but she made herself step back from him, almost careening into the table in her haste to break their connection. Suddenly feeling out of control with him seemed dangerous and it *was* dangerous, she told herself, if it made her act out of character. And whether she liked it or not, everything she had done with Vito was out of character for her.

'We should eat before the food gets cold,' she said prosaically.

'I'll open a bottle of wine.'

'This is an incredibly well-equipped house,' Holly

remarked as he poured the wine he had fetched from the temperature-controlled cabinet in the kitchen.

'The owner enjoys his comforts.'

'And he's your friend?'

'We went to school together.' A breathtaking smile of amused recollection curled Vito's mouth. 'He was a rebel and although he often got me into trouble he also taught me how to enjoy myself.'

'Pixie's like that. We're very close.' Holly lifted the plates and set out the main course.

'You're a good cook,' Vito commented.

'My foster mother, Sylvia, was a great teacher. Cooking relaxes me.'

'I eat out a lot. It saves time.'

'There's more to life than saving time. Life is there to be savoured,' Holly told him.

'I savour it at high speed.'

The meal was finished and Holly was clearing up when Vito stood up. 'I feel like some fresh air,' he told her. 'I'm going out for a walk.'

From the window, Holly watched him trudge down the lane in the snow. There was an odd tightness in her chest and a lump in her constricted throat. Vito had just rebelled against their enforced togetherness to embrace his own company. He hadn't invited her to join him on his walk, but why should he have? Out of politeness? They weren't a couple in the traditional sense and he didn't have to include her in everything. They were two people who had shared a bed for the night, two *very* different people. Maybe she talked too much, maybe he was tired of her company and looking forward to the prospect of some silence. It was not a confidence-boosting train of thought.

Vito ploughed up the steep gradient, his breath steaming on the icy air. He had needed a break, had been relieved when Holly hadn't asked if she could accompany him. A loner long accustomed to his own company, he had felt the walls closing in while he'd sat surrounded by all that cosy Christmas spirit.

And that really wasn't Holly's fault, Vito conceded wryly. Even her cheerful optimism could not combat the many years of bad Christmas memories that Vito harboured. Sadly the stresses and strains of the festive season were more likely to expose the cracks in an unhappy marriage. His mother's resolute enthusiasm had never contrived to melt his father's boredom and animosity at being forced into spending time with his family.

They had never been a family, Vito acknowledged heavily, not in the truest sense of the word. His father had never loved him, had never taken the smallest interest in him. In fact, if he was honest with himself, his father sincerely disliked him. From an early age Vito had been treated like the enemy, twinned in his father's mind with the autocratic father-in-law he fiercely resented.

'He's like a bloody calculator!' Ciccio had condemned with distaste when his five-year-old son's brilliance at maths was remarked on. 'He'll be as efficient as a cash machine—just like his grandfather.'

Only days earlier, Vito's relationship with his father had sunk to an all-time low when Ciccio had questioned his son's visit to the hospital where he was recovering from his heart attack. 'Are you here to crow over my downfall?' his father had asked nastily while his mother had tried to intervene. 'My sins have deservedly caught up with me? Is that what you think?'

And Vito had finally recognised that there was no relationship left to rescue with his father. Ciccio bitterly resented his son's freedom from all financial constraints yet the older man's wild extravagance and greed had forced Vito's grandfather to keep his son-in-law on a tight leash. There was nothing Vito could do to change those hard facts. Even worse, after his grandfather had died it had become Vito's duty to protect his mother's fortune from Ciccio's demands, scarcely a reality likely to improve a father and son relationship.

For the first time Vito wondered what sort of relationship he would have with his son if he ever had one. Momentarily he was chilled by the prospect because his family history offered no encouragement.

Holly had just finished clearing up the dishes when the knocker on the front door sounded loudly. She was stunned when she opened the door and found Bill, who ran the breakdown service, standing smiling on the doorstep.

'I need the keys for Clementine to get her loaded up.'

'But it's Christmas Day… I mean, I wasn't expecting—'

'I didn't want to raise your hopes last night but I knew I'd be coming up this way some time this afternoon. My uncle joins us for lunch and he owns a smallholding a few fields away. He has to get back to feed his stock, so I brought the truck when I left him at home.'

'Thank you so much,' Holly breathed, fighting her consternation with all her might while turning away to reach into the pocket of her coat where she had left the car keys. She passed the older man the keys. 'Do you need any help?'

He shook his head. 'I'll come back up for you when I'm done.'

'I'll get my stuff together.' With a weak smile and with every sensitive nerve twanging, Holly shut the door again and sped straight upstairs to gather her belongings. She dug her feet into her cowboy boots and thrust her toiletries and make-up bag back into her rucksack.

And throughout that exercise she wouldn't let herself even think that she could be foolish enough to be disappointed at being picked up and taken home. Clearly, it was time to *leave*. She had assumed that she would have one more night with Vito but fate had decreed otherwise. Possibly a quick, unexpected exit was the best way to part after such a night, she thought unhappily. There would be neither the time nor the opportunity for awkward exchanges. She closed her rucksack and checked the room one last time. Reminding herself that she still had to pack the Christmas tree, she went back down wondering anxiously if Vito would make it back before she had to leave.

She flipped open her cardboard box and stripped the tree of ornaments and lights, deftly packing it all away while refusing to think beyond the practical. She raced into the kitchen to dump the foil containers she had used to transport the meal, pausing only to lift a china jug and quickly wash it before placing it in the box. That was that then, all the evidence of her brief stopover removed, she conceded numbly.

She didn't want to go home, she didn't *want* to leave Vito, and the awareness of that stupid, hopeless sense of attachment to him crushed and panicked her. He would probably be relieved to find her gone and he would have cringed if he saw tears in her eyes. Men didn't like messy and there could be nothing more messy or embarrassing than a woman who got too involved and tried to cling after one night. *This one-night-and-walk-away stuff is what you signed up for,* Holly scolded herself angrily. There had been no promises and no mention of a future of any kind. She would leave with her head held high and no backward glances.

All the same, she thought hesitantly, if Vito wasn't coming back in time to see her leave, shouldn't she leave a note? She dug into her rucksack and tore a piece of paper out of a notebook and leant on the table. She thanked him for his hospitality and then hit a brick wall in the creative department. What else was there to say? What else *could* she reasonably say?

After much reflection she printed her mobile-phone number at the foot of the note. Why not? It wasn't as if she was asking him to phone her. She was simply giving him the opportunity to phone if he wanted to. Nothing wrong with that, was there? She left the note propped against the clock on the shelf inside the inglenook.

Holly wore a determined smile when Bill's truck backed into the drive. She had her box and her rucksack on the step beside her in a clear face-saving statement that she was eager to get going but there was still no sign of Vito. She climbed into the truck with a sense of regret but gradually reached the conclusion that possibly it was preferable to have parted from Vito without any awkward or embarrassing final conversation. This way, nobody had to pretend or say anything they didn't mean.

Vito strode into the cottage and grimaced at the silence. He strode up the stairs, calling Holly's name while wondering if she had gone for a bath. He studied the empty bathroom with a frown, noting that she had removed her possessions. Only when he went downstairs again did he notice that the Christmas decorations had disappeared along with her. The table was clear, the kitchen immaculate.

Vito was incredulous. Holly had done a runner and he had no idea how. He walked out onto the doorstep and belatedly registered that the old car no longer lay at the foot of the lane in the ditch. So much for his observation powers! He had been so deep in his thoughts that he hadn't even noticed that the car had gone. Holly had walked out on him. Well, that hadn't happened to him before, he acknowledged grimly, his ego stung by her sudden departure. All his life women had chased after Vito, attaching strings at the smallest excuse.

But would he have wanted her to *cling*? Vito winced, driven to reluctantly admit that perhaps in the circumstances her unannounced disappearance was for the best. After all, what would he have said to her in parting? Holly had distracted him from more important issues and disrupted his self-control. Now he had his own space back and the chance to get his head clear. And that was exactly what he should want…

'When you're finished throwing up you can do the test,' Pixie said drily from the bathroom doorway.

'I'm not doing the test,' Holly argued. 'I'm on the pill. I *can't* be pregnant—'

'You missed a couple of pills *and* you had a course of antibiotics when you had tonsillitis,' her friend and flatmate reminded her. 'You know that antibiotics can interfere with contraception—'

'Well, actually I *didn't* know.' Holly groaned as she

freshened up at the sink, frowning at her pale face and dark-circled eyes. She looked absolutely awful and she felt awful both inside and out.

'Even the pill has a failure rating. I don't know…I leave you alone for a few weeks and you go completely off the rails,' the tiny blonde lamented, studying Holly with deeply concerned eyes.

'I can't be pregnant,' Holly said again as she lifted the pregnancy testing kit and extracted the instructions.

'Well, you've missed two periods, you're throwing up like there's no tomorrow and you have sore boobs,' Pixie recounted ruefully. 'Maybe it's chickenpox or something.'

'All right, I'll do it!' Holly exclaimed in frustration. 'But there is no way, just no way on earth that I could be pregnant!'

Some minutes later she slumped down on the side of the bath. Pixie was right and she was wrong. The test showed a positive. The door opened slowly and she looked wordlessly up at her friend and burst into floods of tears.

'Remember how we used to say that the babies we had would be precious gifts?' Pixie breathed as she hugged her sobbing friend. 'Well, this baby is a gift and we *will* manage. We don't need a man to survive.'

'I can't even knit!' Holly wailed, unable to concentrate, unable to think beyond the sheer immensity of the challenges she was about to face.

'That's OK. You won't have time to knit,' her friend told her, deadpan.

Holly was remembering when she and Pixie had talked innocently about their ideal of motherhood. Both of them had been born unwanted and had suffered at the hands of neglectful mothers. They had sworn that they would love and protect their own babies no matter what.

And the vague circumstances suggested by 'no matter what' had actually happened now, Holly reflected heavily, her sense of regret at that truth all-encompassing. Her baby would not be entering the perfect world as she had dreamt. Her baby was unplanned, however, but *not* unwanted. She would love her child, fight to keep him or her safe and if she had to do it alone, and it looked as though she would, she *would* manage.

'If only Vito had phoned…' The lament escaped Holly's lips before she could bite it back and she flushed in embarrassment.

'He's long gone. In fact, the more I think about him,' Pixie mused tight-mouthed, 'the more suspicious I get about the father of your child. For all you know he could be a married man.'

'No!' Holly broke in, aghast at that suggestion.

'Well, what was Vito doing spending Christmas alone out in the middle of nowhere?' Pixie demanded. 'Maybe the wife or girlfriend threw him out and he had nowhere better to go?'

'Don't make me feel worse than I already do,' Holly pleaded. 'You're such a pessimist, Pixie. Just because he didn't want to see me again doesn't make him a bad person.'

'He got you drunk and somehow persuaded you into bed. Don't expect me to think nice things about him. He was a user.'

'I *wasn't* drunk.'

'Let's not rehash it again.' Her flatmate sighed, her piquant face thoughtful. 'Let's see if we can trace him online.'

And while Pixie did internet searches on several potential spellings of Vito's surname and came up with precisely nothing, Holly sat on the sofa hugging her still-flat stomach and fretting about the future. She had already secretly carried out all those searches weeks earlier on Vito and was too proud to admit to the fact, even to her friend.

'I can't find even a trace of a man in the right age group. The name could be a fake,' her friend opined.

'Why would he give me a fake name? That doesn't make sense.'

'Maybe he didn't want to be identified. I don't know…you tell me,' Pixie said very drily. 'Do you think that's a possibility?'

Holly reddened. Of course it was a possibility that Vito had not wanted to be identified. As to why, how could she know? The only thing she knew with certainty was that Vito had decided he didn't want to see her again. Had he felt otherwise, he would have used the phone number she had left him and called her. In the weeks of silence that had followed her departure from the cottage, she had often felt low. But that was foolish, wasn't it? Vito had clearly made the decision that he had no desire to see her again.

And why should she feel hurt by that? Yes, he had said that night with her was amazing but wasn't that par for the course? The sort of thing a man thought a woman expected him to say after sex? How could she have been naive enough to actually believe that Vito had truly believed they were something special together? And now that little bit of excitement was over. What was done was done and what was gone, like her innocence, was gone. Much as her tidy, organised life had gone along with it, she conceded unhappily, because, although she would embrace motherhood wholeheartedly, she knew it would be incredibly tough to raise a baby alone without falling into the poverty trap.

CHAPTER FIVE

Fourteen months later

HOLLY SUPPRESSED A groan as she straightened her aching back. She hated parcelling up the unsold newspapers at the end of her evening shift in the local supermarket but it also meant she would be going home soon and seeing Angelo snugly asleep in his cot.

Picturing her son's little smiling face made her heart swell inside her. There was nothing Holly wouldn't do for her baby. The minute she had laid eyes on Angelo after his premature birth she had adored him with a fierce, deep love that had shaken her to the roots.

Without Pixie's help she would have struggled to survive, but, fortunately for Holly, her friend had supported her from the start. When waitressing had become impossible, Holly had taken a course to become a registered childminder and now by day she looked after her baby and two other children at home. She also worked in the shop on a casual basis. If evening or weekend work came up and Pixie was free to babysit, Holly did a shift to earn some extra cash.

And it was right then when she was thinking about how much she was looking forward to supper and her bed that it happened: she looked down at the bundle of newspapers she was tying up and saw a photograph on the front page of a man who reminded her of Vito. She stopped dead and yanked out the paper to shake it open. It was a financial broadsheet that she would never normally have even glanced at and the picture showed a man standing behind a lectern, a man who bore a remarkable resemblance to the father of her son.

'Are you nearly done, Holly?' one of her co-workers asked from the doorway.

'Almost.' Her shoulders rigid with tension, Holly was frantically reading the italicised print below the photograph. Vittore Zaffari, not Sorrentino. It was a man who resembled Vito—that was all. Her shoulders dropped again but just as she was about to put the newspaper back in the pile she hesitated and then extracted that particular page. Folding it quickly, she dug it into the pocket of her overall and hurriedly finished setting out the newspapers for collection.

It was after midnight before Holly got the chance to check out Vittore Zaffari online. Holly had studied the photograph again and again. He looked like her Vito but the newsprint picture wasn't clear enough for her to be certain. But the instant she did a search on Vittore Zaffari the images came rolling in and she knew without a doubt that she had finally identified her child's father.

'My word,' Pixie groaned, performing her own search on her tablet. 'Now I know why he gave you a fake name and was hiding out on Dartmoor. He was involved in some drugs-and-sex orgy. Hold on while I get this document translated into English.'

'Drugs and sex?' Holly repeated sickly. '*Vito?* It can't be the same man!'

But it was. The photos proved that he was *her* Vito, not some strange lookalike character. Of course, he had never been hers even to begin with, Holly reminded herself doggedly. And it was two in the morning before the two women finished digging up unwelcome facts about Vito, the billionaire banker ditched by his fabulously beautiful blonde fiancée only days before Holly had met him.

'Of course, you don't need to concern yourself with any of that nonsense,' Pixie told her ruefully. 'All you want from him now is child support and he seems to be wealthy enough that I shouldn't think that that will be a big deal.'

Holly lay sleepless in her bed, tossing and turning and at the mercy of her emotions. Vito had lied to her by deliberately giving her a false name. He too had been on the rebound but he hadn't mentioned that either. How would he react when she told him that he was a father? And did she really want to expose her infant son to a drug-abusing, womanising father? The answer to that was a very firm no. No amount of money could make a parent who was a bad influence a good idea.

But that really wasn't for her to decide, she reasoned over breakfast while she spooned baby rice into Angelo, who had a very healthy appetite. She studied her son with his coal-black curls and sparkling brown eyes. He was a happy baby, who liked to laugh and play, and he was very affectionate. Vito had been much more reserved, slow to smile and only demonstrative in bed. Holly winced at that unwelcome recollection. Regardless, Vito had a right to know that he was a father and in the same way she had a right to his financial help. She had to stop considering their situation from the personal angle because that only muddied the waters and upset her.

Angelo was the main issue. Everything came back to her son. Set against Angelo's needs, her personal feelings had no relevance. She had to be practical for his benefit and concentrate on what *he* needed. And the truth was that financially she was really struggling to survive and her baby was having to do without all the extras that he might have enjoyed. That was wrong. Her son didn't deserve to suffer because she had made a bad choice.

On the other hand, if Vito truly was the sort of guy who got involved in sex-and-drug orgies, he wasn't at all the male she had believed him to be. How could she have been so wrong about a man? She had honestly believed that Vito was a decent guy.

Even so, he was still Angelo's father and that was important. She was very much aware of just how much she had longed to know who her own father was. There was no way she could subject Angelo to living in the same ignorance. Nor could she somehow magically estimate whether Vito would be a good or bad influence on his son. The bottom line was that Angelo had the right to know who his father was so that he did not grow up with the same uncertainty that Holly had been forced to live with.

Holly acknowledged the hurt she had felt when Vito failed to make use of her phone number and contact her. Naturally her pride had been wounded and she had been disappointed. No woman wanted to feel that forgettable, but Angelo's birth had cast a totally different light on her situation. She had to forget her resentment and hurt and move on while placing her son's needs first. That would be a tall order but she believed that she loved her son enough to do it. She had to face Vito in the flesh and tell him that he was a father.

One week later, Holly handed over her package to the receptionist on the top floor of the Zaffari Bank in London. 'It's for Mr Zaffari. I would like to see him.'

The elegant receptionist set the small parcel down on the desktop and reached for something out of view. 'Mr Zaffari's appointments are fully booked weeks in advance, Miss…er…?'

'Cleaver. I believe he will want to see me,' Holly completed quietly while she wondered if that could possibly be true. 'I'll just wait over there until he's free.'

'There's really no point in you waiting,' the receptionist declared curtly, rising from her chair as two security guards approached. 'Mr Zaffari doesn't see anyone without a prior appointment.'

Stubbornly ignoring that assurance, Holly walked over to the waiting area and sat down, tugging her stretchy skirt down over her thighs. It had taken massive organisation for Holly to make a day trip to London but she knew that if she wanted to confront Vito she had to take advantage of his current presence in the UK. Her internet snooping had revealed that he was giving a speech at some fancy banking dinner that very evening and was therefore highly likely to be at the Zaffari Bank HQ throughout the day. Pixie had taken a day off to look after Angelo, and the children Holly usually minded were with their grandparents instead.

Holly had made a very early start to her day and had been appalled by the price of the train fare. Pixie had urged her to dress up to see Vito but, beyond abandoning her usual jeans and putting on a skirt with the knee boots Pixie had given her for Christmas, Holly had made no special effort. Why? As she continually reminded herself, this wasn't a *personal* visit and she wasn't trying to impress Vito. She was here to tell him about Angelo and that was all. Her restive fingers fiddled with the zip on her boots while she watched the two security guards carrying off her parcel with the absurdly cautious air of men who feared they could be carrying a bomb. Did she look like a terrorist? Like some kind of a madwoman?

Vito was in a board meeting and when his PA entered and slid a small package in front of him, which had already been unwrapped, he frowned in incomprehension, but when he pulled back the paper and saw the Santa hat and the small sprig of holly, he simply froze and gave his PA a shaken nod of immediate acceptance. Interrupting the proceedings to voice his apologies, he stood up, his cool dark eyes veiled.

What the hell was Holly doing here at the bank? Why now? And how had she tracked him down?

Hearing about that night, Apollo had scoffed. *With all your options you settled for a stranger? Are you crazy? You're one of the most eligible bachelors in the world and you picked up some random woman? A* waitress*?* he had scoffed in a tone of posh disbelief.

In fact, Apollo's comments had annoyed Vito so much that he had fiercely regretted confiding in his friend. He had told himself that it was for the best that Holly had walked away without fanfare, freeing them both from the threat of an awkward parting. He had also reminded himself that attempting to repeat a highly enjoyable experience invariably led to disappointment.

With the information he had had he could have traced her but he had resisted the urge with every atom of discipline he possessed. Self-control was hugely important to Vito and Holly had obliterated his self-control. He remembered that he had acted oddly with her and that memory made him uncomfortable. Even so he still hadn't forgotten her. In fact he was eager to see her because his memories of her had lingered to the extent that he had become disturbingly indifferent to other women and more particular than ever in his choices. He *wanted* to see Holly in full daylight, shorn of the schmaltzy sparkle of the festive season. He was suddenly convinced that such a disillusionment would miraculously knock him back to normality.

But why the hell would Holly be seeking him out now so long after the event? And in person rather than more tactfully by phone? And how had she linked him to the Zaffari Bank? Black brows lowering over cold dark eyes suddenly glittering with suspicion, Vito strode back into his office to await his visitor without an appointment.

Holly smiled and stood up when the receptionist approached her. In spite of her apprehension, Vito *had* remembered her and she was relieved. The Santa hat had been designed to jog his memory. After all, a male who indulged in sex parties might well not recall one night with an ordinary woman from over a year earlier. When it came to a question of morals he was a total scumbag, Holly reminded herself doggedly while walking down the corridor after another woman—even more thin and elegant—had asked her to follow her. She wondered why the other people working there seemed to be peering out of their offices in her direction and staring.

Suddenly she wondered what she was doing. Did she really want a man of Vito's dissolute proclivities in her life and Angelo's? Common sense warned her not to make snap judgements and to give Vito a chance for Angelo's sake. Her son would want to know who his dad was. Hadn't she wondered all her life who had fathered her? Hadn't that made her insecure? Made her feel less of a person than others because she didn't know that most basic fact about herself? No, Angelo deserved access to the truth of his parentage right from the start and that was what Holly would ensure her son had, no matter how unpleasant seeing Vito again proved to be.

Vito was a total scumbag, Holly reminded herself afresh while wondering why she was experiencing the strangest sense of...*elation.* Why was her heart pounding and her adrenaline buzzing? Her guide opened a door and stood back for her to enter. My goodness, he had a big office, *typical scumbag office*, she rephrased mentally. She would not be impressed; she *refused* to be impressed. And then Vito strode in through a side door and she was paralysed to the carpet because he simply looked so drop-dead amazing that she could not believe that she had ever slept with him and that he was the father of her child.

Her mouth ran dry. She felt dizzy. Butterflies danced in her tummy as she focused on those lean, darkly handsome features, and she knew that Pixie would have kicked her hard. *Total scumbag*, she told herself, but her brain would not engage with that fact and was much more interested in opening a back catalogue on Vito's sheer perfection. *To look at—perfect to* look *at*, she rephrased doggedly, striving to get back to the scumbag awareness. *Drugs...sex with hookers*, she fired at herself in desperation.

'The hat and the holly were an original calling card,' Vito drawled, the dark, deep accent tautening every muscle in her already tense body. 'But I *did* remember your name. I didn't need the prompt.'

Holly turned the red-hot colour of a tomato because she hadn't expected him to grasp the reasoning behind her introduction that easily.

'It would have been much easier to phone me,' Vito assured her silkily.

'And how could I have done that without your phone number?' Holly asked stiffly, because she was determined to make no reference to the fact that she had left her phone number with him and that he had decided not to make use of it. Discussing that would be far, far too humiliating.

'Well, maybe you shouldn't have run out on me before I got back to the cottage that day.' Vito smiled suddenly, brilliantly. It almost stopped her heart dead in its tracks as she stared at him. But it had not sat well with Vito that a night he had considered exceptional should have meant so much less to her that she'd walked out without a backward glance. Her reappearance satisfied him. He now felt free to study her with acute appreciation. She was wearing the most ordinary garments: a sweater, a shortish skirt, a jacket and boots, all black and all unremarkable but the glorious hourglass curves he cherished could not be concealed. His dark eyes flamed gold over the swell of her breasts below the wool and the lush curve of her hips before flying up to her full pink mouth, little snub nose and huge blue eyes. Shorn of the schmaltz and the sparkle and in full daylight, Holly was passing the test he had expected her to fail and for the first time in Vito's life, failure actually tasted sweet. He shifted almost imperceptibly as the hot swell of an erection assailed him and he almost smiled at that as well because his diminished libido had seriously bothered him.

'How did you find out who I was?' Vito enquired.

'Yes, that's right…you *lied.* You gave me a false name,' Holly was prompted to recall as she struggled to fight free of the spell he cast over her just by being in the same room.

'It wasn't a false name. I didn't lie. I was christened Vittore Sorrentino Zaffari,' he told her, smooth as glass. 'Sorrentino was my father's surname.'

That smoothness set Holly's teeth on edge. 'You lied,' she said again. 'You deliberately misled me. What I don't understand is why you did that.'

'You must appreciate that I am very well known in the business world. I prefer to be discreet. You coming here today in such a manner…' Vito shifted fluid brown fingers in an expressive dismissive gesture. 'That *was* indiscreet.' From his inside pocket he withdrew a business card and presented it to her. 'My phone number.'

Holly put the card into her jacket pocket because she didn't know what else to do with it. Indiscreet? Coming to see him in the flesh was indiscreet?

Dark golden eyes fringed by inky black, unfairly long lashes surveyed her and her tummy flipped, her heart rate increasing. 'Holly…I have the feeling that you don't understand where I'm going with this but I must be frank. I like to keep my private life *private*. I certainly do not want it to intrude when I'm at the bank. My working hours are sacrosanct.'

My word, he was literally telling her off for approaching him at his place of work, for coming to see him where other people would see her and notice her. A sense of deep humiliation pierced Holly because it had taken so much courage for her to come and confront him with the news she had. His case was not helped by the reality that she had seen a photo of him and his ex-fiancée, Marzia, posing outside the Zaffari Bank in Florence. Evidently, Marzia had enjoyed such privileges because she was someone he was *proud* to be seen with in public. Holly just could not get over Vito's nerve in daring to talk to her like that. Did he really think she was the sort of woman who would let a man talk down to her?

Her blue eyes widened and raked over him but it was pointless to try and put him down that way because she couldn't see a single flaw in his appearance. His dark grey suit fitted him like a tailored glove, outlining his height, breadth and long, powerful legs. And looking at him inevitably sent shards of mortifying memory flying through her already blitzed brain. She knew what he looked like out of his suit, she knew what he *felt* like, she also knew how he looked and sounded when he… *No, don't go there*, she urged herself and plunged straight into punitive speech because he had to be punished for putting such inappropriate thoughts into her head.

'I can't believe you're talking down to me as if you're a superior being,' Holly bit out tightly. 'Why? Because you've got money and a big fancy office? Certainly not because you've been shopped for taking drugs and sleeping with hookers!'

There was a flash of bemused surprise in Vito's brilliant dark eyes before he responded. 'That was a case of misidentification. I was not the man involved.'

'Of course you're going to say that,' Holly retorted with a roll of her eyes. 'Of course you're going to deny it to me but, as I understand it, you never once denied it in public.'

'I had a good reason for that. I never respond to tabloid journalists and I was protecting my family,' Vito returned levelly. 'I assure you…on my honour…that I was not the man involved and that I profoundly disapprove of such activities.'

Holly remained unimpressed. How did she credit that he had honour? How was she supposed to believe him? He had been protecting his family by remaining silent? How did that work?

'I do believe it would be wiser to take this meeting out of my big fancy office to somewhere more comfortable,' Vito continued, his smooth diction acidic in tone. 'I have an apartment in London. My driver will take you and you can relax there until I can join you for lunch.'

Knocked right off balance by that suggestion coming at her out of nowhere, Holly actually found herself thinking about the offer of lunch. Telling him about Angelo in an office setting felt wrong to her as well, and then a little voice in the back of her brain that sounded alarmingly like Pixie told her to wise up and think about the invitation he had made. And at that point the coin finally dropped for Holly and she grasped how Vito had chosen to interpret her sudden reappearance in his life. She wanted to kick herself for not foreseeing that likelihood, but she wanted to kick him even harder for daring to think that he could have a chance with her again. Certainly not with what she now knew about his partying habits!

'I haven't come here for another hook-up,' Holly stated with an embarrassed force that made her voice rise slightly. Behind her mortification lurked a great well of burning resentment.

Did he really think that she was so desperate for sex that she would travel all the way to London for it? How dared he assume that she was that keen, that easy? Well, she certainly hadn't taught him that she was a big challenge the night they first met, Holly conceded grudgingly. *But, my goodness, that one night must have been as good on his terms as he had said it was if he was willing to do it again.* Or maybe he was simply a sex addict? Anything was possible. When Holly had snapped back at him about his money and his fancy office and his debauched partying, she had also picked up on his surprise. He had assumed she was a quiet, easy-going little mouse but Holly wasn't quiet when her temper was roused. And right now her temper was rising like lava in a volcano. The past fourteen months had been very challenging, and working all day after a sleepless night had become her new norm. Having no way of contacting her son's father, who had handicapped her by giving her a false name, had only added to her stress.

Vito tensed. 'I didn't say anything about that. No expectations…' he murmured silkily, lean brown hands sketching an eloquent arc in the air as if to nullify her suspicions.

'Of course you have expectations…but, in this case, I'm afraid it's not going to happen. You had your chance and you blew it!' Holly snapped back, striving to hang on to her temper.

His brows drew together. 'What's that supposed to mean?'

Holly rolled her eyes, her lush mouth compressed. 'A timely little reminder that if you had really *wanted* to see me again I did leave you my phone number.'

'No, you didn't,' Vito insisted.

Holly tensed even more, angry that she had let that reminder fall from her mouth. 'I left a note thanking you for your hospitality and I printed my phone number at the bottom of it.'

Vito groaned. 'I didn't find a note when you left. Where did you leave it?'

'On the shelf in the fireplace.' Holly shrugged dismissively, keen to drop the subject.

'If there was a note, I didn't see it,' Vito assured her.

But then he would say that, wouldn't he? Holly thought, unimpressed. Of course he had found the silly note she had left behind and he had done nothing with it. And in doing nothing he had taught her all she needed to know about how he saw her. She had gone over the events of that morning in her mind many, many times. She was convinced that Vito had gone out for a walk to get a break from her. For him the fun of togetherness had already worn thin. He had ignored her note most probably because he'd been relieved to find her already gone. He had seen that night as a casual one-night stand that he had no desire to repeat.

'Whatever. It's pointless to discuss it after the amount of time that has passed. But let me spell out one fact,' Holly urged thinly. 'I *didn't* come to see you today for anything…er…physical. I came to see you about something much *more* important.'

At her emphasis, Vito raised a level dark brow in cool query mode, his wide sensual mouth tightening with impatience. And she could feel the whole atmosphere turning steadily colder and less welcoming. Naturally. She had taken sex off the lunch table, as it were, and he was no longer interested in anything she might have to say to him. And why would he be interested? She was poor and he was rich. He was educated and she was more of a self-educated person, which meant that she had alarming gaps in her knowledge. He was hugely successful and a high achiever while she worked in dead-end jobs without a career ladder for advancement. It was incredible, she finally conceded, that they had ever got involved in the first place.

'More important?' Vito prompted, his irritation barely hidden.

Defiance and umbrage combined inside Holly. She had held on to her temper but it was a close-run battle. His assumption that she was approaching him for another sexual encounter had shocked her, possibly because she had persuaded herself that they had shared something more than sex. Now she saw her illusions for the pitiful lies that they were, lies she had told herself to bolster her sagging self-esteem while she was waddling round with a massive tummy.

'Yes, much more important,' she confirmed, lifting her chin and simply spilling out her announcement. 'I got pregnant that night we were together.'

Vito froze as if she had threatened to fling a grenade at him. He turned noticeably pale, his strong bone structure suddenly clearly etched below his skin by raw tension. 'You said you were on the pill—'

Holly wasn't in the mood to go into the intricacies of missed pills and antibiotic treatment. 'You must know that every form of contraception has a failure rate and I'm afraid there was a failure. I got pregnant but I had no way of contacting you, particularly not when you had given me a fake name.'

Vito was in shock. Indeed Vito could never recall being plunged into such a state of shock before. Everything he had assumed had been turned upside down and inside out with those simple words...*I got pregnant.*

'And do you usually reintroduce yourself with a very evocative Santa hat and a sprig of holly when this happens?' he heard himself snap without even mentally forming the words. 'Is this some sort of a scam?'

Holly's small shoulders pushed up, along with her chin. 'No, Angelo is not a scam, Vito. He was born eight months after that night.'

'You come here without a word of warning and throw this announcement at me like a challenge,' Vito ground out in condemnation, no fan of major surprises in his life, as yet not even capable of thinking of what she was telling him. The prospect of having a child had long struck him as a possibility as remote as the moon. He had known fatherhood was on the cards somewhere down the line if he married Marzia but he had also known that neither of them were in any hurry to start a family.

'No, I did not. If I challenged you it would be an awful lot tougher!' Holly shot back at him furiously. 'Tough was waitressing until I was eight months pregnant and being in labour for two days before I got a

C-section. Tough is working as a childminder and a shelf-stacker and never getting enough sleep. You wouldn't know tough if it leapt on you and bit you…because in your whole blasted spoilt-rotten life you have had *everything* handed to you on a plate!'

A dark line of colour had delineated Vito's high cheekbones as he viewed her in growing disbelief. 'That is enough.'

'No, it's not enough, and you do *not* tell me when enough is enough!' Holly fired back at him, while pointing at him with an angry finger.

'Ranting at me is not getting us anywhere.'

'I'm entitled to rant if I want to rant!' Holly launched back at him an octave higher, shaking with rage and the distress she was fighting off while wondering if Vito ever lost his temper, because he was still so very controlled. 'And I don't *want* to get anywhere with you. I'm done here. I've told you that you're a father and that's why I came to see you. I saw your photo in a newspaper, incidentally…a *lovely* way to identify the father of your child! But if you want to think Angelo's a scam, you're welcome.'

'Holly…'

Holly yanked open the door and marched down the corridor very fast because she could not wait to get out of the building. She could feel the tears building up and she didn't want them to fall in front of an audience. She ignored Vito's voice when he repeated her name and stabbed the lift button with frantic force.

'Holly…*come back here*!' Vito shouted without warning.

So taken aback was she by that sudden rise in volume from him that she spun round and looked at him. He was only halfway down the corridor, evidently having expected her to return at his urging, and if looks could kill she would have been lying dead at his feet. He did have a temper, though, she registered belatedly, and it made his dark eyes glitter like gold ingots and gave his lean, darkly beautiful features a hard, forbidding edge.

Horribly aware of the number of people openly staring, Holly turned back to the lift just as the doors opened. She dived in as fast as she could but not fast enough to prevent Vito from joining her.

'You should've come back to my office.'

In silence, Holly contemplated his polished shoes because the tears were even closer now and stinging her eyes like angry wasps.

'I have to look into this situation. I need your phone number and your address,' Vito breathed in a raw undertone.

'I wasn't expecting you to be so offensive—funny, how you get the wrong idea about people. I really didn't want to get pregnant, Vito, but I love my son and he is never ever going to hear me admit that because now that he's here he's the *best* thing that ever happened to me,' she bit out shakily, hurriedly stepping out of the lift.

'Phone number. Address,' Vito said again, closing a hand to a slight shoulder to prevent her from walking away through the crowded concourse.

With a heavy sigh, Holly dug into her bag and produced a notebook. He handed her a gold pen. She squinted down at the pen, dimly wondering if it was real gold, and then scolded herself for that stupid thought. She printed out the requested details and ripped out the sheet to hand it back to him. 'Look,' she muttered uncomfortably. 'There's no pressure on you here. If I'm honest I don't really want you in our lives. You're not the sort of man I want around my son.'

And having deprived Vito of breath and speech with that damning final indictment of his character, Holly disappeared into the crowds.

CHAPTER SIX

Well, you made a real screw-up of that, Vito reflected for the first time in his life. But Holly hadn't given him the smallest preparation for what was to come, so it was scarcely surprising that everything that could go wrong *had* gone wrong. He didn't react well to surprises and the delivery of the Santa hat and the holly had seemed suggestively sexual. Was it any wonder he had got the wrong idea? His hard mouth compressed while he wondered about that note she had mentioned. Had she left a note? He had looked in all the obvious places. There had been nothing on the table or the door, and what did it matter now anyway?

What really mattered was that without the smallest warning he was apparently a father…

That was a mind-blowing concept but Vito was primarily ruled by his very shrewd brain and his first call was to his lawyer, who within the hour put him into contact with a London-based specialist in family law. Once all his questions had been answered, Vito was frowning at the realisation that he didn't really have any rights over his own son. Only marriage granted such legal rights. He didn't consult Apollo because he knew that his friend would start talking about demanding DNA tests but he and Apollo lived very different lives and Vito was confident that if Holly had given birth to a baby eight months after that night, it could only be his baby.

He didn't know how he felt about becoming a father, and after he had organised travel to Holly's home town for the following day and informed her by text of his planned visit, he phoned his mother to break the news.

Concetta Zaffari's delight at learning that she was a grandmother tumbled through her every word and then there were questions about Holly that Vito found hard to answer, and some he skipped altogether.

'*Obviously* you'll be getting married,' Concetta trilled cheerfully, and Vito laughed that his mother should even feel the need to say that. Of course they would be getting married. No Zaffari in history had had an illegitimate child and Vito had every intention of being a better parent than his own father had proved to be, although how to go about achieving that ambition he had no very clear idea.

Holly did not respond to Vito's text because it annoyed her. Why did he assume that she was free to drop everything to make herself and Angelo available at a time that suited him? She was working an early morning shift the next day because it was a Saturday and Pixie was taking care of Angelo for her.

As a result, when Vito arrived in his limousine, having been picked up from the helicopter ride that had brought him from London, he was taken aback to be met by Pixie and informed that his son was having a nap.

'Where's Holly?' he demanded, frowning down at

the diminutive blonde, whose facial expression telegraphed her antagonism towards him.

'At work.'

'Where?'

'The supermarket fifty yards down the road,' Pixie advanced reluctantly. 'You can wait in your car. Her shift ends in an hour.'

Infuriated that Holly hadn't thought to warn him so that he could adjust his arrival time accordingly, Vito strode down the road. He was full of righteous indignation until he walked through the busy shop and caught a glimpse of Holly wheeling a trolley bigger than she was through the aisles and pausing to restock shelves. *Tough is working as a shelf-stacker and never getting enough sleep.* Abruptly, he spun on his heel and strode back out of the busy shop again, shamed by the reality that the mother of his child was being forced to work so hard to survive.

Vito would have argued that he had not been spoilt rotten, but he had been born rich and with a near-genius-level IQ, and phenomenal success in almost every field was a reward he took for granted. He had never had to struggle, never had to make the best of two bad choices, never had to do anything he didn't want to do and the sheer undeniable luxury of those realities about his life was finally sinking in on him. With uncharacteristic patience he directed his driver to take him away from the street of tiny terraced houses where Holly lived to a hotel, where he had lunch while imagining Holly going without food, which didn't improve his appetite.

'Vito came, then?' Holly exclaimed as she wriggled out of her overall.

Pixie nodded confirmation. 'Cheese toastie for lunch?'

'Lovely. I should've texted him to say that time didn't suit me. I don't know what it is about Vito but he makes me act completely out of character!' Holly declared guiltily.

'Take it from me, anything other than awe and flattery is probably good for Vito's character. At least he's interested in meeting his son,' Pixie said cheerfully. 'That's good news.'

Holly scoffed down the cheese toastie and touched up her make-up. She couldn't sit down, and she couldn't concentrate either. She wanted to stand at the window waiting for Vito like a kid watching out for Santa Claus arriving. Embarrassment gripped her then and she sat down, only to fly up again when Angelo cried as he wakened from his nap. Changing her son, she gave him a hug and he drank down some water to quench his thirst. It was cold in the small sitting room and she lit the fire to warm it up.

'I'm off out now,' Pixie told her while Holly was strapping a wriggling Angelo into his infant seat.

'But—'

'This is about you and him and Angelo and it's private. Give me a text when he's gone,' Pixie suggested.

Only minutes later the bell went and Holly's heartbeat leapt into her throat, convulsing it. She raced to the front door and then paused to compose herself for several seconds before opening it.

'Holly…' Vito pronounced softly, staring broodingly down at her from his great height. Sheathed in jeans and a sweater teamed with a buttery soft brown leather jacket, he totally took her breath away.

'Come in…' Her wary glance was ensnared by black-fringed dark golden eyes that sent her heart racing. 'Don't stare,' she scolded breathlessly.

'I find you very attractive. Naturally, I'm going to stare, *bellezza mia*.'

He hadn't found her attractive enough to use her phone number, Holly reminded herself ruefully. 'No, don't say insincere stuff like that. All we really have to do here is be polite to each other,' Holly told him in the small, confined hall as he came to a halt beside her.

'I can manage much more than polite,' Vito declared, his long brown fingers settling down onto her slight shoulders and feeling the rigid tension that now gripped her small frame. She had the most luscious mouth he had ever seen on a woman, pink and soft and succulent. His jeans tightened at his groin, his physical reaction instantaneous.

At his touch, Holly turned rigid with discomfiture. 'I meant friendly rather than—'

'*Maledizione!* You want me to be friendly when I can hardly keep my hands off you?' Vito shot at her with raw incredulity. 'I don't think I can manage that.'

'But you have to. I wouldn't be comfortable with anything else,' Holly told him earnestly, convinced that only disaster would follow if she allowed any further intimacy to complicate an already tense relationship.

'*Have* to?' Vito queried, a flash of glittering challenge entering his searching gaze as he stared down at her. 'Have you got someone else in your life…another man?'

Holly dealt him a startled glance. 'No… Why are you asking that?'

Without warning, Vito moved forward, pinning her up against the wall behind her. 'Because if there was

I'd probably want to kill him!' he muttered in a raw undertone.

In wonderment, Holly looked up into his lean, darkly beautiful face and then her view blurred as he hauled her up to his level and opened her mouth with the crushing demand of his own. He tasted so good, all minty and fresh, and the strength in the arms holding her felt even better. Every hard, angular line of his long, lean physique was pressed against her as he braced her hips against the wall. The passion of that hungry kiss threatened to consume her and the anomaly between the cool face he showed the world and the uncontrolled hotness hidden beneath electrified her. The piercing ache she had almost forgotten tugged cruelly in her pelvis as his tongue tangled with hers. His mouth was sublime, the feel of his unyielding muscles, hard against her softer curves, incredible. Insane chemistry…insane behaviour, she translated, pulling back from him with shell-shocked abruptness because she knew with shamed horror that all she really wanted to do with him at that moment was drag him upstairs to her bed to rediscover the amazing pleasure he could give her.

'No, this is not what you're here for…' she muttered in curt reminder, her spine stiff as she turned her back on him to walk into the small sitting room. 'You're here to meet Angelo and that's all.'

'You make it sound so simple when it's anything but simple,' Vito countered with a roughened edge to his voice because she had pushed him away and he had had to resist a powerful urge to turn caveman and yank her back to him.

'If we both make the effort, we can keep this simple and polite,' Holly stated with rigorous resolve.

'I have something I need to explain to you first...' But by that point, Vito could see over the top of Holly's head and his attention zeroed in so quickly on the child in the infant seat that his voice literally trailed away.

And for Vito it was as though the rest of the world vanished. He focused in amazement on the baby who bore a remarkable resemblance to a framed photograph Vito's mother had of her son at a similar age. Huge brown eyes from below a mop of black curls inspected him with sparkling curiosity. A chubby fist waved in the air and suddenly Vito froze, out of his comfort zone and hating it. He had never gone weak at the knees for puppies or babies, had put that lack of a softer side down to his grandfather's rigid discipline. But now he was looking at his son and seeing a baby with his own features in miniature and he finally realised that the very thought of fatherhood unnerved him. His own father had been a hopeless parent. How much worse would he do with Angelo when he had no idea even where to start?

Holly paused beside the child seat to say awkwardly, 'So...er...obviously this is Angelo. He's a little bored at weekends because during the week I look after a pair of toddlers and it's a lot livelier here.'

Vito tried to stand a little less stiffly but in truth he felt much as if someone had swung open the door of a lion's cage and left him to take his chances. 'Why did you call him Angelo?'

'Because you're Italian,' Holly pointed out, wondering why he was questioning the obvious. 'I looked up Italian names.'

Vito forced himself closer to the baby. His hands weren't quite steady as he undid the belt strapping Angelo into his seat. As Vito lifted the baby, Angelo gave his father an anxious, startled appraisal.

'You're used to children,' Holly assumed, rather taken aback by that deceptively confident first move.

'No. I don't think I've ever been this close to a child before. There are none in the family and most of my friends are still single as well,' Vito told her abstractedly, wondering what he was supposed to do with the little boy now that he was holding him.

'Thank you for having him,' Vito breathed in a driven undertone. 'You could have made a different decision but you didn't.'

Nothing about this first meeting was going in any direction that Holly had foreseen. And she was even less ready to hear her baby's father thank her for not opting for a termination. Her eyes prickled with sudden emotion.

'I wanted him from the first, never had any doubts there,' she admitted gruffly. 'He's the only family I have...apart from my friend Pixie.'

As Angelo squirmed and wriggled, Vito lifted him higher and swung him round in aeroplane mode.

The baby's eyes grew huge and he let out a frightened howl before breaking down into red-faced, gulping sobs.

'Let me take him,' Holly urged in dismay as Vito lowered the squalling baby. 'He's not used to the rough stuff. There are no men in his life, really, just Pixie and me...'

Vito settled Angelo back into Holly's arms with more than a suggestion of haste and relief. 'Sorry, I upset him.'

'He needs time to get used to you,' Holly explained. 'I'll put him on the floor to play with his toys.'

Vito was tempted to back off entirely but that struck him as cowardly and he held his ground to crouch down on the rug. Finally recalling that he had brought a gift, he removed it from his pocket and tipped it out of a box. 'It's only a little toy.'

Holly winced as she noted a piece of the toy break off and fall. It had detachable tiny parts and was totally unsuitable for a baby. 'You can't give that to him,' she told Vito apologetically. 'He puts everything in his mouth and he could choke on those tiny pieces.'

In haste, Vito removed the toy and its parts again and grimaced. 'I didn't think. I really don't know anything about babies.'

Holly pulled over Angelo's toy box and extracted a red plastic truck that was a favourite. 'He likes this… Coffee?' she asked.

'Black, no sugar,' Vito murmured flatly, recognising that getting to know his son and learning how to play with him appeared to be even more challenging than he had feared.

Holly made coffee, acknowledging that she was simply delighted that Vito had had enough interest to come and meet Angelo. She could see how awkward he felt with their child and knew that if she didn't make Vito feel more comfortable he might not want to make another visit. Not that he had prepared very well for this first visit, she thought ruefully, wondering what he had thought a baby would do with a miniature brick action figure festooned in even tinier weapons.

When she returned with the coffee, Angelo was sucking on his little red truck and refusing to share the toy with his father. Holly got down on her knees beside them and, with his mother on hand, her son relaxed his grip on the truck and handed it to Vito. For an instant he looked as though he had no idea what to do with the toy and then some childhood memory of his own must have prompted him because he ran the toy across the rug making *vroom-vroom* noises and Angelo gave a little-boy shout of appreciation.

A little of Vito's tension ebbed in receipt of that favourable response. It shook him to appreciate that he had actually craved that first welcoming smile from his son. He wanted the little boy to recognise him as his father, he wanted him to like him and love him, but it was intimidating to appreciate that he hadn't the faintest idea how to go about achieving those things.

Holly parted her lips to say, 'When you first came in you said there was something that you needed to explain to me...?'

Vito's lean, strong profile clenched and he sprang upright. 'Yes. That sex-party scandal that made headlines,' he framed with palpable distaste. 'That wasn't me, it was my father, Ciccio.'

As she too stood up, Holly's mouth dropped open in shock. 'Your...*father*?'

'I didn't deny my involvement because I was trying to protect my mother from the humiliation of having her husband's habits exposed so publicly,' Vito explained grimly.

Holly dropped down on the edge of the sofa behind her. 'Oh, my goodness.'

'My mother could confirm the truth if you require further proof that I wasn't involved. What did happen that night was that I received a phone call in the early hours of the morning telling me that my father had fallen ill and needed urgent medical attention,' Vito told her, his delivery curt.

'The person calling refused to identify herself, and that should've been my warning. My mother was in Paris and I had to take charge. I wondered why my father had taken ill at an apartment owned by the bank but the minute I walked into it I could see what I was dealing with, and that I had been contacted like a clean-up crew in the hope of keeping the wild party under the radar.'

Holly nodded slowly, not really knowing what to say.

'My father had had a heart attack in the company of hookers and drugs,' Vito volunteered grimly. 'I had him collected by a private ambulance from the rear entrance and, having instructed a trusted aide to dispose of all evidence of the party, I intended to join my father at a clinic. Unfortunately the press were waiting outside when I left and I was mobbed. One of the hookers then sold her story, choosing to name me rather than my father even though I had never met her in my life. She probably lied because there was more of a story in my downfall than in that of a middle-aged married man with a taste for sleaze.'

'So you took the blame for your parents' sake?' Holly whispered in wonderment.

'My *mother's* sake,' Vito emphasised drily. 'But my mother worked out the truth for herself and she is currently divorcing my father. She looked after him until he had regained his health and then told him that she wanted a separation.'

'And how do you feel about that? I mean, their divorce means that your sacrifice was in vain.'

'I'm relieved that they've split up. I don't like my

father very much…well, not at all, really,' Vito admitted, his wide sensual mouth twisting. 'He's a greedy, dishonest man and my mother will have a better life without him.'

Utterly amazed by that flood of unrestrained candour from a male as reserved as Vito, Holly continued to scrutinise him with inquisitive blue eyes. 'Why are you telling me all this now?'

'You're family now in all but name,' Vito told her wryly. 'And I couldn't possibly allow you to continue to believe that I am not a fit person to be around my son.'

Holly fully understood that motivation and muttered, 'I'm sorry I misjudged you. I was naive to believe everything I read on the internet about you. I told you before that I don't know who my father is,' Holly admitted, wrinkling her nose. 'My mother gave me several different stories and I challenged her when I was sixteen to tell me the truth but she still wouldn't answer me. I honestly don't think she knows either. In those days she was fairly promiscuous. I've had no contact with her since then.'

'You've never had a father…much like me. Ciccio took no interest in me when I was a child and when I was an adult he only approached me if he wanted something,' he revealed, settling down with striking grace of movement into an armchair. 'My grandfather was my father figure but he was seventy when I was born and he had a Victorian outlook on childcare and education. It was far from ideal.'

Holly was fascinated by what she was learning about Vito's background, although she really wasn't sure why he was choosing to tell her so much. 'I think very few people have an ideal childhood,' she said ruefully.

'But wouldn't it be wonderful to give Angelo that ideal?' Vito pressed, black velvet lashes lifting on glittering gold as he studied her.

Her heart raced and her mouth ran dry. Hurriedly she dropped her gaze from his, only for her attention to fall to the tight inner seam of his jeans stretched along a powerful muscular thigh. Guilty heat surged through her and she shifted uneasily. 'And how could we give Angelo an ideal childhood?' she asked abstractedly.

'By getting married and giving our son a conventional start in life,' Vito spelt out with measured assurance. 'I'm not only here to meet Angelo, Holly…I'm here to ask you to be my wife.'

Disbelief roared through Holly. She blinked rapidly, doubting the evidence of her ears. He was proposing? He was actually proposing marriage to her because she had had his child?

Holly loosed an uneasy laugh and Vito frowned, because that was hardly the response he had envisaged. 'I think your grandfather's Victorian outlook is showing, Vito. We don't need to get married to give Angelo a decent upbringing.'

'How else can I be a proper father when I live in a different country?' Vito demanded with harsh bite. 'I really don't want to be only an occasional visitor in my son's life or the home he visits for a few weeks in summer when he's off school. That is not enough for me.'

Holly watched Vito lean down to lift Angelo, who was tugging at his shoelaces. He closed his arms tentatively round Angelo's small restive body and settled him down on a lean thigh. There was something incredibly sexy about his newly learned assurance with their son and her cheeks coloured at that seemingly tasteless reflection, but the smouldering edge of Vito's sexuality seemed to be assailing her every thought. 'Well, I can see that it would be difficult for you and far from ideal, but marriage…well, that's a whole different ball game,' she told him regretfully. 'I want to marry a man who loves me, not a man who accidentally got me pregnant and wants to do what he feels is the right thing by me.'

'I can't change how we conceived Angelo but with a little vision you should be able to see that where we started isn't where we have to end up,' Vito responded smoothly. 'I may not love you but I'm insanely attracted to you. I'm also ready to settle down.'

'Yes, you were engaged, weren't you?' Holly slotted in rather unkindly.

'That's not relevant here,' Vito informed her drily. 'Stay focused on what really matters.'

'Angelo,' Holly replied, with hot cheeks, while her brain trooped off in wild, unproductive circles.

He was asking her to marry him… He was actually asking her to marry him! How was she supposed to react to that when she had been astonished by his proposal?

'You should also consider the reality that eventually Angelo will be very rich, and growing up outside *my* world isn't the best preparation for that day,' Vito pointed out. 'I want to be his father. A father who is there for him when he needs me. A benefit neither you nor I enjoyed.'

He was making very valid points but Holly felt harassed and intimidated rather than grateful for his honesty. 'But marriage?' she reasoned. 'That's such a huge decision.'

'And a decision only you can make. But there would be other benefits for you,' Vito told her quietly. 'You could set up as an interior designer and live your dream with me.'

'You're starting to sound like a trained negotiator,' Holly cut in.

'I am a trained negotiator,' Vito conceded. 'But I want to give our son the very best start in life he can have, with a genuine family.'

And that was the real moment that Holly veered from consternation and fell deep into his honeytrap. Those emotive words, 'a genuine family', spoke to her on the deepest possible level and filled her head with happy images. That was a goal that she, and surprisingly Vito in spite of his privileged background, both shared, and that touched her. As she studied her son sitting peacefully in his father's arms her heart melted. She had felt ashamed of the lack of caution that had led to her pregnancy. She had been mortified that she had failed her own life goals and could not give her son the family security and the opportunities he deserved. But if she married Vito she would be able to put all her regrets behind her and *give* Angelo two parents and a stable home with every advantage.

'Even people in love find it hard to make marriage work,' Holly reminded him, fighting to resist the tempting images flooding her imagination, and to be sensible and cautious.

'We're not in love. Our odds of success may well be better because we have less exalted expectations,' Vito contended silkily. 'And our arrangement need not be viewed as a permanent trap either. In a few years, should one or both of us be unhappy, we can divorce.

All I'm asking you to do at this moment in time, Holly… is give marriage a chance.'

He made it sound so reasonable, so very reasonable. He was inviting her to *try* being married to him and see if they could make it work. It was a very realistic approach, guaranteed to make her feel that by trying she would have nothing to lose. And she looked back at him in silence with her heart hammering while he raked an impatient hand through his cropped black hair.

'I'll think it over.' Holly fibbed, because she had already thought it over and really there was no contest between what Vito was offering Angelo and what she could hope to offer her son as a lone parent.

'Be more decisive, *bellezza mia*,' Vito urged. 'If you marry me I will do everything within my power to make you happy.'

Holly had known true happiness only a few times in her life. One of those moments had been waking at dawn enfolded in Vito's arms. Another had been the first time she had seen her infant son. But just being with Vito also made her happy and that worried her, implying as it did that she was craving something more than a very practical marriage based on their son's needs. Should she listen to that voice of reason and warning now? Stay on the sidelines where it was safe rather than risk dipping her toes into the much more complex demands of a marriage?

But at the baseline of her responses there was no denying that she wanted Vito Zaffari with a bone-deep, almost frighteningly strong yearning. How could she possibly walk away from that? How could she stand back and watch him take up with other women, as he would, and know that she had given him that freedom?

And the answer was that she couldn't face that, would sooner take a risk on a marriage that might not work than surrender any hope of a deeper relationship with him.

Holly breathed in slow and deep and lifted her head high. 'All right. We'll get married…and see how it goes…'

And Vito smiled, that heart-stopping smile that always froze her in her tracks, and nothing he said after that point registered with her because she was washed away by sheer excitement and hope for the future.

Vito registered the stars in her eyes with satisfaction. Having been driven by the need to secure the best possible arrangement for his son's benefit, he had expended little thought on the actual reality of becoming a married man or a father. He wanted Holly and he wanted his son: that was all that mattered. And Holly would soon learn to fit into his world, he thought airily.

CHAPTER SEVEN

'SMILE!' PIXIE TOLD HOLLY. 'You look totally stupendous!'

Holly smiled to order and gripped her hands together tightly on her lap. The past four weeks had passed in a whirlwind of unfamiliar activity and changes. Now it was her wedding day and hopefully she would finally have time to draw a breath and start to relax. Only not when it was a wedding about to be attended by a lot of rich, important people, she reasoned nervously.

'How are you feeling?' she asked her best friend and bridesmaid, ruefully surveying Pixie's legs, which were both encased in plaster casts.

Her housemate had returned from a visit to her brother badly battered and bruised from a fall down the stairs, which had also broken both her legs. The extent of her injuries had appalled Holly and, although the bruising had faded, she couldn't help feeling that there was more amiss with her friend than she was letting on because Pixie's usual chirpiness and zest for life seemed to have faded away as well. And although she had gently questioned Pixie on several occasions, she could not work out if it was her own imagination in overdrive or if indeed there *was* some secret concern that Pixie wasn't yet willing to share with her.

Predictably, Pixie rolled her eyes. 'I keep on telling you I'm fine. I'll get these casts off in a couple of weeks and I'll get back to work and it'll be as if this never happened.'

'Hopefully you'll be able to come out to visit us in Italy in a few weeks' time.'

'That's doubtful.'

'Er…if it's money—'

'No, I'm not taking money off you!' Pixie told her fiercely. 'You may be marrying Mr Rich but that's not going to change anything between us.'

'All right.' Holly subsided to scrutinise the opulent diamond engagement ring on her finger. Vito wasn't the least bit romantic, she conceded ruefully, because he had sent the ring to her by special delivery rather than presenting her with it. That had been such a disappointment to her. It would have meant so much to Holly if Vito had made the effort to personally give her the ring.

'Let's simply be a normal couple from here on in,' Vito had urged, and seemingly the ring signified that normality he wanted even if it had not entailed him changing his ways.

She had wanted to ask if it was the same ring Marzia, his previous fiancée, had worn but had sealed her lips shut in case that question was tactless. And staging a potentially difficult conversation with a male she had barely seen since she had agreed to marry him had struck her as unwise.

'Of course I'm very busy now. How else could I take time off for the wedding?' Vito had enquired piously on the phone when she'd tried to tactfully suggest that he make more effort to spend some time with her and Angelo.

Vito hadn't even been able to make time for Angelo, whom he had only seen once since their agreement. Of course, to be fair, he *had* suggested that they move into his London apartment *before* the wedding and she had been ready to agree until she had heard from Pixie's brother and had realised that there was no way she could leave her injured friend to cope alone in a house with stairs. She had had to put Pixie first but Vito had not understood that. In fact Vito had called it a silly excuse that was dividing him from his son. After the wedding she needed to explain to Vito just how much of a debt she owed Pixie for her friend's support during her pregnancy and after Angelo's birth, and she needed to explain that she loved Pixie as much as she would have loved a sister. Although, never having had a sibling of his own, he might not even understand that.

And there were an awful lot of things that Vito didn't understand, Holly reflected ruefully. He had been thoroughly irritated when she'd insisted on continuing her childminding until her charges' parents had had time to make other arrangements for their care, but Holly would not have dreamt of letting anyone down, and took her responsibilities just as seriously as he took his own.

Furthermore, in every other way Vito had contrived to take over Holly and her son's lives. He had made decisions on their behalf that he had neglected to discuss with Holly. Maybe he thought she was too stupid and ignorant to make the right decisions, she thought unhappily.

First he had landed her with an Italian nanny, who had had to board at a hotel nearby because there were only two bedrooms in the house Pixie and Holly rented. London-born Lorenza was a darling and wonderful with Angelo, and Holly had needed outside help to cope with shopping for a wedding dress and such things, but she still would have preferred to play an active role in the hiring of a carer for her son.

Secondly, he had landed Holly with a horrible, pretentious fashion stylist who had wanted Holly to choose the biggest, splashiest and most expensive wedding gown ever made. Only sheer stubbornness had ensured that Holly actually got to wear her own choice of dress on her special day. And it was a very plain dress because Holly was convinced that she was too small and curvy to risk wearing anything more elaborate. She stroked the delicate edge of a lace sleeve with satisfaction. At least she had got her dream dress even if she hadn't got any input into any other details because Vito had placed all the organisation into the hands of a wedding planner, whom he had instructed *not* to consult his future wife.

In truth, Vito was extremely bossy and almost painfully insensitive sometimes. He had left it to his social secretary to tell Holly that she had a day at a grooming parlour booked for a makeover. Holly had been mortified, wondering whether Vito thought her ordinary ungroomed self was a mess and not up to his standards. Pixie had told her not to be so prickly and had asked her if she thought there was something immoral about manicures and waxing. And no, of course she didn't think that, it was just that she had wanted Vito to want her as she was, not be left feeling that only a very polished version of her could now be deemed acceptable. After all, she didn't have the security of knowing her bridegroom loved her, flaws and all, and that made a big difference to a woman's confidence, she reasoned worriedly.

'Will you stop it? And don't ask me what you're to stop!' Pixie said bluntly. 'You're worrying yourself sick about marrying Vito and it's crazy. You love him—'

'I don't love him,' Holly contradicted instantly. 'I like him. I'm very attracted to him.'

'You look him up online just to drool over his photos. If it's not love, it's a monster crush. So you might as well be married to him,' Pixie contended. 'Vito's all you think about. In fact watching you scares the hell out of me. I don't think I could bear to love anyone the way you love him, but with a little luck in time he may well return your feelings.'

'Do you think so?'

'I don't see why not,' Pixie responded thoughtfully. 'Vito's the caring type even if he hasn't yet learned to share. Why shouldn't he fall in love with you?'

But it wasn't love she felt, Holly told herself urgently. It was liking, attraction, respect, nothing more, nothing less. Loving Vito without being loved back would simply make her unhappy and she refused to be unhappy. No, she was a very hands-on person and she was going to make the most of what she *did* have with Vito and Angelo, not make the mistake of pining for what she couldn't have. After all, she could plainly see Vito in all his very good-looking and sophisticated glory and she knew she was only getting to marry him because some crazy fate had deposited her as a damsel in distress on his doorstep one Christmas Eve night.

Her foster mother, Sylvia, pushed Pixie down the aisle in her wheelchair while Holly walked to the altar, striving not to be intimidated by the sheer size of the church and the overwhelming number of unfamiliar faces crammed into it. Vito stood beside a guy with black shoulder-length hair and startling green eyes whom she recognised from online photographs as his best friend, Apollo Metraxis. Holly only looked at the bronzed Greek long enough to establish that he was giving her a distinctly cold appraisal before her attention switched quite naturally to Vito, who, unromantic or otherwise, was at least managing to smile that breathtaking smile of his.

Her heart bounced around in her chest to leave her breathless and when he closed his hand over hers at the altar she was conscious only of him and the officiating priest. She listened with quiet satisfaction to the words of the wedding ceremony, grinned when Angelo let out a little baby shout from his place on Lorenza's lap in a front pew and stared down all of a glow at the wedding band Vito threaded smoothly onto her finger. It was her wedding day and she was determined to enjoy it.

When they signed the register, she was introduced to a smiling older woman clad in a lilac suit and hat with diamonds sparkling at her throat.

'I'm Vito's *mamma*, Concetta,' the attractive brunette told her warmly. 'I've met my grandson. He *is* beautiful.'

Unsurprisingly, Holly was charmed by such fond appreciation of her son and her anxiety about how Vito's mother might feel about his sudden marriage dwindled accordingly. Concetta, it seemed, was willing to give her a fighting chance at acceptance. Vito's friend Apollo, however, could barely hide his hostility towards her and she wondered at it. Didn't he realise that this marriage was what Vito had wanted? Did he think she had somehow forced his friend into proposing? Holly's chin came up and her big blue eyes fired with resolution because she was happy to have become Vito's wife and Angelo's mother and she had no intention of pretending otherwise.

After some photos taken at the church they moved on to the hotel where the reception was being held. 'There are so many guests,' she commented with nervous jerkiness when they climbed out of the limo, an easier exercise than it might have been because Holly's closely fitted gown did not have a train.

'My family has a lot of friends but some guests are business acquaintances,' Vito admitted. 'You shouldn't be apprehensive. Invariably wedding guests are well-wishers.'

Apollo's name was on her lips but she compressed it. She didn't think much of the Greek for deciding he disliked her, sight unseen. What happened to giving a person a fair chance? But she refused to allow Apollo's brooding presence to cast a shadow over her day. And although Apollo was supposed to be Vito's best man, and Pixie the chief and only bridesmaid, Apollo snubbed Pixie as well. Of course, he had brought a partner with him, a fabulously beautiful blonde underwear model with legs that could rival a giraffe's and little desire to melt into the background.

As was becoming popular, the speeches were staged before the meal was served. Holly's foster mother, Sylvia, had insisted on saying a few words and they were kind, warming words that Holly very much appreciated. Concetta Zaffari had chosen not to speak and Vito's father had not been invited to the wedding. When Apollo stood up, Holly stiffened and the most excruciating experience of her life commenced with his speech. In a very amusing way Apollo began to tell the tale of the billionaire banker trapped by the snow and the waitress who had broken down at the foot of the lane. Holly felt humiliated, knowing that everyone who had seen Angelo and worked out her son's age was now aware that he had been conceived from a one-night stand.

Vito gripped her hand so hard it almost hurt and hissed in her ear, 'I did not know he was planning to tell our story!'

Holly said nothing. She wasn't capable of saying anything, meeting Pixie's compassionate gaze across the circular table, recognising Concetta Zaffari's compassion on her behalf in her gentle appraisal. She could feel her face getting hotter and hotter and pictured herself resembling a giant blushing tomato and it was a mercy when Apollo had concluded his maliciously polite speech, which had left her pierced by a dozen poisonous darts of condemnation. He had outed her as a slut at the very least and a gold-digger at worst because he had made it sound the most impossible coincidence that her car had gone off the road at that convenient point. But worst of all, he had not uttered a single lie.

'What a bastard!' Pixie said roundly when she had contrived to follow Holly into the palatial cloakroom. 'Vito's furious! He asked me to come and see that you were all right.'

'I shouldn't be ashamed of being a waitress or a woman who fell pregnant after a one-night stand,' Holly muttered apologetically. 'But somehow sitting there in front of all those richly dressed, bejewelled people I felt like rubbish.'

Sylvia joined them at that point and put her arms

around Holly. 'That young man's a rather nasty piece of work,' she opined ruefully. 'That was a very inappropriate speech, in the circumstances. Holly…sticks and stones may break your bones but words can never hurt you.'

'Not true.' Holly sighed, breathing in deep. 'But don't worry about me. I can handle it—'

'But you shouldn't have to on your wedding day, as I told your bridegroom,' Pixie framed angrily.

'No, no, let it go,' Holly urged ruefully. 'I've got over it already. I was being oversensitive.'

Her foster mother departed and Pixie said several rather unrepeatable things about Apollo Metraxis before the two women began to make their way back to the function room. And then suddenly Pixie stopped her wheelchair and shot out a hand to yank at Holly's wrist to urge her into the alcove in the corridor. She held a finger to her lips in the universal silencing motion and Holly frowned, wondering what on earth her friend was playing at.

And then she heard it, Apollo's unforgettable posh British accent honed by years of public schooling. 'No, as you know, he wouldn't listen to me. *No* DNA test, *no* pre-nup…get this? He *trusts* her. No, he's not an idiot. It's my bet he's playing a deeper game with this sham marriage. Maybe planning to go for full custody of his son once he has them in Italy. Vito's no fool. He simply plays his cards close to his chest.'

Holly turned deathly pale because there was not the smallest doubt that Apollo was talking about her and Angelo and Vito. For a split second she honestly wished she hadn't eavesdropped and she could see by her friend's expression that Pixie was now regretting the impulse as well because of what they had overheard. But without a word she planted firm hands on the handles of the wheelchair and moved her friend out of the alcove and back towards the function room.

But Holly was shattered inside and her expressive face was wooden and, after one glance at her, Vito whirled her onto the dance floor and closed his arms round her. Rage with Apollo was still simmering inside Vito like a cauldron. Well aware of his friend's attitude towards his marriage, Vito blamed himself for still including him in the event. He had naively assumed that, after meeting Holly, Apollo would realise how outrageous his cynical outlook was when it came to her. But his misplaced trust in the Greek billionaire had resulted in his bride's hurt on what he very well knew she believed should be a happy day. Even worse, he was still recovering from the unprecedented surge of raw protective reaction he had experienced during that speech. Any individual who wounded Holly should be his enemy, certainly not a trusted confidant of many years' standing.

'I'm sorry, really sorry about Apollo's speech,' he told her in a driven undertone. 'If I'd had the slightest idea what he was planning to say—'

'You should've kept your mouth shut about how we met,' Holly told him in an unforgiving tone. 'If you hadn't opened your big mouth, he wouldn't have known—'

'Holly…I didn't know that we were going to end up together—'

'No, that came right out of left field with Angelo, didn't it?' Holly agreed in a saccharine-sweet tone he had never heard from her before. 'Just boy talk, was it? The brunette slapper I pulled at Christmas?'

Dark colour rimming his high cheekbones, Vito gazed down at her with dark eyes blazing like golden flames. 'Are you seriously saying that you didn't tell Pixie about us?'

Hoist by her own petard, Holly reddened and compressed her lips.

'Thought so,' Vito said with satisfaction and she wanted to slap him very hard indeed. 'We both spoke out of turn but you have the kinder and wiser friend.'

'Yes,' Holly conceded gruffly, tears suddenly shining in her eyes.

'I have spoken to Apollo. If it's any consolation I wanted to punch him for the first time in our long friendship. He's a hothead with a very low opinion of marriage in general. His father married six times,' Vito explained ruefully. 'I know that doesn't take away the sting but, speaking for myself, I don't care how many people know how I met my very lovely, very sexy wife and acquired an even cuter baby. You're a Zaffari now. A Zaffari always holds his or her head high.'

'Is that so?' Holly's heavy heart was steadily lightening because it meant a lot that he was perceptive enough to understand how she felt and that he had made his friend aware that he was angry about that speech.

'Yes, *gioia mia*. We Zaffaris take ourselves very seriously and if one is lucky enough to find a waitress like you in the snow he's grateful for it, not suspicious. Apollo and I have a friendship based very much on the fact that we are opposites in character. He distrusts every woman he meets. He's always looking for a hidden agenda. It must be exhausting,' he said wryly.

Holly rested her brow against his shoulder as they slow-danced and she let the mortification and the anger seep slowly out of her again. It was being with Vito that was important, being with Vito and Angelo and becoming a family that really mattered. And in her heart of hearts she could not credit that Vito was planning a sham marriage purely to try and deprive her of their son. That accusation was hopefully the suggestion of a troubled, misogynistic mind, she reasoned hopefully.

'This is *your* jet…like really? *Your own jet?*' Holly carolled incredulously a few hours later when she scanned the ultra-opulent leather interior of the private jet.

'I travel a great deal. It's convenient,' Vito parried, amused by her wide, shaken eyes.

'As long as sleeping with the cabin crew isn't included,' Holly whispered, her attention resting on the more than usually attractive team overseeing the boarding of Lorenza and Angelo and all the baby equipment that accompanied her son. In consternation Holly realised that she had accidentally spoken that thought out loud.

Predominantly, Vito was shocked by the concept of having sex with anyone who worked for him and then he looked at his bride's burning face and he started to laugh with rare enjoyment. 'No, that sort of entertainment is probably more Apollo than me. Although I did take advantage of *you*.'

'No, you didn't,' she told him before she hurried forward to grasp her son, having missed him during her enforced break from him throughout the day.

'Older, wiser, plied an innocent with wine…' Vito traded, condemning himself for his crime for her ears alone. 'But if I had the chance to go back I would *still* do it again.'

Encountering a lingering sidewise glance from black-fringed dark golden eyes, Holly felt heat lick through her pelvis as she took a seat and cuddled Angelo. For possibly the first time since she had conceived she looked back at that night in the cottage without guilt and regret. No, on that score Vito had hit a bullseye. Given the chance, in spite of the moments of heartache and stress along the way, she would also still have done the same thing again.

And if Vito could be that honest, why shouldn't she match him? Tell him about the phone call she had overheard Apollo making? She would pick her moment, she decided ruefully, and she would ask if he had ever thought of their marriage as a sham and if she had anything to worry about.

Angelo was asleep by the time they landed in Italy. Holly had freshened up, noting with disappointment that her outfit hadn't travelled very well. The fashion stylist had tried to persuade her to buy a whole host of clothes but with Vito already paying for the wedding and her gown she hadn't felt right about allowing him to pay for anything else before they were married. She had teamed an elegant navy-and-white skirt with a matching top but her get-up had creased horribly and looked as though she had worn it for a week rather than only a few hours. Straightening it as best she could, she wondered if Vito would even notice.

Holly was enchanted by the wonderful scenery that enfolded as the four-wheel drive moved deeper into the countryside. Charming low hills rolled across a landscape peacefully dotted with cypresses, serrated lines of fresh green vines and silvery olive groves. Medieval villages slumbered on hilltops while ancient bell towers soared into the cloudless blue sky. Occasionally she caught a glimpse of beautiful, weathered old farmhouses nestling among the greenery and the wild flowers and she wondered if Vito's home resembled them.

'There it is…the Castello Zaffari,' Vito announced with pride as the car began to climb a steep ribbon of road. Dead ahead Holly glimpsed a building so vast it covered the whole hilltop like a village while elaborate gardens decorated the slopes below it. She froze, convinced that that could not possibly be his home because it was a palace, not a mere dwelling. A giant domed portico denoted the front entrance where the car came to a halt.

'Is this it? Is this where you live?' Holly asked in a small voice, wondering crazily if she could hide in the car and refuse to emerge until he admitted that the palace wasn't really his and he had only been joking. It *had* to be a joke, she thought fearfully, because no ordinary woman could possibly learn to live in the midst of such medieval splendour.

Vito picked up on the edge in her voice and frowned at her. 'Yes. What's wrong?'

'Nothing,' she said hurriedly as she took Angelo to allow the nanny to climb out.

'Don't you like it?'

'Of course I like it,' Holly lied in a rush, utterly overpowered by the huge building as she accompanied Vito into a massive marble-floored hall studded with matching lines of columns. 'But you could've at least hinted that you lived like royalty.'

'I don't,' Vito incised in firm rebuttal. 'I live in a historic building that has belonged to my family for centuries. I live a very average, normal life here…'

Please tell me he didn't say that, Holly argued with herself as they rounded the gigantic centrepiece of a winding stone staircase and were faced with a long assembled row of what could only have been household staff all dressed up in uniform as though they had strayed off the set for *Downton Abbey*. *Average? Normal?* On what planet was Vito living?

Sick with the nervous unease of someone totally out of their comfort zone, Holly fixed a smile to her stiff face while Vito conducted introductions. There was a great deal of billing and cooing over Angelo and Vito's own former nanny, Serafina, surged forward to take the baby. Apart from her, Silvestro was the head honcho in the household and little giggly Natalia, it turned out, was Holly's English-speaking maid. With great difficulty Holly kept her face straight at the prospect of having a maid and watched while the two nannies carried Angelo off upstairs.

'Natalia will show you to our room,' Vito informed her at the foot of the stairs and then he paused, a frown etching between his level brows, his dark eyes semi-concealed by his ridiculous lashes as he murmured, 'I should have asked you—do you object to sharing a room?'

The planet he was on was definitely far, far from the moon, Holly thought crazily as she raised her brows. 'Where else would I sleep?'

'Obviously you could have your own room,' Vito told her valiantly.

And Holly almost burst out laughing because Vito was being his extraordinarily polite self and going against his own instincts. She could see it in the tension etched in his lean, darkly handsome face, hear it in the edge roughening his dark, deep drawl. He really, *really* didn't want her to choose a separate bedroom and she wondered why on earth he had made the offer. 'No...' Holly reached for his clenched hand. 'You're not getting rid of me that easily,' she teased.

Vito laughed and smiled almost simultaneously and all the tension vanished. *Silly, silly man*, she thought warmly as she followed Natalia up the stairs. Why had he even given her a choice? Separate bedrooms? Was that how husband and wife normally lived in such a gigantic house? How his parents and grandparents had lived? Well, from here on in Vito was going to have to learn how a normal, average couple lived, and having shared a bed with him once had only made her all the keener to repeat the experience, she acknowledged, her colour rising. But there was just no way of denying that the most unbearable hunger clenched her deep down inside when she looked at Vito.

Months had passed since that night in the cottage but she had learned a lot about herself after that first educational experience. Other men hadn't tempted her the way Vito had and she had always assumed that that'd meant she wasn't a very sensual person. Vito, however, had unleashed her newly discovered appetite for intimacy and taught her differently. He was definitely the right man for her. She could only hope that she would prove to be the right woman for him.

Natalia opened the doors of what had to be the most drop-dead ugly bedroom Holly had ever seen. It was truly hideous. Heavy dark drapes shut out most of the light and made the vast room gloomy. A material that looked and felt like dark red leather covered the walls and every other surface from the high, elaborately moulded and domed ceiling to the furniture, which was heavily gilded in gold. Holly swallowed hard. It looked as though it hadn't been decorated in at least a hundred years and it was very possible that the weird paper was antique like the furniture.

Well, Holly thought as her maid cast open the doors to show her around what appeared to be an entire suite of rooms for their use, she might be keen to share a bedroom with Vito but he might have to move the location of the shared bedroom to make her happy. Natalia beamed and showed her into a large room walled with closets, which she swept open to display the contents.

'Who does all this belong to?' Holly asked, recoiling while wondering if all the garment-bag-enclosed items of clothing had been left behind by Vito's former fiancée, Marzia.

'Is *your* gift…is *new*,' the brunette stressed while showing off a still-attached label to what appeared to be a hand-embroidered ballgown of such over-the-top glamour that it took Holly's breath away.

A gift that could only be from Vito. The gift of an entire wardrobe of clothes? Holly fingered through drawers packed with lingerie and nightwear in little decorative bags and stared at the racks of shoes and accessories Natalia was eager for her to see and appreciate. It was a mind-blowing collection and it was just way too much altogether for Holly, after the wedding, the massive palace Vito lived in and his revealing query about whether or not she was willing to share a bedroom with him. What on earth? What on earth kind of marriage was she in that he had told her so little about his life and yet bought her so much? Did he think flashing around his money made up for his failure to explain all the other stuff?

Catching a glimpse of her creased and tousled reflection in one of the many mirrors in the dressing room, Holly almost groaned. She didn't want to get tricked out in fancy clothes, she simply wanted comfort, and as Natalia opened Holly's single case on the now seemingly pitiful assortment of clothing that had been her lot pre-Vito, Holly bent down to scoop out her one extravagance: a shimmering maxi dress with an iridescent sheen that skimmed her every curve with a flattering fit. She was relieved to see that while the bedroom belonged to a bygone age, the en-suite bathroom, while palatial, was contemporary. Stepping into a wonderful walled rain-forest shower, she rinsed away the tired stickiness of travel and tried to let her anxieties float off down the drain with the soapy water.

A marriage was what you made of it and she had no intention of underestimating the challenge ahead. They had married for Angelo's benefit but their son could only enjoy a happy home life if his parents established a good relationship. Holly's childhood had been damaged by her mother's neglect and self-indulgence, Vito's by his father's indifference. He should've warned her about the giant historic house and the extravagant new wardrobe, but she could no more shout at him for being richer and more pedigreed than she had estimated than she could shout at him for his unvarnished generosity.

Dressed, her black hair tumbling freely round her shoulders, Holly explored the connecting rooms Natalia had briefly walked her through earlier. A door stood ajar on the balcony that led off the sitting room and she strolled out, watching the sun go down over the stunning landscape and the manicured gardens below and slowly veil them in peach, gold and terracotta splendour. Sounds in the room she had vacated alerted her to the arrival of a trolley, and the rattle of cutlery fired her appetite and drew her back indoors.

Vito was framed by a doorway at the far end of the room, his suit abandoned in favour of jeans and a white shirt open at his strong brown throat. Her tummy was awash with butterflies as she instinctively drew in a deep breath and savoured her view of him. He stood there, so tall and dark and devastatingly handsome, watching her with the assessing eyes of a hawk.

Vito finally tore his gaze from his bride's opulent curves, that were so wonderfully enhanced by the fine fabric of her dress, but the words he had been about to speak had vanished from his brain. Holly, he acknowledged simply, was an incredibly sexy woman. Innate sensuality threaded her every movement. It was there in her light gliding walk, the feminine sway of her hips, the swell of her breasts as she straightened her spine and angled her head back to expose her throat.

He had expected Apollo to recognise the sheer depth of Holly's natural appeal, but he couldn't be sorry that his friend's distrust had blinded him because when Vito had seen some of his guests look at his bride with lustful intent, it had annoyed the hell out of him. And that new possessive, jealously protective streak about what was *his* disturbed Vito, who was immensely suspicious of emotional promptings. He had always chosen women who brought out the rational side of his nature but Holly incited much more primal urges.

Vito's butler, Silvestro, moved forward to pour the

wine with a flourish and light the candles on the circular table. Holly tasted the wine with an appreciative sip.

'It's an award-winning Brunello my grandfather laid down years ago. This is a special occasion,' Vito pointed out as he dropped lithely down into his seat and shook out his napkin.

'I cut my teeth on wines that tasted like vinegar.' Holly sighed. 'I'm not much of a drinker.'

'Why would you be if it tasted that bad?' Vito asked with amusement.

'Why didn't you warn me that you lived in a vast house your family have owned for centuries?' Holly asked quietly.

'It didn't occur to me,' Vito admitted with a frown.

'This place was a shock…as was the new wardrobe.'

'You were supposed to shop for clothes at the same time as you chose your wedding dress but the stylist said you weren't interested. So I took care of it for you.'

'Thank you, I suppose…'

As Silvestro left the room, having drawn the trolley close to enable them to serve themselves, Holly embarked on the tiny delicate parcels on her plate. They were exquisitely displayed, and the oriental flavours tasted phenomenal. The courses that followed were even better. Holly had never eaten such fabulous food before.

'Who does the cooking here?' she asked.

'I have a very well-paid chef on staff. When I'm staying at one of my other properties he travels ahead of me.'

Bemused by the concept of a mobile personal chef, Holly blinked. 'You have *other* properties?'

'Here I have the apartment in Florence and a villa

on the shores of Lugano in Switzerland. Those were inherited. But I also own property in the countries I visit most frequently,' Vito admitted.

Holly was frowning. 'What's wrong with hotels?'

'I don't like them. I like quiet and privacy, particularly when I'm working,' Vito advanced smoothly. 'It's my sole extravagance.'

'When I called you a spoilt-rotten rich boy I wasn't far off the mark,' Holly dared.

'Had you ever met my grandfather you would never have awarded me that label. He was a rigid disciplinarian with a punitive approach. He thought my mother was too soft with me.' A rueful smile brought a gentler than usual curve to Vito's wide sensual lips. 'He was probably right.'

'Your grandfather sounds very judgemental. I don't think I would've liked him very much.'

'He was a dinosaur but a well-intentioned one. Since he passed away two years ago, however, I have instigated many changes.'

Holly dealt him a sidewise glance and whispered conspiratorially, 'Our bedroom is a complete horror.'

A flashing grin illuminated Vito's lean, dark features. 'Really?'

'Very dark and depressing.'

'I think I've only been in that room once in my life.'

Her brow furrowed. 'You mean it wasn't yours?'

'No, it's simply the main bedroom in the house and Silvestro has been trying to move me in there ever since my grandfather departed,' Vito confided with amusement. 'But I always resist change and I need the allure of a wife there to entice me.'

Holly compressed her lips as she sipped her wine. 'I

have no allure,' she told him, wrinkling her snub nose in embarrassment.

Vito laughed, lounging back in his chair to study her with gleaming dark golden eyes. 'Being unaware of it doesn't mean you don't have it. In fact that very lack of awareness is incredibly appealing.'

'I should check on Angelo.'

'No, not tonight, *bella mia*,' Angelo intoned as he sprang upright to reach for her hands and raise her slowly from her seat. 'Tonight is ours. Angelo has two nannies and an entire household devoted to his needs. After all, he is the first child in the Zaffari family for a generation, and as such more precious than diamonds to our staff.'

Her throat tightened as he looked down at her with glittering golden eyes fringed by ridiculously long lashes. Suddenly she couldn't breathe or move. 'Er… what are we standing here for?'

'I want to see this horror of a bedroom,' Vito said thickly and then he lowered his head and sealed his mouth to hers with hungry, driving urgency.

Like a flamethrower on a bale of hay his passion ignited hers with instantaneous effect. Her arms closed round him, her small hands roving up over his strong, muscular back to cling to his shoulders. His tongue slid moistly between her lips and an erotic thrill engulfed her in dizzy anticipation. Her nipples prickled into tingling tightness while damp heat surged between her legs. She pressed her thighs together, struggling to get a grip on herself but still wanting him so much it almost hurt…

CHAPTER EIGHT

HAULING HOLLY UP into his arms, Vito carried her into the bedroom and settled her on the foot of the bed to remove her shoes.

'I didn't appreciate how dark it was in here,' Vito admitted as he switched on the bedside lamps. 'Or how hideous. My grandfather liked grand and theatrical.' He sighed.

Holly scrambled back against the headboard and studied him with starry eyes. He stood half in shadow, half in light, and the hard, sculpted planes and hollows of his lean, strong face were beautiful. She marvelled at the fate that had brought two such different people together and rejoiced in it too. Liking, respect, attraction, she listed with resolution inside her head, buttoning down the stronger feelings battling to emerge, denying them.

'Did your parents occupy separate bedrooms?' she asked curiously.

'It was always the norm in this household. I didn't want it for us.' Vito came down on the bed beside her. 'If you only knew how much I've longed for this moment. I wanted you with me in London *before* the wedding.'

'But it couldn't be done. I had responsibilities I couldn't turn my back on.' Holly sighed.

'I could've made arrangements to free you of those duties.'

'Not when they're dependent on friendship, loyalty, and consideration for other people,' Holly disagreed gently, lifting a hand to follow the course of his jutting lower lip and note the stubborn angle of his strong jawline. 'You can't rearrange the world only to suit you.'

'*Sì*…yes, I can,' Vito declared without shame.

'But that's *so* selfish—'

'I will not apologise for being selfish when it comes to your needs and Angelo's.' Vito marvelled at her inability to appreciate that he would always place their needs over the needs of others. What was wrong with that? It was true that it took a certain amount of ruthlessness and arrogance, but he had fought hard in life for every single achievement and saw nothing wrong with an approach that maximised the good things for his family and minimised the bad. The way he saw it, if you made enough effort happiness could be balanced as smoothly as a profit-and-loss column.

With his strong white teeth he nipped playfully at the reproving fingertip rapping his chin.

Holly startled and then giggled and sighed. 'What am I going to do with you?'

'Anything you want… I'm up for *anything*.' Vito savoured her, his dark golden eyes holding hers with explicit need for a heartbeat. He pushed her back against the pillows and then his mouth claimed hers with hungry, delicious force.

Heat unfurled in her pelvis. Her heart raced and the tension went out of her only to be replaced by a new kind of tension that shimmied through her bloodstream like an aphrodisiac and made her heart race. Her breath came in quick, shallow gasps between kisses, each leading into the next until he rolled back and, having established that there was no helpful zip, he gathered the hem of her dress in his hands and tugged it up over her body and over her head to pitch it aside.

'That's better,' he growled, pausing to admire the picture she made in her pretty bridal lace lingerie.

'Except you're still wearing far too many clothes,' Holly objected, embarking on his shirt buttons.

Vito yanked off his shirt without ceremony, kicked off his shoes, peeled off his socks, only to halt there, his long, lean frame trembling while Holly's hands roamed over the hills and valleys of his hard, muscular abdomen. Her reverent fingers took a detour to follow the furrow of dark hair vanishing below the waistband of his jeans.

'I missed you,' she said truthfully. 'I missed *this…*'

Unfreezing, lean dark features rigid with control, he unsnapped his jeans and vaulted off the bed to take them off. 'It was the best night of my life, *bellezza mia*.'

And yet he still hadn't made any mention of seeing her again that night or the following morning. That still stung and Holly said nothing. Had he really not seen her note? Could she believe that?

'That note I left at the cottage for you—' she began breathlessly.

'I didn't see it.'

'Would you have phoned if you'd had my number?' she prompted in a reckless rush.

'I don't know,' Vito responded quietly. 'Certainly I would've been tempted, but on another level I distrust anything that tempts me.'

His honesty cut through her. Even if he had found the

note, he wouldn't have phoned her, she decided painfully. He would have written off their night of passion as a once-in-a-lifetime experience and left it behind. That hurt, but there was nothing she could do about it. She wanted to know who else had since shared his bed but it wasn't a question to be asked on their wedding night even though her heart cried out for reassurance. It would be an unfair question when he had not owed her loyalty. Of course there had been other women in the months they had been apart. That was yet another pain she had to bear.

'I've never wanted a woman the way I want you,' Vito told her thickly.

He flung a handful of condoms down by the bed and stripped naked without inhibition while she watched.

Pink washed Holly's face because he was fully aroused and ready.

'I couldn't get enough of you that night and that unnerved me,' he framed abruptly. 'You were a very unexpected discovery.'

He reached for her again, deftly skimming off her bra and panties, twisting his hips away when she tried to touch him. 'No… If you touch me, you'll wreck me. I'm on a hair trigger after months of abstinence,' he growled, lean brown hands roving over the full curves of her breasts, lingering over her pink pointed nipples to tug and tease until little sounds she couldn't silence broke from between her lips.

Vito flung back the sheet and settled her beneath him to pay serious attention to her swollen mouth and the glorious swell of her breasts.

'Months of abstinence?' Holly encouraged helplessly, her breath tripping in her throat as he sucked on a protruding bud while long, skilled fingers stroked her thigh.

'I'm not an easy lay,' he told her. 'I'm very, very fussy.'

'Nothing wrong with that,' Holly framed in ragged reassurance, all the feeling in her body seemingly centred between her thighs where she was scarily desperate for him to touch her.

And then he did and she gasped and her eyes closed and the fire at the heart of her grew hotter still, hips shifting up and from side to side, the drumbeat of need awakened and throbbing and thrumming through every skin cell. Vito shifted down the bed and parted her thighs. He knew exactly what he was doing. She had discovered that the night Angelo was conceived.

He teased her with the tip of his tongue, slow and then quicker until she could no longer stay silent and whimpers and gasps were wrenched from her. A long sure finger stroked through her wet folds and she quivered, every nerve ending jumping to readiness as the excitement crept higher.

At the height of her climax she cried out his name, lost in the convulsive spasms of erotic pleasure. She was so lost in that pleasure that she struggled to remember what day it was and even where she was. Her lashes flickered when she heard him tear open a condom. As he returned to her she wrapped both arms round him possessively, her body temporarily sated.

He pushed her back and drove into her with a guttural groan of satisfaction. 'Like wet satin,' he bit out appreciatively.

Hunger sizzled through her as his bold shaft stretched her and sank deep. Suddenly she was sensually awake again, her body primed as he angled his lean hips to ensure that she received the maximum enjoyment. His hunger for her was unhidden, his strokes were hard and fast, tormentingly strong. The ache low in her body pinged and climbed in intensity. She wanted, oh, *how* she wanted, craved, needed and longed for that maddening pulse of yearning to be answered, overwhelmed. And then her spine was arching and her body jerking and the waves of hot, drenching pleasure were like a shooting star flaming through her and setting her on fire with the wondrous release from her own body.

'Sexiest, most amazing woman ever…and *mine*,' Vito husked in her ear, his weight heavy on her as he rolled over and pulled her down on top of him. 'That's the most important fact. You're mine, *gioia mia*.'

'Are you mine too?' Holly whispered dizzily.

'Sì…'

'Is sex always this good?'

'Not even half the time. We have our own unique variety of fireworks.'

Holly rested her cheek on a damp bronzed shoulder, her body replete. He smelled so good she drank him in like a drug. She liked being his. She liked that possessive note she heard edging his dark drawl because it made her feel less like Angelo's mother and more like Vito's wife, valued, needed and wanted on her own account. Long fingers traced the path of her spine as he shifted position.

'I have an impossibly fast recovery time with you,' Vito husked, sliding her back onto the sheet on her front, lingering on the soft full curves of her behind.

He reached for another condom. Holly didn't even lift her head. She was still in that place somewhere between total satiation and awareness, shifting obediently as he eased a pillow below her hips, raising her, rearranging her to his satisfaction. And then she felt him rigid and full at her entrance where she was now tender and swollen. He drove in hard and she came suddenly fully awake, eyes wide, throat catching on a breath, heart hotwired back into pounding. He buried himself deep and it felt so good she moaned.

'I like the little sounds you make.' He ground into her with power and energy and a spontaneous combustion of heat surged at the apex of her body.

Excitement crowned with her every cry and snatched breath. She couldn't breathe against the onslaught of raw, surging excitement. With every savage thrust he owned her in a way she had never thought to be owned and she gave herself up to the rise of the hot, pulsing pleasure. The excitement crested with white-hot energy and the sweet waves of deep, quivering pleasure consumed her. Winded, she slumped back down into the pillows.

'Shower time,' Vito told her, lifting her out of bed. 'You're not allowed to go to sleep yet.'

'You and your son have a lot in common.'

'We're both very attached to you?' Vito urged her into the shower.

'You don't sleep at night,' she contradicted. 'Although I have to admit that you're more fun than he is in the middle of the night. Angelo gets grouchy when he's teething.'

'I won't get grouchy with you in my bed,' Vito assured her, leaning back against the tiled wall, lean, bronzed and muscular, a study in male perfection.

Holly was like an energy drink, releasing his tension, refreshing him, leaving him feeling amazingly relaxed. Vito had never done relaxed and wasn't quite sure how to handle it. It was a great deal easier simply to concentrate on working off that surplus energy in bed.

Even with the honeyed ache of sex and satiation Holly wanted to put her hands all over him and explore him with the freedom she had restrained on their first night together. She was so comfortable with him, so indescribably comfortable it almost spooked her. 'I can sleep standing up,' she warned him, resting her damp head down on a strong brown shoulder.

'I have to work tomorrow, *bellezza mia*. Make the most of *now*,' Vito murmured huskily, gathering her close.

Her eyes opened very wide on the tiled wall. He had to work the day after their wedding? Was there some crisis on?

'No. I just like to work,' Vito confided lazily, as if there were nothing the slightest bit strange about his desire to act as though the day after their wedding were just like any other day.

'Are you taking *any* time off?' It was a loaded question but she tried to make it sound casual and unconcerned and then held her breath.

'I'll be home every night...you can bet on that,' Vito growled, nipping at the sensitive flesh below her ear until she shivered helplessly against him and his big hands rose to cup and massage her breasts. 'I'll be keeping you very much occupied.'

Sex, she thought dully. Nothing wrong with his enthusiasm in that department but was that really all he was interested in, all he had ever been interested in? Or simply all she had to offer? Her teeth gritted. What did she have to offer in the intellect category? No, she was never going to be his equal there. Were they going to be one of those couples who never interacted except when their child was around? Would she chatter on relentlessly about Angelo and only ever really get Vito's attention in bed? It sounded a sad and desperate role to her but what was she going to do about it? She couldn't *make* him want more or force him to see her in a different light, could she?

A sham marriage? That overheard phone call returned to haunt her. How hard could it be for Vito to fake being genuinely married when all he intended to do was have sex with her? A chill trickled through her tummy and made her tense. Suddenly fears that she had earlier dismissed were becoming a source of genuine concern. Why had she so easily believed that Apollo was talking nonsense about Vito's intentions? Apollo Metraxis had known Vito since childhood. Apollo probably knew Vito a great deal better than she did and if he suspected that Vito had only married her to gain custody of his son, shouldn't she be sincerely scared?

When she wakened it was still dark, with only the faintest glimmer of light showing behind the curtains. She was deliciously comfortable. Vito had both arms wrapped round her and she was snuggled up to him, secure in the warmth and the wonderfully familiar scent of his skin. He was stroking her hip bone and she stretched in a helpless little movement.

'I want you, *tesoro mia*.'

Her eyes flew wide as he shifted against her back, letting her feel the hard swell of him. *'Again?'*

His sensual mouth pressed into the sensitive skin of her throat. 'Don't move. I'll do all the work.'

And he did, repositioning her, gently rousing her

from her drowsiness and then sinking into her with exquisite precision. She heard herself gasp and then moan and the sweet swell of pleasure surged up and overpowered all her anxious thoughts. Excitement took hold and she trembled with need as his smooth thrusts rocked her sensitised body. She couldn't fight her responses or the uncontrollable wave of ecstatic sensation that swept her to an explosive climax.

'What a wonderful way to wake up,' Vito groaned into her tumbled hair. 'I never dreamt that having a wife could be so much fun. Are you joining me for breakfast?'

Behind her hair, Holly rolled her eyes. She was married to one of those horrid people who came alive around dawn and acted as though it were late morning. Either she stayed in bed and saw very little of him or she changed herself to fit. She lay listening to the shower running and watched him emerge swathed in a towel, the long, lean length of his unspeakably beautiful body mostly exposed. Her mouth ran dry as he disappeared into the dressing room and opened another door. Closet doors were rammed back, drawers opened and closed. She scrambled out of bed and ran for the shower before she could be tempted to backtrack and fall back asleep. Dabbing on minimal make-up, she brushed her hair and extracted some of her new clothes to wear because a pair of jeans and a washed-out cotton top didn't seem quite sufficient for the grandeur of the Castello Zaffari.

Clad in beautifully tailored chinos and a filmy blouse in autumn shades, she slotted her feet into canvas shoes and went out to join Vito. He looked as he had the day she had confronted him at the Zaffari Bank: cool, sophisticated, remote, very much the banker. And at the same time he contrived to look amazing whether he was slotting cufflinks into his cuffs or brushing his cropped black hair.

'Who wears cufflinks these days?' Holly prompted.

Vito shrugged. 'We all use them at the bank.'

'Not at the cutting edge of fashion, then,' she mocked, although his dark suit was incredibly well tailored to lovingly shape wide shoulders, a broad chest, narrow hips and long, powerful legs. Just looking at him, she wanted to touch him.

'Breakfast,' he reminded her, heading for the door.

The *castello* was silent until they reached the ground floor where vague signs of industry could be heard somewhere in the distance. Silvestro entered the hall and looked taken aback to see them. He burst into Italian and Vito responded with quiet amusement.

'Why does everybody think I should be staying home today?' he quipped, leading the way into a sunlit dining room.

'Maybe...because you should be?' Holly dared. 'Just married and all that...'

Silvestro fussed round the table making unnecessary adjustments while Vito translated all the many options Holly could choose for breakfast. As the older man sped off Vito lifted one of the financial newspapers piled at his end of the table and began to read it and Holly wondered whether she should have stayed in bed. She wanted to go and see if Angelo was awake but she didn't want to leave Vito lest he leave for the bank while she was gone.

She had already decided to confront Vito about that phone call she had overheard Apollo making but she had intended to pick and choose the right moment, which might well have been while they were still wrapped round each other in bed. But something about the way Vito lifted that newspaper after dragging her downstairs awakened her temper.

'I overheard Apollo talking on the phone to someone at our reception yesterday.'

Vito lowered the newspaper and frowned at her. 'Overheard?' he questioned.

Below the onslaught of his dark glittering gaze, Holly went pink. 'Well, eavesdropped…I suppose.'

'Are you in the habit of listening in on other people's phone calls?'

'That's not really relevant here,' Holly fudged in desperation, feeling like a child being called to account for misbehaviour. 'Apollo was so obviously talking about us…about our marriage. He was saying that you hadn't had a DNA test with Angelo and that there had been no pre-nup—'

'You're trying to shock me with facts?'

Holly scrambled out of her seat and squared her small shoulders. 'Apollo was sneering about his belief that you trust me.'

'Obviously I won't be trusting you in the vicinity of confidential phone calls,' Vito pronounced, deadpan.

Somehow the confrontation was not proceeding in any expected direction and Holly was stung into anger. 'Apollo thinks our marriage is a sham!'

Vito elevated an ebony brow. 'I think the only two people who can comment on that probability are the two of us.'

'Apollo seemed to believe that you had only married me to get me to move to Italy. He thinks you're planning to go to court and try to claim full custody of our son.'

'I'm not sure whether to be more offended by my friend's low take on my morals or by my wife's,' Vito imparted very softly, marvelling that she could have placed credence in such an unrealistic plot, which smacked very much of Apollo's sensational outlook on life. 'Do you think I would do that to you and Angelo?'

'That's not the point,' Holly protested.

'It is exactly the point,' Vito incised with ruthless bite. 'Why else are you challenging me with this nonsense?'

As Silvestro reappeared with a tray Holly sank back down into her seat. She was angry and mortified at the same time but clung to the comforting fact that Vito had called her concerns 'nonsense'. While food was being laid on the table, Holly studied her pale pink nails and suspected that one day she might possibly throw a coffee pot at Vito for his sarcastic cool.

'To clarify matters,' Vito mused as Silvestro retreated, 'Apollo was most probably talking to a mutual friend called Jeremy, who happens to be a lawyer trained in family law. Although it is ridiculously unnecessary, Apollo tries to protect me from the gold-diggers of this world. If it is any consolation he was no keener on Marzia. He would never marry without a pre-nuptial agreement in place. I deemed it unnecessary because I would not marry a woman I couldn't trust. You're being naive and insecure.'

Holly bridled at that blunt speech. 'I don't see how.'

With precise movements that set her teeth on edge, Vito poured a cup of black coffee. 'I would not deprive my son of his mother. I was sent to boarding school abroad at the age of seven, Holly. I was incredibly homesick and unhappy. Do you honestly think I would subject Angelo to anything similar?'

Holly studied her cup of tea with wooden resolve. Her face was so hot she could feel her ears heating up in concert. No, she could not see him planning to do anything that would damage their son. Boarding school abroad at the tender age of seven? That was brutal, she thought helplessly.

'I *love* my son. I will try hard never to hurt him and I know how much he needs his mother,' Vito framed with measured cool. 'I am also an honourable man. I am not deceitful in personal relationships. I married you in good faith. If eavesdropping on Apollo can rouse your suspicions to this level, what are our prospects for the future? Trust has to work both ways to be effective.'

Holly swallowed hard. Vito was annoyed with her for doubting him and for paying heed to a stupid phone call she shouldn't have been listening to in the first place. She wasn't sure she could blame him for that. On the other hand his determination to head to the bank the day after their wedding was hardly likely to boost her confidence in his attitude towards either her or their marriage.

How much did Vito value her? Just how unimportant was she in his desire for a marriage that would not interfere in his inflexible daily schedule? To thrive, all relationships needed compromise, commitment and the luxury of time spent together. Didn't he appreciate that? And if he didn't, was she clever enough to teach him that she could offer him something more worthwhile than sex? That was a tall order.

Vito rose from his chair and studied her in brooding silence. 'By the way, we're dining out this evening with friends.'

Holly looked up in surprise. 'What friends?'

'Apollo and his girlfriend and Jeremy Morris and his wife. They're currently staying on Apollo's yacht with him.'

The prospect of spending an evening in Apollo Metraxis's radius appealed about as much to Holly as a public whipping. She frowned, studying Vito with incredulous eyes. 'Knowing how I feel about Apollo, why would you arrange something like that?'

Vito compressed his stubborn mouth. 'He's a close friend. He made a mistake. You need to get over it.'

Temper threw colour into Holly's cheeks. 'Do I, indeed?'

Vito gazed expectantly back at her. 'I want it all smoothed over and forgotten…'

'Right, so that's me got my orders, then.' Holly lifted her chin.

'It's not an order, Holly, it's advice. I'm not dropping a lifelong friend because you don't like him.'

'And isn't there some excuse for that dislike?'

'Apollo didn't tell any lies about how we met. Remember that,' Vito retorted with succinct bite.

A painful flush illuminated Holly's face.

'Why shouldn't we have a night out?' Vito fired at her in exasperation. 'I thought you would enjoy getting dressed up and socialising—most women do.'

'That's not my world,' Holly breathed in taut objection.

'It is *now*,' Vito pointed out without hesitation, his impatience unconcealed. 'You need to make an effort to fit in. Why do you think I bought you all those clothes? I want you to have the expensive trappings and to *enjoy* having them.'

As Vito strode out Holly held her breath, feeling a

little like someone trying to fight off a panic attack. He had voiced truths she didn't really want to face. This was his world and, in marrying him, she had become part of that world. He saw no reason why his life shouldn't continue the way it always had and he was making no allowances for Holly's insecurities. No, it was her job to swallow her ire with Apollo and be nice. Well, that certainly put her in her place, didn't it? Vito's long-standing friendship with the Greek billionaire meant more to him than his wife's loss of face at her own wedding. Just as work still meant more to him than settling into marriage and fatherhood. Vito, she recognised painfully, was highly resistant to change of any kind…

CHAPTER NINE

AFTER LUNCH THE same day, Holly lifted Angelo out of the high chair in the dining room and walked outside to settle the baby on a rug already spread across the grass. Her son beamed as she arranged several toys within his reach, enjoying the change of scene.

'Tea,' Silvestro pronounced with decision, having followed her, and he sped off again. Holly made no comment, having already learned that Silvestro liked to foresee needs and fulfil them before anyone could make a request and, truthfully, she did fancy a cup of tea.

She cuddled Angelo and studied the bird's-eye view of the gardens spread out below in an embroidered carpet of multi-hued greens with occasional splashes of colourful spring flowers. Daily life at the Castello Zaffari promised to be pretty much idyllic, she reflected ruefully, feeling ashamed of her negative thoughts earlier in the day when Vito had left her to go to work.

Here she was on a permanent holiday in a virtual palace where she ate fabulous food and was waited on hand and foot. She had beautiful clothes, an incredibly handsome, sexy husband and a very cute baby. What was she complaining about? For the first time ever since Angelo's birth she also had free time to spend with her son. As for the dinner outing? That was a minor hiccup and, having examined her new wardrobe, she had decided to follow the 'little black dress rule' rather than risk being over-or underdressed for the occasion.

A woman in a sunhat with a basket over her arm walked up a gravelled path towards her. Holly tensed, recognising her mother-in-law, Concetta Zaffari.

'Are you on your own?' the small brunette asked. 'I thought I had seen Vito's car drive past earlier but I assumed I was mistaken.'

'No, you weren't mistaken. He's at the bank,' Holly confirmed, as the older woman settled down beside her to make immediate overtures to Angelo.

'Today? My son went into work *today*?' his mother exclaimed in dismay.

Holly gave a rueful nod.

'He should be here with you,' Concetta told her, surprising her.

The rattle of china and the sound of footsteps approaching prompted Holly to scramble upright again. She handed Angelo to Concetta, who was extending her arms hopefully and chattering in Italian baby talk. The two women sat down by the wrought iron table in the shade while Silvestro poured the tea. He had magically contrived to anticipate the arrival of Vito's mother because he had brought an extra cup and a plate of tiny English biscuits.

'A honeymoon isn't negotiable. It should be a given,' Concetta pronounced without hesitation.

'If Vito wants to work, well, then he wants to work,' Holly parried, tactfully non-committal.

'You and this darling little boy are Vito's family

and you must ensure that my son puts you first,' Vito's mother countered. 'That is very important.'

Holly breathed in deep. 'Vito loves to work. I don't feel I have the right to ask him to change something so basic about himself.'

'Priorities have to change once you're married and a parent. As for having the right…' The older woman sipped her tea thoughtfully. 'I will be open with you. I saw your distress after Apollo made that unsuitable speech at the wedding yesterday.'

Holly winced. 'I was more embarrassed than distressed…I think.'

'But why should you be embarrassed by this gorgeous little boy?' Concetta demanded. 'Let me tell you something… When I married Vito's father, Ciccio, thirty-odd years ago, I was already pregnant…'

Holly's blue eyes widened in surprise at that frank admission.

Concetta compressed her lips. 'My father would never have allowed me to marry a man like Ciccio in any other circumstances. He knew that Ciccio was a fortune hunter but I was too naive to see the obvious. I was eighteen and in love for the first time. Ciccio was in his thirties.'

'That's a big age gap,' Holly remarked carefully.

'I was an heiress. Ciccio targeted me like a duck on a shooting range,' the brunette declared with a wry twist of her lips, 'and I paid a steep price for being young and silly. He was unfaithful from the outset but I closed my eyes to it because while my father was alive divorce seemed out of the question. Only when Ciccio dragged our son's reputation down into the dirt with his own did I finally see the light.'

'The scandal in the newspapers?' Holly slotted in with a frown, fascinated by the elegant brunette's candour.

'I could not forgive Ciccio for saving himself at Vito's expense.'

'Vito wanted to protect you.'

'That hurt,' Concetta confided tautly. 'It hurt me even more to see Vito falsely accused and slandered but it also let me see that he was an adult able to handle the breakdown of his parents' marriage. Now I'm making my middle-aged fresh start.'

'It's never too late,' Holly said warmly, noticing how Angelo's sparkling dark eyes matched his father's and his grandmother's.

Concetta confided that she regularly took the flowers from the garden at the *castello* as arranging them was her hobby. Holly admitted that she had never arranged a flower in her life and urged the older woman to keep on helping herself. Vito's mother promised to continue doing the flowers for the house and the two women parted on comfortable, friendly terms.

Holly spent what remained of the day doing her hair and her nails and refusing to think about the evening ahead. Thinking about it wasn't going to change anything. Apollo was Vito's friend and he thought highly of him, she reminded herself. Unfortunately it didn't ease the sting of the reality that her husband seemed to rate Apollo more highly than he rated his wife.

Vito collected her in a limo. He wore a sleek dinner jacket. 'I used my apartment to change,' he admitted, smiling as she climbed into the car. 'You look very elegant.'

But as soon as Holly arrived at the restaurant and saw the other two women she realised she had got it wrong in the frock department because she had played it too safe. Apollo's girlfriend, Jenna, wore a taupe silk dress that plunged at both back and front and was slit to the thigh, while Jeremy's wife, Celia, wore a short fitted scarlet dress that showed off her very shapely legs. Holly immediately felt frumpy and dumpy in her unexciting outfit, wishing that at the very least she had chosen to wear something that displayed a bit of cleavage.

While the men talked, Celia shot inquiries at Holly and it was no surprise to discover that the highly educated and inquisitive redhead was a criminal lawyer. Having her background and educational deficiencies winkled out and exposed made Holly feel very uncomfortable but her attempts to block Celia's questions were unsuccessful and she was forced to half turn away and chat to Jenna to escape the interrogation. Jenna, however, talked only about spa days and exclusive resorts.

'You've never been on a ski slope?' she remarked in loud disbelief.

'I'll teach Holly to ski,' Vito sliced in, smooth as glass.

Holly paled because the idea of racing down a snowy hill at breakneck speed made her feel more scared than exhilarated. As the entire conversation round the table turned to ski resorts and talk of everyone's 'best ever runs', she was excluded by her unfamiliarity with the sport. Jenna's chatter about hot yoga classes and meditation were matched by Celia's talk about the benefits of an organic, *natural* diet, ensuring that Holly felt more and more out of her depth. She was also bored stiff.

'How do you feel about yachting?' Apollo asked smoothly across the table, his green eyes hard and mocking. 'Do you get seasick?'

'I've never been on a yacht, so I wouldn't know. I'm fine on a fishing boat or a ferry, though,' she added with sudden amusement at the amount of sheer privilege inherent in such a conversational topic.

'Who took you fishing?' Vito asked her abruptly.

'Someone way before your time,' Holly murmured, unwilling to admit in such exclusive company that it had been a rowing-boat experience with a teenaged boyfriend.

'Way to go, Holly! Keep him wondering.' Celia laughed appreciatively.

Her mobile phone vibrated in her bag and she pulled it out. 'Excuse me. I have to take this,' she said apologetically, and rose from the table to walk out to the foyer.

It was Lorenza phoning to tell her that Angelo had finally settled after a restless evening. Aware that her son was teething, Holly had asked the nanny to keep her posted. On the way back to the table she called into the cloakroom. She was in a cubicle when she heard Jenna and Celia come in.

'What on earth does a guy like Vito see in a woman like her?' Jenna was demanding thinly. 'She's like a little brown sparrow beside him.'

Angry resentment hurtled through Holly and in the strangest way it set her free to be herself.

'Jeremy thinks Vito must have had a pre-nup written up by another lawyer,' Celia commented. 'There's no way Vito hasn't safeguarded himself.'

Emerging, Holly washed her hands and glanced at the aghast pair of women frozen by the sinks. 'At least I've got a wedding ring on my finger,' she pointed out to Jenna. 'You have to be at least number one hundred in Apollo's long line of companions.'

'We had no idea you were in here,' Celia began sharply, defensively.

'Ah, Celia,' Holly pronounced gently, flicking the tall redhead a calm appraisal in turn. 'I can assure you that there is no pre-nup. My husband *trusts* me.'

And with that ringing assurance, Holly turned on her heel, head held high, and walked back out to the table. And she might resemble a little brown sparrow, she thought with spirit, but she was married to a guy who found little brown sparrows the ultimate in sex appeal. Amused by the level of her own annoyance, Holly returned to her seat and in a break in the conversation addressed Apollo. 'So where's the best place for me to learn to ski?' she asked playfully.

Vito dealt her a bemused look and watched her begin to smile at Apollo's very detailed response because Apollo took his sports very seriously.

A deep sense of calm had settled over Holly. She was still furious with Vito for subjecting her to such an evening with very little warning but, having stood up for herself and spoken up in her own defence, she felt much more comfortable. After all, she could be herself anywhere and in any company. The only person able to make her feel out of her depth was herself and she was determined not to let those insecurities control her reactions again. So, she was more accustomed to stacking shelves in a shop and occasional trips to the cinema but she could do spa days and skiing and yachting trips if she wanted to. It was Vito's world but that wedding ring on her finger confirmed that now it was her world as well and she needed to remember that.

She would have to adapt. But Vito had to learn to adapt too, she reflected grimly. He had told her over the breakfast table that she had to trust him, but so far he had done little to earn that trust. And so far, Holly had been the one to make all the changes. She had given up her home, her country, her friends, and her entire life to come to Italy and make a family with Vito. True, it was a gilded life but that didn't lessen the sacrifices she had made on her son's behalf. When was Vito planning to become a family man, who put his wife and his child first?

'You've been very quiet,' Vito remarked as Holly started up the stairs.

'I want to check on Angelo.'

'There is no need.'

'There is every need. I'm his mother,' Holly declared shortly. 'It's immaterial how efficient or kind your staff are, Vito. At the end of the day they are only employees and none of them will ever love Angelo the way I do. Don't ever try to come between me and my son!'

In silence, Holly went up to the nursery, tiptoeing across the floor to gaze down at the slumbering shape of her little boy lying snug in his cot. Smiling, she left the nursery again.

'I wouldn't try to come between you,' Vito swore.

Holly ignored him and went down to their bedroom, kicking off her shoes before stalking into the bathroom.

'Holly...' Vito breathed warningly from the doorway.

'I'm not speaking to you. You have a choice,' Holly cautioned him thinly. 'Either we have silence or we have it out. *Choose.*'

Vito groaned. 'That's not much of a choice.'

'It's the only one you're going to get and probably more than you deserve.' Holly dabbed impatiently at her eyes with a cotton pad and eye-make-up remover.

'Have it out, I suppose,' Vito pronounced very drily.

Holly tilted her chin. 'You had no business forcing me out to that dinner tonight because I wasn't ready for it. I was uncomfortable, of course I was. Two days ago I was living in an ordinary world with ordinary jobs and meeting ordinary people and now I'm in this *weird* new environment,' she framed between compressed lips. 'And I know everyone seems to think I'm in clover and it *is* wonderful not to have to worry about money any more, but it's strange and it's going to take me time to get used to it. You haven't given me any time. You expect *me* to make all the changes…'

Vito had paled. 'You're making valid points. I'm not a patient man.'

'And you don't always live up to your promises either. You said you'd do everything within your power to make me happy,' Holly reminded him doggedly. 'Then you go back to work within a day of the wedding even though you have a son you barely know and a wife you don't know much better. If you want me to trust you, you have to show me that you value me and Angelo, that we're not just new possessions to be slotted into your busy life and expected not to make any waves. You have to give us your time, Vito, take us places, show us around our new home.'

Holly was challenging him and he hadn't expected that from her. She had thrown his words about trust back at him. And she was also telling him that he was already failing dismally in the successful husband stakes. He had married her one day and walked away the next, acting as though a wedding ring were more than sufficient proof of his commitment.

And had Holly been Marzia it *would* have been sufficient. Marzia had wanted that ring and his lifestyle. She would have thrown a party to show off the *castello* and she would have invited all the most important socially connected people to act as her admiring audience. She would have spent half the day at a beauty salon and the other half shopping for couture garments designed to impress. Vito had lost count of the number of times he had returned to the town house he had once shared with Marzia only to discover that they were hosting a dinner when he was longing for a quiet evening. Marzia had been easily bored and had needed others to keep her entertained. Holly, in comparison, asked for and expected very little. In fact she was asking for something she shouldn't have had to ask for, he acknowledged with a grim look in his dark, unusually thoughtful gaze.

Family came first…*always*. Even his workaholic grandfather had never put the bank before his family. What had he been thinking of when he'd left Holly and Angelo to amuse themselves? They needed him and he hadn't spared them a thought.

'And tonight?' Vito prompted.

'It was bearable. I heard Celia and Jenna bitching about me but I stood up for myself and I couldn't care less about their opinions. But I would've been more equipped to enjoy myself and relax if I'd had more time to prepare.'

'I screwed up,' Vito acknowledged broodingly.

'Yes,' Holly agreed, sliding into bed while he still hovered. 'And sometimes I'll screw up. That's life.'

'I'm not used to screwing up,' Vito told her.

'Then you'll try harder not to make the same mistakes again,' Holly riposted sleepily.

* * *

Holly slept in the following morning. She woke with a start, showered and pulled on jeans to pelt upstairs and spend some time with Angelo. In surprise she stilled in the doorway of the nursery bathroom when she saw Vito kneeling down by the side of the bath and engaged in dive-bombing plastic boats for Angelo's amusement. She had simply assumed that Vito had gone into the bank as usual but it was clear that at some stage, even though he had dressed for work, he had changed his mind. His jacket and tie were hooked on the radiator, his shirtsleeves rolled up.

'Vito...'

Raking damp, tousled black hair off his brow, Vito turned his head and flashed her a heart-stopping grin. 'Angelo emptied his cereal bowl over his head at breakfast and I decided I should stay home.'

Holly moved forward. 'I can see that...'

'I'm very set in my ways but I believe I can adapt,' he told her, laughing as Angelo smacked the water with a tiny fist and splashed both of them.

'He'll grow up so fast your head will spin. You won't ever get this time back with him.' She sighed. 'I didn't want you to miss out and then live to regret it.'

'You spoke up and that was the right thing to do. I respect your honesty. Parenting is a whole new ball game and I still have to get my head around it,' Vito confided, snatching down a towel and spreading it on the floor before lifting Angelo's squirming little body out of the bath and laying him down.

'How to get yourself soaked!' Holly groaned.

'I'm already drenched to the skin,' Vito riposted with quiet pride. 'Angelo and I have had a lot of fun.'

The nursery was empty and Holly rustled around gathering the necessities. 'What have you done with the nanny posse?' she asked curiously.

'I told them to take a few hours off. Being so new to this I didn't want an audience.'

Holly dried Angelo and deftly dressed him. Vito unbuttoned his wet shirt, the parted edges revealing a bronzed sliver of muscular torso. Together they walked downstairs.

'Do you have any photographs of when you were pregnant?' Vito asked, startling her into turning wide blue eyes onto his lean, dark face.

'I don't think so...I wasn't feeling very photogenic at the time. Why?'

'I'm sorry I missed all that. Something else I can't get back,' Vito conceded gravely. 'I really would have liked to have seen you when you were carrying our child.'

Regret assailed her, for she would have loved to have had his support during those dark days of worry and exhaustion. She had struggled to stay employed and earning for as long as possible so as not to be a burden on Pixie.

'As for that challenge you offered me,' Vito mused, walking back to their bedroom to change. 'Draw up a list of places you would like to go.'

'No lists. I'm phobic about lists,' she told him truthfully. 'Let's be relaxed about what we do and where we go. No itineraries laid out in stone. Are you taking time off?'

'Of course. But I'll catch up with my email in the evenings,' he warned her. 'I can't completely switch off.'

'That's OK,' she hastened to tell him. 'But you may be bored.'

'Not a chance, *gioia mia*,' Vito riposted as he cast off his wet shirt. 'You and Angelo will keep me fully occupied from dawn to dusk and beyond.'

'And beyond' was very much in Holly's mind as she studied his muscular brown torso, a tiny burst of heat pulsing between her thighs. It was the desire she never really lost around Vito. Her colour heightened. She was so pleased, so relieved that he had listened to her, but there was a fear deep down inside her that she would not have enough to offer to satisfy him outside working hours.

'When was the last time you saw your mother?' Vito asked lazily as they lay in bed six weeks later.

Holly stretched somnolent limbs still heavy with pleasure and rolled her head round to face him, bright blue eyes troubled. 'I was sixteen. It wasn't the nicest experience.'

'I can deal with not nice,' Vito volunteered, closing an arm round her slight shoulders to draw her comfortingly close.

Holly felt gloriously relaxed and shockingly happy. With every day that passed she was increasingly convinced that Vito was the man of her dreams. He was everything she had ever wanted, everything she had ever dreamt of. But even better, he had proved that he was capable of change.

Six weeks ago, she had reminded Vito that he had to learn how to be part of a family instead of an independent operator seeing life only from a work-orientated point of view. He had started out wanting to make up lists and tick off boxes as if that were the only route to success. He had a maddening desire to know in advance exactly what he would be doing every hour of every day and had only slowly learned to take each day as it came.

Holly had spent several days creating a mood board of her ideas on how to redecorate their hideous bedroom. While she was doing that, Vito had learned how to entertain Angelo. Settling on a colour palate of soothing grey enlivened with spicy tangerine accents, Holly had ordered the required products and utilised a local company to do the actual work. Throughout the entire process, Vito had shown depressingly little curiosity, merely agreeing that it was many years since the *castello* had been decorated and that, as his mother had never had any interest in revitalising the interior, he was sure there was plenty of scope for Holly to express her talents.

Leaving the work team to handle the decorating project, Holly and Vito had taken their son to stay on the shores of Lake Lugano. Vito's family had bought a Swiss villa because, like Zurich and Geneva, Lugano was a major financial centre. Over the generations the Zaffari bankers had found the shores of the lake a convenient business location to stash the family while they worked.

At the villa they had thrown open the shutters on the magnificent lake views and enjoyed long lazy meals on the sun-dappled *loggia*. By day they had explored the water in a private boat, stopping off to ramble around the picturesque little villages on the rugged shoreline. Some evenings they had sat on the lake terrace drinking garnet-coloured Brunello di Montalcino wine while they watched the boats sailing by with twinkling lights. Other nights they had strolled round the cobbled lanes in Lugano to pick a quiet restaurant for dinner, but none had yet lived up to the perfection on a plate offered by Vito's personal chef.

They had visited the Zoo al Maglio, where Angelo had been enchanted by the antics of the monkeys and had struggled fiercely to copy them. They had caught the funicular railway to the top of Monte San Salvatore to enjoy the alpine scenery and on the way back they had stopped off at a chocolate factory, where a peckish Holly had eaten her weight in chocolate and had sworn never to eat it again while Vito teased her about how much he adored her curves.

There had been shopping trips as well, to the designer boutiques on the Via Nassa, where Holly had become bored because her new wardrobe was so expansive she saw no reason to add to it. She had much preferred the bustling liveliness of the farmers' market in the Piazza Riforma, from which she had returned home carrying armfuls of the flowers she couldn't resist. Discovering that arranging them was more of an art than a matter of simply stuffing them in a big vase, she had resolved to ask her mother-in-law for some tips.

'Your mother…' Vito reminded her. 'Are you going to sleep?'

'No. It's only two o'clock in the afternoon.' But in truth she was already smothering a yawn because their post-lunch nap had turned into a sex-fest. 'Mum…' she reminded herself. 'It was the last time I ever lived with her. I thought she wanted me back because I was no longer a child who needed looking after twenty-four-seven. I thought she finally wanted to get to know her daughter. But I got it all wrong—'

'How…?' Vito asked, long fingers inscribing a soothing pattern on her hip bone.

'Mum was living with a guy who owned a little supermarket. She asked me to help out in the shop…' Holly's voice trailed away ruefully. 'It was a crucial school year with exams and I didn't want to miss classes but she insisted she couldn't cope and I fell for it—'

'And…?' Vito prompted when she fell silent again.

'It turned out that she only wanted me working in the shop to save *her* having to do it and they weren't even paying me minimum wage. I was just cheap labour to please her boyfriend and give her a break.' Holly sighed. 'I missed so much school that social services took me back into care. Of course I failed half my exams as well. I haven't seen her since. I realised that she was never going to be the mother I wanted her to be and I had to accept that. She wasn't the maternal type—'

'And yet you're so different with Angelo.'

'And if you compare your relationship with your father, aren't you different with Angelo too? We both want to give our son what we didn't have ourselves,' Holly murmured, rejoicing in the heat and strength of his long, lean length next to hers. 'Why didn't you invite your father to our wedding?'

'I thought it would be too awkward for my mother and our guests, particularly when Ciccio is fighting for a bigger divorce settlement because he stands to lose a lot of things that he's always taken for granted.'

'Concetta seems quite happy…well, for someone going through a divorce, that is,' Holly qualified ruefully.

'With my father gone she has a lot less stress in her life and for the first time she has her independence without the restriction of either a father or a husband. She loves her new home and the freedom she has there.'

'It's a new life for her,' Holly mused drowsily, thinking that her own new life was still in the honeymoon period and wouldn't really officially start until they returned to the *castello* the following day and embarked on a more normal routine.

'I didn't realise that marrying you would be a new beginning for me as well,' Vito admitted thoughtfully, acknowledging that he had not fully thought through the ramifications of marrying and becoming a parent. He had plunged into matrimony, dimly expecting life to go on as it always had only to learn that change was inevitable.

'Do you have regrets?' she whispered fearfully. 'Do you sometimes wish you were still single and unencumbered? I suppose you must.'

'I have no regrets when I'm in bed with you…not a single one.' Vito gazed down at her with dancing dark golden eyes alive with wolfish amusement. '*Sì*, I knew you'd be annoyed by that point but, *Dio mio*…at least I'm honest!'

And as his eyes laughed down at her, her heart swelled inside her and she knew, just *knew* in her very soul that she loved Vito. She loved him the way she had tried not to love him. She had tried so hard to protect herself from feeling more for Vito than he felt for her because that was the hard lesson she had learned in loving her unresponsive mother. You couldn't *make* a person care for you; you couldn't force those feelings.

In any case, it had crossed her mind more than once that Vito's emotions might be quite unavailable in the love category. Holly had met Vito on the rebound, shortly after his fiancée had ditched him. That Christmas theirs had been a classic rebound attraction. Was

Vito still in love with Marzia? Had he tried to return to the beautiful blonde during the fourteen months he and Holly had been apart? Had he mourned the loss of Marzia once he'd decided that he had to marry Holly for his son's sake? And how, when he never ever so much as mentioned the woman, could Holly possibly ask him to tell her honestly how he currently felt about Marzia?

She couldn't ask because she didn't think she could bear to live with the wrong answer.

CHAPTER TEN

TWO WEEKS LATER, Holly shuffled the messy pile of financial publications that Vito always left in his wake and lifted the other, more gossipy newspapers out to peruse. She flicked through the pages, thrilled when she was able to translate the occasional word of Italian.

Her knowledge of the language was slowly growing. She could manage simple interactions with their staff and greetings. Hopefully once she started proper Italian lessons with a local teacher later in the week her grasp of Italian would grow in leaps and bounds. After all, both her son and her husband would speak the language and she was determined not to be the odd one out. Vito's desire that their son should grow up bilingual was more likely to be successful if she learned Italian as well.

Abandoning the papers, she selected a magazine, flipping through glossy photographs of Italian celebrities she mostly didn't recognise until one picture in particular stopped her dead in her tracks. It was a photo of Marzia wearing the most fabulous sparkling ballgown with Vito by her side. She frowned and stared down at it with such intensity that she literally saw spots appear in front of her eyes. She struggled to translate the blurb beneath the picture. It appeared to be recent and it had been taken at some party. The previous week, Vito had spent two nights at his Florence apartment because he had said he was working late. Well, the first time he had been working late, the second time he had actually said that he had to attend a very boring dinner, which invariably would drag on into the early hours…

For dinner, read dinner *dance*, she reflected unhappily. Her entire attention was welded to the photo. Vito and Marzia had been captured at what appeared to be a formal dance with their arms in the air as if their hands had just parted from a clasp. Both of them were smiling. And my goodness, didn't Marzia look ravishing? Not a blonde hair out of place. Holly's fingers crept up to finger through her own tumbled mane. She studied Marzia's perfectly made-up face and thought about her own careless beauty routine, which often consisted of little more than eyeliner, blush and lip gloss. Looking at that gorgeous dress, she glanced down at her own casual silky tee and skirt and low-heeled sandals. She was dressed very nicely indeed in expensive garments but there wasn't even a hint of glamour or sequinned sparkle in her appearance.

Maybe it had only been one dance that Marzia and Vito had shared. And of course they had been photographed for such a potentially awkward moment between former partners was always of interest to others. And they were smiling and happy together. Why not? Her heart had shrunk into a tight, threatened lump inside her chest and her tummy felt as though it were filled with concrete. Vito had spent a couple of years with Marzia. They knew each other well and why should they be enemies? There was no reason why they shouldn't dance together and treat each other like old friends, was there?

Vito hadn't broken any rules. He hadn't told her any lies. All right, he hadn't mentioned the dancing or seeing Marzia, but then he never mentioned his ex, a reality that had made it very difficult for Holly to tackle the subject. Wasn't Vito entitled to his privacy in relation to past relationships? In any case he was not the kind of man who would comfortably open up about previous lovers. Her eyes stung with tears because trying to be reasonable and take a sensible overview was such a challenge for her at that moment.

At the heart of her reaction, Holly registered, was Marzia's sheer glamour and her own sense of inadequacy. Holly didn't do glamour, had never even tried. The closest she had ever got to glamour was a Santa outfit. But what if that kind of gloss, *Marzia's* gloss, was what Vito really liked and admired?

Obviously she had to confront him about the photo and there would probably be a perfectly reasonable explanation about why he had said nothing…

'I knew you would make a fuss,' Vito would be able to point out quite rightly.

She was a jealous cow and he probably sensed that. Although she had never been competitive with other women, having a rival that beautiful and sophisticated could only be hurtful and intimidating. She loved Vito so much and was painfully aware that he did not love her. In addition, she was always guiltily conscious that she had won her wedding ring purely by default. Vito had married her because she was the mother of his son.

Mother of his son, Holly repeated inwardly. Not a very sexy label, certainly not very glamorous. But it didn't have to be that way, she reasoned ruefully. She could walk that extra mile, she could make the effort and dress up too. But she needed the excuse of an occasion, didn't she? Well, at least to begin with… On her passage across the hall, she spoke to Silvestro and told him that she would like a special romantic meal to be served for dinner.

Silvestro positively glowed with approval and she went upstairs to go through her new wardrobe and select the fanciest dress she owned. In the oddest way she would have liked to put on a Santa outfit for Vito again but it wouldn't work out of season. She would tackle Vito the moment he came home. She wouldn't give him time to regroup and come up with evasions or excuses. What she wanted most of all was honesty. He needed to tell her how he truly felt about Marzia and they would proceed from that point.

Did he still have feelings for the beautiful blonde? How would she cope if he admitted that? Well, she would have to cope. Her life, Vito's and Angelo's were inextricably bound to the stability of their marriage. Would he want a separation? A divorce? Her brain was making giant leaps into disaster zones and she told herself off for the catastrophic effect that photo had had on her imagination and her confidence. Since when had she chosen to lie down and die rather than fight?

From the dressing room she extracted the hand-embroidered full-length dress, which glittered with sparkling beads below the lights. It definitely belonged in the glamour category.

Vito knew something strange was afoot the instant he walked into the hall of the *castello* and Silvestro gave him a huge smile. Silvestro had the face of a sad sheepdog and was not prone to smiling.

'The *signora* is on the way downstairs…' he was informed.

Vito blinked and then he saw Holly as he had only seen her on their wedding day, and quite naturally he stared. She drifted down the staircase in a fantastic dress that seemed to float airily round her hourglass curves. It was the sort of gown a woman wore to a ball and Vito suffered a stark instant of very male panic. Why was she all dressed up? What had he forgotten? Were they supposed to be going out somewhere? What special date had slipped past him unnoticed?

Silvestro spread wide the dining-room door and Vito saw the table set in a pool of candlelight and flowers and thought…what the hell? He spun back as Holly drew level with him, her blue eyes bright but her small face oddly tight and expressionless. A pang ran through Vito's long, lean frame because he was accustomed to his wife greeting him at the end of the day as though he had been absent for a week…and in truth he thoroughly enjoyed the wholehearted affection she showered on both him and his son.

'You look magnificent, *bellezza mia*,' Vito declared, while frantically wondering what occasion he had overlooked and how he could possibly cover up that reality rather than hurt Holly's feelings by admitting his ignorance.

She was so vulnerable sometimes. He saw that sensitivity in her and marvelled that she retained it even after all the disappointments life had faced her with. His primary role was to protect Holly from hurt and disillusionment. He didn't want her to lose her innocence. He didn't want her to turn cynical or bitter. But most of all he never ever wanted to be the man who disillusioned her.

'Glad you like the dress,' Holly said a tad woodenly. 'Shall we sit down?'

'I'm no match for your elegance without a shower and a change of clothes,' Vito pointed out with a slight line dividing his black brows into the beginnings of a frown because her odd behaviour was frustrating him.

'Please sit down. We'll have a drink,' Holly suggested, because she had laid that photo of Marzia and him at his place at the table and she was keen for him to see it before she lost her nerve at confronting him in what was starting to feel a little like a badly planned head-on collision.

Maybe she should have been less confrontational and given him warning. Only not if the price of that was Vito coming up with a polite story that went nowhere near the actual truth. She didn't believe he would lie to her but he wouldn't want to upset her and he would pick and choose words to persuade her in a devious way that her concerns were nonsensical.

Vito was on the edge of arguing until he glimpsed the photo, and its appearance was so unexpected that it stupefied him. He stared down at the photo of himself dancing with Marzia in wonderment while Silvestro poured his wine. Why were they apparently celebrating this inappropriate photograph with rose petals scattered across the table and the finest wine? His frown of incomprehension deepened.

'What is this?' he demanded with an abruptness that startled Holly as he swept up the photo.

Consternation gripped Holly because he didn't sound

puzzled, he sounded downright angry. 'I wanted to ask you to explain that picture,' she muttered warily.

'So you set me up with some sort of a romantic dinner and tell me I can't have a shower? And sit me down with a photo of my ex?' Vito exclaimed incredulously. 'This is more than a little weird, Holly!'

Legs turning wobbly as she encountered scorching dark golden eyes of enquiry, Holly dropped reluctantly down into her chair. 'I'm sorry. I just wanted to get it over with and I wanted you to say exactly what's on your mind.'

'Weird!' Vito repeated with an emphatic lack of inhibition, crumpling the photo into a ball of crushed paper and firing it into the fire burning merrily across the room. 'Where did you get that photograph from and when did you see it?'

Holly sketched out the details, her heart beating very fast. She hadn't expected to feel guilty but now she did because taking Vito by surprise had only annoyed him.

'Today?' Vito stressed in astonishment. 'But that photo is at least three years old!'

'Three years old…' Holly's voice trailed off as she studied him in disbelief.

'It was taken at our engagement party. Why on earth would it be printed again now?' he questioned.

Holly scrambled out of her seat and pelted off to find the magazine she had cut the photo from. Reappearing, she planted it into Vito's outstretched hand while Silvestro struggled to set out the first course of the meal.

'Per l'amor di Dio…' Vito groaned. 'You need to learn to read Italian!'

'It's not going to happen overnight,' she grumbled.

'That photo was quite cleverly utilised to symbolise

the fact that I have now cut my ties to the Ravello Investment Bank,' Vito framed in flat explanation. 'Note the way our hands are pictured apart…'

'What does the Ravello Bank have to do with anything? What ties?'

'Marzia is a Ravello,' Vito informed her drily. 'When we got engaged I agreed to act as an investment adviser to the Ravello Bank. When Marzia ditched me her father begged me to retain the position as Ravello was going through a crisis and my resignation would have created talk and blighted their prospects even more.'

Holly blinked. She had become very pale. 'I had no idea you had any business links to Marzia and her family.'

'As of yesterday I *don't*. I resigned the position and they have hired the man I recommended to take my place. Once you and I were married it no longer felt appropriate for Marzia's family and mine to retain that business link,' Vito pointed out wryly.

Holly had been blindsided by an element of Vito's former relationship with Marzia that she could not have known about. A business connection, *not* a personal one. 'You know, I assumed that that was a recent picture of you with Marzia,' Holly confided. 'I thought that dinner you mentioned last week must have been a dinner dance.'

'Had it been I would have taken you with me or bowed out early to get home to you. As it was I was landed with a group of visiting government representatives, whose company I found as exciting as watching paint dry,' Vito told her drily and pushed back his chair. 'May I have my shower now?'

'No, we can't just abandon dinner!' Holly breathed

in dismay. 'Not when Francisco has gone to so much trouble to make us a memorable meal.'

'So, you've been down to the kitchen and have finally met our chef?' Vito gathered in some amusement.

'Yes, he's a real charmer, isn't he?'

'I'm sure he can reheat the food,' Vito pronounced impatiently.

'But we haven't finished talking yet,' Holly protested, all her expectations thrown by Vito's eminently down-to-earth explanation of that photo and its meaning.

'Why are you dressed as though you're about to attend a costume ball?' Vito shot at her.

Holly went red. 'I wanted to show you that if I made the effort I could polish up and look all glam like Marzia.'

Vito groaned out loud. 'You look amazing but I don't want you to look all glam like Marzia.'

'But you bought me all those fancy clothes…'

'Only to cover every possible occasion. And when would you have bothered going shopping?' Vito enquired drily. 'You hate shopping for clothes.'

Holly compressed her lips. 'You don't like me glammed up? Or you don't want me copying Marzia?'

'Both,' Vito told her levelly as he signalled Silvestro and rose from his chair again. 'I like you just to be yourself. You're never fake. I *hate* fake. But why did you think I would be out dancing any place with Marzia?'

'What are you doing?' Holly gasped as he scooped her bodily out of her seat.

'I'm going for my after-work shower and you're either coming in with me, which would sacrifice all the effort you have gone to, or you're waiting in bed for me,' Vito informed her cheerfully.

'I thought you still cared for Marzia,' Holly finally confessed on the way up the stairs. 'I thought you might still love her.'

Vito grunted with effort as he reached the landing. 'I can carry you upstairs but I can't talk while I'm doing it,' he confided. 'I never loved Marzia.'

'But you got engaged to her… You *lived* with her!'

'Yes, and what an eye-opening experience that was!' Vito admitted, thrusting wide the door of their bedroom. 'I asked her to marry me in the first place because she was everything my grandfather told me I should look for in a wife. I wasn't in love with her and when we lived together I discovered that we had nothing in common. I don't want to dance the night away as if I'm still in my twenties but Marzia does. She has to have other people around all the time. She likes to shop every day and will avoid any activity that wrecks her hair… up to and including a walk on a windy day and sex.'

'Oh…' Open-mouthed and taken aback by that information, Holly fell very still as Vito ran down the zip on her dress.

'I was relieved when she ditched me. Not very gallant but it's the truth. We weren't suited.'

'Was my ring…? I've always wanted to ask,' Holly interrupted, extending her ring finger. 'Was it Marzia's before you gave it to me?'

An ebony brow shot up. 'Are you joking? Marzia didn't return her engagement ring and even if she had I hope I would've had more class than to ask you to wear it.'

'You *never* loved her?' Holly was challenged to credit that fact because it ran contrary to everything she had assumed about his engagement.

'When I met Marzia, I had never been in love in my life,' Vito admitted ruefully. 'I got burned young watching my mother trying to persuade my father to love her. I spent my twenties waiting to fall in love, convinced someone special would eventually appear. But it didn't happen and I was convinced it never would. I decided I was probably too practical to fall in love. That's why I got engaged to Marzia the week after my thirtieth birthday. At the time she looked like the best bet I had. Similar banking family and background.'

'My word…that sounds almost…almost callous,' Holly murmured in shock. 'Like choosing the best offer at the supermarket.'

'If it's any consolation I'm pretty sure Marzia settled for me because I'm extremely wealthy.'

Vito yanked loose his tie and shed his jacket. Holly's dress slid down her shoulders and for an instant she stopped its downward progress and then she let it go and shimmied out of it. In many ways she was still in shock from Vito's honesty. He had never fallen in love? Not even with the gorgeous Marzia, who by all accounts had irritated him in spite of her pedigreed background and family. She swallowed hard, trying not to wonder how much she irritated him.

'You're definitely not joining me in the shower,' Vito breathed in a roughened undertone as he took in the coffee-coloured silk lingerie she sported below the dress that had tumbled round her feet. 'You can't deprive me of the fun of taking those off.'

His shirt fell on the floor and she lifted it and the trousers that were abandoned just as untidily to drape them on a chair along with her dress. Sharing a bedroom with a male as organised as Vito had made her clean up her bad habits. Vito had paused to rifle through his jacket and he strode back to her to stuff a jewellery case unceremoniously into her hand. 'I saw it online, thought you'd like it.'

'Oh…' Holly flipped open the case on a diamond-studded bracelet with a delicate little Christmas tree charm attached. 'Oh, that's very pretty.'

'It's very *you*, isn't it?' Vito remarked smugly.

'Why didn't you give it to me downstairs over dinner?' Holly exclaimed, struggling to attach it to her wrist until he stepped forward to clasp it for her.

'I forgot about it. You swanning down to greet me dressed like Marie Antoinette put it right out of my mind.'

'And then you just virtually threw it at me,' Holly lamented. 'There's a more personal way of giving a gift.'

'You mean romantic.' Vito sighed as he strode into the en-suite bathroom, still characteristically set on having his shower. 'Shouldn't the thought *behind* the gift count more?'

Holly thought about that and then walked to the bathroom doorway to sigh. 'You're right. I'm sorry. It's a cute, thoughtful present and I love it. Thank you.'

'My thank you was your face. It lit up like a child's when you saw the Christmas tree,' Vito confided with amusement before he turned the water on.

Holly kicked off her shoes, stared down appreciatively at the bracelet encircling her wrist and lay down on the bed. He had never loved Marzia. Marzia was wiped from Holly's standard stock of worries for ever. Marzia was the past—a past Vito neither missed nor wanted to revisit. That, she decided, was a very encouraging discovery.

All of a sudden hiding her love, being so painfully careful not to let those words escape in moments of joy, seemed almost mean and dishonest. Vito loved Angelo so freely. She witnessed that every day. Her husband hadn't even had to try to love his son and Angelo loved his father back. Perhaps in time Vito could come to love her too, she reflected hopefully. When he had told her that he much preferred her to just be herself around him without the fancy clothes or any airs her heart had taken wings. He liked her as she was. Wasn't that wonderful?

Vito strode out of the en suite, still towelling dry his hair. 'We'll have a very special Christmas this year. For the first time I'll happily celebrate the season. That's the effect you and Angelo have had on my Scrooge-like outlook.'

'I'm grateful because I will always love Christmas.'

'Because that's how we met,' Vito reasoned. 'And I've never forgotten how appealing you looked dressing that little tree at the cottage.'

'Is that so? And yet you made me fight for the opportunity,' Holly reminded him.

'You gave me a fresh look at the world and it's never been the same since,' Vito intoned very seriously as he settled down on the bed beside her and closed her into his arms.

'Meaning?'

'Remember I said I went through my twenties waiting for someone special to appear?'

Holly nodded and rubbed her cheek against a damp bronzed shoulder.

'And then she came along when I was thirty-one years old and, unfortunately, incredibly wary and set in my ways.'

Her brow furrowed because she thought she had missed a line somewhere. '*Who* came along?'

'You did,' Vito pointed out gently. 'And I wasn't waiting or looking for love any more, and my practical engagement had gone belly-up. So, when you appeared and you made me feel strange I didn't recognise that it was special. The sex was incredible but I was blind to the fact that everything else was incredible too.'

'I made you feel...*strange*?' Holly exclaimed in dismay.

'Confused, unsure of myself. I behaved differently with you, I *felt* more with you...and it troubled me. So, like an idiot, I walked away from what I didn't understand,' he completed.

'I wish you'd found my note,' Holly lamented.

'When you walked out first, I told myself that was for the best, that we could never work in the real world. But we *do* work,' Vito told her with quiet satisfaction. 'We work like a dream on every level and I have never been as happy as I am now...'

Holly was thinking about what he had said and a spark of excitement lit inside her.

'If you and Angelo hadn't found me again, where would I be now? The heart and soul of my world was the Zaffari Bank but the bank wasn't enough to satisfy me.'

'Are you trying to tell me that you fell for me that night?' Holly whispered shakily.

'Well, if you have to ask, obviously I'm not doing a very good job of the telling.' Vito groaned. 'What you made me feel unnerved me. I wouldn't even let myself try to trace you because I was too proud. If you didn't want me I wasn't going to chase after you. I tried very hard to forget that night. I even tried to sleep with other women.'

'And how did that go?' Holly broke in to demand.

'It didn't. I made excuses to myself that I was stressed, overtired. I had endless fantasies about you.'

'Me…the temptress,' Holly framed blissfully. 'Who would ever have thought it?'

'You're the love of my life…the *only* love I have ever had,' Vito husked, clamping her to his long, powerful length with strong arms. 'And I fell hard. I fell *so* hard I can't imagine ever living without you and our son. You have brought passion and fun into my daily life and I never had either before.'

'I love you too,' Holly muttered almost shyly.

Vito smiled down at her with burnished golden eyes and her heart skipped a beat. He kissed her with hot, hungry fervour and she ran out of breath. He lifted his tousled dark head and murmured, 'I have one special request. Would you consider having another child?'

'Another?' Holly gasped in astonishment.

'Not immediately,' Vito hastened to assure her. 'I want to share your next pregnancy, *be* there when my child is born, and experience everything I missed out on with our son. If you employ an assistant, even if you get pregnant I don't see why you shouldn't still be able to concentrate on your interior design plan.'

Holly smiled at that prospect. Her very successful bedroom project had quickly spread to include other major rooms at the *castello*. She had had the adjoining reception room done in toning colours before moving on to attack the scarlet Victorian dining room. At present she was well aware that the *castello* was large enough to offer her the chance to utilise her talents and gain proper experience before she considered moving on to tackle outside projects.

'I'll think about another baby,' she told him thoughtfully. 'I would prefer Angelo not to be an only child.'

Vito stared down at her as she gazed up at him with starry eyes. *He loves me, he loves me, he* loves *me,* she was thinking on a happy high. She ran an appreciative hand up over a long, muscular, hair-roughened thigh and sensible conversation ceased around that point. Vito told her he loved her. Holly told him she loved him too. No sooner had they exchanged those sentiments than they both succumbed to an overwhelming desire to dispel the tension with the passion they shared.

Long after, Vito lay studying Holly as she slept, marvelling at how happy he felt. He wondered if he could persuade her into another sexy Santa outfit at Christmas and wondered if it would be a little pushy to buy one for her. Pushiness came so naturally to him that he soon convinced himself that his laid-back bride would simply laugh.

He curved an arm round her slight body.

'Love you...' Holly mumbled automatically.

Vito smiled. 'Love you. You're my happy-ever-after, *amata mia*.'

EPILOGUE

VITO STRODE THROUGH the door and was immediately engulfed in the flying energy of his son, who flung himself at his knees in a classic tackle. Angelo started chattering in a hail of words, only a handful of which were in distinguishable Italian and occasional ones were in English. *Mamma* figured a lot. *Nonna*, as he called his grandmother Concetta, figured too. If Angelo was to be believed, he, his mother and his grandmother had spent the afternoon feeding a dinosaur. A very small dinosaur was waved in Vito's general direction and comprehension set in as he crouched down to dutifully admire the toy.

A giant Christmas tree adorned the hall. It was festooned with ornaments and lights. There were no gifts heaped below the branches because Angelo loved to rip off wrapping paper. Silvestro had been heard to tell a tenant that the Zaffaris were having 'an English Christmas', and Vito's chef, Francisco, had been feeding them turkey for weeks as he fine-tuned his recipes to provide them with an English banquet on Christmas Day. In respect of the Italian traditions, Angelo would receive *la calza*—a stocking full of sweets. The red-suited Babbo Natale would obviously visit on Christmas Eve, but the kind-hearted Italian witch La Befana, who searched for the Christ child in all the houses, would visit at Epiphany with more gifts.

Vito breathed in deep as he saw a small figure clad in white-fur-trimmed scarlet appear at the top of the stairs. 'You're not wearing your hat,' he complained.

Holly stopped midway and jammed it on over her mane of hair and made a face at him. 'Satisfied now?'

Vito angled a lazy, sexy smile at her. 'Don't I have to wait until bedtime for that?'

'Maybe I'll suggest an early night.' Holly remained anchored two steps up so that she was almost level with him.

Vito took the invitation, leaning down to claim that lush pink mouth that he still fantasised about and curving his hands to the swell of her hips to lift her up into his arms. Her hands locked round his neck with satisfying possessiveness and held him fast. He could feel the slight bump of the baby she was carrying against his stomach and he smiled as he lifted his head again.

'I love you,' he groaned.

'Love you madly.' Holly felt ridiculously intoxicated and happy. One kiss from Vito could do that, two were irresistible, and three would only end with her dragging him up the stairs. Evidently falling pregnant sooner than they had expected had done nothing to cool her husband's desire for her and that truly did make her feel as alluring as some legendary temptress. That was very welcome to a woman who was five months pregnant and subject to all the usual aches and complaints of her condition.

Her redecoration schemes at the *castello* had led to an approach from an exclusive interiors magazine, which had taken a whole host of photos. The glossy photo spread and the accompanying article had ensured that within days of the magazine going on sale, Holly was inundated with exciting offers of design work.

This, however, was their first family Christmas and she was revelling in every detail because Vito had really thrown himself into the spirit of the holidays and she didn't think it was solely because he had become a father. She reckoned he had put his sour childhood memories of Christmas behind him. His mother, recently divorced, was joining their festivities and hugely excited about the second grandchild on the way.

'Please tell me turkey isn't on the menu again tonight,' Vito murmured.

'No, we're having steak. I told Francisco I fancied steak,' she admitted.

'When are our guests arriving?' Vito prompted.

'Well, they were supposed to be here for dinner but Apollo's social secretary rang to say they would be late. Why does he need a social secretary?'

'He's always got hundreds of invitations and he's never at home.' Vito paused. 'I appreciate you being willing to give him another chance.'

Holly gave him a soothing smile that concealed her tension. It was past time to forgive and forget—she knew that. After all, Apollo was Vito's closest friend, but Holly had only seen him twice since their wedding. And when she had made the mistake of voicing her opinion on what he considered to be his private business it had been awkward as hell. But she was madly curious to see who he was bringing with him as a guest. Another leggy underwear model? Or his *wife*?

That, Holly supposed, would be another story…

* * * * *

[illegible] that within days of the magazine going on sale [illegible]

[illegible]

Then, Holly supposed, would [illegible]

UNWRAPPING HIS CONVENIENT FIANCÉE

MELANIE MILBURNE

To my dear friend Jo Shearing.

You are such a gorgeous person and I value our friendship so much.

This one is for you. xxxx

CHAPTER ONE

IT WAS THE invitation Violet had been dreading for months. Ten years in a row she had gone to the office Christmas party *sans* partner. *Ten years!* Every year she told herself next year would be different, and yet here she was staring at the red and silver invitation with her stomach in a sinkhole of despair *again.* It was bad enough fielding the *What, no date?* looks and comments from her female colleagues. But it was the thought of being in a crowded room that was the real torture. With all those jostling bodies pressing up so close she wouldn't be able to breathe.

Male bodies.

Bodies that were much bigger and stronger and more powerful than hers—especially when they were drunk…

Violet blinked away the memory. She hardly ever thought about *that* party these days. Well, only now and again. She had come to a fragile sort of peace over it. The self-blame had eased even if the lingering shame had not.

But she was nearly thirty and it was time to move on. More than time. Which meant going to the Christmas party to prove to herself she was back in control of her life.

However, there was the agony of deciding what to wear. Her accountancy firm's Christmas party was considered one of the premier events in the financial sector's calendar. It wasn't just a drinks and nibbles affair. It was an annual gala with champagne flowing like a fountain and Michelin star quality food and dancing to a live band. Every year there was a theme and everyone was expected to be part of the action to demonstrate their commitment to office harmony. This year's theme was *A Star-Struck Christmas*. Which would mean Violet would have to find something Hollywoodish to wear. She wasn't good at glamour. She didn't like drawing attention to herself. She wasn't good at partying full stop.

Violet slipped the invitation between the pages of her book and sighed. Even the London lunchtime café crowd was rubbing in her singleton status. Everyone was a couple. She was the only person sitting on her own. Even a couple pushing ninety were at the table in the window *and* they were holding hands. That would be her parents in thirty years. Still with the magic buzzing between them as it had from the first moment they'd met. Just like her three siblings with their perfect partners. Building their lives together, having children and doing all the things she dreamed of doing.

Violet had watched each of her siblings fall in love. Fast-living Fraser first, racy Rose next and then laid-back Lily. Been to each of their weddings. Been a bridesmaid three times. *Three times. Groan.* She was always in the audience watching romance develop and blossom, but she longed to be on the stage.

Why couldn't she find someone perfect for her?

Was there something wrong with her? Guys occasionally asked her out but it never went past a date or two. Her natural shyness didn't make for scintillating conversation and she had no idea how to flirt… Well, she did if she had a few drinks but that was a mistake she was *not* going to repeat. The problem was that men were so impatient these days, or maybe they always had been that way. But she was not going to sleep with someone just because it was expected of her…or because she was too drunk to say no. She wanted to feel attracted to a man and to feel his attraction to her. To feel frissons of red-hot desire scoot all over her flesh at his touch. To melt when his gaze met hers. To shiver with delight when he pressed his lips to hers.

Not that too many male lips had been pressed to hers lately. She couldn't remember the last time she had been really kissed by a man. Pecks on the cheek from her father and brother or grandfather didn't count.

Violet was rubbish at the dating game. Rubbish. Rubbish. Rubbish. She was going to end up an old and wrinkled spinster living with a hundred and fifty-two cats. With a chest of drawers full of exquisitely embroidered baby clothes for the babies she had longed for since she was a little girl.

'Is this seat taken?'

Violet glanced up at the familiar deep baritone voice, a faint shiver coursing down her spine when her gaze connected with her older brother's best friend from university.

'Cam?' Her voice came out like the sound of a squeaky toy, an annoying habit she hadn't been able to correct since first meeting Cameron McKinnon. She had been eighteen when her brother brought Cam home for the summer—or at least the Scottish version of it—to their family's estate, Drummond Brae, in the Highlands. 'What are you doing here? How are you? Fraser told me you've been living in Greece designing a yacht for someone super-rich. How's it all going? When did you get back?'

Shut up! Funny, but she was never lost for words around Cam. She talked *too* much. She couldn't seem to help it nor could she explain it. He wasn't intimidating or threatening in any way. He was polite, if a little aloof, but he had been a part of her family for long enough for her to get over herself.

But clearly she *hadn't* got over herself.

Cam pulled out the chair opposite and sat down, his knees gently bumping against Violet's underneath the table. The touch was like an electric current moving through her body, heating her in places that had no business being heated. Not by her brother's best friend. Cam was out of her league. Way out.

'I was in the area for a meeting. It finished early and I remembered you mentioning this café once so thought I'd check it out,' he said. 'I've only been back a couple of days. My father is getting remarried just before Christmas.'

Violet's eyes widened to the size of the saucer under her skinny latte. 'Again? How many times is that now? Three? Four?'

His mouth twisted. 'Five. And there's another baby on the way, which brings the total of halfsiblings to six, plus the seven step-siblings, so eleven all together.'

Violet thought her three nephews, two nieces and the baby in the making were a handful—she couldn't imagine eleven. 'How on earth do you keep track of all of their birthdays?'

His half smile looked a little weary around the edges. 'I've set up automatic transfers via online banking. Takes the guesswork out.'

'Maybe I should do that.' Violet stirred her coffee for something to do with her hands. Being in Cam's company—not that it happened much these days—always made her feel like a gauche schoolgirl in front of a college professor. He was an unusual counterpoint to her older brother who was a laugh a minute, life of the party type. Cam was more serious in nature with a tendency to frown rather than smile.

Her gaze drifted towards his mouth—another habit she couldn't quite control when she was around him. His lips were fairly evenly sculpted, although the lower one had a slightly more sensual fullness to it that made her think of long, blood-heating, pulse-racing kisses.

Not that Violet had ever kissed him. Men like Cameron McKinnon didn't kiss girls like her. She was too girl-next-door. He dated women who looked as if they had just stepped out of a photo shoot. Glamorous, sophisticated types who could hold their own in any company without breaking out in hives in case someone spoke to them.

Cam's gaze briefly went to her bare left hand where she was cradling her coffee before coming back to hers in a keenly focused look that made something deep in her belly unfurl like a flower opening its petals to the sun.

'So, how are things with you, Violet?'

'Erm…okay.' At least she wasn't breaking out into hives, but the blush she could feel crawling over her cheeks was almost as bad. Was he thinking—like the rest of her family—*Three times a bridesmaid, never a bride*?

'Only okay?' His look had a serious note to it, a combination of concern and concentration, as if she were the only person he wanted to talk to right then. It was one of the things Violet liked about him—one of the many things. He wasn't so full of himself that he couldn't spare the time to listen. She often wondered if he'd been around to talk to after that wretched party, during her first and only year at university, her life might not have turned out the way it had.

Violet stretched her mouth into her standard everything-is-cool-with-me smile. 'I'm fine. Just busy with work and Christmas shopping and stuff. Like you, I have a lot of people to buy for now with all my nephews and nieces. Did you know Lily and Cooper are expecting? Mum and Dad are planning the usual big Christmas at Drummond Brae. Has Mum invited you? She said she was going to. The doctors think it will be Grandad's last Christmas so we're all making an effort to be there for him.'

Cam's mouth took on a rueful slant. 'My father's decided to upstage Christmas with his wedding on Christmas Eve.'

'Where's it being held?'

'Here in London.'

'Maybe you could fly up afterwards,' Violet said. 'Or have you got other commitments?' Other commitments such as a girlfriend. Surely he would have one. Men like Cam wouldn't go long between lovers. He was too handsome, too rich, too intelligent, too sexy. Too everything. Cam had never broadcast his relationships with women the way her brother Fraser had before he'd fallen madly in love with Zoe. Cam was intensely private about his private life. So private it made Violet wonder if he had a secret lover stashed away somewhere, someone he kept out of the glaring spotlight that his work as an internationally acclaimed naval architect attracted.

'I'll see,' he said. 'Mum will expect a visit, especially now that her third husband Hugh's left her.'

Violet frowned. 'Oh, no. I'm sorry to hear that. Is she terribly upset?'

Cam gave her a speaking look. 'Not particularly. He drank. A lot.'

'Oh...'

Cam's family history was nothing short of a saga. Not that he'd ever said much about it to her, but Fraser had filled in the gaps. His parents went through a bitter divorce when he was six and promptly remarried and set up new families, collecting other biological children and stepchildren along the way. Cam was jostled between the various households until he was sent to boarding school when he was eight. Violet could picture him as a little boy—studious, quietly observing on the sidelines, not making a fuss and avoiding one where it was made. He was still like that. When he came to visit her family for weddings, christenings or other gatherings he was always on the fringe, standing back with a drink in his hand he rarely touched, quietly measuring the scene with his navy-blue gaze.

The waitress came over to take Cam's order with a smile that went beyond *I'm your server, can I help you?* to *Do you want my number?*

Violet tried to ignore the little dart of jealousy that spiked her in the gut. It was none of her business who he flirted with. Why should she care if he picked up a date from her favourite café? Even if she had been coming here for years and no one had asked for *her* number.

Cam looked across the table at her. 'Would you like another coffee?'

Violet put her hand over the top of her latte glass. 'No, I'm good.'

'Just a long black, thanks,' Cam said to the waitress with a brief but polite smile.

Violet waited until the girl had left before she spoke. 'Cra—ack.'

His brow furrowed. 'Pardon?'

She gave him a teasing smile. 'Didn't you hear that girl's heart breaking?'

He looked puzzled for a moment, and then faintly annoyed. 'She's not my type.'

'Describe your type.' *Why had she asked that?*

The bridge between Cam's ink-black eyebrows was still pleated in three tight vertical lines. 'I've been too busy for any type just lately.' His phone, which was sitting on the table, beeped with a message and he glanced at it before turning off the screen, his lips pressing so firmly his mouth turned bone-white.

'What's wrong?'

He forcibly relaxed his features. 'Nothing.'

The phone beeped again and his mouth flattened once more. He clicked the mute button and slipped the phone into his jacket pocket as the waitress set his coffee down on the table between them. 'So, how's work?'

Violet glanced at the invitation peeping out of the pages of her book. Was it her imagination or was it flashing like a beacon? She surreptitiously pushed it back out of sight. 'Fine...'

Cam followed the line of her gaze. 'What's that?'

'Nothing... Just an invitation.'

'To?'

Violet was sure her cheeks were as the red as the baubles on the invitation. 'The office Christmas party.'

'You going?'

She couldn't meet his gaze and looked at the sugar bowl instead. Who knew there were so many different artificial sweeteners these days? Amazing. 'I kind of have to… It's expected in the interests of office harmony.'

'You don't sound too keen.'

Violet lifted one of her shoulders in a shrug. 'Yeah, well, I'm not really a party girl.' Not any more. Her first and only attempt at partying had ended in a blurry haze of regret and self-recrimination. An event she was still, all these years on, trying to put behind her with varying degrees of success.

But secret shame cast a long shadow.

'It's a pretty big affair, isn't it?' Cam said. 'No expense spared and so on, I take it?'

Violet rolled her eyes. 'Ironic when you consider it's a firm of bean counters.'

'Pretty successful bean counters,' Cam said. 'Well done you for nailing a job there.'

Violet didn't like to admit how far from her dream job it actually was. After quitting her university studies, a clerical job in a large accounting firm had seemed a good place to blend into the background. But what had suited her at nineteen was feeling less satisfying as she approached thirty. She couldn't shake off the nagging feeling she should be doing more with her life. Extending herself. Reaching her potential instead of placing limitations on herself. But since that party… Well, everything had been put on pause. It was like her life had jammed and she couldn't move forward.

The vibration of Cam's phone drew Violet's gaze to his top pocket. Not just to his top pocket but his chest in general. He was built like an endurance athlete, tall and lean with muscles where a man needed them to be and where a woman most liked to see them. And she was no exception. His skin was tanned and his dark brown hair had some surface highlights where the strong sunlight of Greece had caught and lightened it. He had cleanly shaven skin, but there was enough dark stubble to suggest he hadn't been holding the door for everyone else when the testosterone was dished out.

'Aren't you going to answer that?' Violet asked.

'It'll keep.'

'Work or family?'

'Neither.'

Violet's eyebrows lifted along with her intrigue. 'A woman?'

He took out the phone and held his finger on the off switch with a determined set to his features. 'Yeah. One that won't take no for an answer.'

'How long have you been dating her?'

'I haven't been dating her.' Cam's expression was grim. 'She's a client's wife. A valuable client.'

'Oh… Tricky.'

'Very. To the tune of about forty million pounds tricky.'

Forty million? Violet came from a wealthy background but even she had trouble getting her head around a figure like that. Cam designed yachts for the super-wealthy. He'd won a heap of awards for his designs and become extremely wealthy in the process. Some of the yachts he designed were massive, complete with marble en suite bathrooms with hot tubs, and dining and sitting rooms that were plush and palatial. One yacht even had its own library and lap swimming pool. But, even so, it amazed her how much a rich person would pay for a yacht they only used now and again. 'Seriously? You're being paid forty million to design a yacht?'

'No, that's the cost of the yacht once it's complete,' he said. 'But I get paid a pretty decent amount to design it.'

How much was *pretty decent*? Violet longed to ask but decided against it out of politeness. 'So...what will you do? Keep ignoring this woman's calls and messages?'

He let out a short, gusty breath. 'I'll have to get the message across one way or the other. I'm not the sort of guy who gets mixed up with married women.' His mouth twisted again. 'That would be my father.'

'Maybe if she sees you've got someone else it will drive home the message.' Violet picked up her almost empty latte and looked at him over the rim of the glass. '*Is* there someone else?' *Arrgh! Why did you ask that?*

Cam's gaze met hers and that warm sensation bloomed deep and low in her belly again. His dark blue eyes were fringed with thick ink-black lashes she would have killed for. There was something about his intelligent eyes that always made her feel he saw more than he let on. 'No,' he said. 'You?'

Violet coughed out a self-effacing laugh. 'Don't *you*

start. I get enough of that from my family, not to mention my friends and flatmates.'

Cam gave her a wry smile. 'I don't know what's wrong with the young men of London. You should've been snapped up long ago.'

A pin drop silence fell between them.

Violet looked at her coffee glass as if it were the most fascinating thing she had ever seen. The way her cheeks were going, the café's chef would be coming out to cook the toast on her face to save on electricity. How had she got into this conversation? Awkward. Awkward. Awkward. How long was the canyon of silence going to last? Should she say something?

But what?

Her mind was blank.

She was hopeless at small talk. It was another reason she was terrible at parties. The idle conversation gene had skipped her. Her sisters and brother were the ones who could talk their way out of or into any situation. She was the wallflower of the family. All those years of being overshadowed by verbose older siblings and super articulate parents had made her conversationally challenged. She was used to standing back and letting others do the talking. Even her tendency to gabble like a fool around Cam had suddenly deserted her.

'When's your office party?'

Violet blinked and refocused her gaze on Cam's. 'Erm…tomorrow.'

'Would you like me to come with you?'

Violet had trouble keeping her jaw off the table and

her heart from skipping right out of her chest and landing in his lap. *Best not think about his lap.* 'But why would you want to do that?'

He gave a casual shrug of one broad shoulder. 'I'm free tomorrow night. Thought it might help you mingle if you had a wingman, so to speak.'

Violet gave him a measured look. 'Is this a pity date?'

'It's not a date, period.' Something about his adamant tone rankled. 'Just a friend helping out a friend.'

Violet had enough friends. It was a date she wanted. A proper date. Not with a man on a mercy mission. Did he think she was completely useless? A romance tragic who couldn't find a prince to take her to the ball? She didn't even *want* to go to the ball, thank you very much. The ball wasn't that special. All those people drinking and eating too much and dancing till the wee hours to music so loud you couldn't hear yourself shout, let alone think. 'Thanks for the offer but I'll be fine.'

Violet pushed her coffee glass to one side and picked up her book. But, before she could leave the table, Cam's hand came down on her forearm. 'I didn't mean to upset you.'

'I'm not upset.' Violet knew her crisp tone belied her statement. Of course she was upset. Who wouldn't be? He was rescuing her. What could be more insulting than a man asking you out because he felt sorry for you? Had Fraser said something to him? Had one of her sisters? Her parents? Her grandfather? Why couldn't everyone mind their own business? All she got these days was pressure. *Why aren't you dating anyone? You're too fussy. You're almost thirty.* It never ended.

The warmth of Cam's broad hand seeped through the layers of her winter clothing, awakening her flesh like a heat pack on a frostbitten limb. 'Hey.'

Violet hadn't pouted since she was about five but she pouted now. She could find a date. Sure she could. She could sign up to one of any number of dating websites or apps and have a hundred dates. If she put her mind to it she could be engaged by Christmas. Well, maybe that was pushing it a bit. 'I'm perfectly able to find my own date, okay?'

He gave her arm the tiniest squeeze before releasing it. 'Of course.' He sat back in his chair, his forehead creased in a slight frown. 'I'm sorry. It was a bad idea. Seriously bad.'

Why was it? And why *seriously* bad? Violet cradled her book close to her chest where her heart was beating a little too fast. Not fast enough to call for a defibrillator but not far off. His touch had done something to her, like he had turned a setting on in her body she hadn't known she'd had. Her senses were sitting up and alert instead of slumped and listless. Had he ever touched her before? She tried to think… Sometimes in the past he would kiss her on the cheek, a chaste brotherly sort of kiss. But lately…since Easter, in fact…there had been no physical contact from him. None at all. It was as if he had deliberately kept his distance. That last holiday weekend at home, she remembered him coming into one of the sitting rooms at Drummond Brae and going straight back out again with a muttered apology when he'd found her curled up on one of the sofas with her embroidery. Why had he done that? What was wrong with her that he couldn't bear to be left alone with her?

Violet picked up her scarf and wound it around her neck. 'I have to get back to work. I hope your father's wedding goes well.'

'It should do, he's had enough practice.' He drained his coffee and stood, snatching his jacket from the back of the chair and slinging it over his shoulder. 'I'll walk you back to your office. I'm heading that way.'

Violet knew the tussle over who paid for the coffee was inevitable so when he offered she let him take care of it for once. 'Thanks,' she said once he'd settled the bill.

'No problem.'

He put a gentle hand in the small of her back to guide her out of the way of a young mother coming in with a pram and a squirming, red-faced toddler. The sizzling heat of his touch moved along the entire length of Violet's spine, making her aware of her femininity as if he had stroked her intimately.

Get a grip already.

This was the problem with being desperate and dateless. The slightest brush of a male hand turned her into a wanton fool. Stirring up needs that she hadn't even registered as needs until now.

But it wasn't just any male hand.

It was Cam's hand...connected to a body that made her think of smoking-hot sex. Not that she knew what smoking-hot sex actually felt like. The only sex she'd had was a surrealist blur with an occasional flashback of two or three male faces looming over her, talking about her, not to her. Definitely not the sort of romantic scene she had envisaged when she'd hit puberty. It was another thing she'd miserably failed at doing. Each of her siblings had successfully navigated their way through the dating minefield, all of them now partnered with their soul mate. *Was* she too fussy? Had that night at that party permanently damaged her self-esteem and sexual confidence? Why should it when she could barely remember it in any detail?

She had been surrounded by love and acceptance all her life. There should be no reason for her to feel inadequate or not quite up to the mark. But somehow love—even a vague liking for someone of the opposite sex—had so far escaped her.

Violet walked out to the footpath with Cam, where the rain had started to fall in icy droplets. She popped open her umbrella but Cam had to bend almost double to gain any benefit from it. He took the handle from her and held the umbrella over both of their heads. Her fingers tingled where his brushed hers, the sensation travelling all through her body as if running along an electric network.

Trying to keep dry, as well as out of the way of the bustling Christmas shopping crowd, put Violet so close to the tall frame of his body she could smell the clean sharp fragrance of his aftershave, the woodsy base notes reminding her of a cool, shaded pine forest.

To anyone looking in from the outside they would look like a romantically involved couple, huddled under the same umbrella, Cam's stride considerately slowing to match hers.

They came to the large Victorian building where the accounting firm Violet worked as an accounts clerk was situated. But just as she was about to turn and say her goodbyes to Cam, one of the women who worked with her came click-clacking down the steps. Lorna ran her gaze over Cam's tall figure standing next to Violet. 'Well, well, well. Things finally looking up for you, are they, Violet?'

Violet ground her teeth so hard she could have moonlighted as a nutcracker. Lorna wasn't her favourite workmate, far from it. She had a tendency to gossip to stir up trouble. Violet knew for a fact their boss only kept Lorna on because she was brilliant at her job—and because she was having a full-on affair with him. 'Off to lunch?' she asked, refusing to respond to Lorna's taunt.

Lorna gave an orthodontist's website smile and aimed her lash-fluttering gaze at Cam. 'Will we be seeing you at the office Christmas party?'

Cam's arm snaked around Violet's waist, a protective band of steel that made every nerve in her body jump up and down and squeal with delight. 'We'll be there.'

We will? Violet waited until Lorna had gone before looking up at Cam's unreadable expression. 'Why on earth did you say that? I told you I didn't want a—'

He stepped out from under the umbrella and placed

the handle back in her hand. Violet had to extend her arm upwards to its fullest range to keep the umbrella high enough to maintain eye contact. 'I'll strike a deal with you,' he said. 'I'll come to your Christmas party if you'll come to a dinner with my client tonight.'

Violet screwed up her face. 'The one with the persistent wife?'

'I've been thinking about what you said back at the café. What better way to send her the message I'm not interested than to show her I'm seeing someone?'

'But we're not…' she disguised a little gulp '…*seeing* each other.'

'No, but no one else needs to know that.'

You don't have to be so darned emphatic about it. Violet chewed at one side of her mouth. 'How are we going to keep this…quiet?'

'You mean from your family?'

'You know what my mother's like.' Violet gave a little eye roll. 'One whiff of us going on a date together, and she'll be posting wedding invitations quicker than you can say *I do*.'

There was another yawning silence.

I do?

Are you nuts? You said the words 'I do' to the man who views weddings like people view the plague!

Something shifted in Cam's expression—a blink of his eyes, a flicker of a muscle in his lean cheek, a stretching of his mouth into a smile that didn't involve his eyes. 'We'll cross that bridge if we come to it.'

If we come to it? There was no *if* about it. That bridge

was going to blow up in their faces like a Stage Five firecracker on Guy Fawkes Night. Violet knew her family too well. They were constantly on the lookout for any signs of her dating. MI5 could learn a thing or two from her mother and sisters. How was she going to explain a night out with Cam McKinnon? 'Are you sure we should be doing this?'

There was a slight easing of the tension around his mouth. 'We're not robbing a bank, Violet.'

'I know, but—'

'If you'd rather not, then I can always find someone—'

'No,' Violet said, not even wanting to think about the 'someone' he would take. 'I'll go. It'll be fun—I haven't been out to dinner for ages.'

He smiled a lopsided smile that made the back of Violet's knees feel like someone was tickling them with a feather. 'There's one other thing…'

You want it to be a real date? You want us to see each other as in 'see each other'? You've secretly been in love with me for years and years and years? Violet kept her face blank while the thoughts pushed against the door of her reasoning like people trying to get into a closing down sale.

'We'll have to act like a normal dating couple,' he said. 'Hold hands and…stuff.'

And stuff?

What other stuff?

Violet nodded like her head was supported by an elastic band instead of neck muscles. 'Fine. Of course.

Good idea. Fab. Brilliant idea. We have to look authentic. Wouldn't want anyone to get the wrong idea… I mean, well, you know what I mean.'

Cam leaned down and brushed her cheek with his lips, the slight graze of his rougher skin making something in her stomach turn over. 'I'll pick you up at seven.'

Violet took a step backwards to enter the building but stumbled over the first step and would have fallen if it wasn't for Cam's hand shooting out to steady her. 'You okay?' he asked with a concerned frown.

Violet looked at his stubble-surrounded mouth that just moments ago had been against the smooth skin of her cheek. Had he felt that same sensation ricochet through his body? Had he wondered in that infinitesimal moment what it would feel like to press his lips to hers? Not in a brotherly kiss, but a proper man-wants-woman kiss? She sent the point of her tongue over the surface of her lips, her breath hitching when he tracked every millimetre of the movement. *Keep it light.* 'For a moment there I thought you were going to kiss me,' Violet said with a little laugh.

The navy-blue of his gaze turned three shades darker before glancing at her mouth and back again. But then his hand dropped from her arm as if her skin had scorched him. 'Let's not go there.'

But I want *to go there. I want to. I want to. I want to.* Violet kept her smile in place even though it felt like it was stitched to her mouth. 'Yes, that would be taking things too far. I mean, not that I don't find you attractive or anything, but us kissing? Not such a great idea.'

There was the sound of heels click-clacking behind her and Violet turned to see Lorna coming back. 'Silly me. I forgot my phone,' Lorna said and with a sly smile at Cam added, 'Aren't you going to kiss her and let her get back to work?'

Violet sneaked a glance at Cam but instead of looking annoyed at Lorna's comment he smiled an easy smile and reached for Violet's hand and drew her against his side. 'I was just getting to that,' he said.

Violet assumed he would wait till Lorna had gone back into the building before releasing her but Lorna didn't go back into the building. She stood three steps up from them with that annoying smirk on her mouth as if daring Cam to follow through. Cam turned his back to Lorna and slipped a hand under Violet's hair, cupping the nape of her neck, making every nerve beneath her skin pirouette.

'You don't have to do this…' Violet whispered.

Cam brought his mouth down to within a whisker of hers. 'Yes, I do.'

And then he did.

CHAPTER TWO

CAM PRESSED HIS lips to Violet's mouth and a bomb went off in his head, scattering his common sense like flying shrapnel. *What are you doing?* But he didn't want to listen to his conscience. He had wanted to kiss her from the moment he'd walked into that café earlier and now her annoying workmate had given him the perfect excuse to do so. Violet's mouth tasted like a combination of milk and honey, her lips soft and pliable beneath his. He drew her ballerina-like body even closer, his body responding with a fierce rush of blood to his groin. Her small breasts were pressed against his chest, her slim hips against his, her hands gripping the front of his jacket as if she couldn't stand upright without his support. Hell, he was having trouble keeping upright himself, apart from one part of his anatomy.

It's time to stop. You should stop. You need to stop. The chanting of his brain was attempting to drown out the frantic panting of his body. *Yes. Yes. Yes.* Clearly it had been too long between drinks. His self-control was usually spot on. But he didn't want the kiss to end.

He felt as though he might *die* if it did. Lust pounded through his body, rampaging, roaring lust that made every cell in his system shudder with need. Intense need. Need that made him think of sweating, straining bodies and tangled sheets and blissful, euphoric release.

She gave a little mewling sound when he shifted position, her mouth flowering open to the hungry glide of his tongue. He explored her sweet interior, his pulse rate going off the scale when her tongue came into play with his. Her tongue was hesitant at first, but then she made another whimpering sound and grew more and more confident, flirting with his tongue, darting away and coming back for the sensual heat of his strokes. He put his hands on her hips, holding her to the throbbing ache of his body.

She felt so damn good, like she was made for his exact proportions. Had he ever felt so aroused so quickly? It was like he was a hormone-driven teenager all over again. He seriously had to get his work/life balance sorted out. How long had it been since he'd slept with a woman? Too long if his trigger was being tripped by just a kiss.

A car tooting on its way past was the only thing that got through to him. Cam put Violet from him, holding her by the hands so as to help her keep her balanced. He did a quick glance over his shoulder but Violet's workmate had disappeared. Not surprising given he'd lost track of time during that kiss.

Violet blinked as if trying to reorient herself. Her

small pink tongue did a quick circuit of her lips and his groin groaned and growled with need. He could almost imagine how it would feel to have that shy little tongue move over his body. He couldn't remember a kiss being so…consuming. He had forgotten where they were. He had darned near forgotten who he was. He might be seriously hot for Violet but he wasn't going to act on it. She was his best mate's kid sister, the baby of the family he adored.

It was a boundary he was determined not to cross. Or at least not to cross any further than he just had.

Cam released her hands and gave a relaxed smile he hoped disguised the bedlam of base needs in his body baying for more. 'That was quite a kiss.'

Violet gave him a distracted little smile that seemed to set off a rippling tide of worry in her toffee-brown eyes. 'Y-you caught me by surprise…'

Right back at you, sweetheart. 'Yes, well, I figured your workmate wasn't going to go away until we got it over with. Is she usually that persistent?'

'You caught her on a good day.'

Cam wondered how much bullying went on in that office. Violet was a gentle soul who would find it hard to stand up for herself in a dog-eat-dog environment. Even within the loving and loud bosom of her family, she had the tendency to shrink away to a quiet corner rather than engage in the lively banter. Before he could stop himself, he brushed a fingertip down the pinked slope of her cheek. 'You're completely safe with me, Violet. You do know that, don't you? Kissing is all we'll do if the need should arise.' *I hope fate isn't listening, otherwise you are toast.*

Her small white teeth sank into the pillow of her lower lip and she lowered her gaze to a point at the base of his neck. 'Of course.' Her voice was not much more than a scratchy whisper.

He stepped back from her. 'I'd better let you get back to work.'

She turned without another word and climbed the steps, not even glancing back before disappearing into the building when she got to the top.

Cam let out a long breath and walked on. It was all well and good to kiss her but that was as far as it could go. He wasn't what Violet was looking for. He wasn't the settling down type. Maybe one day he would think about setting up a home with someone, but right now he had too much going on in his career. That was his focus, his priority. Not relationships.

Marriage might work for some people, but it didn't work for others—his parents and their collection of exes being a case in point. Too many people got hurt when relationships broke down. It was like a boulder dropped into a pond; the ripples of hurt went on for years. He was still sidestepping the pain his parents' divorce had caused. It wasn't that he'd wanted them to stay together. Far from it. They hadn't been happy from the get-go because his mother had been in love and his father hadn't and then his father had dumped his mother for someone younger and more attractive and had been outrageously difficult about the divorce.

His mother had responded by being equally difficult and, inevitably, Cam had got caught up in the middle until eventually he'd been dumped at boarding school and left to fend for himself. In the years since, his parents had changed partners so often Cam had trouble keeping track of names and addresses and birthdays. He'd had to set up a database on his phone to keep on top of them all.

But he needed to get Sophia Nicolaides off his case and taking Violet was the way to do it. Sophia was too crafty to spot a fake. He couldn't bring someone he'd only just met to the dinner. It had to be someone he already felt comfortable with and her with him. Violet was shy around him, but then, she was shy around most people. It was part of her charm, the fact that she didn't flaunt her assets or draw attention to herself. He'd been upfront about the fact it wasn't a date and he was sure she too wouldn't want to compromise the friendship that had built up over the years.

At least they'd got the first kiss out of the way.

And what a kiss. Who knew that sweet little mouth could wreak such havoc on his self-control? He would have to watch himself. Violet wasn't street smart like the women he normally dated. She wasn't the sleep-around type. He wondered if she was still a virgin. Not likely since she was close to thirty, but who knew for sure? It wasn't exactly a question he'd feel comfortable asking her. It was none of his business.

Cam ran his tongue over his lips and tasted her. Even

if he never kissed her again, it was going to take a long time to forget that kiss.

If he ever did.

Violet tried on seven different outfits until she finally settled on a navy-blue velvet dress that fell just above the knee. It reminded her of the colour of Cam's unusual eyes. *Maybe that was why you bought it?* No. Of course not. She'd bought it because she liked it. It suited her. She loved the feel of the fabric against her skin. She slipped her feet into heels and turned to view her reflection in the cheval mirror.

Her flatmate, Amy, popped her head around the door. 'Gosh, you look scrumptious. I love that colour on you. Are you going out?'

Violet smoothed the front of her dress over her stomach and thighs, turning this way and that to check if she had visible panty line. No. All good. 'You don't think it's too...plain?'

'It's simple but elegant,' Amy said, perching on the end of Violet's bed. 'So who's the guy? Have I met him? No, of course I haven't because you've never brought anyone here, that I know of.'

Violet slipped on some pearl drop earrings her parents had given her for her twenty-first birthday. 'He's a friend of my brother's. I've known him for ages.' *And he kisses like a sex god and my body is still humming with desire hours later.*

Amy's eyes danced. 'Ooh! A friends-to-lovers thing. How exciting.'

Violet sent her a quelling look. 'Don't get your hopes up. I'm not his type.' Cam couldn't have been more succinct. *'Kissing is all we'll do.'* She hadn't turned him on… Well, she had, but clearly not enough that he wanted to take things further.

The doorbell sounded and Amy jumped off the bed. 'I'll get it. I want to check out your date to see if he passes muster. Flat twenty-three B has certain standards, you know.'

Violet came out a few seconds later to see Amy giving an impression of a star-struck teen in front of a Hollywood idol. Violet had to admit Cam looked heart-stoppingly fabulous in a suit. He wasn't the designer-wear type, but the sharp tailoring of his charcoal-grey suit fitted his tall frame to perfection and the white dress shirt and blue and grey striped tie highlighted the tanned and healthy tone of his skin and the intense blue of his eyes.

Cam's gaze met Violet's and a tiny invisible fist punched her in the stomach.

'You look stunning.' The deep huskiness of his voice was like a caressing stroke down the entire length of her spine. The way his eyes dipped to her lipgloss-coated mouth made her relive every pulse-racing second of that kiss. Was he remembering it too? How it had felt to have their tongues intimately entwined? How it had felt to taste each other, to feel each other's response? How it had felt to end it without the satiation both their bodies craved?

Violet brushed an imaginary strand of hair off her

face. 'This is one of my flatmates, Amy Kennedy. Amy, this is Cameron McKinnon, a friend from way back.'

When Cam took Amy's hand, Violet thought her flatmate was going to fall into a swoon. 'Pleased to meet you,' he said.

Amy's cheeks were bright pink and her mouth seemed to be having trouble closing. 'Same.'

Violet picked up her coat and Cam stood behind her and helped her into it. His body was so close she could feel its warmth and smell that intriguing blend of his aftershave. He briefly rested his hands on the tops of her shoulders before stepping away. While he was facing the other way, Amy gave her the thumbs-up sign, eyes bright with excitement. Violet picked up her purse and followed Cam to the door.

'Have a good time!' Amy's voice had a sing-song quality to it that made Violet feel like a teen going out on her first date.

Cam led her to his car, parked a few metres down the rain-slicked street. 'How many flatmates do you have?'

'Two. Amy and Stefanie.'

Violet slipped into the plush leather seat of his showroom-perfect convertible. There was no way she could ever imagine a couple of kids' seats in the back. His car was like his lifestyle—free and fast. Not that he was a hardened playboy or anything. But he was hardly a monk. He was a healthy man of thirty-four, in the prime of his life. Why wouldn't he make the most of his freedom? How many women had experienced that divine mouth? That gorgeous body and all the sensual delights it promised?

Probably more than she wanted to think about.

'I'm sorry about Amy back there,' Violet said after they were on the move. 'She can be a bit over the top.'

Cam glanced her way. 'Did I pass the test?'

Violet could feel an annoying blush creeping over her cheeks. 'The girls have a checklist for potential dates. No smokers, no heavy drinkers, no drugs, no tattoos. Must be gainfully employed, must respect women, must wear a condom… I mean during…you know… not at the time of meeting… That would be ridiculous.'

Cam's deep laugh made the base of her spine quiver. 'Good to know I tick all the boxes.'

Violet swivelled in her seat to look at him. 'So what's on your checklist?'

He appeared to think about it for a moment or maybe it was because he was concentrating on the traffic snarl ahead. 'Nothing specific. Intelligence is always good, a sense of humour.'

'Looks?'

He gave a lip shrug. 'Not as important as other qualities.'

'But you've only ever dated incredibly beautiful women. I've seen photos of them. Fraser showed me.'

'Mere coincidence.'

Violet snorted. 'Well-to-do men are selective when choosing a lover. Women, in general, are much more accepting over looks. It's a well-known fact.'

'What are you looking for in a partner?'

Violet looked at her hands where they were clutching her purse. 'I guess I want what my parents have—a partner who loves me despite my faults and is there for me no matter what.'

'Your parents are a tough act to follow.'

She let out a long sigh. 'Tell me about it.'

The dinner was at a restaurant in Soho. Cam's client had booked a private room and he and his wife were already seated at the table when they arrived. The man rose and greeted Cam warmly. 'So good you could join us. Sophia has been excited about it all day, haven't you, *agapi mou*?'

Sophia was excited all right. Violet could see the sultry gleam in those dark eyes as they roved Cam's body like she was mentally undressing him.

Cam's arm was around Violet's waist. 'Nick and Sophia Nicolaides, this is my partner Violet. Darling, this is Nick and Sophia.'

Partner? What was wrong with girlfriend? Partner sounded a little more…permanent. But then he wanted to make sure Sophia got the message loud and clear. 'Darling' was a nice touch, however. Violet quite liked that. No one had ever called her that before. She got 'poppet' and 'wee one' from her parents and her grandad called her Vivi like her siblings did. 'I'm very pleased to meet you both,' she said. 'Cam's told me all about you. Are you in London long?'

'Until New Year,' Nick said. 'Sophia's never had an English Christmas before.'

Sophia looked like all her Christmases and New Year's Eves had come at once when she slid her hand through Cam's arm. 'You're a dark horse, aren't you?' she said. 'You never told us you had a partner. Are you engaged?'

Cam's smile looked a little tight around the edges as he disentangled himself from Sophia's tentacle-like arm. 'Not yet.'

Not yet? Didn't that imply he was actually considering it? Violet had trouble keeping her expression composed. Even though she knew he was only saying it for the sake of appearances, her heart still gave an excited little leap. Not that she was in love with him or anything. She was just imagining what it would be like if she was. How it would feel to have him look at her with that tender look he was sending her way and actually mean it. For real.

Sophia smiled but it didn't crease her eyes at the corners, although that could have been because of Botox. *Meow.* Violet wasn't normally the critical type but something about the predatory nature of Nick Nicolaides' wife irritated her beyond measure. Sophia looked like the type of woman for whom the word 'no' was a challenge rather than an obstacle. What Sophia wanted, Sophia got. No matter what. And Sophia wanted Cam. It was a wonder Nick couldn't see it. Or was Nick so enamoured with his young, stunningly beautiful wife he couldn't see what was right before his eyes?

Violet decided it was time to draw the line, not in

sand but in concrete. She gazed up at Cam with what she hoped passed for besotted devotion. 'I didn't know you were thinking along those lines this early in our relationship.'

He leaned down and dropped a kiss to her upturned mouth. 'It's never too early to say I love you.'

Violet smiled a blissfully happy smile. Who said she couldn't act? Or maybe she wasn't acting. Hearing him say those words, even though deep down she knew he didn't mean them, had a potent effect on her. No one, apart from her family, had told her they loved her. 'I love you, too, baby.' She turned her smile up a notch.

Nick slapped Cam on the shoulder. 'Let's have a drink to celebrate in advance of the announcement.'

Champagne was ordered and served and the glasses held up in a toast to an engagement that wasn't going to happen. It felt weird to be part of such a deception but Violet had no choice but to run with it. Sophia kept looking at her, sizing her up as if wondering what on earth Cam saw in her. Violet didn't let it intimidate her, which was surprising as, under normal circumstances, she would have retreated to the trenches by now.

Dinner was a long, drawn-out affair because Nick wanted to discuss business with Cam, which left Violet to make conversation with Sophia. Never good at small talk, Violet had exhausted her twenty question checklist before the entrées were cleared away.

Cam came to her rescue after what was left of their mains was removed. He excused them both from the table and escorted her out to the restroom. 'You're doing great, Violet. Hang in there.'

'If looks could kill, I'd be lying in a morgue with a tag on my big toe right about now,' Violet said through clenched teeth. 'She is *such* a cow. She's not even trying to hide how she's lusting after you. Why can't Nick see it? She's so brazen it's nauseating.'

Cam's mouth was set in a grim line. 'I think he does see it but he's in denial. I don't want to be the one to take the bullet for pointing it out to him. This project is too important to me. It's the biggest contract I've done and more could follow. Nick has a lot of contacts. Word of mouth is everything in my business.'

Violet studied his tense features for a moment. 'If she weren't married would she be the type of woman you'd be involved with?'

'God, no.' His tone was adamant. 'What sort of man do you think I am?'

'She's incredibly beautiful.'

'So are you.'

Violet moistened her lips. 'You're terrifyingly good at lying.'

His brows came together. 'You think I'm lying? Don't you have mirrors at your flat? You turned every head when you walked through the main restaurant just now.'

Keep it light. Violet smiled a teasing smile to cover her self-consciousness. Compliments had never been her strong point. She knew it was polite to accept them with thanks but she could never quite pull it off with sophisticated aplomb. And if people noticed her when she came into a room, she never saw it. She was always too busy keeping her head down trying *not* to be noticed. 'You *were* lying about the intended proposal.'

His dark blue eyes held hers in a lock that made the base of her spine tingle like sherbet. 'I can be ruthless when it comes to nailing a business deal, but not that ruthless.'

'Good to know.'

His phone pinged with an incoming message. His expression turned sour when he checked the screen.

'Sophia?' Violet's tone was incredulous. 'She texted you while her husband is sitting right next to her?'

Cam expelled a breath and pocketed his phone. 'Go and powder your nose, I'll wait for you here.'

Cam led Violet back to the private dining room. She had reapplied her lipgloss and it made her lips all the more tempting to kiss. *Get a grip.* This was an act, not the real deal. He wasn't interested in the real deal. Not with anyone just now and particularly not with a girl he had viewed as a surrogate sister for the last twelve years.

But then last Easter something had changed.

He had changed.

He had suddenly noticed her. As in *noticed* her. The way she smiled that shy smile that made the corners of her mouth tilt upwards and then quiver, as if uncertain whether to stay there or not. The way she bit her lower lip when she was nervous. The way she moved her body like a graceful dancer. Her beautiful brown eyes that reminded him of caramel. Her creamy skin with that tiny dusting of freckles over the bridge of her nose that he found adorable.

Adorable?

Okay, time to rein it in. He had no right to be thinking about her that way. If he crossed the boundary any further it had the potential to ruin his relationship with her whole family. Three generations of it. He had so many wonderful memories of spending time at Drummond Brae, the big old house set on a Highland estate just out of Inverness. He had met Fraser Drummond in his fourth year at university in London when they were both twenty-two. It felt like a lifetime ago now.

But he still remembered the first time he had visited the Drummond family. It was nothing like any of the families he had been a part of, his nuclear family in particular. He had been struck by their warmth, the way they loved and accepted each other; the easygoing bonhomie between them was something he had never witnessed outside of a television show. Sure, they argued, but no one shouted or swore obscenities or threw things or stormed out in a huff. No one went through an insanely bitter divorce and then refused to have the other person's name mentioned in their presence ever again. Violet's parents were as in love with each other as the first day they'd met. Their solid relationship was the backbone of the family, the scaffolding providing the safety net of stability that allowed each sibling to grow to their full potential. Even the way

Margie Drummond was taking care of her ill ninety-year-old father-in-law Archie was indicative of the unconditional love that flowed in the family.

Cam had become an ancillary part of that family in a way he wouldn't dream of compromising, even if it meant ignoring the persistent drumbeat of lust he had going on for Violet—the baby of the clan. Who was doing an excellent job of pretending to be in love with him at the moment.

But it was far more than the fear of compromising his relationship with her family that held him back. How could he even think about settling down when he was all over the place with work commitments? He was driven to succeed and the only way to succeed was to put everything else on hold. Work was his focus. His first priority. His only priority. If he got distracted now, he could jeopardise everything he'd worked so hard for since the day he'd been left at boarding school. He was used to being an island. Self-sufficient.

Violet resumed her seat next to Cam at the table and looped her slim arm through his, gazing up at him with those big brown eyes as if she thought the world began and ended and only made sense with him. This close he could smell her perfume, a bewitching combination of spring flowers that tantalised his senses until he felt slightly drunk. Or mad. Definitely mad. Mad with lust. He could feel it pounding in his pelvis when she leaned closer, her slim pale hand sliding down to his.

Her touch should not be having this effect on him. He was not a lust-crazed teenager. Normally he could control himself. But if she looked at his lap right now, he'd have some explaining to do. He still had some explaining to do after that kiss. He had been hard for her with one kiss. One kiss, for God's sake! What sort of tragic did that make him? Yes, he hadn't had sex in a while but he'd been busy since Easter… And no, it had nothing to do with seeing Violet that weekend. Nothing to do with noticing her in a way he had never done before.

Or had it?

Had he not pursued the many opportunities he'd had for a casual fling because something had gnawed at him since Easter? The sense that there had to be something more…something more than a few drinks or dinners, a few mostly satisfactory tumbles and a 'goodbye, thanks for the memories'?

For years he had been perfectly content with his lifestyle. He enjoyed the freedom to take on extra work without the pressure of being responsible for someone's emotional upkeep. He had seen both of his parents struggle and fail to meet the needs of each other and their subsequent partners whilst juggling the demands of a career and family. It had always looked like too much hard work.

But there was something to be said for feeling something more than basic lust for a sexual partner. Kissing Violet had felt…different somehow. The connection they had as long-term friends had brought a completely different dynamic to the kiss. He couldn't quite explain it. Maybe he would have to kiss her again… *There's a thought.*

'Smile for the camera,' Sophia said from the other side of the table, holding up her phone.

Cam smiled and leaned his head against Violet's fragrant one, her hair tickling his cheek, her closeness doing something dangerous to his hormones. The photo was taken and Sophia sat back with a Cheshire cat smile. He didn't trust that smile. He didn't trust that woman. He didn't trust his deal with Nick would be secure until the contract was signed, sealed and delivered. But Nick was dragging things out a bit. This trip to London was obviously part of the stalling campaign. Cam couldn't help feeling he was being subjected to some sort of test. Maybe Nick knew exactly what his flirty young wife was up to but wanted to see how Cam would deal with it.

He was dealing with it just fine. With Violet's help. But how long would he have to play pretend? This weekend was fine. But after that? There was only one more week before Christmas. If word got out… His gut seized at the thought. Why had he got himself into this? Seeing Violet in that café earlier had been purely coincidence.

Or had it?

He had felt drawn to that café as if a navigational device inside his body had taken him there. When he'd seen her sitting there all alone something had shifted inside him. Like a gear going up a notch. He had gone from *noticing her* to wanting her…as in *wanting* her. He had offered to take her to the party not because he felt sorry for her but because he couldn't bear the thought of some sleazy colleague trying it on with her.

Green-eyed monster?

You bet.

CHAPTER THREE

VIOLET WASN'T SURE she liked the idea of Sophia having photos of her and Cam but what could she do? She had to play along and pretend everything was fine. Thing was, it *felt* fine. Leaning against him, smiling up at him, looking into those amazingly blue eyes of his that crinkled up at the corners when he smiled—all of it felt so fine she had trouble remembering this was all an act. That it wasn't going to last beyond the weekend.

'Nick and I are going to dance at the nightclub down the road,' Sophia said. 'Come and join us.'

It wasn't an invitation—it was a command. One Violet would have ignored but for the forty million pounds that were hanging in the balance.

And because she didn't want Sophia to think she was one bit intimidated by her. It was how mean girls worked. They manipulated and caused trouble, striking mischief-making matches and standing back to watch the explosion like Lorna had done outside the office.

But there was another reason Violet walked into that nightclub on Cam's arm. She had never danced with anyone. Not since that party. She hated the crush of bodies. The threat of strangers touching her, even by accident as they jostled on the dance floor, had always been too threatening.

But if she danced with Cam it would prove she was moving on. Taking back the control she had lost. She had never danced with him, not even at one of her family's famous *ceilidhs*. He had always refrained from joining into the fun, citing the fact that he had no co-ordination or wasn't a true Scot and there was no way he was ever wearing a skirt. But this would be the perfect opportunity to get him on the dance floor. A legitimate excuse to be in his arms. Where she felt safe.

But Violet hadn't factored in the music. It wasn't the swaying-in-your-partner's arms sort. It was loud, an auditory assault that made conversation other than sign language virtually impossible. The nightclub dance floor was cramped with sweaty, gyrating bodies. It was exactly the sort of place she normally avoided. There wasn't room to swing a cat, let alone a dance partner.

But Sophia and Nick seemed to be enjoying every eardrum-splitting moment. They were jigging about, weaving their way through the knot of dancers as if they did it every day of the week. They waved to Cam and Violet on their way past, shouting over the music, 'Come and join us!'

Violet looked up at Cam, who looked like he was suffering from indigestion. She stepped up on tiptoe and cupped her hand around his ear. 'Are you going to ask me to dance? Because, if so, let me spare you the embarrassment of being rejected.'

'You call that dancing?'

A smile tugged at her mouth and she stepped up to his ear again. 'You ever get the feeling you were born into the wrong century? Give me a traditional Gay Gordon dance any day.'

He drew her closer in a quick squeeze hug that made her breath hitch. 'I feel about a hundred and fifty in here.'

'Age or temperature?'

He gave a crooked smile and took out his handkerchief—*why did classy men always have one?*—and gently blotted the beads of perspiration that had gathered on her forehead. Violet couldn't tear her eyes away from the deep steady focus of his. What was he thinking behind the screen of his gaze? His eyes dipped to her mouth, his lashes going to half-mast, giving him a sexily hooded look that made her belly quiver like someone bumping into an unset bowl of jelly. She moistened her mouth…not because it was dry but because she liked seeing him watch her do so. He moved closer, his thighs strong and muscular, so very male against her trembling legs. She felt the ridge of his arousal. It should have shocked her, would've shocked her, if it had been anyone else.

But it was Cam.

Who desired her even though he didn't want to. It was a force they were both fighting…for different reasons. Violet didn't want to waste time in a relationship going nowhere even if it was with the most desirable man she had ever met. Cam wasn't interested in finding a life partner. He didn't want to be tied down to family life. Understandable, given the atrocious example his parents had set. But Violet couldn't help wondering if deep down he was less concerned about his loss of freedom and more concerned about not being the sort of husband and father he most aspired to be. He was a perfectionist. Doing a good job wasn't enough for someone like Cam. If he put his mind and energy to something he did it brilliantly. That was why he was one of the most celebrated naval architects in the world.

'Let's go someplace else,' Cam said against her ear.

Had he suggested leaving because he knew she was uncomfortable in that environment? Violet couldn't help but be touched by his concern. 'But what about Nick and—?'

'They'll survive without us.' He took her hand and led her out of the nightclub. 'I'll send Nick a text to say we had to leave. He'll think I want to whip you away somewhere private.'

Please do! Violet followed him out of the nightclub to the wet and cold street outside. Within a few minutes they were in the warm cocoon of his car. But instead of driving her back to her flat he turned in the direction of his house in Belgravia. She hadn't been there before...although she'd walked past. Purely to satisfy her feminine interest, of course. During the drive he'd suggested a nightcap, which could have been code for something else but she took it at face value. Besides, going back to her flat, which would be empty now because both Amy and Stef had steady boyfriends and spent most weekends at their homes, was not the most exciting prospect.

Violet had to pretend to be surprised by the outside of the house when he pulled up in front of it. 'Is this your place? Wow! It's gorgeous. How long have you had it? It looks massive.'

'I bought it a year or so ago.' He led her up the black and white tiled pathway to the front door. 'I've done most of the renovations myself.'

Violet knew he was good with his hands; she had the humming body to prove it. But she hadn't realised he was a handyman of this sort of standard. The house was amazing. A showcase similar to those you would see in a home and lifestyle magazine. It was a three storey high Georgian mansion with beautiful features throughout. Crystal chandeliers tinkled above when Cam closed the door against the wintry breeze. The plush Persian carpet runner that led the way down the wide hallway threatened to swallow Violet's feet whole. The antique furniture made her mouth water. Some girls loved fashion and jewellery but anything old and precious did it for her. There were priceless works of art on the walls in gilt-edged frames. Sculptures on marble stands, a white orchid in full bloom on another softening the overall effect.

Cam led her through to a sitting room with a fireplace with a stunning black marble surround with brass trim. Twin cream sofas, deep as a cloud, sat opposite each other with a mahogany coffee table in between. A Louis XV chair was featured in one corner next to a small cedar writing desk next to a full bookcase. It looked like the perfect room for curling up with a book…or cuddling up with the one you loved.

Stop it. You're letting it go to your head.

Violet realised then with a little jolt that this was the first time they had been completely alone. At Drummond Brae there had always been members of her family about the place, if not in the same room. She had never truly been alone with Cam without the threat of interruption.

Violet turned from taking in all of the room to find him looking at her with an unreadable expression. The air seemed to tighten and then to crackle as if an invisible current was being transmitted through their gazes. She could feel her body responding to the magnetic presence of his. She was half a room away but it felt like a force was drawing her to him, a force she could not control even if she wanted to. 'Why are you looking at me like that?' she asked, barely recognising the breathy voice as coming from her.

'How am I looking at you?'

'As if you don't want me to know what you're thinking.'

His mouth lifted in a wry smile that tugged on something deep inside her. 'Believe me, you don't want to know what I'm thinking.'

'Try me.' *Did you just say that? Isn't that flirting? That thing you never do?*

He closed the distance in a couple of strides, standing close enough for her to feel the potent energy of his body calling out to hers. 'This is all sorts of crazy.' He didn't touch her. He just stood there looking down at her with that inscrutable expression on his face.

Violet disguised a tiny swallow. 'What is?'

She heard him draw in a breath, it sounded as if it caught on something on the way through. He lifted his hand, brushing the backs of his bent fingers down the slope of her cheek. 'Being alone with you. It's… ill-advised.'

Ill-advised? Violet wondered what other word he'd considered using. Dangerous? Tempting? Inevitable? All three seemed to apply. She looked at his mouth, knowing it was a signal for him to kiss her. Knowing it and doing it anyway. It was what she wanted. It was what he wanted. She might not be very experienced but she could tell when a man wanted to kiss a woman.

She lowered her lashes over her eyes, swaying towards him. *Kiss me. Kiss me. Kiss me.* She placed her hands on the wall of his chest. The feel of his firm male form beneath her palms sent a thrill through her body. It was like being plugged into a power source. She felt the sensual voltage from her palms to the balls of her feet…and other places. Places she mostly ignored, but not now. Her feminine core responded to his closeness with a tight, clenching ache. His head came down, his mouth hovering within a breath of hers as if some fraying thread of self-control was only just keeping him in check.

Violet took matters into her own hands…or mouth, so to speak. She closed the minuscule distance by placing her lips to his, her heart kicking in excitement when he made a low, deep groaning sound before he took charge of the kiss. His lips were firmer than the last time, not rough but with an undercurrent of desperation as if the self-control he had always relied on had finally let him down. She felt it in the way his tongue came in ruthless search of hers, tangling with it in an erotic dance that made her skin pop all over with goose bumps. The spread of his fingers through her hair made every nerve on her scalp tingle at the roots, his mouth continuing its sensual teasing until she was mindless with longing. His stubble grazed her cheek and then her chin but she didn't care. This was what she'd been hungering for all evening…or maybe for most of her adult life.

The insistent sound of her phone vibrating and chirruping from within her evening bag would have been easy to ignore under normal circumstances, but it was late at night. Late night phone calls usually meant something was wrong. And with her frail grandfather it was hard not to worry something terrible had happened. Violet eased back from Cam's embrace and gave him a wincing look. 'Sorry, better answer that. It might be urgent.'

'Sure.' He rubbed a hand over the back of his neck and stood back while she fished her phone out of her purse.

By the time Violet got her phone out it had stopped, but she frowned when she saw she'd missed six calls from her mother. There were three each from all of her siblings. Her stomach dropped like an elevator with sabotaged cables. She pressed speed dial and looked at Cam with a grimace as she braced herself for bad news.

'Mum? What's wrong? You called me—'

'Poppet, why didn't you tell me?' Her mother's clear voice carried as if Violet had put her on speaker. 'It's all over social media. I've had everyone calling to confirm it. We're so delighted for you and Cam. When did he ask you? Tell me everything. It's just so exciting! Grandad's taken on a new lease of life. He got out of bed and had a wee dram to celebrate. He says he's going to make it to your wedding and no one's going to stop him. Your father's beside himself with joy. Here, speak to him.'

Violet looked wide-eyed at Cam for help, mouthing, *What will I say?*

Cam gestured for her to hand him the phone. He took it and held it to his ear, his eyes on Violet's, his expression was calm on the surface, but she could see a tiny muscle in his jaw going on and off like a miniature hammer. 'Gavin? Yes, well, we were hoping to keep it quiet a little longer but—'

'Congratulations,' her father said. 'Couldn't have asked for a better son-in-law. You have my every blessing, Cam. You're already a big part of the family—this has just made it formal. You and our little Vivi. I'm so thrilled I can barely tell you. I know you'll look after our baby girl.'

After a few more effusive congratulations from both her parents, Cam handed back the phone to Violet and she was subjected to the same. This was the trouble with having parents who were enthusiastic and encouraging in anything and everything their children did. There was barely a space for her to put a word in. Finally her parents ended the call and Violet switched her phone off. Her siblings would be next. There would be another barrage of verbiage she wouldn't be able to contradict for fear of disappointing everyone.

But her brother and sisters would have to wait until she figured out what Cam was up to. Why hadn't he denied it? Why let it continue when so many people would be hurt when the truth came out?

'Okay, so apparently we're now engaged,' she said, shooting him a *please explain* look. 'Any idea how that happened?'

His mouth was set in a rigid line. 'Sophia Nicolaides must have made an announcement on social media with that photo she took of us at dinner. Do you know how many followers she has?' He turned away and let out a stiff curse. 'I should've known something like this would happen.'

'But we could've just denied it.'

He swung his gaze back to hers. 'You heard what your mother said. Your grandfather practically came out of a coma at the news. No, we'll have to run with it—at least until after Christmas.'

Violet's heart was doing a rather good impression

of having some sort of medical event. 'Why till after Christmas?'

'Because I don't want your family's Christmas to be spoilt,' he said. 'It's the time when everyone comes together. Your mother puts such a lot of effort into making it special for everyone. Can you imagine how awkward it would be if we were to tell them it's all a lie?'

Violet chewed her lip. He was right. Of course he was. Christmas was a big thing in her family and it would be ruined if she and Cam put them straight about the charade they were playing. And surely poor old Grandad deserved to have his last Christmas as happy as they could make it? It wasn't like Cam was going to keep this going for ever. He didn't want to settle down. The last thing he would want to do was tie himself down with a woman he wasn't in love with. He liked her, loved her even in a platonic sort of way, but he wasn't in love with her. She wasn't his type. She wasn't anyone's type.

'But we're going to have to tell them some time...'

Cam dragged a hand down his face, momentarily distorting his handsome features. 'I know, but there's too much at stake. And no, I'm not just referring to this deal with Nicolaides.'

'Apart from my family, what else is at stake?'

He let out a ragged-sounding breath. 'There's my family for one thing. I'm not sure I want to show up to my father's fifth wedding on Christmas Eve with a broken engagement under my belt. He'll never let me hear the end of it. I can hear everyone saying it now. *Like father, like son.*'

Violet could understand his point of view. From what she knew of his father, Ross McKinnon would make the most of any opportunity to rub in Cam's mistakes as a way to take the focus off his own behaviour. His mother, Candice, would also not let a chance like that go by, given Cam had been so critical of how both his parents had behaved over the years.

'Right, well, it looks like we run with it then.'

At least her office Christmas party would be less of an ordeal with him there as her fiancé. For once she would be spared the sleazy flirting from male colleagues, and at least there would be no more pitying looks from some of the women who thought it fine sport to make a mockery out of her being single. It was a win-win…she hoped.

Cam picked up his keys from the writing desk where he'd left them earlier. 'I'd better take you home. It's late.'

Violet's spirits slumped in disappointment. Didn't he want to finish the kiss they'd started? 'I don't have to be back by any set time,' she said. 'The girls are sleeping over at their boyfriends' so…'

His sober expression halted her speech. 'Violet.' The way he said her name with that deep note of gravity was a little disquieting to say the least. 'We're not going there, okay?'

There? Where was 'there'? All she wanted was a

little more kissing and…a little fooling around. Okay, *lots* of fooling around. Violet forced a smile.

He looked at her for a long moment, his eyes moving back and forth between each of hers in a searching manner that made her feel like someone was trickling sand down the column of her spine. 'I said we'd kiss and that's all.'

'Fine. No problem. Best to be sensible about this.' The words kept tumbling out. 'Way, way too awkward if we go there. I'm not your type in any case. Not enough experience for one thing.'

His brows formed a bridge over his dark-as-midnight blue eyes. 'How much experience have you had?'

Violet gave a self-deprecating grimace. 'Well…let's put it this way. I haven't been around the block, I got to the corner and then got kind of lost.'

His frown deepened. 'What do you mean?'

What are you doing? You haven't ever told anyone about…that.

Violet pressed her lips together, wondering if she should go any further. Would it make him see her differently? Make him judge her for being a naïve little fool to get into such a situation? But something about his concerned expression made her realise he would be the last person to pass judgement on her. 'I'd rather not talk about it…'

'You can tell me, Violet.' Cam's voice was so steady, so strong, so calm. But then he had always been a good listener. Violet remembered an occasion during her teens when she'd found herself telling him about the mean girls at school who had taunted her for not wearing the right label of clothes to a party. *What was it with her and parties?* Cam had listened to her frustrated rant and then assured her the girls were probably jealous because she didn't need designer wear to look gorgeous. Violet remembered blushing to the roots of her hair but feeling a strange sense of warmth every time she recalled that conversation since.

Telling him about what happened at that university party was not on the same level of having a moan about a bunch of vacuous schoolgirls at a teenage birthday bash. Telling him about the trauma of her first sexual experience would be laying herself bare. Opening old wounds that had never properly healed. But there was something about Cam that gave her new strength. Maybe it was time to get it off her chest so she could breathe without that lingering pinching feeling of shame.

'During my first year at university, I went to a party…' She took a short breath before continuing. 'I was trying to fit in instead of being on the outer all the time. I had a couple of drinks—too many drinks, really…'

Violet glanced up to see him frowning so intensely his eyebrows met over his eyes. But it wasn't a frown of disapproval or judgement, it was one of raw concern. It gave her the courage to continue. 'Things got a little hazy and I…well, I woke up and there were three…' She took a painful swallow. 'At first I wasn't sure if it was a dream—a nightmare or something. I was on a bed and there was a man, not someone I knew…'

'Did he…rape you?' Cam's voice came out sounding rusty as if he had trouble getting the words through his throat.

This time Violet couldn't quite meet his gaze but aimed it at a point just below his chin. 'I'm not sure… I don't remember that part. Can you call it rape if you don't remember anything? There wasn't just one man… I'm not sure if they were just…watching or…'

He took her by the hands and drew her close but not quite touching his body as if he was worried about making her feel uncomfortable after her confession. 'Did you report it?'

Violet shook her head. 'I couldn't bear anyone knowing about it. I didn't tell anyone, not even Mum or Rose or Lily. I felt so ashamed I'd got myself into that situation. I just locked it away and…and, well, I quit my studies. I couldn't help feeling people were looking at me differently around the campus…you know? I just thought it best to move on and pretend it never happened.'

He drew her against him in a gentle hug, resting his head on top of hers. 'I wish I'd been at that party because there's no way those lowlife creeps would have got away with that.' The deep resonance of his voice from his chest where it was pressed against hers was a strange sort of comfort. She felt safe in a way she hadn't felt in years. If only he had been there. If only she had been able to run to him and have him hold her, protect her. He was that type of man. Honourable. Chivalrous. There was no way he would spike anyone's drink and take advantage of a woman when she was too out of it to give proper consent. The world needed more men like Cam. Men who weren't afraid to stand up to bullies. Men who were brave and steadfast in their values. Men who treated women as equals and not as objects to service their needs.

Violet looked up at him. 'Thank you.'

He gently stroked her hair back from her face. 'It wasn't your fault, Violet. What those men did was wrong. You're not the one who should be feeling ashamed. They committed a crime and so did anyone else at that party who witnessed it and didn't report it.'

'I was so worried there might be...photos...'

He winced as if someone had stabbed him in the gut. 'Do you remember anyone taking any?'

Violet shook her head. 'No, but there was so much I didn't remember so I could never be sure one way or the other. It's made the humiliation of that night go on and on. For ten years I've worried someone out there has photos of me...like that, and I can't do anything about it.'

Cam's expression was tight with rage on her behalf. There were white tips around his mouth and his jaw was locked. 'Think of it this way. If photos were to surface they could be used as evidence in court. You could identify the perpetrators and lay charges.'

Violet hadn't thought of it that way and it was like a weight coming off her, like taking off a heavy backpack after a long, exhausting walk. She leaned her head against his chest, breathing in the clean male scent of him. He continued to stroke her head, gentle soothing strokes that made her feel as if she was the most precious person in the world instead of someone dirty, tainted, someone to be used for sport and cast aside.

Violet didn't know how long they stood there like that. It could have been seconds, minutes or even half an hour. All she knew was it felt as if she had come to a safe anchorage after years of tossing about in an unpredictable sea.

But finally he eased back from her, still holding her, his thumbs rhythmically stroking the backs of her hands. 'I want you to know something, Violet. You will always be safe with me. Always.'

Violet wasn't sure she wanted to be safe. The feelings she had for him were dangerous. Dangerous and exciting. 'Thanks…' *I think.* 'But please, I'd rather you didn't mention this to my family. I want to put it behind me. For good.'

'Am I the only person you've told?'

Violet nodded. 'Weird, huh? You of all people.'

His frown was still pleating his forehead. 'Why me of all people?'

She shifted her gaze. 'I don't know… I never thought I'd tell you. I guess I didn't want you to think of me… like that.'

He brought her chin up so her gaze came back to his. 'Hey.' His eyes were as dark as sapphires, his voice low and deep as a bass chord. 'I could never think of you like that and nor should you think of yourself that way. You're a beautiful person who had an ugly thing happen to her. Don't keep punishing yourself.'

Violet had spent years berating herself for being in the wrong place at the wrong time with the wrong personality. If she'd been less reserved, less trusting, more able to stand up for herself, then maybe it wouldn't have happened. For so long she had blamed herself for allowing herself to get into such a situation. But now that she had opened up to Cam, she could see how futile that blame game was. It was time to let it go and accept that it could have happened to anyone. She had been that *anyone* that fateful day.

Violet looked into his dark, caring eyes. Did this mean it was still hands-off? She still wanted him to kiss her. She wanted to be free from her past and experience being in a relationship with a man who respected her and treated her as an equal. Why couldn't Cam be that man? Cam who listened to her as if she were the only person in the world he wanted to hear talk. Cam, whom she'd trusted enough to tell her most shameful secret to, which, strangely enough, didn't feel so shameful now that she had shared it with him.

Cam's phone started ringing and he took it out of his pocket and grimaced when he saw the caller ID. 'Fraser.' He pressed the mute button. 'I'll call him later.'

Violet bit down on her lip. Fraser wouldn't give up in a hurry. She had yet to talk to him and her sisters. How soon before one of her family began to suspect things weren't quite as they seemed? What if it jeopardised Cam's contract? She didn't want to be responsible for ruining that for him, but nor did she want to be responsible for wrecking everyone's Christmas. 'This situation between us is getting awfully complicated… I'm not a very good liar. What if someone guesses this isn't for real?'

His hand cupped one side of her face, his touch gentle fire licking at her flesh. 'No one will guess. You're doing a great job so far.'

That's because I'm not sure I'm still pretending.

CHAPTER FOUR

CAM DROVE VIOLET back to her flat half an hour later. He was still getting his head around what she'd told him earlier. He'd had trouble containing his rage at what had happened to her. The frustrated anger at the way she had been treated gnawed at him. He had the deepest respect for women and felt sickened to his gut that there were men out there who would act so unconscionably. For all these years since, Violet had lived with the shame of being in the wrong place at the wrong time with the wrong people. It saddened him to think she blamed herself. *Still* blamed herself. No wonder she had no dating life to speak of. Why would she want to fraternise with men if she didn't know if she could trust them?

He didn't trust himself around her. Not that he would ever do anything she didn't want, but still. The attraction that had flared up between them was something he was doing his best to ignore. It was all very well pretending to be engaged for a couple of weeks. Kissing and holding hands and stuff was fine to add a little authenticity. More than fine. But taking it any further?

Not a good idea.

A dumb idea.

An idea that had unfortunately taken root in his brain and was winding its tentacles throughout his body like a rampant vine. He had only to look at Violet and those tentacles of lust coiled and tightened in his groin.

But how could he act on it? Even if it was what she wanted? It wouldn't be fair to her to get her hopes up that he could offer her anything more than a casual relationship. He hated hurting people. If he broke Violet's heart he would never forgive himself. Her family would never forgive him either.

Engaged via social media.

What a nightmare. How had he got himself into such a complicated mess?

Cam walked Violet to the door of her flat but when they got there it was slightly ajar. She stopped dead, cannoning back against his body standing just behind her. 'Oh, no…' Her voice came out as a shocked gasp.

Cam put his hands on her shoulders. 'What's wrong?' And then he saw what she had seen. The lock had been jemmied open, the woodwork around it splintered. 'Don't touch anything,' he said, moving her out of the way. 'I'll call the police.'

Within a few minutes the police arrived and investigated the scene. The police told Cam and Violet that several flats in the area had been targeted that night in the hunt for drugs and cash. Once they were allowed inside, Cam held Violet's hand as she inspected the mess.

And it was a mess. Clothes, shoes, books, kitchen items and even food thrown around and ground into the carpet as if the intruders were intent on causing as much mayhem as possible.

Cam could sense Violet's distress even though she was putting on a brave face. Her bottom lip was quivering and her brown eyes were moving from one scattered item to the next as if wondering how on earth she would ever restore order to the place. He was wondering that himself. 'I… I've got to call Amy and Stef,' she said in a distracted tone, fumbling for her phone in her purse and almost dropping it when she found it.

Cam would have led her to the sofa to sit down but it had been slashed with a sharp object, presumably one of the kitchen knives the police had since bagged and taken away for fingerprinting. He shuddered at the thought of what might have happened if Violet had been alone inside the flat when the intruders broke in. Who knew what this new class of criminals were capable of these days? It didn't bear thinking about. He picked up an overturned chair instead and set it down, making sure it was clean first. 'Here, sweetie. Come and sit down and I'll call the girls for you.'

Violet's expression was a mixture of residual fear and gratitude. 'Would you? I'm not sure I can think straight, let alone talk to anyone just now.'

Cam spoke to both of Violet's flatmates, telling them what had happened and that everything was under control now as he was organising an emergency locksmith to repair the lock. 'And don't worry about Violet,' he added. 'I'm taking her back to my place.'

Of course he would have to take her home with him. There was no question about it. He couldn't leave her in the trashed flat to lie awake all night in terror of being invaded again. Or worse. It was the right thing to do to take her home with him. What friend wouldn't offer a bed for a night or two? He wasn't one for sleepovers. He liked his space too much. But this was Violet. A friend from way back.

It was a pity his body wasn't so clear on the friend factor, but still. His hormones would have to get control of themselves.

While the locksmith was working on the lock, one of Violet's elderly neighbours shuffled along the corridor to speak to her. 'Are you all right, Violet?' the wizened old man said. 'I didn't hear a thing. The sleeping pills the doctor gave me knock me out for most of the night.'

Violet gave the old man a reassuring smile. 'I'm fine, Mr Yates. I'm glad you weren't disturbed. How's your chest feeling? Is your bronchitis better?'

Cam thought it typical of Violet to be more concerned about her elderly neighbour than herself. The old man gave her a sheepish look. 'The doc reckons I should give up smoking but at my age what other pleasures are there?' He turned his rheumy gaze to Cam. 'And who might you be, young man?'

'I'm Violet's—'

'Friend,' Violet said before Cam could finish his sentence.

Mr Yates's bushy brows waggled. 'Boyfriend?'

'Fiancé, actually,' Cam said with a ridiculous sense of pride he couldn't account for or explain. He knew it was beneath him to be beating his chest in front of an elderly man like some sort of Tarzan figure but he couldn't help it. *Boyfriend* sounded so…juvenile, and *lover*, well, that was even worse. Violet wasn't the sort of girl to take a lover.

Mr Yates smiled a nicotine-stained smile. 'Congratulations. You've got a keeper there in Violet. She's the nicest of the girls who live here. Never could understand why she hasn't been snapped up well before now. You're a lucky man.'

'I know.'

Once the locksmith had finished and Mr Yates had shuffled back to his flat, Cam led Violet back out to his car with a small collection of her belongings to see her through for a few days. Not that she could bring much as most of it had been thrown about the flat. The thought of putting on clothes that some stranger had touched would be horrifying for her. It was horrifying to him.

He glanced at her once they were on their way. She was sitting with a hunched posture, her fingers plucking at her evening bag, her face white and pinched. 'How are you doing?'

'I don't know how to thank you…' She gave a little hiccupping sound as if she was fighting back a sob. 'You've been so amazing tonight. I really don't know what I would've done without you.'

Cam reached for her hand and placed it on top of his thigh. 'That's what friends—or rather, fake fiancés—are for.' His attempt at humour didn't quite hit the mark. Her teeth sank into her lower lip so hard he was worried she would puncture the skin. She looked so tiny and vulnerable it made his chest sting. It made him think of how she must have been after that wretched party—alone, terrified, shocked, with no one she felt she could turn to. If only he had known. If only he had been there that night, he could have done something to protect her. Violet was the sort of girl who made him want to rush off for a white horse and a suit of armour. Her trust in him made him feel…conflicted, truth be told.

He wanted to protect her, sure, but he wanted her, period. Which was a whole lot of capital *T* trouble he could do without right now. Bringing her home with him was the right thing to do. Of course it was. Sure, he could have set her up in a hotel but he sensed she needed company. Her parents were too far away in Scotland to get to her in a hurry, so too were her brother and sisters, who lived in various parts of the country.

Cam was on knight duty so it was up to him to hold her hand.

As long as that's all you hold.

Violet had held off tears only because Cam had done everything that needed to be done. He'd taken charge in a way that made her feel supported and safe. The horror of finding all her possessions strewn around the flat had been such a shock. She felt so violated. Someone—

more than one someone, it seemed—had broken in and rifled through her and her roommates' things. They had seen her photo with the girls at Stef's last birthday celebration stuck on the kitchen door, which meant she might one day pass them in the street and they would know who she was but she would have no idea who they were. It was like being back on the university campus after that party. She didn't know who the enemy was. They had touched her clothing, her underwear. Invaded her private sanctuary and now it was defiled, just as her body had been defiled all those years ago.

Cam kept glancing at her and gently squeezing and stroking her hand. It was enormously comforting. Violet could see the concern, and the anger he was doing his best to suppress on her behalf. Was he thinking of what might have happened if she'd been in that flat alone? She was thinking about it and it was terrifying. How fortunate that he had walked her to the door. But then, of course he would do that. It was the type of man he was. Strong, capable, with old-fashioned values that resonated with hers.

His offer to have her stay with him at his house was perfectly reasonable given their friendship and yet… she wondered if he was entirely comfortable with it. Would it make it harder for him to keep things platonic between them?

Once they were back at his house, Cam carried her small bag of belongings—those she could stomach enough to bring with her—to one of the spare bedrooms. But at least her embroidery basket had been left intact. She was halfway through making a baby blanket for Lily's unborn baby and couldn't bear the thought of anyone destroying that.

'I'm only a door away over there.' Cam pointed to the master bedroom on the other side of the wide hallway. 'I'll leave my door open in case you need me during the night.'

I need you now.

'Thanks…for everything.'

He gave her one of those lopsided smiles of his that made her heart contract. 'You're welcome.'

Violet shifted her weight. 'Do you mind if I have a hot drink? I'm not sure I'm going to be able to sleep. Maybe a hot milk or something will help.'

'Of course.'

Violet followed him back down to the spacious kitchen and perched on one of the breakfast-bar stools while he went about preparing a hot chocolate for both of them. It was a strange feeling to be alone with him in his house, knowing she would be sleeping in one of his beds. Not *his* bed. He'd made that inordinately clear. But the possibility he could change his mind made her feel a thrill of excitement like someone had injected champagne bubbles into her bloodstream. She couldn't stop looking at his hands, couldn't stop imagining how they would feel touching her, stroking her. He had broad hands with long fingers with neat square nails. Capable hands. Careful hands. Hands that healed instead of hurt. Every time he touched her she felt her body glow with warmth. It was like she was coming out of cold storage. His touch awakened the sensuality that had been frozen by fear all those years ago.

He slid the hot chocolate towards her with a spoon and the sugar bowl. 'There you go.'

Violet took a restorative sip and observed him while he stirred his chocolate. He still had a two-fold crease between his eyes as if his mind was still back at her flat thinking up a whole lot of nasty scenarios, similar to the ones she was trying her best not to think about. 'I'll only stay tonight,' she said into the silence. 'Once the girls and I tidy up, I'll go back.'

His frown wasn't letting up any. 'Is that such a good idea? What if you get broken into again? The security there is crap. You don't even have a security chain on the door. Your landlord should be ashamed of himself.'

'It's actually a woman.'

'Same goes.'

Violet cradled her drink between her hands, looking at him over the rim of her cup when she took another sip. He had abandoned his drink as if his mind was too preoccupied. There were lines of tension running down either side of his mouth. 'I know this must be awkward for you…having me here…' she said. 'You know, after our conversation earlier about…only kissing.'

His gaze went to her mouth as if he couldn't help himself. 'It's not awkward.' His voice came out so husky it sounded like it had been dragged along a rough surface.

'I could go to a hotel or stay with a—'

'No.' The word was delivered with such implacability it made Violet blink. 'You'll stay here as long as you need to.'

How about for the rest of my life? Violet took another sip of her chocolate before setting the mug down. She had to stop this ridiculous habit of imagining a future with him. She was being a silly romantic fool, conjuring up a happy ending because she was almost thirty and Cam was the first man to treat her the way she'd always longed to be treated. It was her hormones…or something. 'I guess it kind of makes sense, me being here, since we're supposed to be engaged.'

'Yes, well, there's that, of course.'

Violet slipped off the stool and took her mug over to the sink, rinsing it first before putting it in the dishwasher. She turned and found Cam looking at her with a frowning expression. 'I'm…erm…going to bed now,' she said. 'Thanks again for everything.'

He gave her a semblance of a smile that softened the frown a smidgen. 'No problem. Hope you can get some sleep.'

Violet was about to turn for the door when, on an impulse she couldn't explain let alone stop, she stepped up to where Cam was standing and, rising on tiptoe, pressed a soft kiss to his stubble-roughened cheek. His hands went to her hips as if he too couldn't stop himself, drawing her that little bit closer so her body was flush against his. His eyes searched hers for a long moment before dipping to her mouth. 'We really shouldn't be doing this, Violet. It only makes things more—'

'More what?' Violet said, pressing herself closer,

feeling the hardened ridge of him against her belly. 'Exciting?'

His hands tightened on her hips but, instead of drawing her closer, he put her from him, dropping his hold as if her body was scorching hot. His frown was severe but she got the feeling it was directed more at himself than at her.

'You're upset after the break-in,' he said. 'Your emotions are shot to pieces. It would be wrong of me to take advantage of you when you're feeling so vulnerable.'

Take advantage! Take advantage! Violet knew he was being the sensible and considerate man she knew him to be, but the fledging flirt in her felt hurt by his rejection. Why shouldn't they have a fling? It was the perfect chance for her to let go of her past and explore her sensuality without shame, without fear, with a man she not only trusted but admired and cared about. Why couldn't he see how much she needed him to help wipe away the past? 'I'm sorry for misreading the signals. Of course you wouldn't want to sleep with me. No one wants to sleep with me unless I'm coma-drunk. Why am I so hopeless at this?'

Cam took her by the shoulders this time, locking his gaze on hers. 'You're not hopeless at anything, sweetheart. You're a beautiful and talented young woman who deserves to be happy. I'm trying for damage control here. If we take this further, it will blur the boundaries. For both of us.'

Violet planted her hands on his chest, feeling the thud-pitty-thud-pitty-thud of his heart beneath her palm. The battle was played out on his features: the push of pulsating desire and the pull away of his sense of duty. Push. Pull. Push. Pull. It was mirrored in the rhythm of a muscle flicking in his jaw. 'But you want me…don't you?' she said.

He brought her up against his body, pelvis to pelvis, his eyes holding hers. 'I want you, but—'

'Let's leave the "but" out of it,' Violet said. 'If I were anyone else, you'd have a fling with me, wouldn't you?'

He let out a short breath. 'You're not a fling type of girl so—'

'But what if I was? What if I wanted to have a fling with you because I'm so darn tired of being the girl without a date, the girl who hasn't had proper consensual sex? I'm sick of being that girl, Cam. I'm turning thirty in January. I want to find the courage to embrace my sexuality and who better with than you? Someone I trust and feel safe with.'

It was clear she had created a dilemma for him. His expression was a picture of conflict. His hands tightened on the tops of her shoulders, as if torn between wanting to bring her closer and pushing her away. 'I don't want to hurt you,' he said. 'That's the last thing I want.'

'How will you hurt me?' Violet asked. 'I'm not asking you to commit to anything permanent. I know that's not what you want and I'm fine with that.' *Not exactly true, but still.* 'We can have a fling for as long as our pretend engagement lasts. It will make it appear more authentic.'

He cupped her face with the broad span of his hand while his thumb stroked back and forth on her cheek. 'Looks like you've thought all of this through.'

'I have and it's what I want. It's what you want too, isn't it?'

His frown hadn't gone away but was pulling his brow into deep vertical lines between his eyes. 'What about your family?'

'What about them?' Violet said. 'They already think we're…together. Why shouldn't we therefore actually be together?'

'There's something a little off with your logic but I'm not sure what it is.'

'What's logical about lust?'

His frown was back. 'Is that all this is?'

'Of course.' Violet suspected she might have answered a little too quickly. 'I love you but I'm not *in* love with you.'

His eyes did that back and forth thing that made her feel as if he was looking for the truth behind the screen of her gaze. 'The thing is…good sex can make people fall in love with each other.'

Violet cocked her head. 'So, I'm presuming you've had plenty of good sex. Have you ever fallen in love?'

'No, but that doesn't—'

'Then what makes you think you will this time?'

He blinked as if he was confused about her line of argument. 'I'm not worried about me falling in love, I'm worried about you.'

Violet raised her brows. 'What makes you think you'll be immune to falling in love?'

He opened and closed his mouth, seemingly lost for an answer. 'Sex for me is a physical thing. I never allow my emotions to become involved.'

'Sounds like heaps of fun, just getting it on with someone's body without connecting with them on any other level.'

His brows snapped together and he dropped his hands from her hips. 'Damn it. It's not like that. At least I know their names and make sure they've given full and proper consent and are conscious.'

Violet wasn't going to apologise for her straight talking. In her opinion he was short-changing himself if he stuck to relationships that were based on mutual lust and nothing else. What about sharing someone's life with them? What about growing old together? What about being fully present in a relationship that made you grow as a person?

All the things she wished for but hadn't so far been able to find.

'You remind me of Fraser before he met Zoe. He was always saying he'd never fall in love. Look what happened to him. A chance meeting with Zoe and now he's married with twins and he couldn't be happier.'

Cam blew out a frustrated-sounding breath. 'It's different for your brother. He's had the great example your parents have set. He's had that since he was a baby—all of you have. I had a completely different example, one I wouldn't wish on a partner and certainly not on any children.'

Violet studied his tense expression, his even more rigidly set body and the way his eyes glittered with bitterness. And the way he had put some distance between their bodies as if he didn't trust himself not to reach for her. 'What exactly happened between your parents that you're so against marriage?'

It was a moment or two before he spoke. 'They only got married because my mother got pregnant with me. They were pressured into it by both of their families, although to be fair my mother was in love with my father, but unfortunately he didn't feel the same. It was a disaster from the word go. The earliest memories I have are of my parents fighting. They're the only memories I have, really.'

'But that doesn't mean you'd conduct a relationship like that,' Violet said. 'You're not that type of person.'

He gave a short laugh that had a note of cynicism to it. 'Thanks for the character reference but it won't be needed. I'm fine with how my life is now. I don't have to check in with anyone. I'm free to do what I want, when I want, with whomever I want.'

'As long as they're not married to your richest client or are your best friend's kid sister,' Violet said with a pointed look.

He pressed his lips together as if checking a retort. 'Violet…'

'It's fine.' Violet turned away with an airy wave of one hand. 'I get the message. You don't want to complicate things by sleeping with me. I'm not going to beg. I'll find someone else. After our engagement is over, of course.'

It was a great exit line.

And it would have been even better if she hadn't stumbled over the rug on her way out.

CHAPTER FIVE

CAM SWORE AND raked his hand through his hair until he thought he'd draw blood. Or make himself bald. What was he doing even *thinking* of taking her up on her offer of a fling? Violet was the last girl he should be thinking about. Tempted by. Lusting over. She was so innocent. So vulnerable. So adorable.

Yes, adorable, which was why he had to be sensible about this. She wasn't someone he could walk away from once the fling was over and never see or think of again. He would see her every time he was at a Drummond family gathering. He could avoid them, of course, but that would be punishing her family as well as himself.

Not that he didn't deserve to be punished for dragging her into this farce. If he hadn't asked her to that wretched dinner, none of this would have happened.

But if the dinner and the Christmas party tomorrow night weren't bad enough, now he had her under his roof in one of the spare bedrooms. Now he would spend the night, or however many nights she would be here, in a heightened state of arousal. Forget about cold showers, he would have to pump in water from the North Sea to deal with this level of attraction.

What was wrong with him?

Where was his self-control?

Why had he kissed her? That had been his first mistake. The second was to keep touching her. But he couldn't seem to keep his hands off her. As soon as she came within touching distance, he was at it again.

He had to stop thinking about making love to her. Stop picturing it. Stop aching for it. Just stop.

But truth was it was *all* Cam had been thinking about since running into Violet at that café. Which was damned annoying, as he'd never seen her that way before last Easter. For years she'd been one of the Drummond girls, just like Rose and Lily—a sister to him in every way other than blood. But it had all changed that last time he'd visited Drummond Brae. He could sense the exact moment when she turned her gaze on him. His body picked up her presence like a radar signal. His stomach rolled over and begged when she smiled at him. His skin tingled if she so much as brushed past him in a doorway. When his knees bumped hers under the table in the café he'd felt the shockwave travel all the way to his groin.

Even though she was safely in the spare room, he couldn't get her out of his mind. Her neat little ballerina-like figure, gorgeous brown eyes the colour of caramel, wavy chestnut hair that always smelled of flowers, a mouth that was shaped in a perfect Cupid's bow that drew his gaze more than he wanted it to. He had fantasies about that mouth. X-rated fantasies. Fantasies he shouldn't be having because she was like a sister to him.

Like hell she is.

Was that why he'd offered to bring her back here? Had some dark corner of his subconscious leapt at the opportunity to have her under his roof so he could take things to the next level? The level Violet wanted? The level that would change everything between them? Permanently. Irrevocably. How would he ever look at her in the future and not remember how her mouth felt under his? He was having enough trouble now getting it out of his mind. He could think of nothing else but how her mouth responded to his. How her lips had been as soft as down, her tongue both playful and shy. How her body felt when she'd brushed up against him. How her dainty little curves made him want to crush her to him so he could ease this relentless ache of need. How he wanted to explore every inch of her body and claim it, nurture it, release it from its prison of fear.

But how could he do that, knowing she had so much more invested in their relationship? She was after the fairytale he was avoiding because loving someone to that degree had the potential to ruin lives. If—and it was a big if—he ever settled down with a partner, he would go for a companionable relationship that was based on similar interests rather than the fickleness of love that could fade after its first flush of heat. His mother had paid the price—was still paying it—for loving without caution. It hadn't just ruined her life but that of several others along the way, as well. He didn't want that sort of emotional carnage. He already had feelings for Violet. Feelings that could slip into the danger zone if he wasn't careful. Having her here under his roof was only intensifying those feelings. The thought of her being only a few doors away was a form of torture. Making love with Violet would be exactly that: making love. Encouraging love, feeding love, nurturing it to grow and blossom. Sex was easy to deal with if he kept his feelings out of it. But having sex with Violet would be all about feelings. Emotions. Bonding. Commitment. All the things he shied away from because they had the potential to disrupt the neat and controlled order of his life.

He had to be strong. Determined. Resolute. Violet was looking for someone to give her heart to. She was vulnerable and it would be wrong of him to give her the impression an affair between them could go anywhere.

Why couldn't it?

Cam slapped the thought away like he was swatting away a fly. But it kept coming back, buzzing around the edges of his resolve, making him think of how it would be day after day, week after week, month after month, year after year with Violet in his life. Having her not just as a temporary houseguest but as a permanent partner. He wasn't so cynical that he couldn't see the benefits of a long-term marriage. He had only to look at Violet's parents to see how well a good marriage could work.

But how could he guarantee his would work? There were no guarantees, which was what scared him the most.

Violet didn't expect to sleep after the evening's disturbance. She thought she'd have nightmares about her flat being invaded but the only dreams she had were of Cam kissing her, touching her, making her feel things she'd never expected to feel. With time to reflect on it, she understood his caution about getting involved with her sexually. Of course it would be a risk. It would change everything about their relationship. Every single dynamic would be altered. You couldn't undo something like that. Every time she saw him at family gatherings in the future it would be there between them—their sensual history. He had only kissed her and held her and yet she was going to have a task ahead of her to forget about it. It was like his touch had seeped through every pore of her skin, tunnelling its way into her body so deep she instinctively knew she would never feel like that with anyone else. How could she? His touch was like a code breaker to her frozen sensuality. It unlocked the primal urges she had hidden away out of shame. He'd awoken those sleeping urges and now they were jumping up and down in her body like hyperactive kids on a trampoline.

Violet threw off the bedcovers and showered but when she looked at her overnight bag of belongings she'd hastily packed last night she knew she could never bring herself to touch them, let alone wear them. How could she know for sure if the intruders had touched them? What if she wore them and then out on the street the burglars recognised them as the ones they had rifled through last night? She had only the clothes she'd been wearing for the dinner last night. She didn't fancy putting them on again after her shower and, besides, the velvet cocktail dress was hardly Saturday morning wear. It was way too dressed up. If she went out in that get-up, she would look like she had been out all night. She rinsed out her knickers and dried them with the hairdryer she found in one of the drawers in the bathroom. There was a plush bathrobe hanging on the back of the bathroom door so she slipped it on over her underwear.

Cam was in the kitchen pouring cereal into a bowl when she came in. He looked up and Violet saw the way his eyes automatically scanned her body as if he was imagining what she looked like underneath the bathrobe. He cleared his throat and turned back to his cereal, making rather a business of sealing the inside packet and folding down the flaps on top of the box. 'Sleep okay?'

'Not bad…'

He took a spoon out of one of the drawers and then turned and opened the fridge for the milk. Violet drank in the image of him dressed in dark blue jeans and a black finely woven cashmere sweater with a white T-shirt underneath. There should be a law against a man looking so good in casual clothes. The denim hugged his trim and toned buttocks; the close-fitting sweater showcased the superb musculature of his upper body. His hair was still damp from a shower and it looked like his fingers had been its most recent combing tool, for she could see the finger-spaced grooves between the dark brown strands.

'What would you like for breakfast?' he said, turning from the fridge. 'I'm afraid I can't match your mother's famous breakfast spreads but I can do cereal, toast and fruit and yoghurt.'

'Sounds lovely.' Violet perched on the stool opposite him. 'Can I ask a favour?'

His gaze met hers. 'Look, we had this discussion last night and the answer is—'

'It's not about…that.' Violet captured her lip between her teeth. Did he have to rub it in? So he didn't want to sleep with her. Fine. She wasn't going to drag him kicking and screaming to the nearest bedroom. 'It's about my clothes. I need to get new ones. I can't bear wearing any of mine from the flat, not even the ones I brought with me, and I don't want to wear my cocktail dress because I'll look like I've been out all night.'

A frown pulled at his forehead. 'You want me to go…shopping for you?'

Did he have to make it sound like she'd asked him to dance naked in Trafalgar Square? 'I'll give you my credit card. I just need some basics and then I can do the rest myself once you bring those couple of things back.'

He blew out a breath and reached for a pen and a slip of paper, pushing it across the bench. 'Write me a list.'

* * *

Cam had never shopped for women's clothing before. Who knew there was so much to choose from? But choosing a pair of jeans and a warm sweater wasn't too much of a problem. The problem was he kept looking at the lingerie section and imagining Violet in the sexy little lacy numbers. He had to walk out before he was tempted to buy her the black lace teddy with the hot pink feathers. Or the red corset one with black silk lacing. Once he'd completed his mission, he was making his way back to his house when he walked past a jewellery store. He'd walked past that store hundreds, if not thousands, of times and never looked in the window, let alone gone in. But for some reason he found himself pushing the door open, going inside and standing next to the ring counter.

It's just a prop.

Violet's office party was tonight and what sort of cheap fiancé would he look if he hadn't bought her a decent ring? No need to mortgage the house on a diamond but that one at the back there looked perfect for Violet's hand. He didn't have too much trouble guessing her ring size; he had thought of her hands—holding them, feeling them on his skin—enough times to know the exact dimensions. Actually, he knew pretty much the exact dimensions of her whole body. They were imprinted on his brain and kept him awake at night.

Cam paid for the ring, placed it in his pocket and walked out of the store. Just as he was about to turn the corner for home, he got a call from Fraser. He couldn't avoid the conversation any longer, but something about lying to his best mate didn't sit too comfortably. 'Hey, sorry I haven't returned your calls,' he said. 'Things have been happening so fast I—'

Fraser gave a light laugh. 'You don't have to apologise to me, buddy. I saw the way you were looking at Vivi at Easter. Is that why you skived off to Greece? So you wouldn't be tempted to act on it?'

Maybe it had been, now that he thought about it. Cam often had to travel abroad at short notice in order to meet with a client, but the chance to go to Greece for a few months had been exactly the escape hatch he'd needed. He'd felt the need to clear his head, to get some perspective, to have a little talk to himself about stepping over boundaries that couldn't be undone. But the whole time he'd been away, Violet had been on his mind. 'Yeah, well, now that you mention it.'

'Great news, man,' Fraser said. 'Couldn't be more delighted. Zoe reckons this is going to be the best Christmas ever. Did you hear about Grandad? Talk about a turnaround. He's so excited for your wedding.'

The wedding that wasn't going to happen… Cam sidestepped the thought like someone avoiding a puddle. 'Yeah, your mum told me. It's great he's feeling better.'

'So when's the big day? Am I going to be best man? No pressure or anything.'

Cam affected a light laugh. 'I've got to get my father's fifth wedding out of the way first. We'll set a date after that.'

'What's your new stepmother like?'

'Don't ask.'

'Like that, huh?'

'Yep,' Cam said. 'Like that.'

Violet looked around Cam's house while he was out. It was a stunningly beautiful home with gorgeous touches everywhere but on closer inspection it didn't have a personal touch, nothing to hint at the private life of its only occupant. There were no family photos or childhood memorabilia. Unlike her family home in Scotland, where her mother had framed and documented and scrapbooked each of her children's milestones, Cam's house was bare of anything to do with his childhood. There were no photos of him with his parents. None of him as a child. It was as if he didn't want to be reminded of that part of his life.

Violet turned from looking at one of the paintings on the wall in the study when Cam came in carrying shopping bags. 'You've been ages,' she said. 'Was it frightfully busy? The shops can be a nightmare at this time of year. I shouldn't have asked you. I'm sorry but I—'

'It was fine.' He handed her the bags. 'You'd better check I've got the right size.'

Violet took the bags and set them on the cedar desk. She took out the tissue-wrapped sweater and held it against her body. It was the most gorgeous baby-blue cashmere and felt soft as a cloud. The other wrapped parcel was a pair of jeans. But there was another tiny parcel at the bottom of the second shopping bag. Her heart gave a stumble when she picked it up and saw the high-end jewellery store label on the ribbon that was tied in a neat bow on top. 'What's this?'

'An engagement ring.'

Violet's eyes rounded. Her heart pounded. Her hopes sounded. *Did this mean...? Was he...?* 'You bought a ring? For me?'

His expression was as blank as his house was of his past. 'It's just for show. I figured everyone would be asking to see it at your office party tonight.'

Violet carefully unpeeled the ribbon, her heart feeling like a hummingbird was trapped in one of its chambers. She opened the velvet box to find a beautiful diamond in a classic setting in a white gold ring. It was more than beautiful—it was perfect. How had he known she wasn't the big flashy diamond sort? She took it out of the box and pushed it onto her ring finger. It winked up at her as if in conspiracy. *I might be just a prop but don't I look fabulous on your hand?* She looked up at Cam's unreadable expression. 'It's gorgeous. But I'll give it back after Christmas, okay?'

'No.' There was a note of implacability to his tone. 'I want you to keep it. Think of it as a gift for your help with the Nicolaides contract.'

Violet held up her hand, looking at the light dancing off the diamond. She didn't like to think it might be the only engagement ring she ever got. She lowered her hand and looked at him again. 'It's very generous of you, Cam. It's beautiful. I couldn't have chosen better myself. Thank you.'

'No problem.'

Violet gathered up her new clothes and the packaging. 'I'm going to get dressed and head out to replenish my wardrobe. What are your plans?'

'Work.'

'On the weekend?'

He gave her a *that's how it is* look. 'I'll catch up with you later this evening. What time is your office party?'

'Eight.'

'I'll be back in time to take you. Make yourself at home.' He reached past her to open the drawer of the desk and took out a key on a security remote. He handed it to her. 'Here's the key to the house.'

Violet took the key and a rush of heat coursed from her fingers to her core when her hand came into contact with his. He must have felt it too for his gaze meshed with hers in a sizzling tether that made her wonder if he was only going to work to remove himself from the temptation of spending time with her. Doing…things. Wicked things. Things that made her blood heat and her stomach do cartwheels of excitement. 'Cam?' Her voice came out croaky and soft.

His eyes went to her mouth and she saw the way his throat moved up and down over a tight swallow. 'Don't make this any harder than it already is.' His tone was two parts gravel, one part honey, and one part man on the edge of control.

With courage she had no idea she possessed, Violet moved closer, planting her hands on his chest, bringing her hips in contact with his. 'Don't I get to kiss you for buying me such a gorgeous ring?'

His eyes darkened until it was impossible to tell where his pupils began and ended. His body stirred against hers, the swell of his erection calling out to her. Desire burned through every lonely corridor of her body, every network of nerves, every circuit of her blood. She became aware of her breasts pushed up against the fabric of her bathrobe, the nipples already tight, her flesh aching for human touch—Cam's touch. Her courage increased with every pound of his heart she could feel thundering under her palm.

His head came down at the same time she stepped up on tiptoe, their mouths meeting in the middle in an explosion of lust that sent a shockwave through Violet's body. It sent it through Cam's, too, for he grabbed her by the hips and pulled her hard against him, smothering a groan as his mouth plundered hers.

His tongue didn't ask for entry but demanded it, tangling with hers in a sexy combat that mimicked the intimacy both of them craved. This wasn't a chaste kiss between old friends. This was a kiss of urgency, of frustration, of long-built-up needs that could wait no longer for satiation.

Cam's mouth continued its thrilling exploration of hers while his hands slipped beneath the opening of her bathrobe, exposing her breasts. Violet shivered as the feel of his hand shaping her, cupping her, caressing her threatened to heat her blood to boiling. She'd had no idea her breasts were that sensitive. No idea how wonderful it felt to have a man's hand cradle her shape while his thumb moved back and forth across her nipple.

But it wasn't enough. Her body wanted more. More contact, more friction, more of the sensual heat his body promised. She pushed her lower body against his, relishing the delicious thrill it gave her to feel the potency of his arousal. She had done that to him. Her body stirred his as his stirred hers. It was a combustible energy neither of them could deny nor ignore any longer.

'This is madness,' Cam said just above her mouth.

Violet didn't give him a chance to pull away any further. She pressed closer, stroking her tongue over his lips, the top one and then the lower one, a shiver coursing through her when he gave another rough groan and covered her mouth in a fiery kiss. His hands gripped her by the hips, holding her to his rigid heat, the contact making Violet's inner core tingle and tighten with anticipation. How had she survived so long without this magical energy rushing through her body? Cam's touch made every nerve in her body cry out for more.

He pulled his mouth away, his breathing a little unsteady. 'Not here, not like this.'

Violet kept her arms around his waist, reluctant to give him the opportunity to break the intimate contact. 'Don't say you don't want me because I know you do.'

He gave her a rueful look. 'Not much chance of hiding it, is there? But I want you to be comfortable and making love on a desk or the floor is not my idea of comfortable.'

Before Violet could say anything, he scooped her up

in his arms. She gave a startled gasp and held on, secretly delighted he was taking charge like a romantic hero out of an old black and white movie.

They came to his bedroom door and he shouldered it open and carried her to the end of the bed, lowering her to the floor, but not before trailing her body down the length of his, leaving her in no doubt of his erotic intentions. He pressed another lingering kiss to her lips, exploring the depths of her mouth with a beguiling mix of gentleness and urgency. Sensations rippled through her body in tiny waves, making her skin sensitive to his touch like he had cast a sensual spell on her. But then he had. From the moment he had walked into that café, she had been under the heady spell of sexual attraction.

Violet pulled up his sweater and T-shirt so she could glide her hands over his naked skin. Warm, hard male flesh met the skin of her palms; a light smattering of masculine hair grazed her fingertips, the scent of his cologne teased her nostrils. She explored the tiny pebbles of his nipples, and then the flat plane of his stomach with its washboard ridges that marked him as man who enjoyed hard physical exercise.

Cam untied the waist strap of her bathrobe and sent his hands on their own sensual journey. Violet shuddered when his hands glided around her ribcage, not quite touching her breasts but close enough for her to feel she would die if he didn't. He brought his mouth to the upper curve of her right breast. He didn't seem in a hurry, but maybe he was giving her time to get used to this level of intimacy. He brushed his thumb over her nipple, a back and forth movement that made her body contract with want.

Rather than undress her any further, he set to work on his own clothes, taking each item off while his gaze was trained on hers.

Finally, he was in nothing but black underpants, and then and only then did he remove her bathrobe. Violet's belly did a somersault an Olympic gymnast would have been proud of when she saw the way his eyes feasted on her breasts. He cupped them in his hands with exquisite care, rolling his thumb over each nipple before lowering his mouth to subject her to an intimate torture that made her senses spin in dizzying delight.

He lifted his mouth off her breast and, kneeling in front of her, continued to kiss his way from her sternum to her belly button. Violet sucked in a breath, her hands on his shoulders, not sure she could handle what he was planning.

'Relax, sweetheart.'

Easy for you to say. Violet held her breath while he peeled away her knickers. The warmth of his breath on her intimate flesh made her spine weaken as if someone had unbolted her vertebrae. His mouth came to her softly, a light as air touch that made her knees tremble. He gently parted her, stroking her with his tongue, the sensation so powerful she pulled away. 'I—I can't…'

His hands were gentle but firm on her hips. 'Yes, you can. Don't be frightened of it. Trust me.'

Violet glanced down at him worshipping her body, his touch so tender, so respectful it made her see her body differently, not as something to be ashamed of and hidden away, but as something that was not only beautiful and capable of receiving pleasure, but also of giving it too. The rhythmic strokes of his tongue sent a torrent of tingles through her body, concentrating on that one point—the heart of her femininity. The tension grew to a crescendo until she was finally catapulted into a vortex that scattered her thoughts until all she could do was feel. Feel the power of an orgasm that swept through her like a hot wave, rolling through every inch of her flesh, trickling over every nerve ending, sending showers of goose bumps over her body, leaving no part of her immune. She was limbless, dazed, out of her mind as the aftershocks pulsed through her.

Cam brought his mouth back up over her stomach and ribcage, then her breasts, leaving a blistering trail of kisses on her tingling skin. He stood upright, drawing her closer, his mouth settling back on hers in a mind-altering kiss, the eroticism of it heightened by the fact she could taste her own essence on his lips and tongue.

Violet had thought herself too shy to draw his briefs from his body but somehow her hands reached for the elastic edge of the waistband and slid them away from his body. She took him into her hand—hot, hard, and quintessentially male. She stroked him with experimental caresses, her fingers drawing down from the base to the head and back again. It was so empowering to be an active part of a sexual encounter. The deep guttural noises he made added to her sense of agency.

She was doing this to him. She was the one he wanted. She was the one exciting him, pushing him to the limit of control.

Cam gently moved her hand away and guided her to the mattress behind her, coming down over her in a tangle of limbs, balancing his weight on his arms so as not to crush her. 'Comfortable?'

'Yes.' Violet was surprised she was capable of thought, let alone speech. The way he made her feel, so safe, so treasured, made the shame she had carried for so long slip further out of reach, like an old garment stuffed at the back of the wardrobe. It was still there but she could no longer see it.

Cam stroked her face with his fingertip, his eyes dark and lustrous. 'We don't have to go any further if you're not ready.'

I'm ready! I'm ready! Violet touched the flat of her palm to his stubbly jaw, looking into his eyes without reserve. 'I want you inside me.'

A flash of delight went through his gaze. 'I won't rush you and you can stop me at any point.'

He reached for a condom in the bedside drawer and deftly applied it before coming back to her. The choreography of their bodies aligning themselves for that ultimate physical connection was simple and yet complex. It was like learning the steps to a dance, one leg this way, the other that, her breasts pressing against the wall of his chest, her arms winding around his body to anchor herself. He gently probed her entrance, allowing her time to adjust to him just...being there. She felt the weight and heft of him waiting there but it wasn't threatening in any way.

He slowly entered her, waiting for her to relax before going any further. Violet welcomed him inside her body with soft little gasps as the sensation of him stretching her, filling her, tantalising her gained momentum. He began a slow rhythm that sent shivers of delight through her body, the friction of male against female making her aware of her body in a way she had never been before. Nerves she hadn't known existed were firing up. Muscles that had been inactive for most of her life were now being activated in a deeply pleasurable workout that had one sure goal. She could feel that goal dangling just out of reach, the thrill of her flesh building and building but unable to go any further. It was a frustrating ache, a restless urging for more. But, as if Cam could read her silent pleas for release, he brought his hand down between their bodies and sought the heart of her arousal. The stroking of his fingers against her tipped her into a free fall of spinning, whirling, dizzying sensations. They ricocheted through her in giant shudders, making her lose her grasp on conscious thought. She was in the middle of a vortex, vivid colours bursting like thousands of tiny fireworks behind her squeezed-shut eyelids.

Then the slow wash of a wave of lassitude… She was drifting, drifting, drifting…

But then she became aware of the increasing pace of Cam's thrusts as his own release powered down on him. She experienced every second of it through the sensitised walls of her body, his tension building to a final crucial point before he pitched forwards against her, his deep primal cry making something in her belly shiver like a light wind whispering over the surface of a lake.

Violet lay in his embrace, her fingertips moving up and down his spine while his breathing gradually slowed. She couldn't find the words to express what her body had just experienced. She felt reborn. As if the old her had been sloughed away like a tired skin. Her new skin felt alive, energised, and sensitive to every movement of Cam's breathing as his chest rose and fell against hers.

Should she say something? What? *How was it for you?* That seemed a little trite and clichéd somehow. How many times had he lain here like this with other women? How many other women? He might not be the fastest living playboy on the planet but he wasn't without a sex life. He just kept it a little more private than other men in his position. How many women had lain here in his arms and felt the same as her? Was what she had experienced with him run-of-the-mill sex? Or was it different? More special? More intense?

Violet knew she was being a fool for allowing her feelings to get involved. But this was Cam. Not just some hot guy she happened to fancy. Cam was a friend. Someone she had known for years and years and always admired.

They had stepped into new territory and it felt… weird, but not horribly weird. Nicely weird. Excitingly weird. Would he make love to her again? How soon? Would he get so hooked on having sex with her he would extend their 'engagement'? What if he fell in love with her? What if he decided marriage and kids wasn't such a bad idea? What if—?

Cam dealt with disposing of the condom and then looked down at her with a soft smile that made his eyes seem even darker. 'Hey.'

Violet hoped he wasn't as good at reading her mind as he was at reading her body. Her thoughts were running like ticker tape in her head. *Please fall in love with me. Please.*

'Hey…'

He brushed some stray strands of hair back from her face, his smile fading as a frowning concern took up residence instead. 'Did I hurt you?'

Violet had trouble speaking for the sudden lump in her throat. 'N-not at all.'

He picked up another strand of hair and gently anchored it behind her ear, holding her gaze with his. 'Sure?'

How was she supposed to keep her feelings out of this when he looked at her like that? When his hands touched her as if she were something so eminently precious to him he would rather die than hurt her? 'I'm sure.'

He leaned down to press a soft kiss to her mouth. 'You were wonderful.'

Violet traced the line of his mouth with her fingertip. 'This won't…change things between us, will it? I mean, no matter what happens, we'll always be friends, won't we?'

A flicker of something moved through his gaze like a passing thought leaving a shadow in its wake. 'Of course we will.' He took her hand and quickly kissed the ends of her fingertips before releasing it. 'Nothing will ever change that.'

Violet wasn't so sure. What if she couldn't cope with going back to normal? He might be able to go back to relating to her as he had always done, but she wasn't confident she would be able to do the same to him. How could she look at him and not think of how his mouth felt against her own? How could she not think of how his hands had stroked her most intimate flesh? How could she not think of how his body had awakened hers and made her feel things she hadn't thought were possible to feel?

Not just physical things, but emotional things.

Things that might not be so easily set aside once their fling was over.

CHAPTER SIX

CAM WAITED WHILE Violet had a shower and got changed. He would have joined her but he was conscious of allowing her time to recover. God, *he* needed time to recover. So much for keeping his distance. So much for his self-control. Where had that gone? He hadn't been able to resist the temptation of making love to her. So apparently they were having a fling. It didn't feel like any fling he'd ever had before. He had never known a partner the way he knew Violet. Her trust in him had heightened the experience. Every touch, every kiss, every stroke, every whimper or gasp of hers had made his pleasure intensify. It was like having sex for the first time but not in a clumsy, awkward way, but in a magical, mutually satisfying way that left his body humming like a plucked string.

Somehow the thought of spending the afternoon working didn't hold its usual appeal. Even a yuletide cynic like him had to agree there was no greater place to be before Christmas than in London. He wasn't much of a shopper but Violet needed a new wardrobe and he would rather spend the time with her than chained to his desk.

Violet came down the stairs wearing the jeans and baby-blue sweater he'd bought her. Cam had trouble keeping his hands to himself. He ached to slide his hands under the sweater and cradle the perfection of her breasts. To feel those pink nipples embed themselves into his palm. To feel her body quake with pleasure when he touched her.

She smiled at him shyly, her cheeks going a faint shade of pink as if she too were recalling their earlier intimacy. 'I thought you were going to work?'

Cam shrugged. 'It can wait.' He took her hand and brought it up to his mouth. 'I probably should warn you I'm not the world's best shopper but I'm pretty handy with carrying bags.'

Her eyes shone as if the thought of him accompanying her pleased her as much as it pleased him. 'Are you sure you're not too busy? I know how much men loathe shopping. Dad and Fraser are such pains when we try to get them through a department store door.'

Cam looped her arm through his. 'I have a vested interest in this expedition. I have to make sure Cinderella is dressed appropriately for the ball tonight.'

A flicker of worry passed through her gaze. 'I never know what to wear to the office party. There's a theme this year… *A Star-Struck Christmas*. Last year it was *White Christmas*. The year before it was *Christmas on the Titanic*.'

'You could turn up in a bin liner and still outshine everyone else.'

Her smile made something in his chest slip sideways. 'I really appreciate you coming with me. I can't tell you how much I hate going alone.'

Cam bent down to press a kiss to her forehead. 'You're not alone this year. You're with me.'

Cam wasn't much of a party animal but even he had to admit Violet's firm put on a Christmas extravaganza that was impossible not to enjoy. It occupied the ballroom of one of London's premier hotels and the decorations alone would have funded a developing nation for a year. Giant green and gold and red Christmas bells hung from silken threads just above head height. Great swathes of tinsel adorned the walls. A fresh Christmas tree was positioned to one side of the room, covered with baubles that looked like they had been dipped in gold. Maybe they had. There was an angel on the top whose white gown glittered with Swarovski crystals. The music was lively and fun. The food was fabulous. The champagne was top-shelf and free flowing.

Or maybe he was having a good time because he was with the most beautiful girl at the party. The shimmery dress he'd helped Violet choose skimmed her delicate curves so lovingly his hands twitched in jealousy. The heels she was wearing put his mind straight in the gutter. He couldn't stop imagining her wearing nothing but those glossy black spikes and a sexy come-and-get-me smile.

Cam had been ruminating all afternoon over whether he had done the right thing in making love to Violet. Who was he kidding? He was *still* ruminating. It was like a loop going round and round in his head. *What have I done?*

It was fine to put it down to hormones, but he wasn't some immature teenager who didn't know the meaning of the word self-control. He was a fully grown adult and yet he hadn't been able to walk away.

Had he done the wrong thing?

His body said *Yes.*

His mind said *Yes, but.*

The *buts* were always going to be the kicker. Violet wasn't like any other casual lover he'd met. She'd been in his life for what seemed like for ever. He'd seen her grow from a gangly and shy teenage girl to a beautiful young woman. She was still shy but some of that reserve had eased away when they'd made love. Sharing that experience with her, being the one to guide her through her first experience of pleasure with a partner had been special. More than special. A sacred privilege he would remember for the rest of his life. Her trust in him had touched him, honoured him, and made him feel more of a man than he had ever felt before.

But...

How could he give her what she wanted when it was the opposite of what he wanted right now? Violet came from a family where marriage was a tradition that was celebrated and treasured and believed in. She wanted the fairytale her parents and siblings had.

It wasn't that Cam was so cynical he didn't think marriage could work. It did work. It worked brilliantly, as Margie and Gavin Drummond demonstrated and their parents before them. But Cam's parents' example had made him see the other side of the order of service: the stonewalling, the bitter fights, the disharmony, the petty paybacks, the affairs and then the divorce lawyers, not to mention years of estrangement where the very mention of the other person's name would bring on an explosive fit of temper.

While Cam didn't think he was the type of person to walk out on a commitment as important as marriage, how could he be sure life wouldn't throw up something that would challenge the standards he upheld? The promises people made so earnestly in church didn't always ring with the same conviction when life tossed in a curve ball or two.

It was all well and good to be confident he would stand by his commitment, but it wasn't just about his commitment. The other person would have to be equally committed. How could he be sure Violet, as gorgeous and sweet as she was, would feel the same about him in ten weeks, let alone ten years or five times that? Watching his parents go through their acrimonious divorce when he was a young child had made him wary about rushing into the institution.

He had never had any reason to question his decision before now. It had always seemed the safest way to handle his relationships—being open and honest about what he could and couldn't give. Yes, some lovers might have been disappointed there was no promise of a future. But at least he hadn't misled them.

But sleeping with Violet had changed things. Changed *him*. Made him more aware of the things he would be missing out on rather than the things he was avoiding. Things like walking into a party hand in hand, knowing he was going to leave with that hand still in his. Knowing the smile she turned his way was for him and no one else. Recognising the secret look she gave him that told him she was remembering every second of his lovemaking and she couldn't wait to experience it again. Feeling the frisson of awareness when she brushed against him, how his body was so finely tuned to hers he could sense her presence even when she was metres away.

Had he ever felt like that with anyone else? No. Never. Which wasn't to say he wouldn't with someone else…someone other than Violet. His gut swerved at the thought of making love to someone else. He couldn't imagine it. Couldn't even picture it. Couldn't think of a single person who would excite him the way she excited him.

It will pass. It always does.

Lust for him was a candle not a coal ember. It would flare for a time and then snuff out. Sometimes gradually, sometimes overnight.

But when he looked at Violet, he couldn't imagine his desire for her ever fading. Because his desire for her wasn't just physical. There was another quality to it, a quality he had never felt with anyone else. When he'd made love to her it had felt like an act of worship rather than just sex. Her response to him had been a gift rather than a given. The fact she trusted him enough to feel able to express herself sexually was the biggest compliment—and turn on—he had ever experienced.

But...

How was he going to explain the end of their 'engagement' to her family? How was he going to go back to being just friends? How would he be able to look at her and not remember the way her mouth had felt when she'd opened it for him that first time? How her shy little tongue had tangled with his until his blood had pounded so hard he'd thought his veins would explode? How would he be able to be in the same room as her without wanting to draw her into his arms? To feel her slim body press against his need until he was crazy with it?

Maybe he was crazy. Maybe that was the problem. Making love to her was the craziest thing he'd done in a long time.

But...

He wanted to make love to her again. And again and again.

God help him.

Violet was coming back from a trip to the ladies' room when she was intercepted by three of her workmates, including Lorna.

'Congratulations, Violet,' Lorna said, eyeing her engagement ring. 'Gracious me, that man of yours was quick off the mark.' Her gaze flicked to Violet's abdomen. 'You're not pregnant, are you?'

If there was one time in her life Violet wished she didn't have the propensity to blush, this was it. Could Lorna tell the engagement wasn't real? After all, Violet hadn't mentioned anything about dating anyone, not that she talked about her private life that much at work. But women working together for a long time tended to pick up on those things. Besides, conversations around the water cooler tended to show how boring her life was compared to everyone else's. 'No, not yet but it's definitely on the to-do list.' *Why did you say that?*

Lorna's smile didn't involve her eyes. 'When's the big day?'

'Erm…we haven't decided on a date yet,' Violet said. 'But some time next year.' *I wish.*

'So how did he propose?'

Violet wished she'd talked this through a little more with Cam. They hadn't firmed up any details of their story apart from the fact—which was indeed a fact—they had met via her older brother. How would Cam propose if he were going to ask her to marry him? He wasn't the bells and whistles type. There wouldn't be any skywritten proposals or football-stadium audiences while he got down on bended knee. That was the sort of thing his father did, even on one memorable occasion making the evening news. Cam would choose somewhere quiet and romantic and tell her he loved her and wanted to spend the rest of his life with her. Her heart squeezed. *If only!* 'It was really romantic and—'

'Ah, here's Prince Charming himself,' Lorna said as Cam approached. 'Violet's been telling me how you proposed.'

Cam's smile never faltered but Violet knew him well enough to notice the flicker of tension he was trying to disguise near his mouth. He slipped an arm around Violet's waist and drew her close against him. 'Have you, darling?'

Violet's smile had a hint of *help me* about it. 'Yes, I was saying it was terribly romantic…with all the roses and…stuff.'

'What colour?' Lorna asked.

'White,' Violet said.

'Red,' Cam said at exactly the same time.

Lorna's artfully groomed brows rose ever so slightly. But then she smiled and winked at Cam. 'You have good taste. Violet's a lucky girl to land a man who knows his way around a diamond dealer.'

'She deserves the very best,' Cam said.

'Yes, well, she's waited long enough for it,' Lorna said and with a fingertip wave moved on to return to the party.

Violet released a long jagged breath. 'She suspects something. I know she does. We should've talked about the proposal.' She spun around so her back was to the party room. 'I feel such an idiot. And, for the record, I hate red roses.'

'I'll make a note of it.'

Violet searched his expression but he had his blank-wall mask on. 'So how would you propose if you were going to?'

His brows moved together over his eyes. 'Is that a trick question?'

'No, it's a serious one,' Violet said. 'If, and I know it's a very big "if", but if you were to ask someone to marry you how would you go about it?'

Cam glanced about him. 'Is this the right venue to talk about this?'

Violet wasn't going to risk being cornered by another workmate for details of their engagement. Nothing would out a charade faster than someone cottoning on to a clash of accounts of an event from witnesses. 'We're out of earshot out here. Come on, tell me. What would you do?'

He blew out a short breath. 'I'd make sure I knew what the girl would like.'

'Like what colour roses?'

He gave her a droll look. 'What have you got against red roses?'

Violet gave a lip shrug. 'I don't know… I guess because they're so obvious.'

'Right, then I'd make sure we were alone because I don't believe in putting a woman under pressure from an audience.'

'Like your father did with wife number three?'

'Number two and three.' Cam's eyes gave a half roll.

'So no TV cameras and news crews?'

'Absolutely not.'

Violet looked back at the party in the next room. 'We should probably go and mingle...'

'What's your dream proposal?' Cam asked.

She met his gaze but there was nothing to suggest he was asking the question for any other reason than mild interest. 'I know this sounds a bit silly and ridiculously sentimental, but I've always wanted to be proposed to at Drummond Brae. Ever since I was a little girl, I dreamed of standing by the loch near the forest with the house in the distance and my lover going down on bended knee, just as my father did with my mum and my grandfather did with my grandmother.'

'Your would-be fiancé would have to have a meteorological degree to predict the best time to do it.' Cam's tone was dry. 'Nothing too romantic about being proposed to in sleet or snow.'

Violet's smile was wistful. 'If I was in love I probably wouldn't even notice.'

Half an hour later, Violet turned back to Cam after listening to a boring anecdote from one of her co-workers who'd had one too many drinks. Cam was staring into space and had a frown etched on his brow. 'Are you okay?' she said, touching him on the arm.

He blinked as if she'd startled him but then he seemed to gather himself and smiled down at her. 'Sure.' He slipped an arm around her waist and drew her closer. 'Did I tell you you're the most beautiful woman in the room?'

Violet could feel a blush staining her cheeks. Did

he mean it or was he just saying it in case other people were listening? She felt beautiful when she was with him. What woman wouldn't when he looked at her like that? As if he was remembering every moment of making love to her. The glint in his dark eyes saying he couldn't wait to do it again. 'Don't you feel a little… compromised?'

'In what way?'

She glanced around at the partying crowd before returning her gaze to his, saying sotto voce, 'You know… pretending. Lying all the time.'

He picked up her left hand and pressed a kiss to the diamond while his eyes stayed focused on hers. 'I'm not pretending to want you. I do and badly. How long do we have to stay?'

Violet's inner core tingled in anticipation. 'Not much longer. Maybe five, ten minutes?'

He dropped a kiss to her forehead. 'I'm going to get a mineral water. Want one?'

'Yes, please.'

'Hey, Violet.' Kenneth from Corporate Finance came up behind her and placed a heavy hand on her shoulder. 'Come and dance with me.'

Violet rolled her eyes. She went through the same routine with Kenneth every year at the Christmas party. He always had too much to drink and always asked her to dance. But, while she didn't want to encourage him in any way, she knew Christmas for him was a difficult time. His wife had left him just before Christmas a few years ago and he hadn't coped well with the divorce.

Violet turned and gently extricated herself from his beefy paw. 'Not tonight, thanks. I'm with my…fiancé.'

Kenneth looked at her myopically, swaying on his feet like his body couldn't decide whether to stand or fall. 'Yeah, I heard about that. Congrats and all that. When's the big day?'

'We haven't got around to settling on that just yet.'

He grabbed her left hand and held it up to the light. 'Nice one. Must've cost a packet.'

Violet didn't care for the clammy heat of his hand against hers. But neither did she want to make a scene. The firm had strict guidelines on sexual harassment in the workplace but she felt sorry for Kenneth and knew he would be mortified by his behaviour if he were sober. 'Please let me go, Kenneth.'

He lurched forwards. 'How about a Christmas kiss?'

'How about you get your hands off my fiancée?' Cam said in a tone as cold as steel.

Kenneth turned around and almost toppled over and had to grab hold of the Christmas tree next to him. Violet watched in horror as the tree with all its tinsel and baubles came crashing down, the snow-white angel on the top landing with a thud at Violet's feet, her porcelain skull shattering.

The room was suddenly skin-crawlingly quiet.

But then Kenneth dropped to his knees and picked up the broken angel and held it against his heaving chest. His sobs were quiet sobs. The worst sort of sobs because what they lacked in volume they made up for in silent anguish.

Violet went down beside him and placed a comforting hand on his shoulder. 'It's all right, Kenneth. No one cares about the tree. Do you want us to give you a lift home?'

To her surprise Cam bent down on Kenneth's other side and place his hand on the man's other shoulder. 'Hey, buddy. Let's get you home, okay?'

Kenneth's eyes were streaming tears like someone had turned on a tap inside him. He was still clutching the angel, his hands shaking so much the tiny bits of glitter and crystals from her dress were falling like silver snow. 'She's having a baby… My ex, Jane, is having the baby we were supposed to h-have…'

Violet had trouble keeping her own tears in check. How gut-wrenchingly sad it must be for poor Kenneth to hear his ex-wife was moving on with her life when clearly he hadn't stopped loving her. She exchanged an agonised glance with Cam before leaning in to one-arm-hug Kenneth. She didn't bother trying to search for a platitude. What could she say to help him recover from a broken heart? It was obvious the poor man wasn't over his divorce. He was lonely and desperately sad, and being at a party where everyone was having fun with their partners was ripping that wound open all over again.

After a while, the music restarted and the crowd went on partying. Cam helped Kenneth to his feet while some other men helped put the tree back up.

Violet collected their coats and followed Cam and Kenneth out to the foyer of the hotel where the party was being held. She waited with Kenneth while Cam brought the car to the door and within a few minutes they were on their way to the address Kenneth gave her.

He lived in a nice house in Kensington, not unlike Cam's house, but Violet couldn't help thinking how terribly painful it must be for Kenneth to go home to that empty shell where love had once dwelled, where plans had been made and dreams dreamt.

Once they were sure Kenneth was settled inside, Cam led Violet back to his car. 'Sad.'

'I know…'

'Did you see all the photos of his ex everywhere?' Cam said. 'The place is like a shrine to her. He needs to find a way to move on.'

'I know, but it must be so hard for him at Christmas especially.'

He gave her hand a light squeeze. 'Sorry for being a jerk about him touching you.'

'That's okay, you weren't to know.' She let out a sigh. 'It must be terrible for him, seeing everyone else having a good time while he comes back here to what? An empty house.'

'Does he have any other family? Parents? Siblings?'

'I don't know…but even if he did, wouldn't being with them just remind him of what he's lost? It's hard when you're the only one without a partner.' Violet knew that better than anyone.

Cam nodded grimly. 'Yeah, well, divorce is harder on some people than others.'

Violet glanced at him. 'Your mother took it hard?'

The line around his mouth tightened. 'I was six years old when they finally split up. A week or two after my father moved out to live with his new partner, I came downstairs one morning to find her unconscious on the sofa with an empty bottle of pills and an empty wine bottle beside her. I rang Emergency and thankfully they arrived in time to save her.'

No wonder he was so nervous about commitment. Seeing the devastation of a breakup at close quarters and at such a tender age would have been nothing short of terrifying. 'That must have been so scary for you as a little kid.'

'Yeah, it was.' He waited a beat before continuing. 'Every time I went back to boarding school after the holidays I was worried sick about her. But she started seeing another guy, more to send a message to my father than out of genuine love. It was a payback relationship—one of many.'

'No wonder you break out in a rash every time someone mentions the word marriage,' Violet said.

'Divorce is the word I hate more. But you can never know if it's going to happen or not. No one can guarantee their relationship will last.'

Violet wanted to disagree but deep down she knew what he said was true. There were no guarantees. Life could change in a heartbeat and love could be taken away by disease or death or divorce. Just because you were in love didn't mean the other person would remain committed. She knew many women and men who'd been devastated by their partners straying. But she believed in love and commitment and knew she would do her best when she fell in love to nurture that love and keep it healthy and sustained.

What do you mean—when you fall in love? Haven't you already?

Violet waited until they'd gone a few blocks before speaking again. 'Cam? I have to do something about my flat tomorrow. I really should have done something about it today but I couldn't bring myself to face it. But I can't leave that mess for the girls to clean up on their own.'

'Do you have to go back there?'

Violet glanced at him again. 'What do you mean? It's where I live.'

'You could live somewhere else. Somewhere safer, more secure.'

'Yeah.' Violet sighed. 'Somewhere heaps more expensive too.'

There was a silence broken only by the swishing of the windscreen wipers going back and forth.

'You could stay with me for as long as you like,' Cam said. 'Until you find somewhere more suitable, I mean. There's no rush.'

Violet wondered what was behind the invitation. Was it solely out of consideration for her safety or was he thinking about extending their relationship until who knew when? 'That's a very generous offer but what if you want to start seeing someone else after we break up after Christmas? Could be awkward.'

'Everything about this situation is awkward.'

Violet looked at the tight set of his features. 'Are you regretting…what happened this morning?'

He relaxed his expression and reached across the gear console and captured her hand, bringing it over to rest on top of his thigh. 'No. Maybe I should, but I don't.'

'I don't regret it either.'

His eyes met hers when he parked the car. 'Your family is going to be hurt when we…end this.'

Why had he hesitated over the word 'end'? Who would end it? Would it be a mutual decision or would he suddenly announce it was over?

'Yes, I feel bad about that. But at least it's not for long,' Violet said. 'Once Christmas is over we'll say we made a mistake…or something and go back to normal.'

He studied her for a long moment. 'Will you be okay with that?'

Violet gave him a super-confident smile. 'Of course. Why wouldn't I be? It's what we agreed on. A short-term fling to get me back on my dating feet.'

His expression clouded. 'You have to be careful when you're dating guys these days. You can't go out with just anyone. It's not safe when there are so many creeps on the prowl. And don't do online dating. Some of those guys lie about their backgrounds. Anyone can use a false identity. You could end up with someone with a criminal past.'

Violet wondered if he was cautioning her out of concern or jealousy or both. 'You sound like you don't want me to date anyone else.'

He paused before responding. 'I care about you, Violet, that's all. I don't want you to become a crime statistic.'

'I'm sure I'll manage to meet and fall in love with some perfectly lovely guy, just like my sisters have done,' Violet said. 'I'm just taking a little longer than they did to get around to it.'

He opened his car door and came around to hers but, instead of tension, this time there was a self-deprecating tilt to his mouth. 'Sorry about the lecture.'

Violet smiled and patted his hand where it was resting on the top of the doorframe. 'You can lecture me but only if I can lecture you right on back. Deal?'

He bent down to press a kiss to the end of her nose. 'Deal.'

CHAPTER SEVEN

CAM WOKE FROM a fitful sleep to find the space next to him in the bed was empty. He sat bolt upright, his chest seizing with panic. Where was Violet? When he'd drifted asleep she had been lying in his arms.

Calm down, man. She's probably gone to the bathroom.

He threw off the bedcovers and, snatching up a towel, wrapped it around his hips and padded through his house, checking each room and bathroom upstairs but there was no sign of her.

'Violet?' His voice rang out hollowly. His blood chugged through his veins like chunks of ice. His skin shrank away from his skeleton. He was annoyed at his reaction. What did it say about him? That he was so hooked on her he couldn't let her out of his sight? Ridiculous. She had a right to move about the house without asking permission first. Maybe she'd had trouble sleeping with him in the bed beside her. After all, she'd never been in a proper relationship before. Sharing a bed with someone took some getting used to, which was why he generally avoided it.

'Violet?'

Where could she be? Had she gone outside? He tugged the curtains aside but the back garden was as quiet and deserted as a graveyard. It was three in the morning and it was bitterly cold. Had she gone back to her flat? No. She wouldn't go there without backup. He flung open the sitting room door, then the study.

All empty.

'Are you looking for me?' Violet appeared like a ghost in the doorway of the study.

Relief flooded through Cam like the shot of a potent drug. 'Where were you?'

Her eyes did a double blink at the edginess of his tone. 'I was reading in the breakfast room.'

Cam frowned so hard his forehead pinched. 'Reading?'

Her tongue snaked out and left a layer of moisture over her lips. 'I was…having trouble sleeping. I didn't want to disturb you. You seemed restless enough without me putting on the light and rustling pages.'

Cam forked a hand through his already tousled hair. 'You should've woken me if I was disturbing you. Was I snoring?'

'No, you were just…restless like you were having a bad dream or something.'

He had been having a bad dream. It was coming back to him now in vivid detail. He had been alone in a run-down castle. The drawbridge was up and there was no way in or out. Loneliness crept out from every dark corner, prodding him with tomb-cold fingers. The yawning emptiness he felt was what he had seen on Kenneth's face when they'd returned him to his home last night: the absence of hope, the presence of despair, the bitter sting of regret.

But it was a dream. It didn't mean anything. It was just his mind making up a narrative while his body rested. It didn't mean he was worried about ending up alone in a castle with nothing but cobwebs and shadows to keep him company. It didn't mean he was subconsciously regretting his stance on marriage and commitment. It meant he was dog-tired and working too hard. That was what it meant. That. Was. All. 'Sorry for wrecking your beauty sleep. Next time just give me a jab in the ribs, okay?'

Violet's shy smile tugged like strings stitched on to his heart. 'It was probably my fault more than yours. I've never spent the night with anyone before.'

Of course she hadn't. She might have felt all sorts of uncomfortable about sharing the night with him in his bed. Cam put his hands on her hips and brought her closer. 'I'm not much of a sleep-over person myself.'

A flicker of concern appeared in her gaze. 'Oh... well, then, I can sleep in one of the spare rooms if you'd—'

'No.' Cam brought his mouth down to within an inch of hers. 'I like having you in my bed.' *More than I want to admit.*

Her hint of vanilla danced over his mouth. 'I like it too.'

Cam covered her mouth with his, a shockwave of need rushing through him as her lips opened beneath his. He moved his lips against hers, a gentle massage to prove to himself he could control his response to her. But within seconds the heat got to him, the flicker of her tongue against his lower lip unravelling his self-control like a dropped ball of string. He splayed his fingers through her silky hair, holding her face so he could deepen the kiss. She gave a soft whimper of approval that made his body shudder in delight.

Her body pressed against his, her breasts free behind the bathrobe she was wearing. Knowing she was naked underneath that robe made him wild with need. He untied the waistband, still with his mouth on hers, letting it fall to her feet. He glided his hands over her breasts and then he brought his mouth to each one in turn, caressing the erect pink nipples with his tongue, gently taking them between his teeth in a soft nibble. She smelt of flowers and sleep and sex and he couldn't get enough of her.

He brought his mouth back to hers, his hands holding her by the hips so she could feel what she was doing to him. The ache of need pounded through his body, the primal need to mate driving every other thought out of his brain.

He should have taken her upstairs to the bed but he wanted her now. *Now.*

The hunger was in time with his racing pulse. He

wanted her on the floor. On the desk. On the sofa. Wherever he could have her. He dragged his mouth off hers. 'I want you here. Now.'

Violet's eyes shone with excitement. She didn't say anything but her actions spoke for her. She stroked her hands down his chest to his abdomen, deftly unhooking the towel from around his waist and taking him in her hands. Her touch wreaked havoc on his control. Red-hot pleasure shot through his body, luring him to the abyss where the dark magic of oblivion beckoned.

Cam had to stop her from taking him over the edge. He drew her hand away and guided her to the floor. He kissed his way down from her breasts to her belly, lingering over her mound, ramping up her anticipation for what was to come. She squirmed and whimpered when he claimed his prize, her body bucking within seconds of his tongue moving against her. Her cries of pleasure made him want her all the more. Her passion was so unfettered, so unrestrained it made him wonder if she would find the same freedom to express her sexuality with someone else.

Someone else...

Cam tried to push the thought aside but it was impossible. It was ugly, grotesque thinking of Violet with some other guy. Someone who might not appreciate her sensitivity and shyness. Someone who might pressure her into doing things she wasn't comfortable with doing. Someone who wouldn't protect her at all times and in all places.

That's rich coming from the guy who hasn't got a condom handy.

Violet must have sensed Cam's shift in mood for she propped herself up on her elbows to look at him. 'Is something wrong? Did I do something wrong?'

Cam took her by the hand and helped her to stand. 'It's not you, sweetheart. It's me.' He handed her the bathrobe before picking up his towel and hitching it around his waist. 'I didn't bring a condom with me.'

'Oh...'

'Unlike other men, I don't have them strategically planted in every room of the house.' *But maybe I should.*

Her lips flickered with a smile. 'That's kind of nice to know...'

'I'm selective when it comes to choosing partners.' He only ever chose women he knew he wouldn't fall in love with: safe, no-strings women who were out for a bit of fun and a tearless goodbye at the end of it. Women who didn't look at him with big soulful brown eyes and pretend they didn't feel things they clearly felt.

How was he going to end this?

Do you even want to?

Cam played with the idea of extending their affair. But how long was too long and how short was too short? Either way, it still left him with the task of facing her family and saying the happy ever after they were hanging out for wasn't going to happen.

And that wasn't even the half of it. What about what Violet felt? No matter how much she said she was only after a short fling, he knew her well enough to know she was only saying that to please him. Would it be fair to continue this, knowing she was probably falling in love with him? God knew he was having enough trouble keeping his own feelings in check. Feelings he couldn't explain. Feelings that crept up on him at odd moments, like when Violet looked at him a certain way, or when she smiled, or when she touched him and it sent a lightning zap of electricity through him. Feelings he couldn't dismiss because Violet wasn't a temporary fixture in his life.

The longer he continued their affair, the harder it would be to end it. He knew it and yet…and yet…he couldn't bring himself to do it. Not until after Christmas. Grandad Archie surely deserved to have his last Christmas wish?

Violet made a business of tying the bathrobe back around her waist. 'I suppose you're careful to choose partners you're not likely to fall in love with.'

'It's easier that way.' Maybe that was why he never felt fully satisfied after an encounter even when the sex was good. Something always felt a little off centre. Out of balance, like only wearing one shoe. He never let a relationship drag on for too long. A month or two maximum. It made him look like a bit of a player but that was the price he was prepared to pay for his freedom.

Violet gave him a smile that didn't quite make the grade. 'Lucky me.'

Cam frowned. 'Hey, I didn't mean I chose you for that reason. You're different, you know you are.'

'Not different enough that you'll fall in love with me.'

'Violet—'

She held up her hand. 'It's okay, I don't need the lecture.'

Cam took her by the shoulders again. 'Are you saying you're in love with me? Is that what you're saying?'

Her eyes did everything they could to avoid his. 'No, I'm not saying that.' Her voice was hardly more than a thread of sound.

Cam tipped up her chin, locking her gaze with his. 'This is all I can give you. You have to accept it, Violet. Even if we continued our relationship past Christmas, it would still come down to this. I'm not going to get married to you or to anyone just now.'

Her shoulders went down on a sigh. 'I know. I'm being silly. Sorry.'

He brought her head against his chest, stroking her silky hair with his hand. 'You're not being silly. You're being normal. I'm the one with the commitment issues, not you.'

Her arms snaked around his waist. 'Can we go back to bed now?'

Cam lifted her in his arms. 'What a great idea.'

Violet had arranged with Cam to take her back to her flat on Sunday afternoon to help Amy and Stef with the clean-up, but while she was getting breakfast ready while Cam checked some emails, Amy phoned.

'You're not going to believe this,' Amy said. 'But last night old Mr Yates in twenty-five was smoking in bed and started a fire—'

'Is he all right?' Violet asked.

'Just a bit of smoke inhalation but both our flats are uninhabitable from the water damage,' Amy said. 'The landlady is furious and poor Mr Yates won't want to face her in a hurry.'

'So what will we do?' Violet asked. 'Are we expected to clean it up or will a professional cleaning service do that?'

'Cleaning service,' Amy said. 'I'm not going in there until the building's secure. The ceiling might come down or something. Stef's going to move back in with her mum and I'm going to move in with Heath. We've talked about moving in together for ages so this nails it. What about you? Will you stay with Cam now that you're officially engaged?'

'I… Yes, that's what I'll do,' Violet said. What else could she say? *No, Cam doesn't want to live with anyone*?

Cam came in at that point and smiled. It never failed to make her shiver when he looked at her like that. He stroked a hand down her back while he reached past her to take a mug out of the cupboard next to her. It was the lightest touch but it sent a tremor of longing through her flesh until her legs threatened to buckle.

Violet said goodbye to Amy and put her phone on the bench. 'I have a slight problem…'

'What's wrong?'

She explained about the fire and the water damage. 'So, I have to find somewhere else to live.'

It was hard to read his expression beyond the concern it showed while she had related the events of last night's fire. He turned to one side to take out a tea bag from a box inside the pantry. 'You can stay here as long as you need to. I told you that the other day.'

'Yes, but—'

'It's fine, Violet, really.'

'No, it's not fine,' Violet said. 'A couple of weeks is okay, but any longer than that and things will get complicated.' *More complicated than they already were.*

'What if I help you find a place?'

'You don't have to do that.'

'I'd like to,' he said. 'It'll mean I can give the security a once-over.'

Violet gave him a grateful smile. 'That would be great, thanks.' She waited a beat before adding, 'What's happening with the contract with Nicolaides? Is it secure yet?'

'Not yet.' Cam pulled out one of the breakfast-bar stools. 'I have some drawings to finalise. Sophia keeps altering the design, I suspect because she wants to drag out the process.'

'Has she sent you any more texts?'

'A couple.'

Jealousy surged in Violet's gut. 'When's she going to get the message? What is wrong with her?'

He gave a loose shrug. 'Some women don't know the meaning of the word no.'

Violet would have to learn it herself and in a hurry. 'I think it's disgusting how she openly lusts over you while her husband is watching. Why does he put up with it?'

'He's too frightened to lose her,' Cam said. 'She's twenty years younger than him. And she brings a lot of money to the relationship. Her father left her his empire. It's worth a lot of money.'

'I wouldn't care how much money someone had. If I couldn't trust them, then that would be it. Goodbye. Have a good life.'

He stroked a fingertip down her cheek, his smile gently teasing. 'If you think Sophia's bad, wait till you meet my father's fiancée.'

Violet frowned. 'You want me to meet her?'

'My dad's organised drinks on Wednesday night,' Cam said. 'If you'd rather not go, then—'

'No, it's okay. Of course I'll go. You went to my boring old office party, the least I can do is come with you for drinks with your father.'

Cam's father, Ross, had arranged to meet them at a boutique hotel in the centre of London. Violet hadn't met Ross McKinnon before but she had seen photos of him in the press. He was not quite as tall as Cam and his figure showed signs of the overly indulgent life he led. His features had none of the sharply chiselled definition of Cam's, and while he still had a full head of thick hair, it was liberally sprinkled with grey. His eyes, however, were the same dark blue but without the healthy clarity of Cam's. And they had a tendency to wander to Violet's breasts with rather annoying frequency.

'So this is the girl who's stolen my son's hard heart,' Ross said. 'Congratulations and welcome to the family.'

'Thank you,' Violet said.

Ross pushed his fiancée forward. 'This is Tatiana, my wife as of next weekend. We should have made it a double wedding, eh, Cameron?'

Cam looked like he was in some sort of gastric pain. 'Wouldn't want to steal your thunder.'

Violet took the young woman's hand and smiled. 'Lovely to meet you.'

Tatiana's smile came with a don't-mess-with-me warning. 'Likewise.'

Cam was doing his best to be polite but Violet could tell he was uncomfortable being around his father and new partner. Ross dominated the conversation with occasional interjections from Tatiana, followed by numerous public displays of affection that made Violet feel she was on the set of a B-grade porn movie. Clearly she wasn't the only one as several heads kept turning at the bar, followed by snickers.

Ross showed no interest in Cam's life. It shocked Violet that his father could sit for an hour and a half in his son's company and not once ask a single question about his work or anything to do with his private life. It made her feel sad for Cam to have had such a selfish parent who acted like a narcissistic teenager instead of an adult.

Violet was relieved when Cam got to his feet and said they had to leave.

'But we haven't told you what we've got planned for the honeymoon,' Ross said.

'Isn't that supposed to be bad luck?' Cam said with a pointed look.

Ross's face darkened. 'You can't help yourself, can you? But Tatiana is the one. I know it as sure as I'm standing here.'

'Good for you.' Cam's tone had a hint of cynicism to it and Violet wondered how many times he had heard exactly the same thing from his father. Ross was the sort of man who treated women as trophies to be draped on his arm and summarily dismissed when they ceased to pander to his bloated ego.

Violet quickly offered her hand to Ross and Tatiana. 'It was lovely to meet you. I hope the wedding goes well.'

Ross frowned. 'But aren't you coming with Cameron?'

Violet realised her gaffe too late. 'Erm…yes, of course, if that's what you'd like.'

'You're part of the family now,' Ross said. 'We'd be delighted to have you share in our special day, wouldn't we, babe?'

Tatiana's smile was cool. 'But of course. I'll aim the bouquet in your direction, shall I?'

Violet's smile felt like it was stitched in place. 'That'd be great.'

Cam took her by the hand and led her out of the hotel. 'I did warn you.'

'How on earth do you stand him?' Violet said. 'He's impossibly self-centred. He didn't ask you a single thing about your work or anything to do with you. It was all about him. How amazing he is and how successful and rich. And Tatiana looks like she's young enough to be his daughter. What on earth does she see in him?'

'He paid for her boob job.'

Violet rolled her eyes. She walked a few more paces with him before adding, 'I'm sorry about the wedding gaffe. I didn't think. Do you think they suspected anything was amiss?'

'Probably not,' Cam said. 'They're too focused on themselves.'

'Poor you,' Violet said.

He gave a soft smile. 'You want to grab a bite to eat before we go home?'

Go home. How...permanent and cosy that sounded. 'Sure. Where did you have in mind?'

'Somewhere on the other side of the city so there's no chance my father and Tatiana will chance upon us.'

Violet gave him a sympathetic look. 'I swear I am never going to complain about my family ever again.'

'There's no such thing as a perfect family,' he said. 'But I have to admit yours comes pretty close.'

Violet adored her family. They were supportive and loving and always there for her. But the pressure to live up to the standards her parents had modelled for her always made her feel as if she wasn't quite good enough, that she would never be able to do as brilliant a job as they had of finding love and keeping it. It was one of the reasons she had never told her mother or her sisters about what had happened at that party. Although she knew they would be nothing but supportive and concerned, she'd always worried they would see her differently…as damaged in some way.

'I know, but it's hard to live up to, you know? What if I don't find someone as perfect as my dad is for my mum? They're such a great team. I don't want to settle for less but I'm worried I might miss out. I want to have kids. That makes me feel under even more pressure. It's all right for guys; you can have kids when you're ninety. It's different for women.'

'If it's going to happen it'll happen,' he said. 'You can't force these things.'

'Easy for you to say. You have a queue of women waiting to hook up with you.'

He gave her hand a tiny squeeze. 'I'm only interested in one woman at the moment.'

At the moment.

How could she forget the clock ticking on their relationship? It was front and centre in her mind. Each day that passed was another day closer to when they would go back to being friends. Friends *without* benefits. It would be torture to be around Cam without being able to touch him, to kiss him, to wrap her arms around him and feel his body stir against her. It would be torture to see him date other women, knowing they were experiencing the explosive passion and pleasure of being in his arms.

What if she never found someone as perfect for her as Cam? What if she ended up alone and had to be satisfied with being an aunty or godmother instead of the mother she longed to be? She had been embroidering baby clothes since she was a teenager. She'd made them for her sisters and brother's wife Zoe each time they were expecting but she had her own private stash of clothes. It was her version of a hope chest. Every time she looked at those little vests and booties and bibs she felt an ache of longing. But it wasn't just about having a baby, she realised with a jolt. She wanted to have *Cam's* baby. She couldn't think of anything she wanted more than to be with him, not just for Christmas but for ever.

After dinner they walked hand in hand through the Christmas wonderland of London's streets. Violet had always loved Christmas in her adopted city but being with Cam made the lights seem all the brighter, the colours all the more vivid, the hype of the festive season all the more exciting. When they walked past the Somerset House ice-skating rink, Cam stopped and looked down at her with a twinkling look. 'Fancy a quick twirl to work off dinner?'

Violet looked at the gloriously lit rink with the beautifully decorated Christmas tree at one end. She had skated there a couple of times with Stef and Amy but she'd felt awkward because they had brought their boyfriends. The boys had offered to partner her but she'd felt so uncomfortable she'd pretended to have a sore ankle rather than take them up on their offer. 'I'm not very good at it…' she said. 'And I'm not wearing the right clothes.'

'Excuses, excuses,' Cam said. 'It won't take long to go home and change.'

Within a little while they were back at the rink dressed in jeans and jackets and hats and gloves. Violet felt like a foal on stilts until Cam took her by the hand and led her around until she felt more secure. He looked like he'd been skating all his life, his balance and agility making her attempts look rather paltry in comparison.

'You're doing great,' he said, wrapping one arm around her waist. 'Let's do a complete circuit. Ready?'

Violet leaned into his body and went with him in graceful sweeps and swishes that made the cold air rush past her face. It was exhilarating to be moving so quickly and with his steady support she gained more and more confidence, even letting go of his hand at one point to do a twirl in front of him.

Cam took her hand again, smiling broadly. 'What did I tell you? You're a natural.'

'Only with you.' *And not just with skating.* How would she ever make love with someone else and feel the same level of pleasure? It didn't seem possible. It wasn't possible because there was no way she could ever feel the same about someone else.

Once they had given back their skates, they walked to the London Eye, where Cam paid for them to go on to look at the Christmas lights all over London. Violet had been on the giant Ferris wheel a couple of times but it was so much more special doing it with Cam. The city was a massive grid of twinkling lights, a wonderland of festive cheer that made all the children and most of the adults on board exclaim with wonder.

Violet turned in the circle of Cam's arms to smile at him. 'It's amazing, isn't it? It makes me get all excited about Christmas when usually I'm dreading it.'

A slight frown appeared on his brow. 'Why do you dread it? I thought you loved spending Christmas with your family.'

Violet shifted her gaze to look at the fairyland below. 'I do love it…mostly, it's just I'm always the odd one out. The one without a partner. Apart from Grandad, of course.'

His hand stroked the small of her back. 'You won't be without a partner this year.'

But what about next year? Violet had to press her lips together to stop from saying it out loud. Once Christmas was over so too would their relationship come to an end. All the colour and sparkle and excitement and joy would be snuffed out, just like someone turning off the Christmas lights.

'No one knows what the next year will bring,' Cam

said as if he had read her thoughts. 'You could be married and pregnant by then.'

I wish...but only if it were to you. 'I can't see that happening.' Violet waited a moment before adding, 'Would you come to my wedding if I were to get married?'

Something flashed across his face as if pain had gripped him somewhere deep inside his body. 'Would I be invited?' His tone was light, almost teasing, but she could sense an undercurrent of something else. Something darker. Brooding.

'Of course,' Violet said. 'You're part of the family. It wouldn't be a Drummond wedding if you weren't there.'

'As long as you don't ask me to be the best man,' he said with a grim look. 'My father's asked me to be his and that'll be four times in a row.'

'Wow, you must be an expert at best man speeches by now.'

'Yeah, well, I hope this is the last time but I seriously doubt it.'

Violet thought of her parents and how loving and committed they were to each other and had been from the moment they'd met. They renewed their wedding vows every ten years and went back to the same cottage on the Isle of Skye where they'd spent their honeymoon on each and every anniversary. How had Cam dealt with his father's casual approach to marriage? Ross McKinnon changed wives faster than a sports car changed gears. How embarrassing it must be for Cam to have to go through yet another wedding ceremony knowing it would probably end in divorce. 'Maybe this time will be different,' she said. 'Maybe your dad is really in love this time.'

Cam's expression was a picture of cynicism. 'He doesn't know the meaning of the word.'

CHAPTER EIGHT

THE NEXT DAY Cam came home from work with the news that his contract with Nick Nicolaides had been signed that afternoon.

'Let's go out to celebrate.' He bent down to kiss Violet on the mouth. 'How was your day?'

Violet looped her arms around his neck. 'My day was fine. You must be feeling enormously relieved. Was Sophia there at the meeting?'

'Yes, but she was surprisingly subdued,' he said. 'I think she might've been feeling unwell or something. She got up to leave a couple of times and came back in looking a bit green about the gills. Too much to drink the night before, probably.'

Violet's brow furrowed. 'Could she be pregnant?'

He gave a light shrug. 'I wouldn't know, although, now that I think of it, Nick was looking pretty pleased with himself. But I thought that was because we finally finalised the contract.'

'Maybe being pregnant will help her settle down with Nick instead of eyeing up other men all the time,' Violet said.

Cam stepped away to shrug off his coat, laying it over the back of a chair. His expression had a cloaked look about it, shadowed and closed off. 'A Band-Aid baby is never a good idea.'

Violet knew he was bitter about his parents and the way they had handled his arrival in the world. Did he blame himself for how things had turned out? How could he think it was his fault? His parents were both selfish individuals who ran away from problems when things got the slightest bit difficult. They moved from relationship to relationship, collecting collateral damage along the way. How many lives had each of them ruined so far? And it was likely to continue with Ross McKinnon's next marriage. No wonder Cam wanted no part of the type of marriage modelled by his parents. It was nothing short of farcical. 'True,' she said. 'But a baby doesn't ask to be born and once it arrives it deserves to be treasured and loved unconditionally.'

A frown pulled at Cam's forehead. 'We haven't discussed this before but are you taking any form of oral contraception?'

Violet felt her cheeks heat up. It was something she had thought about doing but she hadn't got around to making an appointment with her doctor to get a prescription. There hadn't seemed much point when she wasn't dating regularly. But now…now it was imperative she kept from getting pregnant. The last thing Cam would want was a baby to complicate things further, even though she could think of nothing more wonderful than falling pregnant with his child. 'I'm not but I'm sure it won't be a problem—'

'Condoms are not one hundred per cent reliable,' he said, still frowning.

Violet felt intimidated by his steely glare. Why did he have to make her feel as if she was deliberately trying to get pregnant? There were worse things in the world than falling pregnant by the man you loved. Much worse things. Like not getting pregnant at all. Ever. 'I'm not pregnant, Cam, so you can relax, okay?'

A muscle tapped in his cheek. 'I'm sorry but this is a big issue for me. I don't want any mishaps we can't walk away from.'

Violet cast him a speaking look. 'You'd be the one walking away, not me.'

His frown deepened. 'Is that what you think? Really? Then you're wrong. I would do whatever I could to support you and the baby.'

'But you wouldn't marry me.' It was a statement, not a question.

For once his eyes had trouble meeting hers. 'Not under those circumstances. It wouldn't be fair to the child.'

Violet moved away to fold the tea towels she had taken out of the clothes dryer earlier. 'This is a pointless discussion because I'm not pregnant.' *And I wouldn't marry you if I were because you don't love me the way I long to be loved.*

'When will you know for sure?'

'Christmas Day or thereabouts.'

A silence ticked past.

Cam picked up his jacket and slung it over his arm. 'I'm going to have a shower.' He paused for a beat to rub at his temple as if he was fighting a tension headache. 'By the way, thanks for doing the washing. You didn't need to do that. My housekeeper will be back after Christmas.'

'I had to do some of my own so it was no bother.'

He gave her a tired-looking smile. 'Thanks. You're a darling.'

Violet disguised a despondent sigh. *But not* your *darling.*

Cam couldn't take his eyes off Violet all evening. They had gone to one of his favourite haunts, a piano bar where the music was reflective and calming. She was wearing a new emerald-green dress that made her creamy skin glow and her brown eyes pop. Her hair was loose about her shoulders, falling in soft fragrant waves he couldn't wait to go home and bury his head in.

But there was something about her expression that made him realise he had touched on a sensitive subject earlier. Babies. Of course he'd had to mention contraception. He had the conversation with every partner. It was the responsible thing to do. A baby—*he*—had ruined his mother's life. It had changed the direction of her life, her career plans, her happiness—everything. A thing she unfortunately reminded him of when she was feeling particularly down about yet another broken relationship.

But Violet wanted a baby. And why wouldn't she? Her siblings were growing their young families and she was the only one left single.

Not quite single...

Cam picked up his glass and took a measured sip. Weird how he felt...so committed and yet this was supposed to be temporary.

Violet raised her glass, a smile curving her lips. 'Congratulations, Cam. I'm so happy for you about the contract.'

'Thanks.' He couldn't think of a single person he would rather celebrate his contract with. It wasn't as if either of his parents were interested, and while Fraser was always thrilled for him when he won an award or landed a big contract, it wasn't the same as having someone who wanted your success more than their own.

'About our conversation earlier...' Cam said.

'It's fine, Cam,' Violet said. 'I understand completely.'

'It's tough on women when they get pregnant. I realise that,' Cam said. 'Even today when there is so much more support around. It's a life-changing decision to keep a baby.'

'Did your mother ever consider...?' Violet seemed unable to complete the sentence.

'Yes and no.' Cam leaned forward to put his glass down. 'She kept me because by doing so she thought she'd be able to keep my father. But when that turned sour, she decided she wished she'd got rid of me so she could have continued her studies.'

Violet frowned. 'She told you that?'

He gave an I'm-over-it shrug. 'Once or twice.'

'But that's awful! No child, no matter how young or old, should hear something like that from a parent.'

'Yes, well, I was an eight-pound spanner in the works for my mother's aspirations. But I blame my father for not supporting her. He got on with his career without a thought about hers.' Cam passed Violet the bowl of nuts before he was tempted to scoff the lot. 'Have you ever thought of going back and finishing your degree?'

Her mouth froze over her bite into a Brazil nut. She took it away from her mouth and placed it on the tiny, square Christmas-themed napkin on the table between them. 'No… I'm not interested in studying now.'

'But you were doing English Literature and History, weren't you?' Cam said. 'Didn't you always want to be a teacher?'

Her eyes fell away from his and she dusted the salt off her fingers with another napkin. 'I'm not cut out for teaching. I'd get too flustered with having to handle difficult kids, not to mention their parents. I'm happy where I'm working.'

'Are you?'

Her eyes slowly met his. 'No, not really, but I'm good at it.'

'Just because you're good at something doesn't mean you should spend your life doing it if it bores you,' Cam said. 'Why don't you study online? Even if you don't teach, it will give you some closure.'

Violet pushed her glass away even though she had

only taken a couple of sips. Her cheeks were a bright shade of pink and her mouth was pinched around the edges. 'Can we talk about something else?'

Cam leaned forwards, resting his forearms on his thighs. 'Hey, don't go all prickly on me. I'm just trying to help you sort out your life.'

Her eyes flashed with uncharacteristic heat. 'I don't need my life sorting out. My life is just fine, thank you very much. Anyway, you need to sort out your own life.'

He sat back and picked up his glass. 'There's nothing wrong with my life.'

Her chin came up. 'So says the man who only dates women who won't connect with him emotionally. What's that about, Cam? What's so terrifying about feeling something for someone?'

Losing them.

Like his mother had lost his father and gone on to lose every other partner since in a pattern she couldn't break because the one person she had loved the most hadn't wanted her any more.

Cam didn't want to be that person. The person left behind. The person who gave everything to the relationship only to have it thrown away like trash when someone else more exciting came along.

He was the one in control in his relationships.

He started one when he wanted one.

He left when it was time to go.

'We're not talking about me,' Cam said. 'We're talking about you. About how you're letting a bad thing that happened to you rob you of reaching your full potential.'

'But isn't that what you're doing? You're letting your parents' horrible divorce rob you of the chance of long-term happiness because you're worried you might not be able to hang on to the one you love.'

So what if he was? He was fine with that. It wasn't as if he was in love with anyone anyway. *You sure about that?* Cam blinked the thought away. Of course he loved Violet. He had always loved her. But it didn't mean he was *in* love with her.

Yes, you are.

No, I'm not.

The battle went back and forth in his head like two boxing opponents trying to get the upper hand. He was confusing lust with love. The sex was great—better than great—the best he'd ever had. But it didn't mean he wanted to tie himself down to domesticity. He was a free agent. Marriage and kids were not on his radar. Violet was born to be a mother. Any fool could see that. She went dewy-eyed at the sight of a baby. She embroidered baby clothes for a hobby, for goodness' sake. Even puppies and kittens turned her to mush. She had planned her wedding day since she was a kid. He had seen photos and home videos of her and her sisters playing weddings. Violet had looked adorable wearing her mother's veil and high heels when she was barely four years old.

How could he ask her to sacrifice that dream for him?

Violet began chewing at her lip. 'Are you angry at me?'

Cam reached across and took her hand. 'No, of course not.' He gave her hand a gentle squeeze. 'Would you like to dance?'

Her eyes lit up. 'You want to dance?'

'Sure, why not?' He drew her to her feet. 'I might not be too flash with a Highland fling but I can do a mean waltz or samba.'

Her arms linked around his neck, bringing her lower body close to the need already stirring there. 'I didn't mean to lecture you, Cam. I hate it when people do that to me.'

Cam pressed a soft kiss to her mouth. 'I'm sorry too.'

Violet had always been a bit of a wallflower at her home town's country dances. She stood at the back of the room and silently envied her parents, who twirled about the dance floor as if they were one person, not two. But somehow in Cam's arms she found her dancing feet and moved about the floor while the piano played a heartstring-pulling ballad as if she was born to it. His arms supported her, his body guided her and his smile delighted her. 'If you tell your brother about this I'll have to kill you,' Cam said.

Violet laughed. 'Someone should be videoing this because no one's going to believe I've got through three songs without doing you an injur— Oops! Spoke too soon.' She glanced down at his feet. 'Did I hurt you?'

'Not a bit.' He guided her around the other way, drawing her even closer to his body.

Violet loved the feel of his arms around her, but

the slow rhythm of the haunting melody of lost love reminded her of the time in the not too distant future when those words would apply to her. How long had she been in love with him? It wasn't something she could pin an exact time or date to. She had always thought falling in love would be a light bulb moment, a flash of realisation that this was *The One*. But with Cam it had been more of a slow build, a gradual awareness the feelings she had towards him were no longer the platonic ones she had felt before. It was an awakening of her mind and body. Every moment she spent with him she loved him more. Which would make the end of their affair all the more difficult to deal with. Had she made a mistake in letting it go this far? But then she would never have known this magic. She would never have known the depth of pleasure her body was capable of giving and receiving.

The song ended and Cam led her back to their table in the corner to collect their coats. Violet suppressed a shiver when his hands pulled her hair out from the back of her collar when he helped her into her coat. She turned back around to face him and her belly did a flip at the smouldering look in his eyes. 'Time to go home?' she asked.

His mouth tilted in a sexy smile. 'If I make it that far.'

They barely made it through the door. Violet slipped out of her coat and walked into Cam's arms, his head coming down to connect his mouth with hers in a hungry kiss that made her whole body tingle. His tongue entered her mouth with a determined thrust that mimicked the intention of his body. She sent her tongue into combat with his, stroking and darting away in turn, ramping up the heat firing between them.

His hands went to the zipper at the back of her dress, sending it down her back, his hand sliding beneath the sagging fabric to bring her closer to the hardened length of him. His mouth continued its passionate assault on her senses, his teeth taking playful nips of her lower lip, pulling it out and releasing it, salving it with his tongue and then doing it all over again.

Desire roared through Violet's body with a force that was almost frightening in its intensity. She clawed at his clothing like a woman possessed, popping buttons off his shirt but beyond caring. She had to feel his hot male skin under her hands. *Now.* She unzipped him and dragged down his underwear, taking him in one hand, massaging, stroking up and down until he was fighting for the control they'd lost as soon as they'd stepped through the door. She sank to her knees in front of him, ignoring his token protest and put her mouth to him.

He allowed her a few moments of torturing him but finally hauled her upright, pushing her back against the wall, ruthlessly stripping her dress from her, leaving her in nothing but her tights and knickers and heels. He cupped her mound, grinding the heel of his hand against her ache of longing, his mouth back on hers, hard, insistent, desperate.

Violet fed off his mouth, her hands grasping him by the buttocks, holding him to the throb of her female flesh. 'Please...*please...*' She didn't care that she was begging. She needed him like she had never needed him before.

Cam pulled off her tights, taking her knickers with them. He left her hanging there while he sourced a condom, swiftly applying it and then coming back to her, entering her in one deep thrust that made her senses go wild. He set a furious pace, unlike anything he had done before. It was like a force had taken over his body, a force he couldn't control. The same force that was thundering through her body, making her gasp and whimper and arch her spine and roll her hips to get the friction where she needed it most.

He hooked one of her legs over his hip and caressed her with his fingers, triggering an earthquake in her body. It threw her into a tailspin, into a wild maelstrom of sensations that powered through her from head to toe. Even the hairs on her head felt like they were spinning at the roots.

Cam followed with his own release in three hard thrusts that brought a harsh cry out from between his lips.

Violet's legs were threatening to send her to a puddle of limbs on the floor at his feet. She grasped at the edges of his opened shirt, which she hadn't managed to get off his body in time. 'Wow, we should go dancing more often.'

He gave a soft laugh, his breathing not quite back to normal. 'We should.'

Violet pulled her clothes back on while he dealt with

the condom and his own clothes. If anyone had told her she would have acted with such wanton abandon even a week ago, she would have been shocked. But with Cam everything felt…right. She had the confidence to express herself sexually with him because she knew he would never ask her to do something she wasn't comfortable with. He always put her pleasure ahead of his own. He worshipped her body instead of using it to satisfy himself.

'We'll have an opportunity to dance at my father's wedding on Saturday,' Cam said once they had gone upstairs to prepare for bed.

Violet stalled in the process of unzipping her dress. 'You're not really expecting me to go with you, are you?'

He was sitting on the end of the bed, reaching down to untie his shoelaces, but looked up with a partial frown. 'Of course I want you there. We can fly up to Drummond Brae that evening. The wedding's in the morning so we should make it plenty of time for Christmas.'

Violet sank her teeth into her lip. 'I don't know…'

'What's wrong?'

'Your father won't mind if I don't show up. He won't even notice.'

'Maybe not, but I want you there. I'm the best man. Dad's arranged to have you with me at the top table.'

Violet thought about the wedding photos that would be taken. How she would be in all the family shots that for years later everyone would look at and say, *'There's the girl who was engaged to Cam for two weeks.'* It was bad enough with it being all over social media. But at least everyone would forget about it after a while. But a wedding album wasn't the same as cyberspace. It would be a concrete reminder of a charade she should never have agreed to in the first place.

However, it wasn't just the fallout from social media that had her feeling so conflicted about his father's wedding. It was the wedding ceremony itself, the sanctity of it. How she felt she would be compromising someone else's special day by pretending to be something she was not. How could she cheapen a ceremony she held in such high esteem? It would be nothing short of sacrilege. 'I don't think I belong at your father's wedding.'

He got up from the bed and tossed his loosened tie to the chest of drawers. 'You do belong there. You belong by my side as my fiancée.'

Violet pointedly raised her brow. 'Don't you mean your *fake* fiancée?'

A flicker of annoyance passed over his features. 'You didn't have any problem with lying to your workmates and your family. Why not stretch it to my family as well?'

'I'm not going, Cam. You can't make me.'

Cam came up to her and placed his hands on her shoulders. 'We're in this together, Violet. It's only till after Christmas. Surely it's not too much to ask you to come with me.'

Violet held his gaze. 'Why do you want me there? It's your father's fifth marriage, for pity's sake. It'll be a farcical version of what marriage is supposed to represent. I can't bear to be part of it. It would make me feel as if I'm poking fun at the institution I hold in the highest possible regard. Why is it so important to you that I be there?'

He dropped his hands and stepped away, his expression getting that boxed up look about it. 'Fine. Don't go. I don't blame you. I wish I didn't have to go either.'

Violet realised then how much he was dreading his father's wedding. Just like he had dreaded meeting his father for drinks. If she didn't go to the wedding then he would have to face it alone. Surely it was the least she could do to go with him and support him? He'd supported her at her office Christmas party. He'd supported her through the ordeal of her flat being broken in to. He'd been there for her every step of the way. It was a big compromise for her but wasn't that what all good relationships were about? She came up behind him and linked her arms around his waist. 'All right, I'll go with you but only because I care about you and hate the thought of you going through it alone.'

He turned and touched her gently on the cheek with his fingertip. 'I hate putting you through it. If it's anything like his last one it will be excruciating. But it'll be over by mid-afternoon and then we can fly up to Scotland to be with your family.'

Violet stepped up on tiptoe to plant a kiss to his lips. 'I can't wait.'

* * *

The church was full of flowers; every pew had a posy of blooms with a satin ribbon holding it in place. On each side of the altar was an enormous arrangement of red roses and another two at the back of the church. Violet sat in the pew and looked at Cam standing up at the altar with his father. Ross was joking and bantering with the other two groomsmen and, even though Violet was sitting a few rows back, she wondered if he was already a little drunk. His cheeks were ruddy and his movements were a little uncoordinated. Or perhaps it was wedding nerves? No. Ross McKinnon wasn't the type of man to get nervous about anything. He was enjoying being the centre of attention. He was relishing it. It was jarring for Violet, being such a romantic. She loved weddings where the groom looked nervous but excited waiting for his bride to arrive. Like her brother Fraser, who had kept checking his watch and swallowing deeply as the minutes ticked on. It had been such a beautiful wedding and Cam had been a brilliant best man.

Violet looked at Cam again. He looked composed. Too composed. Cardboard cut-out composed. He met her gaze and smiled. How she loved that smile. He only did it for her. It was *her* smile. The way his eyes lit up as if seeing her made him happy. She was glad she'd come to the wedding. It was the right thing to do even if the wedding was every type of wrong.

The organ started playing the 'Wedding March' and every head turned to the back of the church. There were three bridesmaids who were dressed in skimpy gowns that didn't suit their rather generous figures. Had Tatiana deliberately chosen friends who wouldn't upstage her? Not that anyone could upstage Tatiana. Violet heard the collective indrawn breath of the congregation when the bride appeared. Tatiana's white satin gown was slashed almost to the waist, with her cleavage on show as well as the slight bulge of her pregnancy. Violet looked on in horror as Tatiana's right breast threatened to pop out as she walked—strutted would be a more accurate description—up the aisle. The back of Tatiana's dress was similarly slashed, this time to the top of her buttocks, which her veil was not doing a particularly good job of hiding.

Ross looked like he couldn't wait to get his hands on his bride and made some joking aside to Cam that made Cam's jaw visibly tighten. Violet felt angry on his behalf. What a disgusting display of inappropriateness and poor Cam had to witness every second of it.

It got worse.

Ross and Tatiana had written the vows but they weren't romantic and heartfelt declarations but rather a travesty of what a marriage ceremony should be. Finally they were declared man and wife and Ross and Tatiana kissed for so long, with Ross's hand wandering all over his new bride's body, that several members of the congregation snickered.

The reception was little more than a drunken party. How Cam managed to get through his speech while his father cracked inappropriate jokes and drank copious amounts of champagne was anybody's guess.

When Cam sat back down beside her, she took his hand under the table and gave it a squeeze. 'This must be killing you,' she said.

'It'll be over soon.' He gave her a soft smile. 'How are you holding up?'

Violet curled her fingers around his. 'I'm fine, although I feel a bit silly up here at the top table. Tatiana doesn't like it. She keeps giving me the evil eye.'

'That's because you outshine her,' Cam said.

Violet could feel herself glowing at his compliment. His look warmed her blood. The look that said *I want you*. 'I'm going to powder my nose. Can we leave after that, do you think, or will we have to wait until your father and Tatiana leave?'

He glanced at his watch. 'Let's give it another hour and then we'll go.'

On her way back from the ladies' room, Violet saw Cam's father leading one of the bridesmaids by the hand to a corner behind a large arrangement of flowers. The bridesmaid was giggling and Ross was leering at her and groping her. Violet was so shocked she stood there with her mouth hanging open. Did Ross have no shame? He'd only been married a matter of hours and he was already straying. Did the commitment of marriage mean nothing to him?

Violet swung away and went back to where Cam was waiting for her. She couldn't stay another minute at this wretched farce of a wedding. Not. One. Minute.

She felt tainted by it. Sullied. Defiled by listening to people mouthing words they didn't mean and watching them behaving like out of control teenagers. No wonder Cam was so against marriage. Apart from her brother and sisters' weddings, all he had seen was the repeated drunken mockery of what was supposed to be the most important day in a couple's life. No wonder he was cynical. No wonder he couldn't picture himself getting married in the near future.

'What's wrong?' Cam said when she snatched up her wrap from the back of the chair.

'I can't stay here another minute,' Violet said. 'Your father is feeling up one of the bridesmaids out in the foyer.'

Cam's expression showed little surprise about his father's behaviour. 'Yes, well, that's my father for you. A class act at all times and in all places.'

Violet tugged his arm. 'Come on. Let's get out of here. My flesh is crawling. Oh, God, look at Tatiana. She's got her tongue in the groomsman's ear. She's practically doing a lap dance on him.'

Cam took Violet's hand and led her out of the reception room. 'Sorry you had to witness all that craziness. But I'm glad you came. It would've been unbearable without you there.'

Violet was still seething about his father's and Tatiana's behaviour when they got home to change and collect their bags for their evening flight to Scotland. 'I can't believe you share any of your father's DNA. You're nothing like him. You're decent and caring and principled. I'm sure if you were to get married one day in the future you won't be off canoodling with one of the bridesmaids within an hour or two of the ceremony. What is wrong with him?'

Cam paused in the action of slipping off his coat. But then he resumed the process of shrugging it off and hanging it on the hallstand with what seemed to Violet somewhat exaggerated precision. 'We've had this conversation a number of times before,' he said. 'I don't want to get married.'

Violet felt his words like a rusty stake to her heart. Not married? *Ever?* She had heard him say it before but hadn't things been changing between them? Hadn't *she* changed things for him? He cared about her. He talked to her. *Really* talked. About things he'd not spoken of to anyone else. He had invited her into his home. Was his heart really still so off-limits? How could he make love to her the way he had and not have felt anything? He'd bought her an engagement ring, for goodness' sake. He could have bought something cheap but he'd chosen something so special, so perfect, it surely meant he cared more than he wanted to admit.

Violet understood now why he was so wary of marriage. But deep down she had harboured hope that he would see how a marriage between them would be just like the marriage between her parents: respectful and loving and lasting. 'You don't really mean that, Cam. Deep down you want what I want. What my parents and siblings have. You've seen how a good marriage is conducted. You can't let your father's atrocious behaviour influence you like this. You're not living his life, you're living yours.'

Cam's expression went into lockdown. Violet knew him well enough to know he felt cornered. A frown formed between his eyes, his mouth tightened and a muscle ticked in his lean cheek. 'Violet.'

'Don't *do* that,' Violet said, frustrated beyond measure. 'Don't use that schoolmaster tone with me as if I'm too stupid to know what I'm talking about. You're not facing what's right in front of you. I know you care about me. You care about me much more than you want to admit. I can't go on pretending to be engaged to you when all I want is for it to be for real.'

The tenseness around his mouth travelled all the way up to his eyes. They were hard as flint. 'Then you'll be waiting a long time because I'm not going to change my mind.'

Violet knew it was time for a line to be drawn. How long could she go on hoping he would come to see things her way? What if she stayed in a relationship with him for months and months, maybe even years, and he still wouldn't budge? All her dreams of a beautiful wedding day with her whole family there would be destroyed. All her hopes for a family of her own would be shattered. She couldn't give that up. She loved him. She loved him desperately but she wouldn't be true to herself if she drifted along in a going nowhere relationship with him. She had to make a stand. She couldn't go on living in this excruciating limbo of will-he-or-won't-he? She had to make him see there was no future without a proper commitment.

No fling.

No temporary arrangement.

No pretend engagement.

Violet drew in a carefully measured breath, garnering her resolve. 'Then I don't want you to come home to Drummond Brae with me. I'd rather go alone.'

It was hard to tell if her statement affected him for hardly a muscle moved on his face. 'Fine.'

Fine? Violet's heart gave a painful spasm. How could he be so calm and clinical about this? Didn't he feel anything for her? Maybe he didn't love her after all. Maybe all this had been a convenient affair that had a use-by date. *Be strong. Be strong. Be strong.* She knew he was expecting her to cave in. It was what she did all the time. She over-adapted. She compromised. She hated hurting people's feelings so she ended up saying yes when she meant no. It had to stop. It had to stop now. It was time to grow a backbone. 'Is that your final decision?' she said.

'Violet, you're being unreasonable about—'

'*I'm* being unreasonable?' Violet said. 'What's unreasonable about wanting to be happy? I can't be happy with you if you're not one hundred per cent committed to me. I can't live like that. I don't want to miss out on all the things I've dreamt about since I was a little girl. If you don't want the same things then it's time to call it quits before we end up hurting each other too much.'

'It was never my intention to hurt you,' Cam said.

You just did. 'I have to go now or I'll miss the flight.' Violet moved past him to collect her bag from his room upstairs. Would he follow her and try and talk her out of it? Would he tell her how much he loved her? She listened for the sound of his tread on the stairs but there was nothing but silence.

When she came back downstairs with her overnight bag he was still standing in the hall with that blank expression. 'I'll drive you to the airport,' he said, barely moving his lips as he spoke.

'That won't be necessary,' Violet said. 'I've already called a cab.' She took off her engagement ring and handed it to him. 'I won't be needing this any more.'

He ignored her outstretched hand. 'Keep it.'

'I don't want to keep it.'

'Sell it and give the money to charity.'

Violet placed the ring on the table next to his keys. Did it have to end like this? With them acting like stiff strangers at the end of the affair? She'd taken a gamble and it hadn't paid off. It was supposed to pay off! Why wasn't he putting his hands on her shoulders and turning her around and smiling at her with that tender smile he reserved only for her? She turned back to face him but if he were feeling even half of the heartache she was, he showed no sign of it. 'Goodbye, Cam. I guess I'll see you when I see you.'

'I guess you will.'

Violet put on her gloves and rewound her scarf around her neck. *Do* not *cry.*

'Right, that's it then. I'll have to collect the rest of

my things when I get back. I hope it's okay to leave them here until then?'

'Of course it is.'

Another silence passed.

Violet heard the telltale beep of the taxi outside. Cam took her bag for her and opened the front door and helped her into the taxi. He couldn't have given her a clearer message that he was 'fine' with her decision to leave without him.

Violet slipped into the back of the taxi without kissing him goodbye. There was only so much heartbreak she could cope with. Touching him one last time would be her undoing. She didn't want to turn into a mess to add insult to injury. If it was over then it was over. Better to be quick and clean about it. Apparently he felt the same way because he simply closed the door of the taxi and stood back from the kerb as if he couldn't wait for it to take her away.

'Going home for Christmas?' the cabbie asked.

Violet swallowed as Cam's statue-like figure gradually disappeared from view. 'Yes,' she said on a sigh. 'I'm going home.'

CHAPTER NINE

CAM STOOD WATCHING the taxi until it disappeared around the corner. *What are you doing?* Being sensible, that was what he was doing. If he chased after her and begged her to stay then what would it achieve? A few weeks, a few months of a relationship that was the best he'd ever had but could go no further. That was what he would have.

He walked back into his house and picked up the engagement ring off the table. It was still warm from being on Violet's finger. Why was he feeling so… numb? Like the world had dropped out from under him.

Violet had blindsided him with her ultimatum. He was already feeling raw from his father's ridiculous sham of a wedding. She couldn't have picked a worse time to discuss the future of their relationship. Seeing his father act like a horny teenager all through that farce of a service, and then to hear via Violet he had been feeling up one of the bridesmaids at the reception had made Cam deeply ashamed. So ashamed he'd wanted to distance himself from anything to do with weddings. The word was enough to make him want to be ill. Why had she done that? Why push him when they'd already discussed it? He had been honest and upfront about it. He hadn't told her any lies, made any false commitments, allowed her to believe there was a pot of gold at the end of the rainbow. They hadn't been together long enough to be talking of marriage even if he was the marrying type. If he were going to propose for real—*if*—then he would do it in his own good time, not because it was demanded of him.

Go after her.

Cam took one step towards the door but then stopped. Of course he had to let her go. What was the point in dragging this out till after Christmas? It wasn't fair to her and it wasn't fair to her family. She wanted more than he was prepared to give. She wanted the fairytale. Damn it, she *deserved* the fairytale. All her life she had been waiting for Mr Right and Cam was only getting in the way of her finding him.

He paced the floor, torn between wanting to chase after her and staying put where his life was under his control. He blew out a long breath and went through to the sitting room. He sat on one of the sofas and cradled his head in his hands. His chest felt like someone had dragged his heart from his body, leaving a gaping hole.

If this was the right thing to do then why did it feel so goddamn painful?

Violet hadn't worked up the courage to tell her parents she and Cam were finished when her mother texted to ask what time they would be arriving. She told her mother they would be arriving separately due to his father's wedding commitments. She knew it was cowardly but she couldn't cope with their disappointment when hers was still so raw and painful. Checking into that flight at Heathrow had been one of the loneliest moments of her life. Even as she'd boarded the plane, she had hoped Cam would come rushing up behind her and spin her around to face him, saying he had made the biggest mistake of his life to let her leave.

But he hadn't turned up. He hadn't even texted or phoned. Didn't that prove how relieved he was that their relationship was over? By delivering an ultimatum she had given him a get-out-of-jail-free card. No wonder he hadn't argued the point or asked for more time on their relationship. He had grabbed the opportunity to end it.

Violet's mother met her at the airport and swept her into a bone-crushing hug. 'Poppet! I'm so happy to see you. Your father's at home making mince pies. Yes, mince pies! Isn't he a sweetheart trying to help? But you should see the mess he's making in the kitchen. We'll be cleaning up flour for weeks. Now, what time is Cam coming? There are only two more flights this evening. I've already checked. I hope he doesn't miss whichever one he's on. I've made up the suite in the east wing for you both. It's like a honeymoon suite.'

Violet let her mother's cheerful chatter wash over her. It reminded her of the time when she'd come home after quitting university. She had kept her pain and shame hidden rather than burst her mother's bubble of happiness at having her youngest child back home. It wasn't that her mother wasn't sensitive, but rather Violet was adept at concealing her emotions.

Her father was at the front door of Drummond Brae wearing a flour-covered apron when Violet and her mother arrived. He came rushing down the steps and gathered her in a hug that made her feet come off the ground. 'Welcome home, wee one,' he said. 'Come away inside out of the cold. It's going to snow for Christmas. We've already had a flurry or two.'

Violet stepped over the threshold and came face to face with a colourful banner hanging across the foyer that said: *Congratulations Cam and Violet*. Helium balloons with her and Cam's names on them danced in the draught of cold air from the open door, their tinsel strings hanging like silver tails.

Her grandfather came shuffling in on his walking frame, his wrinkled face beaming from ear to ear. 'Let's see that ring of yours, little Vivi,' he said.

Violet swallowed a knot that felt as big as a pine cone off the Christmas tree towering in the hall in all its festive glory. She kept her gloves on, too embarrassed to show her empty ring finger. How on earth was she going to tell them? The rest of the family came bursting in, Fraser and Zoe with their twins Ben and Mia and then Rose and Alex with their boys Jack and Jonathon. And, of course, Gertie the elderly golden retriever who looked like the canine version of Grandad with her creaky gait and whitened snout.

'Aunty Violet! Did you bring me a present?' Ben

asked with a cheeky grin, so like her brother Fraser it made Violet's heart contract.

'Can I be your flower girl?' Mia asked, hugging Violet around the waist.

Rose and Lily greeted her with big smiles and even bigger hugs. 'We've already started on the champagne,' Rose said. 'Well, not Lily, of course, but I'm drinking her share.'

'When's Cam arriving?' Lily asked.

'Erm…' Violet felt tears burning like acid behind her eyes. 'He's…hoping to make it in time for Christmas dinner.' *Coward.*

Her brother Fraser came forward and gave her a big hug. 'So pleased for you guys. Always knew Cam had a thing for you.'

'I thought so too,' Rose said, grinning. 'He wasn't himself at Easter, do you remember, Lil? Remember when I asked him to take in a hot cross bun to Vivi and he got all flustered and said he had to make a call? Classic. Absolutely classic.'

Lily's smile made her eyes dance. 'I'm so thrilled for you, Vivi. All three of us will be married. How soon will you start a family? It'd be so cool to have our kids close in age.'

Gertie came up to Violet and slowly wagged her tail and gave a soft whine as if to say, *What's wrong?*

Violet could stand it no longer. 'I—I have something to tell you…'

Rose's eyes lit up as bright as the lights on the Christmas tree she was standing near. 'You're pregnant?'

Violet bit her lip so hard she thought she would break the skin. 'Cam and I are…not engaged.'

The stunned silence was so profound no one moved. Not even the children. Even the tinsel and baubles on the Christmas tree seemed to be holding themselves stock-still. Everyone was looking at her as if she had just told them she had a disease and it was contagious.

'Oh, poppet.' Her mother came to her and gathered her in her arms, rocking her from side to side as if she were still a baby. 'I'm so sorry.'

Her father joined in the hug, gently patting her on the back with soothing 'there, there's' that made Violet sob all the harder.

Rose and Lily ushered the children away and Fraser helped Grandad back into the sitting room near the fire. Lily's husband Cooper and Rose's husband Alex came in late and, taking one look at the scene, promptly walked back out.

'What happened?' Violet's mother asked. 'Did he break it off?'

'No, I did. But we weren't even engaged. We were pretending.'

Her mother frowned. 'Pretending?'

Violet explained the situation through a series of hiccupping sobs. 'It's my fault for being so pathetic about going to the office Christmas party on my own. I should've just gone alone and not been such a stupid baby. Now I've hurt everyone and ruined my friendship with Cam and spoilt Christmas for everyone too.'

'You haven't spoilt anything, poppet,' her mother

said. 'Take the banner down, Gavin. And get the kids to pop the balloons. I'll take Violet upstairs.'

Violet followed her mother upstairs, not to the suite prepared for her and Cam but to her old bedroom. All her childhood toys were neatly arranged on top of the dresser and some on her bed. Violet's books were in the bookshelves, waiting for her like old friends. It was like stepping back in time but feeling out of place. She wasn't a child any more. She was an adult with adult needs. Needs Cam had awakened and then walked away from as if they meant nothing to him.

As if *she* meant nothing to him.

Her mother sat on the edge of the bed beside Violet. 'Are you in love with him?'

'Yes, but he doesn't love me. Well, he does but not like that.'

'Did you tell him you loved him?'

Violet gave a despondent sigh. 'What would be the point? He never wants to get married. He doesn't want kids either.'

'I expect that's because of his parents,' her mother said. 'But he might change his mind.'

'He won't.'

Her mother hugged her again. 'My poor baby. I wish there was something I could do or say to help you feel better.'

Violet wiped at her eyes with her sleeve. 'I love him so much but he's so cynical about getting married. Deep down, I don't really blame him after attending his father's fifth wedding today. It was awful. So awful you wouldn't believe.' She described some of what went on and her mother made tut-tutting noises and shook her head in disgust.

'Did you press him for a commitment after you came back from the wedding?' her mother asked.

Violet looked at her mum's frowning expression. 'You think I should've waited?'

Her mother squeezed her hand. 'What's done is done. At least you were honest with him. No point pretending you're happy when you're not.'

Violet's bottom lip quivered. 'He's the only one for me, Mum. I know I won't be happy with anyone else. I just know it.'

Her mother gave her a sad smile. 'For your sake, poppet, I hope that's not true.'

Cam packed up Violet's things for when she was ready to collect them. He could have done it any time between Christmas and New Year because she wouldn't be back till the second of January as they had planned to spend the week with her family. But he was feeling restless and on edge. He kept telling himself it was better this way. That it was wrong to drag things out when he couldn't give her what she wanted.

But when he came to her embroidery basket, his heart gave a painful spasm. He opened the lid and took out the creamy baby blanket Violet was in the process of embroidering with tiny flowers. He held it to his face, its softness reminding him of her skin. He could even smell her on the blanket—that sweet flowery scent that made him think of spring. He put the blanket back inside the basket and took out a pair of booties. They were so tiny he couldn't imagine a baby's foot small enough to fit them. He started to picture a baby…one he and Violet might make together: a little squirming body with dimpled hands and feet, a downy dark head with eyes bright and clear and a little rosebud mouth.

What if Violet were pregnant? They had been careful but accidents could happen. Should he call her? No. Too soon. He needed more time. Time to get his head together. He wasn't used to feeling this level of emotion. This sense of…loss. The sense of loss was so acute it felt like a giant hole, leaving him empty and raw.

Cam picked up a tiny jacket that had sailing boats embroidered around the collar. He rubbed his thumb over the meticulous stitches, wondering what it would be like to have a son. His father hadn't been an active father in any sense of the word, but Cam couldn't imagine not wanting to be involved in your child's life. How could you not be interested in your own flesh and blood? Being there for every milestone, watching them grow and develop, reading to them at bedtime—all the things Violet's parents had done and were now doing for each of their grandchildren when they came to stay.

He put the sailing boat jacket down and picked up a pink cardigan that was so small it would have looked at home on a doll. There were tiny rosebuds around the collar and the cuffs of the sleeves. What would it be like to have a daughter? To watch her grow from babyhood to womanhood. To be there for her first smile, her first tooth, her first steps. *Gulp.* Her first date. Walking her down the aisle. One day becoming a grandfather…

Cam had never thought about having his own children. Well, he had thought about it but just as quickly dismissed it. Like when he had walked into the sitting room at Drummond Brae at Easter and seen Violet curled up on the sofa with a baby's bonnet in her hands. It had been a jarring reminder of the responsibility he'd spent his adult life actively avoiding.

But now he wondered why he was working so hard when he had no one to share it with. What was the point? Would he end up some lonely old man living out his end days alone? Not surrounded by a loving family like Grandad Archie in the winter of his life. No one to tell him they loved him, no one to be there in sickness and in health and everything in between. No laughter-filled Christmases with all the family gathered around the tree exchanging gifts and smiles and love.

Cam put the pink cardigan back inside the basket and closed the lid. What was he doing? It was best this way. Violet was better off without him and his crazy family who would do nothing but stir up trouble between them if given half a chance. He wasn't cut out for marriage and commitment. He was too driven by his career, by achieving, by the next task waiting on his desk. He didn't have the time to invest in a long-term relationship.

Cam had been to three of his father's previous weddings and never once taken much notice of the vows. But when he'd heard his father make all those promises earlier that day it had made Cam's gut churn to realise his father didn't mean a word of them. They were just words, empty, meaningless words because his father had no intention of committing to his new wife other than in an outward way by standing up in church in front of family and friends. His father didn't mean them on the inside, in his heart where it counted. Anyone could say they would love someone for the rest of their life but how many people actually meant it? Violet's parents obviously had. So had her grandad Archie and Maisie Drummond when they had married sixty-five years ago.

Cam knew if it were him up there saying those words with Violet by his side, he would make sure he meant them. His heart gave a kick as the realisation dawned. This was why he had avoided marriage and commitment all this time—because he had never been able to picture himself saying those words with any sincerity. But with Violet they meant everything. He loved her with all his heart and mind and soul. He worshipped her with his body, he wanted to protect her and stand by her in sickness and in health, in pregnancy and childbirth.

What a damn fool he had been. Letting her walk away when he loved her so much. Loved her more than anything, more than his freedom, which wasn't such a great thing anyway. True freedom was in your ability to love someone without fear, without conditions, loving without restraint.

The love he felt for Violet was bigger than his fear of abandonment. It was bigger than the need to protect himself from hurt. He couldn't control life and all its vagaries. Life happened, no matter how carefully you laid plans. He thought of Violet's poor workmate Kenneth, so hung up on his ex-wife he was unable to move on with his life. Cam didn't want to be like that. Too afraid to love in case he lost it.

He loved Violet and he would make sure nothing and no one destroyed that love. They would face the future together, a dedicated team who had each other's backs no matter what.

Cam glanced at his watch. He would have to hotfoot it but he could make the last flight if he was lucky.

Violet was determined her family's Christmas would not suffer any more disturbance after her tearful confession. She joined in with the family board games—a Drummond tradition late at night on Christmas Eve while everyone drank eggnog—and laughed at her father's corny jokes and patiently repeated everything for Grandad, who was hard of hearing. Her mother kept a watchful eye on her, but Violet did her best to assure her mum she was doing just fine, even though on the inside she felt a cavern of emptiness.

She couldn't stop wondering what Cam was doing. Was he spending Christmas with his mother or alone? Or had he hooked up with someone new? It wasn't like him to do something like that but what if he wanted to press home a point? He wanted his freedom, otherwise wouldn't he have come after her by now? Called her? Texted her? Given her a fragment of hope? No. He hadn't. It didn't seem fair that she was up here in the Highlands of Scotland nursing a broken heart while he was in London living the life of a playboy. Did he miss her? Was he thinking about her?

'Well, we're off to bed,' Fraser announced, taking Zoe's hand. 'The kids will be up at four, looking for their presents.'

Zoe gave Violet a sad look. 'Are you okay, Vivi?'

Violet put on a brave smile. 'Rose and I are going to work on that bottle of champagne over there, aren't we, Rose?'

Rose gave her an apologetic look and reached for her husband Alex's hand. 'Sorry, Vivi, but I've had too much already.'

'Don't look at me,' Lily said, placing a protective hand over her belly. 'I'm knackered in any case.'

'Will you take Gertie out for a wee walk, poppet?' her mother asked. 'Your father and I have to stuff the turkey.'

Violet shrugged on her coat and put on her gloves and took the dog outside into the crisp night air. There were light flurries of snow but it wasn't settling. So much for a magical white Christmas. Maybe it was going to be one of those miserable grey and gloomy ones, which would be rather fitting for her current state of mind.

Gertie wasn't content with waddling about the garden and instead put her nose down to follow a scent leading down to the loch. Violet grabbed a torch from the hall table drawer and followed the dog. The loch was a silver shape in the moonlight, the forest behind it a dense dark fringe.

Violet stood at the water's edge, feeling the biting cold coming off the sheet of water while Gertie bustled about in the shadows. An owl hooted, a vixen called out for a mate.

A twig snapped under someone's foot.

Violet spun around, shining the torch in the direction of the sound. 'Who's there?'

Cam stepped into the beam of light. 'It's me.'

Violet's heart gave an almighty lurch. 'Cam?'

He shielded his eyes with his arm. 'Will you stop shining that thing in my face?'

'Sorry.' She lowered the torch. 'You scared the heck out of me.'

He came up closer, the moonlight casting his features into ghostly relief. Gertie padded over and gave him an enthusiastic greeting as if she had suddenly turned into a puppy instead of the fifteen-year-old dog she was. Cam leaned down to scratch at the dog's ears before straightening. 'I'm sorry about earlier today. I was wrong to let you leave like that. I got flooded with feelings I didn't want to acknowledge. But I'm acknowledging them now. I love you, Violet. I love you and want to spend the rest of my life with you. Will you marry me?'

Violet stared at him, wondering if she was hearing things. 'Did you just ask me to marry you?'

He smiled so tenderly it made her heart skip a beat. Her smile. The one he only used for her. 'I did and I want to have babies with you. We can be a family like your family. We can do it because we're a team who are batting for each other, not against each other.'

Violet stepped into his waiting arms, nestling her head against his chest. 'I love you so much. It tore my heart out to leave you but I had to. I wasn't being true to myself or to you. Your father's wedding brought it home to me. I couldn't go on pretending.'

'After you left I started thinking about my father and that ridiculous sham of a wedding,' Cam said. 'He doesn't love Tatiana enough to die for her. He's using her as a trophy to prove his diminishing potency. He uses every woman he's ever been with like that. I know I won't do that to you. I couldn't. You mean the world to me. I couldn't possibly love anyone more than I love you.'

Violet gazed up at him. Was this really happening? Cam was here. In person. Asking her to marry him. Telling her he loved her more than anyone else in the world. 'It was a bit mean of me to push you on commitment so close to your father's wedding,' she said. 'No wonder you backed away. The mere mention of the word *wedding* after that debacle of a ceremony would've been enough to make you run for cover.'

He gave her a rueful smile. 'Your timing was a little off but I got there eventually. I'm sorry you had to go through an awful few hours thinking we were over. After you left I sat in numb shock. Normally when a relationship of mine comes to an end I feel relieved.

Not this time. Can you forgive me for being so block-headed?'

Violet linked her arms around his neck. 'I'm never leaving again. Not ever. You've made all my dreams come true. You've even proposed to me by the loch.'

He grinned and drew her closer. 'I reckon we've got about sixty seconds before your family come down here to check if there's a reason to celebrate Christmas with a bang or we both freeze to death. Will you marry me, my darling?'

Violet smiled so widely her face ached. 'Yes. A million times yes.'

'Once will be more than enough,' Cam said. 'From here on I'm a one-woman man.'

She stroked his lean jaw, now dark and rough with stubble. 'I've been a one-man woman for a lot longer. I think that's probably why I never dated with any enthusiasm. I was subconsciously waiting for you.'

His eyes became shadowed for a moment as if he was recalling how close to losing her he had come. 'How could I have been so stupid not to see how perfect you are for me all this time?'

Violet smiled. 'Mum saw it. She's going to be beside herself when she hears you're here. Did anyone see you coming up the driveway?'

'I'm not sure. When I pulled up I caught a glimpse of you heading towards the lake with Gertie so I came straight down here.'

'They made a banner for us,' Violet said. 'It was a

bad moment when I saw it hanging in the hall. I hadn't told them we were over at that point.'

He winced. 'Poor you. Well, we'd better tell them the good news. Ready?'

Violet drew his head down to hers. 'Not yet. Let's treasure this moment for our kids. I want to tell them how you kissed me in the moonlight, just like Grandad did to my grandmother in exactly this spot.'

'Hang on, I'm forgetting something.' He took out the ring from his pocket and slipped it on her finger. 'I don't want to see that come off again.'

Violet smiled as she twirled the ring on her finger. Her hand had felt so strange without it there. Like someone else's hand. The diamond winked at her as if to say, *I'm back!* 'I can't believe this is happening. I felt so lonely and lost without you.'

'Me too,' he said. 'I was so afraid of losing you that I ended up losing you. I will regret to the day I die not following you out of my house and bringing you back. I wanted to but I kept thinking you were better off without me.'

There was the sound of twigs snapping and a few hushed whispers. Cam's eyes twinkled. 'Looks like the family has arrived. Shall we make an announcement?'

Violet drew his head down to hers. 'Let's show them instead.'

EPILOGUE

Christmas Eve the following year...

CAM LOOKED AROUND the sitting room at Drummond Brae where all Violet's family were gathered. Correction. *His* and Violet's family. The last few months since his and Violet's wedding in June had shown him more than ever how important family was and how much he had missed out on having a proper one growing up. But he was more than making up for it now. He glanced at Violet where she was sitting almost bursting to tell the family her good news. *Their* good news. He still couldn't believe they were having a baby. Violet was just past the twelve-week mark and there could be no better Christmas present for her parents than to tell them they were about to have another grandchild.

He smiled when Violet's gaze met his. He never tired of looking at her; she was glowing but not just because of being pregnant. She had completed her first semester of an English Literature degree. He couldn't have been prouder of her. Of course she topped her class.

Grandad Archie was sitting with a blanket over his legs and a glass of whisky in his hand and looking at Violet with a smile on his face. That was another miracle Cam felt grateful for. Grandad Archie, while certainly not robust in health, was at least enjoying life surrounded by his beloved family. Even Kenneth, Violet's workmate, had started dating again. Cam had introduced him to a young widow who worked part-time in his office and they'd hit it off and had been seeing each other ever since.

Poor old Gertie, the golden retriever, hadn't been so lucky; her ashes were spread out by the loch not far from where Cam had proposed to Violet. But there was a new addition to the family, a ten-week-old puppy called Nessie who was currently chewing on one of Cam's shoelaces.

'Vivi, why aren't you drinking your eggnog?' Grandad Archie asked with a twinkle in his eyes. 'Is there something you have to tell us?'

Cam took Violet's hand just as she reached for his. He squeezed it gently, his heart so full of love he could feel his chest swelling like bread dough. 'We have an announcement to make,' he said. 'We're having a baby.'

'Ach, now I'll have to live another year so I can wet the wee one's head,' Grandad said, grinning from ear to ear.

Violet's mother grasped her husband's hand and blinked back happy tears. 'We're so thrilled for you both. It's just the most wonderful news.'

Violet placed Cam's hand on the tiny swell of her

belly and smiled up at him with her beautiful brown eyes brimming with happiness. 'I love you.'

Cam bent down and kissed her tenderly. 'I love you too. Happy Christmas, my darling.'

'Okay, knock it off you two,' Fraser said with a cheeky grin. 'The honeymoon's been over for six months.'

Cam grinned back. 'Not this honeymoon.' He gathered Violet closer. 'This one's going to last for ever.'

* * * * *